More praise for *Fair and Tender Ladies*

"Reading Lee Smith's work is like coming home again, to find everything just as you remembered: worn quilts on the brass bed, cat dozing in the most comfortable chair by the fire, peach cobbler in the oven. And Ivy Rowe, the heroine of *Fair and Tender Ladies*, is just the sort of friend we want to find waiting for us."

The Washington Post

"In this book, Smith reins in her humor to listen to one voice, the joltingly clear sound of Ivy Rowe, whose passion for letter writing yields a poignant chronicle of enduring pride."

People

"Lee Smith's fast-moving, tender folk tale about an endearing mountain beauty may be her best book yet; certainly warmhearted, willful Ivy Rowe is her deepest, best-developed character. Woven into her story are many of the fabled things of Smith's native Appalachia—mysterious, seductive strangers, independent, hard-working people whose pride transcends poverty, foolishness for love, and the everlasting pull of the Virginia hills themselves."

The Virginia-Pilot/The Ledger-Star

"There is only one voice covering four generations in a typical backwoods family. But the voice of Ivy Rowe is positive, joyful and irrepressible even in the face of hardship, disappointment and family tragedy."

The Seattle Times

ALSO BY LEE SMITH

The Last Day the Dogbushes Bloomed
Something in the Wind
Fancy Strut
Black Mountain Breakdown
Cakewalk
Oral History
Family Linen
Me and My Baby View the Eclipse
The Devil's Dream

Fair
and
Tender
Ladies

Lee Smith

Ballantine Books • New York

This edition published by arrangement with G. P. Putnam's Sons, a division of The Putnam Berkley Group, Inc.

The author gratefully acknowledges permission to quote the following: Excerpt from lyrics of "Oh! How I Hate to Get Up in the Morning" by Irving Berlin, at pages 128–129. © Copyright 1918 Irving Berlin. © Copyright renewed 1945 Irving Berlin. © Copyright assigned to Ruth H. (Mrs. Ralph J.) Bunche, Joe DiMaggio, and Theodore R. Jackson as Trustees, God Bless America Fund. Reprinted by permission of Irving Berlin Music Corporation.
Lyrics from "Heartbreak Hotel" by Mae Boren Axton, Tommy Durden, and Elvis Presley, at pages 283–284. Copyright © 1956 Tree Publishing Co., Inc. Copyright renewed. All rights reserved. International copyright secured. Used by permission of the publisher.

Library of Congress Catalog Card Number: 92-97544

http://www.randomhouse.com

ISBN 0-345-38399-0

Cover design by James R. Harris
Cover art by Bob Sabin

Manufactured in the United States of America

First Ballantine Books Trade Edition: July 1993

20 19 18 17 16 15 14 13 12 11

For Amity

Weep-Willow

At night she watched the road
and sang. I'd sigh and settle on the floor
beside her. One song led
to one more song. Some unquiet grave.
A bed of stone. The ship that spun round
three times ere it sank,
near ninety verses full of grief.
She sang sad all night long

and smiled, as if she dared me
shed a tear. Sweet Lizzie Creek swung low
along the rocks, and dried beans rattled
in the wind. Sometimes her black dog howled
at fox or bear, but she'd not stop,
no, not for God Himself, not even if he rode
astride a fine white horse and bore the Crown
of Glory in his hands. The dark was all
she had. And sometimes moonlight
on the ceaseless water. "Fill my cup,"

she'd say, and sip May moonshine
till her voice came back as strong as bullfrogs
in the sally grass. You whippoorwills
keep silent, and you lonesome owls go haunt
another woman's darkest hours. Clear,

clear back I hear her singing me to sleep.
"Come down," she trolls,
"Come down among the willow
shade and weep, you fair
and tender ladies left to lie alone,
the sheets so cold,
the nights so long."

from *Wildwood Flower*, by Kathryn Stripling Byer

Fair
and
Tender
Ladies

"Oh Ivy, sing ivory, rosebud and thorn . . ."

I

Letters from Sugar Fork

My dear Hanneke,

Your name is not much common here, I think it is so pretty too.
I say it now and agin it tastes sweet in my mouth like honey or
cane or how I picture the fotched-on candy from Mrs. Browns
book about France, candy wich mimicks roses. Have you seed any
such as this? I have not. I have seed them in her red book that is
all. My teacher is called Mrs. Brown. She is from far away also,
she has lived in the city of St. Louis oncet with buggies and street-
ligts, I know all about it now. And I know all how you live too,
we have seed the pictures, I cannot feature it all so flat ther with
flat water so brigtly blue and never a mountain nor nary a cloud
in the sky. You are lower than the sea so that oncet a boy has had
to stick his finger in the wall to hold back the water, this is scary
to me. I have nare seed the ocean nor has anyone I know seed it
althogh Daddy has been to the city too, he did not like it with
bad water and no air and no mountains like Bethel Mountain
yonder, Daddy says he needs a mountain to rest his eyes aginst.
But in the book I have seed those fields of flowers, tulips, we
think you have wooden shoes. Momma makes all of our clothes
we have storeboghten shoes thogh they are black, they have copper
on the toes so as not to wear out very fast. I disgust them and
wish for wooden shoes and a lace cap like yourn and such pretty
long white stockings, you look like a little Queen. I know it is not
you in the book but I think it is you. I hope you will be my Pen
Friend.

My momma had also a white dress with lace as a girl, I have
seed the picture. She stands by the door it is a fancy door of a
house in a town I know is Rich Valley where she has growed up
and ther is her big father smiling holding her hand but now a
hardness has come up between them. He has a black suit and a
black mustashe and a gold watch chain hanging down in the picture,
he is rich, his name is Mister Castle and we do not know him atall.
He is smiling but he is mean. My momma Maude was then fifteen,
her momma had died of her lungs in the year 1886 so that Maude
was the ligt of her daddys life, and the only joy of his hart.

Then my daddy come to Rich Valley and she took up with him,
and her and him set to walking out together of an evening like
you do.

Mister Castle said NO I forbid it, he has no prospects, and said
he wuld send my momma to her mothers sister in Memphis Ten-

essee where my momma never had been or even heard tell of, to learn her some sense and how to act like a lady at last. Instead my momma packed up her own mommas silver brush and comb which was all she took, and lit out in the dead of nigt for Sugar Fork with my daddy John Arthur Rowe. He is a redheaded man he had been over ther in Rich Valley with his brother trading mules. My momma and him rode double astride on daddys horse Lightning. She was glad to leave, she said, and never looked back nor cared for a thing but my daddy.

They carried a pine knot that burned in the nigt to show them the way. They passed throgh Squeeze Betsy in the Pound Gap it is so black at nigt the rocky-clifts is so high they nearabout black out the moon. And then you come up on Bethel Mountain wich is high and lonesome and a hoot owl screeched out in the nigt it like to have scarred my momma to death she was a town girl she like to have plum lost hart then and ther, Daddy says. He says the pine knot was burning yaller and you culd see little critters eyes all shining yaller in the ligt from the edge of the woods. They is still bears and catamounts up on Bethel Mountain, to this day.

Well Momma and Daddy come on to Slate Creek and follered it down to Home Creek where they forded it at the grist mill and Momma got down in the dark and wetted her face with the water, she said her face was burning as hot as fire she was all atremble from what she had done and they never knowed at that time if Mister Castle wuld of sent a posse out after them or not. My daddy a Batcheler was considerable older than her. Momma said she seed her face in the still black pool by the pine knots yaller ligt and she looked so wild, she culd not of said who she was, she culd not of called her own name. But she said that the water in Home Creek was so cool, and tasted the sweetest of any she ever had. And Daddy kissed her, and they got up agin on Lightning thogh Momma was so sore by then that she like to have died, she said she was down in the back atterwards for days and days.

So they rode on alongside Home Creek and by then it was getting ligt, on the prettest path you have ever seed, it is still rigt here, it runs throgh sprucey-pines and he-balsams and past three little old waterfalls. When you get to that third one you start looking out for them two big cedar trees and you leave Home Creek rigt ther where Sugar Fork comes into it and foller Sugar Fork up and up, you will ford it twicet, its the loudest and sing-ingest little old creek you ever dreamed of, and direckly when you cant go no further youl be here, here in my daddys house which was his daddys house afore him way up here on Blue Star Mountain.

And it aint nobody up here but usuns.

Daddy had lived up here farming all by hisself since his own daddy died of his hart and his momma died of the bloody flux and his sister had maried and gone off and his brother Revel had took to helling around so. Sometimes Daddy wuld go down the mountain somewhere and holp Revel with his buisness, which is mules. But then he wuld come back up here direckly, Daddy wuld, he dont love noplace in the world he says like he loves Sugar Fork.

Well it was getting on for daybreak when my daddy and my momma come riding up there plum wore out, and Lightning so puny he is going on dead, he never was the same horse after that nigt Daddy said, you can see for why. Uncle Revel wanted to trade him after he got so puny but Momma said NO and she fed him out of her own hand and wuld not let nobody ride him but her until the day he died, wich was not long in coming. That ride had used him teetotally up.

The sun come peeping up then over the top of Hell Mountain like a white hot firy ball rising up from the fog that always hangs on the mountaintop of an evening. It will burn off in the day.

Momma looked around.

She saw Sugar Fork sparkle in the sun like a ladys dimond necklace.

She saw Pilgrim Knob rise up direckly behind the house, and Blue Star Mountain beyond. They call it that because of how blue it looks from down below, along Home Creek and Daves Branch, why you can see Blue Star Mountain clear from Majestic on a pretty day. And you can see the Conaways and the Rolettes and the Foxes cabins, coming up Home Creek from the schoolhouse like her and daddy had done that morning, now you can see all them neghbor peoples houses fine but you cant see ourn, nor get to it nether, without wanting to. You are not going to happen upon us, is what I mean. And Blue Star Mountain dont seem so blue nether, when your up here. But it is the prettiest place in the world.

And so my momma looked all around, and she seed all of that.

She seed the shining waters of Sugar Fork go leaping off down the mountain into the laurel slick. And she seed that this is a good big double cabin here with a breezeway in between where it is fine to set and look out and do your piecework. And she seed the snowball bush in the yard and the rosybush here by the porch all covered with pink-pink flowers. It was June. And Momma looked up in the sky she said and she seed a hawk gliding circles around and around without never flapping his wings, agin that big blue sky. She said that hawk made three circles in the sky, and then Daddy turned to her real formal-like and cleared his throat and said Maude, it is what I have to give you. It is all I have. But she knowed this, she had knowed it all along. It will do, John, is what she said. Then she busted out laghing and my daddy picked her up and carried her in the house wich is where I live today, in Virginia, in the United States of America. But you must put Majestic, Virginia, U.S.A. and many stamps on the outside of your letter Mrs. Brown said or it will not come here.

Now I am glad I have set this all down for I can see my Momma and Daddy as young, and laghing. This is not how they are today. For I have to say they did not live haply ever after as in Mrs. Browns book. I reckon that migt even of been the lastest time my Daddy ever lifted her up, or lifted ary thing else heavy. Because before long a weakness was to come upon him, from the hart.

Now this is Daddys bad hart, wich he has to this day, he is the disablest one up here rigt now. You can hear his bad hart for yourself iffen you come over and put your ear up agin his chest, it goes dum-DUM dum-DUM like our banty rooster that goes coo-COO coo-COO of a morning on Pilgrim Knob. You can hear Daddys bad hart just thumping away irreglar in his chest. He is little now too, hardly no meat atall on his bones, but his hair is still thick and red and his eyes are so blue and just as lively as Sugar Fork. He will still tell a story. He is little thogh like a brownie in Mrs. Browns McGuffey Reader.

Do you have a reader? Do you like to read? I love it bettern anything and mostly poems such as Thanatopses and the little toy soldier is covered with dust but sturdy and stanch he stands and the highwayman came riding riding up to the old inn door. I love that one the bestest.

Mister Brown is a forren preacher from the North but does not preach he is the husband of Mrs. Brown my teacher. He says to her, what is your substance whereof are you made? and other poems. He carries bunches of flowers up from the creek for her and one time it was about a month ago he brung them rigt into the schoolhouse and give them to her with a funny little bow like a Prince you ougt to of seed him, we was all rigt ther when he done it. Her cheeks turned as red as a apple, I wuld of had a fit if it was me.

For I take a intrest in her and Mister Brown and in what I have told you, the story of my Momma and Daddy. I take a intrest in Love because I want to be in Love one day and write poems about it, do you? But I do not want to have a lot of babys thogh and get tittys as big as the moon. So it is hard to think what to do. My momma was young and so pretty when she come riding up Sugar Fork, but she does not look pretty now, she looks awful, like her face is hanted, she has had too much on her. Too much to contend with she says.

So next I will write you about my Life, it is what Mrs. Brown said to do, I want to be a writter, it is what I love the bestest in this world. Mrs. Brown says I have a true tallent she thinks, she gives me books to read but Momma gets pitched off iffen I read too much, I have to holp out and I will just fill my head with notions, Momma says it will do me no good in the end.

My hair is long and yaller-red it comes down to my waist and Silvaney holps me to wash it, we spread it over a chairback to lift it to dry in front of the fire. Momma come in last night when we was all drying our hair, Silvaney and Beulah and me and Ethel. Silvaneys hair is real long and curly and wellnigh white, and Ethels is real ligt yaller, and Beulahs hair is as red as that sourgum tree rigt now up on Pilgrim Knob, she takes after Daddy the mostest. Momma just set to starring with her eyes as big as a plate and then she commences to weeping out loud.

Now Maude whats the matter, Daddy said to her from his pallet up next to the fire, we keep him up there so close but he cant hardly get warm even thogh it is not but October and we aint yet had a killing frost. Whatevers the matter now Maude, Daddy said.

These girls is all so pretty she said theyd be better off ugly, these girls is all so pretty theyd be better off dead.

Hush now Maude you just hush she dont mean it girls, shes just wore out, Daddy said to us. She is all wrogt up dont pay her no mind now girls, Daddy said.

He is there on his pallet pulled up by the fire we are all in a row with our hair spreaded out on the chairbacks to dry.

So this is the members of my Family, I will tell you as Mrs. Brown said. And of my Chores and our Culture too. I wuld like to see your face, I feature your face as white as ice and your eyes so blue, like the Ice Queen but smiling with cherryred lips. I know you have windmills and big pieded black and white cows in the flat green fields. Well we have got a cow too her name is Bessie but she is close to give out at this time.

We grow nearabout all we eat, and mostly the corn wich will work you to death. So I cant go to school sometimes in the spring when we plant it or later on you have got to get out there and hoe it to beat the band, and the side of Blue Star Mountain is so steep youve got to hill it good or it wont grow atall. And we used to grow us a patch of cane too and then we wuld make molasseys, folks wuld come from all around and holp, but we have not got no cane this year as Daddy is poorly, he has to lay down.

And we grow cabbages and sweet taters and white taters both and shucky beans and we have got some apple trees too but Bess as I said is sick, this is fidgeting Momma to death what to do, for the twins is so little yet, we need the milk for Danny is always weak. They is chickens and turkeys grabbling out in the woods and guinea hens up by the house. They say pot-rack, pot-rack. I hate it when Momma kills them, you dont want to get you a pet hen, you will be sorry, nor a pet pig nether like Lizzy that was mine.

But we raise what we need, we dont go to the store for nothing but coffee and shoes and nails and to get the mail, we do not get any mail much but sometimes a letter from Daddys sister in Welch or Mommas friend Geneva Hunt from childhood or a pattern Momma sent off for. Momma can sew anything. She culd sew so pretty if she had the time. Beulah and Ethel sews too now. The store is at Majestic it is the P.O. too. This is where Mrs. Brown will take my letter to you, then Bill Waldrop will put it in his saddlebag and carry it over the mountain, a ship will carry it over the sea. Does this seem magicle to you? It seems so to me.

I wish you culd see Stoney Branhams store at Majestic, they is a woodstove at the back where all the men gathers round and spits tobaccy and waits for Bill Waldrop to come, and lays bets on what time he will get ther. They talk and talk about who has seed a bear or who is laying up in the bed sick or who has been bit by a snake or where lightning has struck last, or they will tell a tale, and the womenfolks that is in ther will be looking at thread or may be some flowered piecey-goods. Stoney Branham sends to-baccy back to Daddy who coughs so deep now it is just like thunder over Hell Mountain when he coughs now it is relly terible. They is more wrong with him now than his hart.

Do ye reckon John Arthur will make it throgh the winter, Stoney said to Granny Rowe it was a week ago Monday I heerd him myself, anybody culd of heerd him, that had ears. Wich means Silvaney who got all wroght up something awful, she run out back of Stoney Branhams store and cried, she knows a lot more than you think.

I will tell you of my Family now and she will be first, I love Silvaney the bestest, you see. Silvaney is so pretty, she is the sweetest, all silverhaired like she was fotched up on the moon. She takes after a Princess in a story, Silvaney does. Her and my brother Babe was twins, wich runs in the Family. Silvaney is five years oldern me.

But something is wrong with Silvaney, she had brain fever as a baby, now she will never be rigt in the head. It dont matter, shes so sweet, but she scares easy, sometimes she will put her apron up over her head and start in crying and other times she will get to laghing and she cant stop, you have to pour a gourdfull of water down over her face. Momma says she run a fever for days and days it has burned out a part of her brain. So Silvaney dont go to school to Mrs. Brown but you cant tell it just to see her, she is the prettest thing. So Silvaney is bigger and oldern me, but it is like we are the same sometimes it is like we are one. We have slept in the same bed all of our lives and done everything as one, I am smart thogh I go to school when I can and try to better myself and teach Silvaney but she cant learn.

Lord me and her have had some fun thogh, just usuns, we get a piece of tin sometimes and some rocks and sneak off and build us a little stove rigt out in the woods and gather up sticks and make us a little cookfire under the tin then we have got a little stove. Then I will take out the meal I have stole from the chest on the porch and wound up in my skirt, and get some water from Sugar Fork, and we will make up some little pancakes and have us a play-party rigt there in the woods by the creek in our secret place. We put black-eye susans and Queen Annes lace in our hair.

We have party names too, I am the Princess Lucia she is the Princess Melissa Clarissa and Beulah used to play too sometimes, she was Miss Margaret White, who knows where she got that name? But Beulah will not play no more, she is courting Curtis

Bostick from Poorbottom, he rides up here on his listed horse and takes her walking. I do not know what they will do when it gets cold and they cannot go walking, as we are so many here in the house and Curtis Bostick dont know how to court good inside a house Beulah says he just sits like a bump on a log. He is not a bit good at sweethearting, to do it as much as he does.

Anyway now we do not have Miss Margaret White so we have made up a Miss France who wears a big pink hat and sticks out her finger and laghs la-la-la, I cannot tell if Silvaney knows that Miss France is made up or not. Well Ethel is only nine but she will not play party, when I say I have some scrumptious cake she says it is only pone and when I say, hear the lovely music Miss Ethel it is violins, she says <u>my name is nothing but Ethel, just plain Ethel, and that is birds.</u>

Ethel will not even play Town but Victor will watch sometimes and Garnie will preach. What you do is make you some little houses outen sticks and you can chink up your logs with mud iffen you wish to, and you can have some rocks for furniture, all covered over with moss that you find by the creek where it gets so little and bouncy starting up Pilgrim Knob. Now this will be your fancy furniture, that is your bed and chairs and all, and you will make corncob people, you can have pinecones for pigs, and a cow and the chicks in the yard.

And your own people can come to and fro, they can go courting and have a baby and die or get saved or whatever you want to happen. One time me and Victor, this is my elder brother, he wont play no more nether, one time me and Victor stoled us some thread and hitched up some big old bugs and made us horses named Buck and Berry. And iffen you want little old Garnie to play, you have got to let him preach a funeral and sing, been a long time travelling here below, been a long time travelling here below, been a long time travelling from my home, to lay this body down. But then you will have to pour water on Silvaneys face, she crys so hard at a funeral. Momma said, stop this, this is awful, and Silvaney is too old to play. But we sneak off, we have us a time, I guess.

What do you all play?

Mrs. Brown said I should tell you about our Chores but they are never over, it is so hard on a farm without no mule we had one but it died a year ago come April I think it was. And Daddy has had a big falling-out with Revel now so we cant get no more mules from him, aint none of us set eyes on Revel for over a year. So we go down on Home Creek and get the loan of one from the Rolettes. Folks is real nice, they know Daddy is sick. So Victor he runs the farm, and Momma, the bestest they can, and I will get up in the morning before full ligt and milk Bessie, and Beulah she will start in cooking and Ethel will dress the younguns and Silvaney looks for eggs. And then I will bring up the milk and strain it and put it in the churn and rinch out the strainer and things, and hang them up, and later on I will have to churn or go out and hoe the corn and such as that, it is always something to do on a farm.

The next leastest has to watch out for the leastest ones, and I loved to do that, I used to take Garnie and Ethel up under the rocky-clifts by the cornfield to watch them while everbody was working, its fun in there you can go way back and keep so cool. One time we was up there and I seed a rattlesnake all quiled up and singing to beat the band, I had to snatch up Ethel, she thogt it was a play-pretty.

Babe killed it with a hoe. He loves to kill things, Babe does. I am so glad he is gone from here now, I hope he is gone for good. This is my eldest brother named Clarence Wayne but called Babe, he is mean as a snake hisself. He works for Frank Ritter Lumber Company now in Bone Valley we think, he dont send us hardly a thing.

When we was all real little I recall Daddy showing us how to make frog houses out in the yard, this is where you put your bare foot down in the dirt and push up the dirt all around it and then you take out your foot and you have got you a house, you would leave them there of a summer nigt for the frogs to come. But Babe used to stomp them down. They say he takes after my daddys brother Revel Rowe and this is so, but Revel is funny too and a handsome man even iffen he is sorry as they say.

I will stop now and fold up this letter which I have writ as neat and as small as posible, it has took days and days, I hope you will enjoy to read it, and be my Pen Friend always. I will carry this letter down to Mrs. Brown when next I go, I have not been to school for a long time now nor has any one of us, as my daddy is not doing any good atall, nor is Danny, and it is coming on for winter at this time we have to pull the fodder now and get it down offen the mountain on the woodsled, this is very hard without no mule. We have all holped to do this Chore.

I wonder very much what your Chores are, and do you grow very tired, also? And are you afeared sometimes of things you cannot put a name to, as I am? Sometimes I am afeared so and I culd not tell you for why, it is like a fire in my hart when my daddy coughs so loud or Momma sets her face agin us and will not speak. And I look at Silvaney who smiles with the ligt in her eyes that scares me for she does not understand. So I will love to have a Letter from you. I hope your family is gayly I remane your devoted Pen Friend I am hoping.

Ivy Rowe.

Dear Mrs. Brown,

Victor says he will bring this letter to you, he will come by on his way to Majestic where he is going to see old Doc Trout to try and get some medicine for Daddy who is not doing good at all. Daddy is cold all the time and his face is so dreamy it seems. We keep that fire just roaring we are like to burn down the house Momma says, but it does him no good. He eats scarcely a bite these days and looks so little, like ther is nothing in the bed at all. We have got him under the rising star quilt that Granny Rowe made and given us. We have got him rigt up by the fire too, it does no good. So you see I can not come to school now and for why.

I am so thankful for all the writting paper you have sent to me, and for the poems of Eugene Field. I read them out loud to my daddy, this is all that will bring a smile. He loves to hear of the Sugar Plum Tree in the garden of Shut-Eye Town. My bestest is Wyncken Blinken and Nod one nigt sailed off in a wooden shoe, Sailed on a river of crystal ligt, Into a sea of dew.

But Mrs. Brown this poem makes me so sad too because of the wooden shoe, I have wanted a Pen Friend always ever since I learned of them and I do not understand what you mean that my letter is too long and not approprite. I did not know you wuld read my letter ether. So I have written another letter to send to

Miss Hanneke Van Veldt I will send it to you also by Victor, it is very short.

Granny Rowe has come to holp us, she chews tobaccy and spits in the fire. Granny Rowe is my antie I think not my granny relly. Granny Rowe has give Daddy a potion it dont do no good, he has vomited yaller insted. Momma is given him whisky and honey its bettern nothing at best but it makes him dreamy. Theys ice in the water of Sugar Fork now it hangs to the rocks on the side it shines out so pretty of a morning when the sun comes up. It is cold up here now we are keepen the younguns inside iffen we can do it, it is hard to make those twins do ary a thing thogh and Momma is acten so funny sometimes she sits out in the cold at the back of the house and oncet I follered her up Pilgrim Knob, she tried to hold later that she was chasing after chickens but she was not.

She was standing there on the rocky-clift looking out in the wind and her hair blowed all around her face but she never cared. Who knowed what she was thinking? and they was never a chicken in sight. I think of you so and I think, does she still wear the purple dress, and the hat with the fether? And the ladys face so fine on the pretty pin I think it is camio. Another one I love is the Little Boy Blue but it makes us cry and mostly Silvaney. We do not know what is a trundle bed. I hope you are keeping fine, I shall remane forever your devoted,

Ivy Rowe.

My dear Hanneke,

I am a girl 12 years old very pretty I have very long hair and eight brothers and sisters and my Mother and my Father, he is ill. We live on a farm on the Sugar Fork of Home Creek on Blue Star Mountain the clostest town is Majestic, Virginia. It is so pretty up here but rigt now it is so cold.

I want to be a famous writter when I grow up, I will write of Love.

My Chores are many but sometimes we have some fun too, as when we go hunting chestnuts away up on the mountain beyond

Pilgrim Knob which we done yesterday, Victor taken us. Daddy loved this so but he cant go no more as he is sick.

We start out walking by the tulip tree and the little rocky-clift ther on Pilgrim Knob where the chickens runs but then we keep rigt on going follering Sugar Fork for a while, you get swallered up in ivy to where it is just like nigt, but direckly you will come out in the clear. You will be so high then it gives you a stitch in your side you have to stop then and rest, and drink some water from Sugar Fork which is little up there and runs so gayly. And so you go along the footpath where the trees grow few and the grass is everywhere like a carpet in the spring but now in winter the grass is all froze and you can feel it crunch down when you step, you can hear it too. We was having a big time crunching it down. When the sun shined on it, it looked like dimond sticks, a million million strong.

Now this was me and Ethel and Beulah and Silvaney and Garnie. Victor taken us. I am wearing Daddys old black coat, I resemble a hant, we are laghing and laghing. When we get to the chestnut trees they is four of them, and Victor says hush now, you hush Silvaney we will play a trick on Garnie whose never been up here before.

So we get Garnie jumping up and down on the froze-grass, and crushing it down, and Victor he runs around behind this great big old rock up there and grabs aholt of the leastest tree and we walk over there with Garnie, not acting like nothing is happening.

Get you some chestnuts Garnie, Ethel says.

Wheres the chestnuts, Garnie says.

Dont you know how to get no chestnuts honey, Beulah says, you just start picking them up like this, look at me, it is all they is to it honey, Beulah says.

So we all bend over and act like we are putting chestnuts in the poke but Garnie cant see no chestnuts.

Wheres the chestnuts? Wheres the chestnuts? he axes pulling on Ethel so hard that he liked to of pulled her over.

Then Victor he starts hollering and shaking that leastest chestnut tree real hard, and the chestnuts come falling down all around us like a big hard rain, and Garnie he just stands ther he is so suprised and then he starts laghing and dancing all around crunching down on the icy grass.

And then we was all doing it, and laghing, and then we have to get Silvaney quite, now this is hard, and then we filled our pokes up plum to the top and started down. We was not but halfway up Blue Star Mountain but you culd feel the wind already, they is a famous endless wind on the clift at the tip top of the mountain, I have never been up ther. You roast a chestnut in the fire, they taste so sweet. Victor carried Garnie on his sholders all the way down.

I see I have writ so long agin, nevermind I will give this letter to Victor anyway. I have got a scar on my wrist like a little moon from one time I cut it when I was cleaning a trout fish, what else? My eyes are blue and my hair is red, I will remane forever I hope your devoted Pen Friend,

Ivy Rowe.

Dear Mrs. Brown,

My daddy John Arthur Rowe says Thank you very much but I may not come we will not be beholden in any way, he says to say that he is better, he is not. I will come to school agin another time may be Ethel will come too and Garnie, after the thaw, the Rolettes will drive us as before, they have a wagon you know. So we will walk down to Home Creek sometimes and come with them.

So please do not let Mister Brown try to come up here it is not a good idea atall, even Victor says, do not come.

No Granny Rowe is not here right now, she has had to go back over on Dimond Fork to get Tenessee who will run after men if you leave her alone so Granny Rowe has to watch her, she cant keep her hands off the men. These are Daddys aunts is who they are.

To anser your questin, Yes I will be so happy to play with your nice when she comes to visit I will be so happy to do so.

Victor is going over to Bone Valley now where Babe works for the Frank Ritter Lumber Company, Victor hopes to find work ther too, he will send us money, he will come back to plant in the spring. So we will be fine. Do not worry please, and here is your book, do not let Mister Brown come here please as Daddy says he has not got no use for him or his prayers. To anser your questin, my momma sits out in the snow and crys, she says shes a fool for love. What is the name of your nice? We thank you for your kindness we are fine. I do not know wether you will recive this letter or not thogh I remane forever your devoted,

Ivy Rowe.

Dear Mister Castle,

You do not know me, I am your grand-daghter, Ivy Rowe. The daghter of your girl Maude who left Rich Valley to come to Blue Star Mountain with my daddy John Arthur Rowe. My daddy is sick now Momma is not pretty no more but crys all the time now I thoght you migt want to know this I thoght you migt want to help out some iffen you knowed it and send some money to us at the P.O. at Majestic, Va., you can send it to me, Ivy Rowe. I am hopen you will send us some money. I am hopen you will get this letter I will send it to you at Rich Valley, Va. by Curtis Bostick he comes up here courting Beulah who has not been bleeding for a while now, we do not know iffen she will marry Curtis Bostick or not his momma is pitching a fit agin it so they say. It is one more thing to contend with, Momma says. Beulah says she wuldnt have him on a stick but she wuld I bet, nevermind what she says. We have not got hardly a thing up here now but meal and taters and shucky beans, Danny has a rising like a pone on the side of his neck and Daddy breths awful. Please if you are alive now send us money, tell no one I am writting you this letter they wuld kill me for axing but I know you are a rich man I will bet you are a good man too. I remane your devoted granddaghter,

Ivy Rowe.

My dear Hanneke,

I hate you, you do not write back nor be my Pen Friend I think you are the Ice Queen insted. I do not have a Pen Friend or any friend in the world, I have only Silvaney who laghs and laghs and Beulah who is mad now all the time and Ethel who calls a spade a spade. I know you are so rich with all your lace and those fine big cows. I know you have plenty to eat. I know I am evil and I wish evil for you too. Mister Brown told us one time that God is good, but He is not good or bad ether one, I think it is that He does not care. I hope that the sea will come in the hole in the dike and flood you out and you will drown. I will not send this letter as I remane your hateful,

Ivy Rowe.

Dear Mrs. Brown,

I am writing to thank you for the meal and the flour and coffee and the beans you have sent us, Green Patterson come up here with them, he says Mister Brown has payed to send them from Stoney Branhams store. We are so thankful to have them. Things is better up here now as I will relate.

To anser your questin, yes we did have Christmas it is different we do not have a tree here nor have ever seed one. Oakley Fox said you and Mister Brown have made a tree and hanged it with play-prettys I wuld admire to see it so. On December 25 they is not a thing happening as a rule but on Old Christmas Eve that is Janury 5 this is when Gaynelle and Virgie Cline comes over and tells storys all nigt with Daddy as they did it when Daddy was young, this is Christmas to us.

So to anser your questin, on December 25 they was not a thing happening up here on Sugar Fork nor even down at Home Creek but that folks drinks likker and shoots off ther guns, I do not mean us we have got no likker here now but Ethel and me shot the gun. It was fun you culd hear them bang like thunder up and down the Fork and clear down on Home Creek. Ethel and me was out in the snow I was wearing Daddys coat and his old black hat, Momma says he will never wear them agin.

It had froze all the previous nigt so when I walked out ther Mrs. Brown, it was so pretty that it like to have took my breth away. Ice just shining on each and evry limb of evry tree and isickles thick as your arm hanging down offen the house. It was like I looked out on the whole world and I culd see for miles, off down the mountain here, but it was new. The whole world was new, and it was like I was the onliest person that had ever looked upon it, and it was mine. It belonged to me.

Now it is new for me to feel this as I have not had hardly ever a thing of my own, it is handmedowns and pitching in and sharing everything up here on Sugar Fork, they is so many of us up here as you know. But I looked out over all them hills, and the land was sloped so diffrent, from the snow. And every tree was glittering, and Sugar Fork black and singing along mostly under the ice. The snow come plum up to my knees. Nobody else had got up yet and I reckon I was the onliest one in the world. My breth hung like clouds in the air and the sun come up then, it liked to have blinded me. Well now this is the time I know Mrs. Brown when you pray, but to anser your questin if I pray, I can not. So I know I am evil but I do not feel evil.

And this is what happend next.

I heerd them guns popping all threw the hills and then I knowed it was Christmas wich I had clean forgot. All the rest of them was sleeping in the house. ETHEL I hollered, and direckly she come, wearing Daddys dead mommas old coat, she looked so funny I liked to of died. Get the gun I hollered, and whilst she was doing it I layed rigt down in the snow and made angels, I must of made a thousand angels but I never got wet, that snow was as dry as powder. Lord it was a pretty pretty day. Then I stands up and brushes off Daddys coat real good and drawed in my breth real good, it was like I was brething champane.

And I says, I am the Ice Queen, rigt out loud. I felt so good.

Then Ethel come running out with the guns and we fired them, I love that blue smoke and the way they smell. Well this woken everbody up a course and they flung open the door and all come running out hollering even Beulah who is big now and little Danny he is sick was laghing and crying at once.

And then do you know what happend next?

Our Momma tied back her hair and smiled and popped popcorn on the fire, did you ever hear the like of popping corn for breakfast? It beat all. So now that was what happend on the morning of Dec. 25, and next I will tell you of what follered which is so strange I cannot credit it yet at all.

It was along about evening and Ethel and Garnie and me was all gathered up close around the fire trying to get dryed out, we had done gone all the way down to Home Creek and slid on the ice with the neghbor people, the Conaways and the Rolettes and the Foxes, they was all out there sliding, and Delphi Rolette he was playing the fool, he brung a little old rocky chair out there and took to pushing all the littluns on the ice. One time his old woman Reva Rolette come out from there crying and twisting her hands and says oh Delphi come on back to the house, you know you are crazy drunk you are going to hell for sartin. But Mister Delphi Rolette he laghs a great big lagh and pushes little old Dreama Fox, the leastest one of them Foxes, around on the ice. I have heerd tell how Mister Delphi Rolette is so bad to drink, but you cannot tell it, I think he is nice but his old woman is touched for sure. She is crazy religios too, Oakley Fox says she talks out of her head and will swaller her tonge iffen the rest of them does not hold her down and grab it. She is a big large fleshy woman and real religios so they say. And Oakley Fox is telling me all of this. Then he says, come up to the house now, my momma says to bring you all up there afore you set off for home. Now Oakleys momma Edith Fox is real sligt and ashy-pale, her hair is as ligt as Silvaneys. Oh honey, she says to me, how are you keeping? Shes not as big as a minit, Edith Fox. And then she just up and kisses me, which set me off crying, I cant say for why thogh. It is like Oakleys momma is little and soft and sweet but my momma is hard as a rocky-clift, and her eyes burns out in her head.

Looky here younguns, Oakleys momma says, and she given us a hunk of apple stack-cake apiece it was the bestest thing I have put in my mouth so far. And Oakley and Dreama and Ray get stack-cake whenever they want it I reckon, ther daddy lives in a camp at Coeburn he has got a big job in the lumber mills ther and dont come home of a week. Ethel and me says no thank you mam after one hunk but that little old Garnie just eats and eats, I dont reckon hes ever had such as that before. Dreama and Ray is spoilt I think but Oakley is real nice in fact he is TOO nice, I gess I am like Daddy and hate to be beholden for ary a thing. Oakley has freckles and a big smile like his mommas I cannot smile back, insted I want to hit him, I can not tell why.

So we make our manners and clumb up Sugar Fork, it was coming on for dark then and all the shadders was blue. We cross Sugar Fork one, two times on the crackly ice, and then we come walking up the lastest rise, me and Ethel pulling Garnie by the hands atwixt us, and him just fussing, and then we can see the house sticking up there outen the snow with smoke rising from the chimbly and snow on the roofshakes and isickles hanging down offen the roof. The cedars looks so diffrent all bowed down with snow, and blue shadders underneath coming creepen up towards the house. Law, it looked like a picture book!

This here is Christmas, I says to Garnie and Ethel, now you all mark it.

And when we come in, my hands was too froze to work good. Did you all have a good time? Momma axed us and we said, Yesm. Her and Beulah was carding wool by the fire and Daddy was sound asleep on his pallet rigt there. You could hear his breth all around it is like a rattle way down inside him. Silvaney was looking out the winder she can look for hours and hours at the snow it is like she has never seed any such thing, she takes on so about the snow. So I go over and look out with her.

It was coming on for dark real fast then, everthing was blue and gray and white and silver, it did not look like Sugar Fork no more it looked like Fairyland out ther as nigt come on. Then the air growed as thick and as dark as the waters of that big swimming hole down on the Levisa River where Daddy taken us oncet, and when we looked out the winder it was like looking down in that swimming hole where we culd see the forms of the silver trout-fish go flashing by way down so deep in the water that you culdnt exackly see them, you just thoght you culd. Well looking out the winder was like that, I thoght I culd almost see things or the shapes of things, moving behind the dark behind the cold thick air. Silvaney and me held hands.

I know I am telling to much Mrs. Brown, it may not be approprite nether.

But this come next, you will not belive it!

We was looking out real quiet at the snow, and Momma and Beulah was carding the wool and Ethel and Garnie asleep on the floor, you culdnt hear a thing but the crackling fire and a pop ever now and then if a isickle cracked offen the roof, when all of a sudden they comes the loudest whistle you ever heerd, rigt up close to the house.

So Silvaney commences to blubbering and runs and gets down in the bed. Beulah throws down her wool and comes over ther to look out but it is dark now, you cant see nothing.

Then we hear that whistle agin, real loud and real close to the house. It dont sound like anything I ever heerd, it sounds like a screech owl but it aint a screech owl, it sounds like a shreeking hant.

Lord Lord, my momma says. I look back at her and in the fires red ligt she looks almost pretty, I swear her face is diffrent all of a sudden, she touches her hair with a hand that shakes like a moth flying.

Well that set me back some, I will tell you.

But then I looked over at Daddy, and Lord it was the biggest suprise I had seed yet. Daddy set rigt up in the bed and throwed Granny Rowes quilt rigt down on the floor and swang his legs around like he was fixing to stand up, like he was a man that culd get up outen the bed.

While now outside, this whistling has switched to a tune, they never was a bird that culd whistle as good as that.

What is it, what is it? axes Beulah and me.

Lord Lord, is all Momma says.

Then they comes a loud pounding on the door, and then Daddy turns and grins the biggest grin and I recollected all of a sudden how he used to look, how he used to be such a handsome man, and what all he used to do. He keeps on grinning.

It is Revel, is what he says.

Well let him in girls, he said then, and I run to open the door and sure enough it is our uncle Revel that we have not seed for years, not since I was a little girl and him and Daddy fell out so bad. Revel lets out a big whoop and a holler and comes rigt on in and gives Daddy a hug. John Arthur, he says, and Daddy says, Revel. Then they look at each other for a long time and then Revel goes over and says Maude, how are you? to Momma who is trying to stay mad, but she cant do no good with that. Well shut the door then Revel, your letting out all the heat, Momma says, and he done so. And all the time, uncle Revel's big black dog is wagging hisself all over the house and licking at people and jumping up. Ethel wakes up scarred to death and crying and so does Garnie.

You hush now, Momma says, this is your uncle Revel, that you have heerd tell of, and then Revel says Sit to his dog and it does. This dog is named Charly, we come to learn. It minds the best and is the smartest of any dog I ever seed, Ill say that. Charly goes everwhere with uncle Revel.

And now I will tell you of uncle Revel hisself and what he looks like, he wears a big black hat like a cowboy hat and black boots and a long dark coat, he has a black beard and a mustashe and kind of pale silver eyes but he is not as scarry looking as this sounds. No, but Revels eyes is just jumping, just full of fire and foolishness. When he smiles, his teeth is like a slash of white in his face. His lips is as red and full as a pretty womans. Well then he goes out, and then he comes back in with a poke, and then we see he has brung us jawbreaker candy from town, and even Silvaney comes creepen down outen the loft to get hern, and uncle Revel looks at her and says, Lovely. He has brung whisky to drink and his banjer to play, he sings like a man on the radio. Mrs. Brown, you have never heerd such-like in all your life. And Daddy is setting up now and he axes for his guitar and Momma gets it but he cant do nothing except just pluck at it a little bit, Momma lays it there alongside of him on his pallet by the fire. Uncle Revel sings a bunch of funny songs. Now I have heerd tell all my life how uncle Revel cannot keep his hands off the women nor stay outen truble but what I think is, he is just a natural antic, he gets us all to laghing so hard we cant hardly stop. We sing oh I will go to meeting, I will go to meeting, I will go to meeting in a old tin pan. We sing Bile Them Cabbage Down and other tunes.

One time Revel looks at Momma and jerks his head at me and says, Thats the one Maude, she takes after you shel be truble all rigt, shel be wild as a buck like you, just wait and see, but Mommas face turns as dark as a stormcloud and she says Revel, Revel, all that is past, Revel your crazy, youl never grow up.

I hope not Maude, says Revel.

We sing Skip Tum Aloo and Saro Jane. Daddy has fell asleep by now and Revel gets up and gets Daddys guitar real gentle-like and hangs it back up where it goes. He kneels down by Daddy like he is praying and tuches his face. Dont nobody say a word. Then Revel stands up and puts on his hat and pulls on his gloves and tips up the bottle and drinks the rest of that whisky down. Ho Charly, he says. Cant ye stay the nigt, Revel? axes Momma, but uncle Revel says No Maude, Ive got to get on down the road now, and then he winks at her, and I am the onliest one besides Momma that sees it. In this wink they is a woman someplace waiting on him, and all of a sudden Oakley Fox pops up in my mind, this makes me so mad I liked to of died. Oakley Fox is stupid, hes too nice. I stomped on one foot with the othern, I was that mad, and Revel grinned at me, and said, Thats the one to watch Maude, to Momma. Then he picked me up and hugged me to him. His beard and mustashe is scratchy he smelled wonderful like tobaccy and whisky and out-of-doors.

Ho Charly, he said.

And then he was gone.

So uncle Revel has come to call on Christmas Day I reckon, and has gone on his way agin, he has given us all them jawbreaker candys and also money, Momma says. She says thank God.

So I am wishing you a Merry Christmas Mrs. Brown and Mister Brown too down ther, it has been a lot happening, we are fine thogh and I remane your devoted,

Ivy Rowe.

My dear Hanneke,

I know you will not get this letter.

I know I will not send it, you are the Ice Queen so cold with your icy blue eyes and your cap like a snowflake and your long white stockings as white as the snow.

But it is snowing now and so I think of you, and sometimes it seems to me like you are more real than all of my Family, you seem more real to me now than the days that pass. It seems like I can not talk to my Family they is so many of us here in the house in the snow we have to keep the younguns in you can not bath yourself nor nothing and little Danny crys. They is noplace here you can go to get away from him crying, it is only when I am writting you this letter late in the nigt that I dont hear. And Daddy my sweet Daddy sleeps in the ligt of the fire now, he wont hardly wake up for a thing. The snow is driften plum up to the roof on the north side of the house and ever time you get the water from the spring youve got to bust the ice, and then youve got to haul it throgh all this snow, it is so hard, we have not got but one pair of gloves amongst us.

Yesterdy when I was the one hauling the water, it was coming on for dark, I slipped and fell coming down the hill and spilled my whole bucketfull of water, I just layed in the snow and cryed and it was getting dark all around me, I just layed there crying while nigt come on, and before long I culd feel my tears freezing on my face I was so cold, and all the air was blue. I tell you, I wanted nothing more than to lay ther, that blue air seemed so pure and sweet. I culd hear the wind go whoosh real gentle-like throgh the cedar tree and come whooshing acrost the snow and it was so quite there, the wind whooshed acrost my face.

But then Momma hollered out where was I, and the third time she hollered I said I was coming, and I went back up ther and got us some more water, and then I went on in the house. My leg had got cut and bleeding but I never even knowed it till I seen it in the ligt. I wuld of layed there forever if I culd of. Do you think this is evil? It is true thogh, belive you me.

Well that was yesterdy evening, and then we et us some sweet taters Momma had roasted in the fire and a pot of soup beans she had cooked with some fatback in them, and some cornbread Beulah made, her cornbread is bettern Mommas. So this was good. And Garnie and Ethel is getting some meat back on ther bones now Im proud to say, and Johnny he grows like a weed but Danny dont do no good, he carrys his head to the side and walks on a slant, it seems.

And then all of a sudden, in comes Gaynelle and Virgie Cline! Never even knocked nor hollered nor nothing, just pushed open the door and poked those old black bonnets around it, Silvaney and Beulah screamed bloody murder and Ethel she went for the gun.

Law, law, Momma said, but Daddy he slep on.

So the Cline sisters comes on in laghing like silver bells, then they see Daddy and goes over ther and bends way down and tuches him here and ther, ther hands is fluttering like butterflys down by Sugar Fork in the spring. Oh oh they said, John Arthur is going, and they tuched his forehead, he stirred but he never awoke. He is going they said, Oh la. For they had not knowed this, they never leave ther cabin hardly ever wich is way away up on Hell Mountain, Daddy used to take us up ther to hear ther storys.

Lord you orter see how they live! ther cabin is so little it is like a dolly cabin with everthing just so. They is two pallets ther with the prettest quilts, and two little old rocky chairs by the fire, and two cups and two plates on the table and two little brooms, and not a thing else. Gaynelle and Virgie Cline are maiden ladys, and have not been apart for a minute. They sit on the porch in little strate-back chairs with seats of woven hickory, smoking pipes. Ther faces are little and squnched up like apple dolls, they are teeny-tiny with curly white hair and dont way hardly a thing. Dont nobody know how they live exackly Daddy said, they do not farm nor raise a thing but beans and flowers in the yard, nor have a cow, but folks takes them food just to hear ther storys.

I think myself they live on storys, they do not need much food.

But I am telling how they come in here last nigt and like to have frigted us outen our wits and then Silvaney, now mark you it was Silvaney, I swear she knows moren folks think, <u>Silvaney</u> says, oh it must be Old Christmas! for this is when they used to come ever year, Janury 5 like clockwork and stay up all nigt and drink coffee and tell storys with Daddy, they did it when he was not but a child living here with his own momma and daddy and his sister Vicey and brother Revel. Daddy allus said it seemed to him that they were old ladys then, so dont nobody know how old they migt be now.

So Gaynelle and Virgie Cline were talking back and forth amongst therselves, and looken at Daddy, ther talking was too soft to hear good and it sounded like a nother langage almost, like bells in the snow. You culd tell they didnt know iffen twuld be better to stay nor go. Danny and Johnny was holding onto Ethels legs and peeping outen her skirt with ther eyes as big as a plate.

And you culd hear our daddy drawing ever breth.

I looked at Momma wich werent no good, Momma was looking wild and she bit at her lip, she had bit it so much it was all ready bleeding. Her hair was all over her head. She clutched up her skirt in her hands. And all I culd think of I sware was that snow outside I sware, where I had layed as I said for upwards of a hour and where it was so quite and peacefull. Lord it was like it drawed me out the door almost, it was like I was being pulled.

But then all of a sudden I heerd myself say, and it was <u>me,</u> mind you, I was the one that said it, Well now that youve come so far we hope you will stay, take off your bonnets come close to the fire and tell us a story. For it seemed to me that the only way I culd keep from running back out in the snow was to hear a story! Momma looked ill as a hornet at me but then she looked down at Daddy and then she told Beulah to make some coffee wich Mrs. Brown had sent us up here by Green Patterson. And the ladys sat down by the fire and we all gathered up around.

Dont tell Bloody Bones begged Beulah, whatever you do.

And just the mention of it set Silvaney off, I had to wet her face down to make her hush.

Tell Old Dry Fry, I said. This one is funny and Daddys faverite.

Well Old Dry Fry was a preacher man, one of the ladys started, but you cant tell Gaynelle from Virgie, its not worth your truble to try. And when they tell a story it goes back and forth, first one to the other you know. She said, everbody knowed Old Dry Fry. And Old Dry Fry liked to eat so much, he wuld eat at two or three houses sometimes after meeting, and one time when he was eating, he et so much that he up and died. Well in the house where he died lived a man named Ray Doolittle and he said, Law me! We will be hung for murder! and so he wrapped Old Dry Fry up in a quilt and taken him down the road and leaned him up agin another fellers door. And when this other fellers old woman opened the door that follering day, why Old Dry Fry fell in the house and everbody said, Law me! its Old Dry Fry dead, we will be hung for murder! For everbody knowed Old Dry Fry.

So they put him in a corncrib and then they taken him out in the dead of nigt and set him up in the bresh by the high road, and direckly a rich man come along, and some highway robbers come up and shot at him until they had cotched him and took all his money, and then they let him go. This rich mans name was Old Moneybags Macintosh, and he run off crying to beat the band.

Then it got full ligt, and them highway robbers seed Old Dry Fry setting up there dead in the bresh by the side of the road, and they said, Law me! its Old Dry Fry dead as a post, we will be hung for murder! For everbody knowed Old Dry Fry.

So they taken Old Fry down to the riverbank and propped him up by a willer tree, and he stayed rigt there until a little old fiesty boy come along and said Ho there, Old Dry Fry! For everbody knowed Old Dry Fry. And when Old Dry Fry didn't say nothing, this little fiesty boy said, I reckon you think you are too good to talk, Old Dry Fry, and when Old Dry Fry didnt say nothing then, why this little fiesty boy just poked him in the river with a willer stick and run off down the road. Now there was a old woman down there fishing for bass-fish and Lord, she cotched Old Dry Fry. And she said, Law me! Hit is Old Dry Fry as dead as a stone, I will be hung for murder! For everbody knowed Old Dry Fry.

And the sisters passed the story around, back and forth between them, and by and by we was all laghing and laghing, even serios Ethel and glummy little old Garnie and even Momma, well she was not laghing but she had set down ther by Daddy and she had left off clutching her skirt. They is something very funny about saying Old Dry Fry over and over. So the story goes on, it goes back and forth betwixt Gaynelle and Virgie Cline until at the end of it, we was dubbled up laghing and Old Dry Fry had ben put in a poke and tyed onto a horse and the last anybody knowed, the horse was galloping off for Kentucky under the ligt of the moon.

And then they toled a bunch more including Mutsmag wich Silvaney asked for, now you see how good she can recollect. So the sisters toled Mutsmag wich is about a old woman that had three gals, Poll, Betts and Mutsmag, but they all treated Mutsmag mean, she had to do all the work while theyd lay in bed of a morning and not give her nothing to eat but leftovers and old sour milk. Then the old woman up and died, and the girls had to go in the world to seek ther fortune and they said Mutsmag, you come too, but she had to carry all ther plunder and they wuldnt give her no journey cakes. But after many adventures a giant comes along, and he eats up Poll and Betts, and then he turns into a handsome Prince and tuck Mutsmag off to a faraway country where she was the Queen.

I loved that one. But now it was late and the littluns had fell asleep and even Ethel was fixing to fall asleep, you culd tell by her eyes drooping down. The Cline sisters stirred and rustled as if they was fixing to go. Me and Silvaney was the onliest ones still up and listening. And I recollected how, if Daddy had not been so sick, he wuld of been telling too, he loved the old storys so, and I recollected what all he used to say about Old Christmas Eve, how alder buds will bust and leaf out, and bees will roar in a beegum like ther fixing to swarm, and briars will blossom and animals will speak, and if you go up on a real high hill, you migt see a big star rise.

Daddy allus said Old Christmas was a time to stay home and think on what will last. And what will last? I said to myself rigt then, and I looked over at Daddy ther fixing to die, and the fire was dying too. It was real late but I wasnt one bit sleepy. Nothing lasts, I said to myself, nothing not nary a thing.

And then the sisters, who had been stirring to go, sat back and said, Well now Ivy, this one is for you.

And they toled it then in a whisper so low it was like it was toled in my very own head.

There was a man with three daghters who was fixing to go to town, and he axed, What do you want me to bring you girls? for he loved them very much. The eldest one axed for a new silk dress the color of evry bird in the sky, and the second eldest axed for a new silk dress the color of evry color in the rainbow, and the youngest, who was the fathers faverite, axed for white roses.

Well the onliest white roses in the whole town was on a rosybush in the churchyard and when the father comenced to brake these roses, he heerd a voice that said, You brake them and I will brake you. And then he comenced to brake them agin, and then he heerd it agin, and then he thoght about his youngest daghter and how bad she wanted them white roses. But then finely he heerd the voice say, Give me what meets you first at the gate, you can brake all you want till your basket is full. And he thoght of his old hound dog that allus run out to the gate, and said that wuld be all rigt.

But when he rode up carrying his roses, who shuld run out but his youngest girl, she said, Daddy Daddy!

Get back sugar, he hollered, but she come on anyways and give him a big kiss and tuck the roses. So the father was truble, but he didnt say nothing, nor tell it, and then as soon as dark come, they heerd a big voice say, Send out my pay.

So the father he tryed to send out the old hound dog, but the voice come agin, Send out my pay.

So the father he went out there hisself, and then the eldest girl she went, but the voice come agin, Send out my pay! and finely the youngest girl she give them all a kiss and gotten her bonnet and coat and gone out the door where she was suprised to find the biggest white bear she had ever seed, who said Get up on my back, and she done it, but she was crying so hard that her nose bled, and three drops of blood fell on the white bears back.

But he kept running on and on.

And finely he come to a nice cabin, and lit the lamp, and lo and behold he was a good-looking young feller and as soon as she seed him, she thoght the world of him.

But now she had to choose. He said his name was Whitebear Whittington and he had been witched so that he culd be a man of a nigt and a bear of a day, or a bear of a nigt and a man of a day, now wich will it be? axed Whitebear Whittington.

She picked a man of a nigt.

So in the daytime hed be a bear and lay around in the woods outside whilst she kept house, and then come nigt and hed be a man, and she was as happy as she culd be. For she loved him with all her hart. She had three babys and time past and she wanted to show them to her daddy, she knowed he was getting old.

Well you can do this said Whitebear Whittington, but dont you never speak my name no matter what you do, and she said she wuld never do so. So he tuck them on his back next morning to her fathers gate.

Now I am so happy to see you honey, her father said, but he kept on axing whose was these babys and finely because she loved him so, she said, Whitebear Whittington.

Well Lord then it lightninged and thunder roled and when she raised up her eyes, she seed her husband going up Pine Mountain and on the back of his shirt was three drops of blood.

Oh how she hollered and cryed then, for she loved him.

So she left her children with her father and set out after him, and she walked the mountains for seven long years and whenever she lost hart, a white bird wuld fly over and drop a fether with a red speck on it, so she wuld keep on going, and sometimes she wuld come to a house wher theyd tell her about a fine young man who had ben ther only the nigt before, with three drops of blood on the back of his shirt. And she kept walking for seven years. She wuld of give up if she had not come upon a old woman who gave her three gold nuts, a walnut and a hickry nut and a chinkypin, and said for her to foller the river and she wuld find her man. So she done so.

But what she found was a bunch of women warshing his shirt, for whoever culd get out the blood culd have him. So she grabbed it away from them women and in a minute it come clean, but then another woman jerked it away, and so this other woman got him and tuck him home, and all this time he never knowed her. He looked her strate in the eye and never knowed her. So the girl gave the woman her gold chinkypin just to sleep with him one nigt, and so she did, and in the nigt the girl said, Three drops of blood Ive shed for thee, three little babes Ive born for thee, Whitebear Whittington turn to me. But the old lady had done give him a sleepy dram, and he wuld not wake.

And then the girl give the woman her gold hickry nut so she culd sleep with him the next nigt but the same thing happend, and he slept on, and she culd not rouse him.

Finely she gave the old woman her gold walnut, and it was all she had, and this evening her husband spit out his sleepy dram, and did not swaller it. So when the girl said, Three drops of blood Ive shed for thee, three little babes Ive born for thee, Whitebear Whittington turn to me, he done so, and when she said his name he waked up, and he knowed her. And the next morning that old woman found the door locked as tigt as a drum, and she culdnt get in no way and she was mad as fire but there wasnt nothing she culd do as the spell was finely broke and they walked back over the mountains together and got ther three children and went on home, and Whitebear Whittington never was a bear again.

I think this is the bestest story I have ever heerd.

By the time the sisters had quit telling it, it was real late and everbody but me and Silvaney was sleeping, so we helped the sisters get ther bonnets and ther coats where we had hanged them up to dry and they said over and over they had to go, they wuld not spend the nigt, which we knowed anyway, they never will stay the nigt but walk in all wethers home. Goodbye then we said, we culd not see ther faces under ther bonnets nor hear what they said, wich sounded like fairy bells in the snow. When they tell a story, you can hear them. Silvaney stood in the door and watched them go, and I come and stood in the door behind her, and Momma raised up and hollered at us for letting out heat. So we went out and closed the door behind us and stood barefoot in the snow, it was not even cold a bit, watching the lady sisters skitter like waterbugs over the snow, moving faster and faster it seemed until they were lost in the shadders of trees as they headed up Hell Mountain so fast it seemed they were flying.

Silvaney and me stood with our arms around each others waists and looked at everthing, the moon on the snow so brite it was almost like day, the snow shining back at the moon.

The sisters dissapeared.

But when I was straining to see them I seed something else and

I will sware it, you culd see in that moonligt as plain as day, and what I seed was Whitebear Whittington walking into the dark trees, and them three drops of blood on his back. I grabbed Silvaney hard it made her lagh out loud she thoght I was funning her, and then she culdnt stop laghing, it tuck awhile. I said Silvaney Silvaney, did you see him? and she said, who? But Silvaney dont know what she sees. And I seed him myself I tell you, seed his white shirt and fine gold hair all shining, Whitebear Whittington I seed him as plain as day, but I cant tell it to nobody else so I have writ it down for you cold Hanneke, Hanneke Queen, or for nobody, or may be it is for me as I remane forever always,

Ivy Rowe.

My dear Mrs. Brown,

I thank you kindly for yor letter but to anser yor questin, no I do not pray, nor do I think much of God. It is not rigt what he sends on people. He sends too much to bare.

Listen here.

My daddy died to anser yor questin a week ago Thursday.

And it was a funny thing, it being rigt after that big rain, and little freshets of water was busting out everwhere around here and the sky so blue it was like you culd smell spring in the air and the birds is all coming back now too, they was twittering. I had took off my long undershirt two weeks before, and Silvaney and Ethel and the littluns had done the same, and we had took the asafiddity offen around the littluns necks. Ethel and them was taking on so that morning for I had found three little chicks just hatched and nearabout drowned up on Pilgrim Knob, and I had brung them in the house and put them in a little box up here by the stove and we was all watching them. So wasnt nobody paying much mind to nothing but that, when all of a sudden Silvaney comes busting in the door and screams and falls down on the floor by Daddys pallet. Now I culdnt tell you where Silvaney had been nor what in the world she was up to. She has took to wandering the mountain since the thaw, cant none of usuns keep her in the house, and after all she is growed, Silvaney is a big girl now.

And that awful screem she lets out as she falls is like a knifeblade in my hart.

Silvaney lays on the floor crying.

Lord what is it now, Momma says and she turns from the stove where she has been cooking a mess of cabbage. Then she thows down her paddle on the floor and runs over there and flings herself acrost Daddy, laying her ear to his puny chest. John, John Arthur, she says. Then she lays plum still for a minute acrost his pallet, and her hair had come loose now outen its knot, and it splayed black and gray everwhere like a witches hair, covering Daddys face. You culdnt hear a thing in the house but Silvaney crying and the boy-babys banging ther little gourds on a old tin pan Beulah had give them to play with. Then Momma looked up and looked around at all of us.

He is gone, Momma said. Yor Daddy is gone now, dear God I never thogt Id live to see this day. I knowed it was coming I gess but I never thogt it wuld relly come, dear God, may his sweet soul rest in peace.

Mommas face was like thunder and lightning, it was terible to see. Then she leaned back down and give Daddy a big kiss on the lips. Oh Momma Momma, Ethel and Beulah and me started crying, and we come over to her, and she said girls, holp me up now.

Daddy just layed ther as slite as a boy, with nary a line on his face, he looked so young in death, like he must of looked when Momma run off with him, all those years ago. Now she looked 20 years oldern him. But a course he had not done nothing but layed ther, just layed ther was all he culd do for years while Momma had been out fighting the world alone. We come over one by one and kissed our Daddy on the cheek or just tuched him, Beulah culd not bring herself to kiss him she toled me later, but it was not bad atall, his cheek was still warm and his beard scratchy as in life, I culdnt get it in my head that he was dead.

Momma took off her apron and pinned up her hair.

Theys a lot to do now girls, Momma said. Ivy you go on down to Home Creek and tell all the neghbor people, and ax if one of them Conaway boys can go for Victor, we will want Victor home now, and get somebody to tell Early Cook we will need a coffin for John. And Ethel you go on over to Dimond Fork for Granny Rowe and Tenessee, and Silvaney, you get up from there rigt now, get up this minit Im telling you. And Garnie you have got to let go of yor Daddys hand now it aint rigt, yor Daddy is dead, Garnie let go of his hand now, let go. Ivy cant you do something with Garnie now Momma said, and she and Beulah went and got Silvaney up and took her over in the other side of the house to sleep. Silvaneys skirt was all muddy and twisted, who knowed where Silvaney migt of been? Beulah was as big as a house, she had to move real slow, and Curtis Bostick had not come up here courting since afore that big snow in Janury. Momma said it was just one more cross to bare. Beulah leaned way back when she walked, balancing her belly, you culd tell it was hard for her.

They went off with Silvaney and I said Garnie, Garnie! This is not one of yor play funerals now Daddy is relly dead now. Will we sing? Garnie axed and I said no honey, I reckon not, we will berry Daddy, it is a good thing the thaw has come so we can do it. Then one day this summer they may be a funeral when the preacher comes it wont be for months you know this Garnie, get up now, and he done it at last but his face was so odd-like Ill never forget it, so serios and brigt-eyed like a funny little rat.

Where is Daddy now? he said and I said, he is dead Garnie, he has gone to Heaven I reckon where his chest dont hurt no more and he can breth good, but I knowed in my hart this was not so for ever since he got sick he has not gone to meeting nor prayed, this is years now. I can scarce recall meeting myself, and Momma is not religios ether, she has not took us to meeting since Daddy got sick and she took up figting agin the world.

Garnie looked at Daddy real hard. He aint in Heaven, Garnie said, and something about the way he said it given me the all-overs and I shivered just like I was froze.

Well he is too, iffen I say he is, I toled Garnie, and I says, who are you, such a crazy little old boy, to say any diffrent? Who are you to say whose in Heaven and whose in Hell?

So Garnie shet his mouth then and never said another word, but his little eyes was shiny and dark as the buttons that go up the front of Granny Rowes good dress. Garnie is too intrested in dying and Heaven, it is not rigt Mrs. Brown, mark my words.

Daddy layed ther real peacefull like a sleeping boy like he wuld of been so suprised at all of the hulla baloo. Go ring the bell, Momma said to Garnie, coming back, and he done so, and I heerd its ringing ever afterwards as I started down the mountain for Home Creek. Water was running everwhere, water water bounding offen ever little clift and shining in the sun, and the sky just as blue as a piece of cloth in Stoney Branhams store. Buds had busted out on all the bushes and trees. It was hard walking in all the mud. I got it clear up to my ankles I kept slipping on stones I was crying too, it was like I culdnt hardly stop crying.

For Daddy had loved the spring. He used to plow and hold the plowed earth to his face, he loved how it smelled, I recall him doing that when I was not but a little thing, and him saying to Babe, isnt this good now? and dont this smell just like spring? and Babe rolling his eyes and snorting like Daddy had lost his mind. Farming is pretty work, Daddy said. But Babe hated farming, he run off as soon as he culd, and I for one was glad to see him go and hope he is gone for good. Daddy loved the dogwood and the redbud and the sarvis and how they looked blooming all by ther-selves up here on Blue Star Mountain afore everthing else got green. He used to take us way up on the mountain in the wee early spring to tap a birch and get the sap, he cut off a big piece of bark for us to lick the inside, it tasted so sweet, I recall he said to me one time Now Ivy, this is how spring tastes. This is the taste of spring. I rembered how he took us down to the creek to look for tadpoles, and how he played his guitar outside after sup-per, propped back in a chair on the porch playing fast tunes like Cripple Creek. By the time I got down there to Home Creek I had mud clear up my ankles and had tucked up my skirt all around my waist, I didnt care who saw what, I didnt care for nothing. Daddy Daddy was all I thogt. And coming down that mountain, sick with crying, I heerd Garnie ringing and ringing and ringing that bell, Mrs. Brown it has rang in my head now for days. DAD-dy, DAD-dy, DAD-dy is what it says.

Well I got myself down to Home Creek I reckon and went to the Foxes house but I do not recall this so good, I was all wroght up as I said. And all what happend next I do not recall so good nether. It was like Garnie ringing that bell had switched on some big awful machine that started rolling and going and wuldnt quit nor slow down for nothing, it kept on rolling till things was finished and done with.

Tomorry Ill tell you the rest.

Early Cook made the coffin for Daddy and then him and Mister Delphi Rolette come up here in Mister Delphis wagon as far as they was able, and highsted the coffin up here on ther sholders the rest of the way. Mister Delphi got so red in the face he had to take off his coller and lay in the yard for a wile before him and Early Cook culd start on back. Early Cook is a thin old pokerface man who dont say a thing unlessen you drag it out of him. Momma paid him cash money for the coffin, she said thank God for Revel Rowe, it is Revels money wich will get John Arthur berried.

Then Victor come busting in, he had rid all nigt to get there, and hugged us all. Momma never shed a tear afore she saw Victor, but as soon as he come in the door, she started in crying, and culdnt stop for a thing. It scarred Silvaney so to see Momma like that, for as a rule our Momma never cryed nor smiled nor nothing, but Granny Rowe who was there by then said No Silvaney, it is good for Maude to cry, Maude has got crying backed up to last her years, now you get up from ther and let yor momma cry, and Silvaney done it to my suprise, she will mind Granny Rowe bettern she will mind anybody else. Granny Rowe got Silvaney and Ethel out there making mudpies with Johnny and Danny to keep them outen the house, and she got Beulah in ther making coffee and ginger biskit for them that wuld come direckly, she got Garnie a-halling wood and she got Momma to set on the porch finely iffen Victor wuld set beside her, wich he done.

Victor has growed up a big handsome man, you wuldnt hardly know him, he has got the clearest dark brown eyes and a big sweet grin. He is a man now thogh, he is smoking cigarets. He said, I reckon I will lay off awile now Im here and not go back till we get done planting, wich was the first I had heerd one of usuns ever telling Momma what was what.

Momma nodded and sighed, it was like she scarcely heerd him, holding onto the arms of that rocker and starring down the mountain towards Home Creek throgh the springy washed-clean air.

Or do ye reckon to plant at all? Victor axed her, Have ye thogt of selling this land and moving to town? You used to be a town girl, Victor said. Victor grinned at Momma.

Momma looked at Victor like he was talking in a forren langage, as in French. Why Victor this is John Arthurs land and it was his fathers land before him and itll be yourn now, when you want it, I will keep this land for you. Momma looked at Victor like he was crazy.

But Victor shuck his head and ducked his chin and grinned and said oh Momma, I dont know, we will start in planting tomorry iffen hits good wether, but I dont know iffen I aim to farm or not,

I will tell you the truth as I see it. My boss man Cord Estep says they is a golden oppertunity in the lumber trade for a man like me.

A man like you, my foot! hollers Momma. You aint a man yet. You shet up all this foolishness, you have gone and got your head full of fancy notions is all, now I wont hear another word, Momma says with all the old fire, and Victor says yessum, but I knowed he was telling a lie. I knowed he wuld take off when he got good and ready and seek his fortune, as in the storys.

And I got to feeling agin like I felt when Garnie was ringing that bell, like it was a big machine rolling and rolling on and I culd not do nothing but hang on the back and holler.

Momma starred off down the mountain smoking one of Victors cigarets, I had never knowed her to smoke a cigaret before.

By God I will run this farm, she said.

Ethel! Ivy! Come in here now girls and holp me, Granny Rowe said then, and we done what all she said. You never know what you can do iffen you dont have to do it, now thats the truth. Granny Rowe sent Ethel up to the spring for water whilst we undressed Daddy and when Ethel come back, we warshed him off. He was so little it was like warshing a little bitty child, or a little shadder of a man, it did not seem like our daddy. And then Momma come in with the white wool berrying socks and we put them on him, and his good black suit, and his tie. Granny wet the comb and parted his hair but when Momma saw it she screemed, she said it was parted on the wrong side, so Granny changed it. Momma wuldnt tuch him herself now, she just cryed and cryed. We had to do everthing.

They was a lot of people coming up the holler by then, they was all out in the yard by the daffodils wich was blooming ther crazy heads off. Then Momma got the berrying quilt and they rapped him up in that, his own Momma had made it, years before. When Momma got it up out of the hope chest they was a nother quilt in ther that I had not seed before, a real pretty mostly blue crazy quilt, and I said, I have never seed this quilt before nether, and Momma said no, this-uns for me, and so we left it laying rigt ther.

Now I think this is <u>awful</u> Mrs. Brown, do you? I will not keep a berrying quilt nor any socks, so holp me God. I think it is awful, I had to warsh his face, we put quarters on his eyes to keep them shut, after Victor and them lifted him into the coffin and Granny

Rowe tyed a rag under his chin to keep his mouth closed, and put a camphor cloth acrost his nose and mouth so he wuldnt turn black.

Garnie come in at this time and wuldnt hardly leave Daddy alone a minit so it got to be his job to stay there by the coffin and get that rag ever oncet in a wile and put more camphor on it. Beulah culdnt stand the smell, she went over on the other side of the house to lay down, she was feeling faint anyway.

The house was the fullest of people Mrs. Brown that it has ever been before or since. Everbody come up there from Home Creek, Mister Delphi Rolette and his crazy wife who acted like she was the one dying, she took on so, and all the Foxes including Oakleys sweet momma Edith and Oakley hisself and Dreama and Ray and his daddy, and bald-headed Thurman Conaway who has got a goiter and his wife Maxie who was a Breeding, and all ther children. They was about ten children out in the yard, so Victor went up in the loft and got down that old blowed-up hog bladder for them to play with. Daddy used to make us a playball outen the hog bladder ever time we killed a hog.

Poor little old Johnny and Danny was scarred to death, they hadnt hardly ever seed no other kids, they hung back and helt onto each other just peeping around the side of the house. When you see a whole passel of children like that, you know for sure it is something wrong with Danny, he goes along slaunchways as I said.

Then Green Patterson come up here, and Stoney Branham and a bunch of other men from the store that had knowed Daddy all ther lifes and used to play poker and tell tales with him afore Momma put a stop to him drinking so. This was Dove Yates and Troy Counts and Woody Elswick and a whole bunch of others, and they had brung some likker, and the women had brung food. Lord it was the mostest food you have ever seed, devilled eggs and chicken and dumplings and sweet tater pie and blackberry jam cake and such as that, setting all over ever place, and that little Garnie he et and et. And Daddy in his coffin was laying there in the middle of it all, with his eyes shut down by silver money and his mouth covered up by the camphor cloth.

Momma sat by him in a strate-back chair and helt his hand. Finely she had let Ethel and me pin back her hair, and she had put her lace coller on. It smelled awful in the house, even with the winder open, and the door, from all that camphor, but Momma just set there and people wuld come and set with her and finely as the evening come on, they was a lot of folks ther on the porch and in the yard too, they was all eaten and drinking.

Dont you recollect the time when John Arthur and Revel got that dynamite and took and blowed up Sugar Cave? said Mrs. Kirk.

Lord yes and dont you recollect that time the high Sheriff come all the way up here after Revel, they said he had daddied a baby down there in Majestic, it was the Sheriffs nice as I recall, and Revel put on a old ladys dress and bonnet, it must of been his mommas or his grannys, and set on the porch there smoking his pipe and allowing as how Revel had just lit out of here the day before, headed for Wheeling, West Va.?

They all toled storys about Revel and Daddy, and after a while when it started getting dark, Momma toled agin how she had come ther, and the midnigt ride. I rember I was setting on the top step then and listening to Momma tell it inside and I was all full up with wanting, wanting something so bad, I culd not of said what it was. The smell of the camphor was making me sick and the moon was coming up full. It was kindly cold on the porch but the house was so full of folks.

Here Ivy, here Ivy, said Oakley Fox and put a pint jar of corn likker in my hand.

Lord Oakley, where did you get this much likker? I said, and Oakley said he had got it out back where the men were, by the smokehouse, and they was plenty more where that come from.

Lets me and you get drunk, he said but Mrs. Brown I am proud to say that we did not for I said No Oakley, but we drunken some of it, just to taste you know, it tasted awful I thoght and then Oakley give the rest to my aunt Tenessee who was sitting there on the steps too, now this was a big mistake as I will relate to you now.

You know my aunt Tenessee is not quite rigt in the head but she isnt quite crazy ether. In fact she is smack inbetween I gess you wuld have to say, but more crazy than not. Tenessee hasnt never lived apart from her sister Garnett, this is Granny Rowe, who does everthing for her, even shell the beans! So Tenessee dont do a thing, but she dresses up as much as she can, and thinks she is beutiful. Some of her get-ups looks so bad you wuld die to see it, she laghs la-di-da and thows back her head. Her hair was so blond and fine at one time but now it is nearly white only she dont know it, she dont know she has gotten old. The bad thing about Tenessee is, she will go up and show herself to men some-times, everbody around here knows it and buttons her up and takes her back over on Dimond Fork or down to the store where they will keep her until somebody can get up with Granny.

But I have heerd tell that one time something nasty happend to Tenessee, and yet a nother time, a drummer come to Majestic and seed her ther in the store and fell plum in love with her and took her walking and give her a perl necklace and then axed ther daddy for her and wuld not take no for an anser nor listen to any sense. When he finely said yes, they say that Garnett, this was Granny then, took to her bed weeping. But this drummer was in love, and proposed to take Tenessee over to his people in Hun-tington West Va. wich he done, but after a wile he brung her back! and carried her up this holler in a buggy as far as they culd go. She was wearing a new green suit wich he had boght her, and a big yaller hat. Carried a new little bead purse.

This drummer he walked her up to the porch dressed fit to kill whilst Garnett and aunt Vicey and Daddy and ther Momma and Daddy was all setting there watching them climb the holler and not knowing what to say. And then that drummer, they say he clicked his heels together like a man in a play and he said, <u>Well my love, it has been an honor,</u> and he give a little bow to her and then a little bow to all of them, and walked off down the holler without so much as a bye-your-leave, and them all watching too suprised to say ary a thing, Tenessee waving goodbye goodbye with a little lace hankerchief that she pulled out of her black bead purse.

She has got it still Mrs. Brown, that lace hankerchief wich is now all gray and soiled from her holding it. She still keeps it in the bead purse and takes the bead purse everwhere. Why she had it ther sitting on the steps, the nigt we berried my daddy.

And Tenessee never has said one word about where all she went or what she done in those three months she was gone, or even if she got maried. I gess she dont know if she did or not. It dont matter anyway. The drummer went into politics we have heerd, and lives in Charleston West Va. where he is famous.

So my aunt Tenessee was drinking this likker wich Oakley had give her, when Mister Green Patterson stood up on the porch and cleared his throat like he was fixing to say something, now he is real important at a berrying, and Tenessee giggled. Mister Green

Patterson cleared his throat agin and says, Well, is everbody here that is coming? and Victor says yes. Clarence Wayne is not coming in for the berrying? Mister Green Patterson axed and Victor said no, nor was anybody else yet to come, he said. Then Mister Green Patterson said we had best get on with it, and him and the other men went in and lit some more lamps that they had brung up from the store, and stood up around the coffin.

Do you want a prayer Maude, Mister Patterson axed Momma, and she said Lord no, Green.

But aunt Tenessee out on the porch started laghing and laghing, she said, Father Son and Holy Ghost, the one that drinks the fastest can have the most. And so Granny come and taken her back in the other side of the house. The men stood ther around the coffin the rest of the nigt, it is just what you do, with little Garnie standing amongst them so big-eyed like a little owl. Momma stood too with her face as hard as a mans face, not crying now nor looking like she ever culd of cryed, and they stood ther all nigt, and come first ligt they nailed the coffin shut and carried it outside, Early Cook put drawer handles on the sides to carry it with, and off we went, everbody that had stayed the nigt and was not drunk.

It was the softest palest prettest morning. Everthing smelt so new because of the rain, it was like Genesis in the Bible. They caried Daddy in the box real easy, he didnt way hardly a thing, with me and Momma and Granny and Ethel and Garnie and Tenessee follering. We left Danny and Johnny back at the house with Beulah. Victor had gone ahead with some boys to dig him a grave at the berrying ground, and Silvaney run off in the woods. We past by the smokehouse and then we was on our way throgh the orchard it was like the ocean I think thogh I have never seed it, or it was like clouds, white clouds on ever side. Somehow in the pale perly ligt these apple trees seemed the prettest I have ever seed them, and smelled the sweetest, and this on the day we berried my daddy wich shuld of been the worstest in my life, but somehow it was not. It was not. For he had been sick so long, and had got so little, that it was not like we had talked to him there on his pallet by the fire for a long time, Mrs. Brown. It was like we had talked to ourselves.

Now, I thoght, Daddy is free to go, and the sun come up then and those white flowers looked even pretier, bees buzzing all throgh them.

Get away, get away, said Tenessee, batting at a bee with her hand, and it obeyed her. Tenessee is good with animals, she has got a house cat that follers her everwhere around ther cabin at Dimond Lick, and one time she trained a deer but Major Little shot it by mistake.

We past throgh the apple trees and past by Pilgrim Knob where our chickens run, and then we started up Blue Star Mountain on the trail we took when Victor taken us up ther after chestnuts, it seemed like years ago. We past by sarvis and redbud and dogwood, and all the trees had little pale green leaves on them now I saw, the oak trees had leaves as big as squirrel paws, all was a pale pale green. Tenessee talked to herself all the way in her singsong voice, but Momma clumb with her jaw shut tigt and her eyes set strate ahead. Are you all rigt? I axed her one time, and she said yes. We past by the path that went to the bald where the chestnut trees is, and we past by the rocky-clifts where Daddy used to bring us after blackberrys, and this was the fartherest I had ever been up ther before. We was out of the tall woods by then, moving throgh scrub pines, so you culd see the sky wich was blue as blue culd be, I reckon it was about seven in the morning by then, and one or two hawks was flying circles up ther. Ethel pointed up but did not speak. Tenessee and Granny had dropped behind.

Ho! Victor said and then we were ther. It was not much to see. Him and the Conaway boys had dug a big hole and the dirt was all red and muddy, piled up beside it. It was a little clearing on the hillside, that is all, where the trees dont grow. I dont know exackly how I thoght it wuld be, may be like the sematary at the Methodist Church in Majestic wich is pretty with flowers and gravestones. Well they is none of that here at the Rowe berrying ground up on Blue Star Mountain. Theys little mounds, that is all, and some so old they have sunk in insted of humped up, and some old wooden markers you cant hardly read and some you can. And theys four lattice houses bilt up ther, two of them falling in, one of them bilt over the grave that holds Daddys daddy and momma, to keep out animals I reckon.

They put Daddys coffin down into the grave.

It was Mister Green Patterson and Mister Delphi Rolette and Stoney Branham and Roland Fox and Dove Yates and Victor, all of them sweating by then, and they taken off ther hats and bowed ther heads and everbody was looking out of the side of ther eyes at Momma who looked for a minit as if she wuld speak, but then she bit her lip and set her jaw and turned away, and the Conaways started shovelling.

Rest in peace, Victor said just about to himself, he looked down at the ground when he said it.

I went over and sat on a rock by myself while they shovelled, but after a wile we heerd the sweetest singing, this was Tenessee who had got up ther at last. She stood on the edge of the woods and sang When I can read my title clear, to mansions in the skys, I will bid farewell to evry care, and wipe my weep-ing eyes. Been a long time travelling here below, to lay this body down. It was Garnies song wich he used to sing at his preachings, when we wuld play Town. But Garnie did not sing. Instead he was starring down into the grave wile they filled it up until you culdnt see the coffin any more. Momma looked up in the sky, shading her eyes with her hand, and I looked too and seed them hawks still circling. They was a little wind up ther, clean and cold. Silvaney come out of the woods and watched Tenessee singing God be with you till we meet agin and I sat on the rock.

Then they were done shovelling and Tenessee was done singing and Momma turned to me and smiled the first smile she had smiled since Christmas and said Gentlemen, I thank you. And I felt my soul lift up like the hawk flying.

It was over.

I know Victor and Early Cook will go back up ther and build a little lattice house to cover his grave, I heard them say it, and I know the preacher man will pray for Daddy too bye and bye when next he comes, iffen Momma will allow it. But it is finely over.

And you will not belive what has happend next!

When we come back to the house the firstest thing we saw was Danny and Johnny out in the muddy yard wearing nothing but ther drawers, this was so irreglar as you will gess.

Hidy! Hidy! they hollered. Beulah has got a baby.

Lord lord, Momma said and we come busting in as fast as we culd and sure enogh, Beulah was laying in the bed all warshed out looking and smiling, and blood everwhere.

Holp me Granny, Beulah said, and Granny Rowe done all the rest of it, and I got to hold the baby wich is named John Arthur after Daddy, a little boy. Granny Rowe says that sometimes it happens like that, one spirit goes and a nother one comes direckly, but you cant make too much out of it. Granny Rowe says it is nothing but natural, that is all. Tomorry, Victor says, we will start to plant.

And so I remane your devoted,

Ivy Rowe.

My dear Mrs. Brown,

To anser your questin, YES I will love to come! My momma has said at first that No I may not come, it will spoil me rotten, but now she says yes I may come, to get me out of her hair, I will have to be good and watch my Ps and Qs. So I may come when your nice is visiting, Victor will carry me down to your house on his way back to work with the company as he has got our garden put in now, and they think so highly of him over ther.

I remane your exited and grateful,

Ivy Rowe.

PS, I will see you soon!

Dear All,

I know you will want to hear from me and how I am getting along. Well the anser is, fine. Molly Bainbridge is the nice of Mrs. Brown, her whole name is Margaret Mae Bainbridge wich I love so much I culd eat it with a spoon. It is like a Party name isnt it? I know you rember our Play Parties in the woods. Now as I write this letter I am sad all of a sudden, I dont know what has come over me, I think of you All so. Please do not think I am fancy, nor spoilt, nor putting on Airs. It is not so, as I will tell you direckly. Things is not all what they seem ether.

But Molly is real sweet and you wuld love her too. Molly is my age 14 she has shiny dark brown hair that curls all down her back, she has a million diffrent ribands for it too, they lay in the drawer of her trunk just like a rainbow, it is the prettest thing, all the colors you can think of, some you cant. The first time ever I seed them all laying ther like that, I starred and starred and cotched my breth, they was so beutiful. So Molly said, Why what are you looking at Ivy?

And when I told her, she laghed and said, Oh Ivy go on. That is how she says it, Oh go on.

Molly laghs a lot, also she talks all the time. The firstest two days I was here, I got plum wore out just trying to foller what all she said, now I am keepen up pretty good. Molly looks so much like Mrs. Brown you wuld take them for sisters. Mollys momma is the elder and Mrs. Brown is the younger one. Molly can cross her eyes grate, also she can stick her tonge out all rolled up, and she is so full of notions Momma, if you think I am full of notions you shuld see Molly Bainbridge. I cant hold a candle to her.

So far Molly and me have played cowboy, queen, city, and goldrush. The way you play goldrush is, go to the creek with a seve and pan for gold. You migt find some. A boy found a ruby not far from here down in North Carolina, Mister Brown showed us this in a newspaper. Also now we are writting a play, we will give it for Mister and Mrs. Brown. Also Molly has got a jumprope so we jump rope a lot we sing songs too and play jumprope games.

One time Mrs. Brown come out and jumped rope too, she is not like a lady some ways she is just like a girl. Molly says that Mrs. Brown wants children the worst in the world, but so far her and Mister Brown has not had any luck. I thoght, if Molly comes up on the mountain to see us we culd get Granny Rowe to send Mrs. Brown something to holp her out. I will write more of this later.

Now I will tell you what all Molly has in her trunk, this is a Chinese red trunk with brass straps, inside it she has

17 Hair Ribands

5 Dresses

3 Skirts

4 Camisoles

3 Shirtwaists

Pink Stationary

A White Bible

Ballay Shoes!

A Bathing Costume!

She will not need the last two up here, belive you me! This is what Mrs. Brown toled her. She toled Molly that mountain girls do not dance ballay, nor swim in a bathing costume. But we have swum down at the swimmen hole in the bend of the Levisa many times when Daddy took us fishen, I said as much. Of coarse we did not ware a bathing costume to do so, I rember I wuld ware Victors old jeans and a shirt.

Molly lets me ware anything, so when I look in the glass sometimes I think it is her but insted, it is me!

Molly wants to have freckles moren anything just like mine but I hate them, I want to have dark dark hair like hers and Mrs. Browns, not red like mine, dark is more royal I think. When we pull up our hair the same way and put Mollys ribands in it, when we put our faces together then starring into Mrs. Browns glass, why then it is hard to tell who is who, and who has got freckles and dark hair, and who aint. One time I started a sentence and Molly finished it, and one nigt we dremp the same dream about walking down a long, long road.

Molly is so smart thogh, she has read ever book in the world it seems like.

But Molly is a only child. So she axes me and axes me, Where do you all sleep? What do you all eat? What is it like to have so many? I can not say. Molly has everthing she wants without lifting a finger, this is clear. But she is not spoilt.

In fact she is so sad sometimes and cries like her hart is braking, this is because her Momma is indisposed. It is what Mrs. Brown says, indisposed. It means her Momma is laying in a hospital due to her nerves, while her Father practices Law, Molly says he is very grand and very busy, he has hired a German lady to cook and take care of Molly. Molly has not met her yet but if she hates her she will run away to New York City and join up with a show! This is what she says. Molly is so full of spunk she has wore out her Father who just grubs after the almighty doller acording to Mister Brown, he said if he had to live with Robert Bainbridge he too wuld be indisposed. Molly crys to think of her Mother, she cryed to hear Mister Brown talk so mean about her Father.

So althogh Molly the nice has everthing I wuld want in the whole world including a cocker spanel at home that can do five tricks and a house as big as a hotel with running water and who knows what all, she has so many trubles and crys and is not happy, now are you all suprised?

I wish she culd live here forever with Mister and Mrs. Brown but her Father will not let her do so. He says Mister and Mrs. Brown are mining fools gold anyway, but they are not mining atall so far as I can tell, except for Molly and me in the creek with our seve.

I am writting this letter at Mister Browns desk, it is a real desk with many little drawers to put things, I wuld so love to have a desk like this one. Early Cook made it for Mister Brown and brung it over here, he is so proud of it too. He has not ever had a call to make nothing like it before. For Mister Brown is a writter I think not a preacher atall, he walks the mountain for pleasure, carrying a walking stick and a notebook, and does not come home all day long. He has many notebooks I see here numbered one, two, three. Molly says he has studdied to be a preacher but he does not preach as you know, nor does he act like one. I have never knowed anybody to act like him atall!

First off, well you have seed Mister Brown and you know how he looks, aint nobody looks like him nether, that wild white hair sticking out around his head like dandelion fluff it is so fine, and his eyes real blue and extra big behind his glasses with the little gold frames. His hair is prematerly white Molly says, and says it runs in his family, but I think myself that it migt of turned white from all the books he has read, you can look in Mister Browns eyes and tell he knows moren most folks has ever thoght of.

Mister Brown calls me Brigt Eyes and talks to me a lot. One time when I toled him mine and Mollys favorite poem rigt now is young Lochinvar, he grabbed up both my hands and said, Oh lovely lovely Brigt Eyes! as if he wuld cry, now why wuld he act this way?

What I did not tell is, young Lochinvar reminds me of Whitebear Whittington, some way. Because sometimes when I say things, Mister Brown writes them down in his notebook and then I feel like whatever I have said isnt mine any more, its a funny feeling.

I thoght that Mister and Mrs. Brown have come here to live

and run our school, and this is true, but they is considerable more to it than that I think. Mister Brown is a reglar card as Granny wuld say and a mistery to me. I have never seed the beat of Mister Brown.

I will tell you one thing he done for an instance, now this was yesterday, he come out on the porch where me and Molly was stringing beans for Mrs. Brown and he brung the Bible too, I thoght, Oh no now he will preach, but insted he read out loud to Mrs. Brown like he was an acter.

Mister Brown read, now this is outen the Bible mind you, Rise up my love my fair one and come away, for lo the winter is past, the rain is over and gone, the flowers apear on the earth, the time of the singing of birds is come, and the voice of the turtle is heerd in the land. I toled Molly, A turtle aint got no voice, for this is so. And we got to giggling and laghing so bad but we was trying not to, now it was hard. For Mister Brown was all wild and waving the Bible around. His forehead is big and white and peaky, it has lumps, you can tell he is so smart. He is real real thin.

Then Mister Brown says, Thy lips Oh my spouse drop as the honeycomb, honey and milk are under thy tonge, and the smell of thy garments is like the smell of Lebanon. He is reading all this outen the Bible!

Oh honnestly David, says Mrs. Brown. Do stop, you are embarassing the girls.

But Mister Brown read that she is a garden inclosed and a spring shut up. You cant hardly tell if hes funning her or not.

My word David, says Mrs. Brown. Oh my mercyful soul.

You are a fountain sealed, he hollers, and with that she puts down the pan of beans and stands up and smooths out her skirt. Mrs. Browns cheek is as red as fire and little dark curls of hair springs up everwhere around her face. David, come inside for a minute, she says, and the way her face looks, you cant tell iffen she is real happy or real mad. Sometimes she just dont know what to do with him, this is clear. Sometimes Mister Brown actes like he is plum tetched in the head he is so crazy about her, but other times he gives her a lecture like she is still in school.

He is considerable oldern Mrs. Brown. Molly says that Mister Brown was her teacher, this is how come them to meet in the first place, Mrs. Brown says he swep her offen her feet. Well this may be so, but sometimes now I think he will talk her to death. It is a funny thing to see Mrs. Brown in the schoolhouse and note how she keeps even them big boys like Claude Presnell and Monk Lester in line, and dont put up with no sass, and everbody dotes on her, and then to note how she actes at home with Mister Brown, how she is just like a little girl agin, it dont make no sense to me. She actes jolly and laghing and happy as a child, and does for him all the time. Why Mister Brown dont have to lift a finger, not even to chop up the wood for the cookstove. Green Pattersons boy comes and does it for them, now what do you all think of that?

But they is other times too, and I will tell you one of them wich I seed with my own eyes, even iffen I wasnt supposed to. It was real early morning and I was up and listening to all the birds, Molly and me sleeps on pallets up ther in the loft it is like your plum up in the trees. They is a little winder what looks out on leaves and at nigt you look out into stars. So I wake up afore Molly ever day, and ever day the firstest thing I think is, now I have to go and milk old Bess, and then I rember wher I am and I dont. I lay ther and think of you All and of lots of things.

But so this one morning I was just laying ther and I heerd Mister Brown in the kitchen going on and on, now it was too early in the morning for one of them lectures of hisn and anybody with any sense culd of told him so. But I heerd him going on and on, and on and on, and then direckly I heerd something crash and brake, like a glass or a plate or something, and I heerd somebody running so ligt acrost the porch I knowed it was probly Mrs. Brown, and then I get up and go over ther and look out the little winder and what do I see? I see the back of her pretty blue dress just flashing along throgh the cherry trees, and then she stops by the well and puts her hands up to her face, and then she sinks down to the grass it is clear she is crying. And then direckly of coarse Mister Brown he comes out ther after her looking all wild and crazy, he tuches her sholder real easy but she jerks away. He dont leave, however. Then after a time Mrs. Brown stands up and rubs her face and takes Mister Browns hand and they walk back to the house together as grave and proper as dolls. In fact they put me in mind of dolls, I seen it all throgh the little winder wich has made a frame around it in my mind.

Now what I think is this. I think Mister Brown loves Mrs. Brown too much, is what I think, he is like to kill her with it but you cant blame him I reckon, I love Mrs. Brown too, and Molly who is so like her. And I love what all they have got down here in old

Miss Leonas cabin like storeboghten soap and cans of food and Hershy bars and oranges that come in a box on the train, books and writting paper and pens does too. I reckon old lady Leona wuld of died to see how her house looks now, she culd not of featured it. They is a picture on the wall of some people walking a road in a place you have never seed, with big old trees like fethers around them, it is very beutiful, they is a nother picture of a fancy lady smiling very misterios.

Mister Brown has come in here now, poking all around. He says, What are you writting Brigt Eyes, that is the longest letter in the world! But he is tickled, you can tell it, and says he will take my letter over to the store tomorry, and send it up ther someway.

So I will have to close, but Momma I beg you, can Molly come back up ther with me and stay for a day or so? At first Mrs. Brown said No but then Mister Brown said Hell yes, let her go, lets give Robert Bainbridges daghter a fine education! So she can come if you will say so. Mrs. Brown is sending you a letter about this, I know she will send you money too, I urge you to swaller yor pride and take this as they is plenty more wher that came from belive you me! I do not mean no disrespect but my life is like a dream here, and I will be so happy to come back up ther and see what you all are up to, for I have not got spoilt a bit and belive me I remane forever yor devoted,

Ivy Rowe.

My dear Molly,

I am writting you this letter to tell you a secret that you can not tell to nobody, cross your hart and hope to die, you can not tell a sole.

Do you rember that day when it was raining so bad and we got Mommas needle outen her sowing box and stuck our fingers with it and mixed up our blud and swor it on the Bible we wuld tell each other iffen we ever kist a boy? I am writting you to say, I have done it. It was not so bad nor was it so good nether, this is what happend.

We was all going berry picking up on Blue Star Mountain wich is what you do come August, it was me and Silvaney and Ethel and Oakley Fox and a whole bunch of Conaways that had clumb up here from Home Creek, they is a famous berry patch away up ther by the rocky-clifts that everbody has heerd tell of. We took off carrying buckets, and the Conaways had them some sacks althogh Momma said, A sack is no good for berrys.

Well we took off walking up the path past Pilgrim Knob wher we seed a snake, it wernt nothing but a blacksnake, mind you, come sliding acrost the path, and Silvaney starts up hollering and then ligts out for home. Drop yor pail, leave yor pail honey, the Conaways hollerd, and we heerd it falling, and they scrambled down and got it and took it on. She is scarred to death of a snake. Well Silvaney is scarred of everthing, you know how Silvaney is.

So then it is just me and Ethel and Oakley and Ray Fox and the Conaway boys, and we clumb up ther, and it was hot as hell going up that path until we got up a ways and then it started cooling off and getting better. The Conaway boys was funning us, they wuld holler Snake, snake, watch out honey its a snake, and such as that. They are big old fat boys now and one of thems face is all broke out terible. Oakley clumb ahead with a snake stick. They was butterflys flying around us, and little flowers everwhere, Indian paintbrush and jack in the pulpit and I dont know what all. I was glad I had wore a bonnet, the sun was so hot on my head. Well we got up ther direckly, and insted of going strate on up by the chestnut trees, Oakley taken us off on this other path that goes to the side where they is a long ridge and a rocky-clift going around it over towards Hell Mountain. Berrys will grow good by a rocky-clift, in sunshine.

Pretty soon we are there and Lord it is true, you have never seed so many blackberrys, just glissening in the sun. Hoo ha! the Conaway boys hollered, and they must of eat for ten minutes sollid afore they even started picking. So we got ahead of them, me and Ethel, and we had our buckets full while they was still going at it.

I belive I will just lay down rigt here and rest a minit, Ethel says, and she lays down in the shade of a junipper, but I say, Well I will walk up this ridge a minit, dont nobody leave without me, and I done so.

The air felt so good up ther Molly, a little breeze come along and cooled me off. It is the highest up I have ever been on Blue Star Mountain so far, I aint never gone plum to the top. I took off my bonnet and looked around. All the leaves was that deep dark shiny green they get rigt at the end of summer, like they are putting on the last act of a show wich in a way they are, I reckon. I had brung a handfull of berrys along and I was eating them one by one, ever time I ate one it was like a reglar explosion in my mouth.

Then I seed a shadder over ther behind the bushes, and when I got up close to it, it was a cave sure enogh, and I went over ther and poked my head in. It was black as nigt in ther, you culdnt see nothing atall, but it felt like it migt be a good sized cave. Hello, I said and my voice come back to me, Hello hello hello.

So I stepped in ther. Hello, I said agin, and this time, somebody rigt behind me said, Hello Ivy.

Well I spun around like a top belive you me but I culdnt see nothing for a minit, the sun out ther was glarring so it blinded me, but it was the black form of somebody all rigt, and he come up and took me by the sholders, and it was Oakley Fox.

You better come out of here now Ivy, we are fixing to go, its not safe nether, said Oakley Fox. My hart was just racing. He had liked to of scarred me to death, but I wasnt going to let on of coarse, so I said, Well then, what are we waiting for?

But Oakley just stood ther holding onto my sholders, and then he stepped up even closer and before I had any inkling what he was up to, he was kissing me. It may be that Oakley did not know what he was up to nether.

Well Molly I just stood ther with my mouth open while he was kissing me and did not close my eyes, and Oakley Fox did not close his eyes nether. Do you rember how we wonderd where you wuld put your tonge, I do not know the anser to this questin yet. We did not get to the tonge part. This kiss was not a bit bad nor was it good ether as I said, and it was not a thing like anything else that has ever happend to me before, I will say that. It culd not of lasted hardly a minit, but it seems to me like it went on for about a year! When he was done kissing me, Oakley kind of stumbled back out in the sun like he was drunk and I came too, and he turned and walked ahead of me back to wher the others were waiting. We walked that ridge with nary a word, but I seed that somehow I had got berry juice all over my skirt and on Oakleys shirt too, I gess I had squashed them in my hand when we was kissing. I knowed that Momma wuld have a fit about the berry-stains, wich she has done. You cant get a berrystain out to save your neck.

We went on down the mountain, and it was hard work carrying all them berrys and we was plum tuckered out when we got to the house, but Oakley and them just took a drink of water and went on. I looked at Oakley good wile he was drinking. He is a serios boy and he is not a bad looking boy nether, but he is not Lochinvar. Do you rember, so daring in love, and so dauntless in war, have ye err heerd of gallant like young Lochinvar? I think that Lochinvars hair wuld stand out around his face like the rays of the sun. Oakley has got brown hair.

After we came down the mountain I culd not look strate at him, for the life of me. I had to look at him while he was drinking.

Oh Molly, do you rember that time we put out the pans of cornmeal with the slugs in them and left them overnigt like Granny toled us, to spell out the firstest letters of who all we wuld mary? And yourn was SL and mine was SS and Ethel said, May be a slug dont know no letters but S? I am going to mary somebody that makes me feel like a poem thats for sartin, not Oakley Fox. Oakley finished drinking and grinned like he allus grinned, then I knowed he never wuld mention that kiss agin in this world, nor wuld I, it was like a streak of lightning or like nothing, like something that did not happen.

Now Molly, do you think I am evil?

Has anybody kissed you yet?

I am sorry to hear that yor momma is still laying up in the hospital, I am sorry you do not like the German lady, she sounds terible. When will you go to yor new school, are you exited? I will ask Mrs. Brown, What is a nun?

Please write to me soon for I remane forever yor best friend,

Ivy Rowe.

My dear Molly,

Yor trip to New York City sounds like a dream. Also it seems to
me that yor Father cannot be so mean if he takes you on such a
big trip and bys you everthing, I wuld try to love him some if I
was you. I am sorry to here that your Momma is worser. I am
sorry that you do not like your new school with the nuns, it sounds
grate to me with books and gray dresses, I wuld love so to have
a gray dress with a white coller as you tell. I do not belive that
they are maried to Jesus thogh, it does not seem like a good idea
atall, they must be as crazy as my auntie Tenessee. Oh and Molly
I love yor new pink stationary, did you by it in New York City?
And I am so happy to have a real frend to write to, let us be best
frends and pen frends always whatever befalls.

Yes yor aunties school has started up agin I am toled, I can not
go to it now, nor never I sometimes think althogh I can not stand
to think this. It is like a big hot black cloud has come down on
my sole. It seems to me now like all our long blue springtime was
a dream. Do you rember when Mister Brown took us down to
the Levisa swimming and you wore yor Bathing Costume? Do you
rember our play about the Queen and the errant night? It seems
to me like years and years ago.

It is dog days here. This is when its hot as hell day after day
and everthing is dying in the garden and iffen you get sick, or get
you a sore place, it wont heal up unlessen the dog days is over. I
have to say, we are not doing so good here now, none of usuns
is what you wuld call gayly in these days. Danny is doing the
worstest. He wont eat hardly a thing and he is growing so puny.

Momma and me and Ethel taken him over to old Doc Trout
he says Danny has got a weakness of the blood it seems to him,
he dont think ther is anything to be done for it. Wate and see,
Doc Trout says. He smelt like likker the day we was in ther, they
say he drinks to much but he is smart. He give us all a peppermint
stick and a tonick for Danny, he says, This is free of charge, now
you all let me know how he is doing, and little Danny just smiled,
he is the cutest thing. I do not think I will have any children ever
as they will brake yor hart. Wile Momma and me and Ethel was
down ther in Majestic, we sent word to Victor to come on home
and holp us. Now this was the start of all our trubles as I will relate.

But wile we was in the store down ther, Mister Branham who
runs the store he says, Now Maude, you know my old woman is

poorly so we culd use a girl around the house I reckon, to sweep up and watch the baby and such as that, I will pay her a little I reckon, now what do you say? And Momma said, Ethel will come. I was thinking of the otherun, Mister Branham said, meaning me, and Molly my hart leaped up I have to say, for I wanted so to come. But Momma says, Cant nobody but Ivy do a thing with Silvaney, I have to keep Ivy at home, and so it was desided and Ethel stayed down ther with Mister and Mrs. Branham they have the gray house on the corner next to the Methodist Church. The last I seen of Ethel, she was sweeping ther front walk and grinning like crazy.

So Momma and me taken little Danny back up on the mountain, and he is taken his tonick, it dont seem to do no good. I miss Ethel moren I thoght, and ever day the sun comes up so hot like a ball of fire, and dust devils dance in the yard. When I look down the holler its like it is shimmying, its so hot. But that aint all.

The worst is that Babe is back.

Now this is my eldest brother Clarence Wayne Rowe, he come up here and toled us that the message come for Victor but Victor cant come, he is gone off with the lumber company out West, so Babe reckons he will come home and stay a spell! Beulah says she heerd that Babe got fired, this is how come him to leave over ther at Poorbottom, but dont nobody know for sure, nor know what Babe is up to nether. It is all that Beulah and Momma and me can do to look after the littluns and hoe the corn and such as that, and Babe is in and out all the time now, he dont do no real work nor lift his hand in the garden. He says he has got business everwhere but he dont say what this business is, we know it is something bad.

I hate it when Babe is here. It is like a dark wind blowing down from the mountain and filling up the house when he is here, he is so mean, he slapped the fire out of Garnie for getting in his way and talks mean to Momma.

One nigt it was so hot I culdnt sleep good and so I got up and went out on the porch and Babe was sitting out ther drinking by hisself and he said, Well looky here it is Ivy, come over here honey and sit down, and I shuld of knowed better but it was hot and dark out ther and sometimes when you get up in the nigt your lonesome, and think that things is diffrent from what they are. Come out here and set with me Ivy, Babe said and in the dark his voice sounded just like Daddys. Then Babe lit a cigaret and when the match flarred up his face looked like Revels face. Babes face looks like Revels a lot in general but twisted, everthing is sligtly out of whack. But in the ligt of the match he looked like Revel for an instant, and my hart went soft.

What are you up to anyway, Babe? I asked him.

And he said Well Ivy, Ive got some prospects, and he laghed, and so I laghed to and then he said, Your sure growing up pretty honey and tuched me on the titty. I jumped up and spit in his face and ran in the house but I culd heer him laghing, laghing after me.

Shoot fire, I didnt mean nothing by that Ivy, Babe said to me the next day, I was just fooling with you, your as bad as Silvaney, scarred of shadders and clouds, I aint never seed the beat of you all.

Momma says we need Babe rigt now to hall the water and get in the corn, that it is life and death wether we can hold onto this land or not, but he dont holp much it seems to me. He is gone for days, I am glad when he leves, and since Ethel is gone now, Silvaney is acting so funny I do not mean funny ha ha nether. Beulah is tired so much, she is nursing that baby and working her hands to the bone, mooning over Curtis Bostick. She migt have a baby but she still has a broken hart.

Molly Molly I miss you so. I think of you in school with your gray dress and the white coller and the bells that ring evry hour, please think of me. Sometimes lately it thunders and lightnings way off in the sky but this dont mean much, it is not a thing but heat lightning, it will be dog days forever it seems with Babe filling up this house with his cigaret smoke and the smell of swet for he dont ware a shirt half the time. Oh Molly this heat pushes down on my head and the heat lightning dont mean a thing. But think of me some for I remane yor devoted frend,

Ivy Rowe.

Dear Victor,

I will send this letter to the Frank Ritter Lumber Co., I do not know wether it will ever reach yor hands or not. We got the monney and thanks. We know you are doing good. We know you are out West learning the business it is the chance of a lifetime, we are so proud of you too, but Victor, I wish you wuld come home. I implore you, as it is the dog days here and things is going from bad to worse. We have got some meal and we are eating outen the garden rigt now but it is so dry that we are not putting up a thing, we will not have a thing come fall, we are halling water to the corn I have bruses on my hands from halling buckets but it dont seem to do no good. The creek is not but a trickle now.

They was three men on horses come up here yesterdy looking for Babe, they was awful mean looking men too, forreners Momma said, and she said, Why Clarence Wayne is not here, I do not know where he is nor when to expect him nether, and they rared up and rode off but one of them shot at the bell as they past. It has rang in my mind ever since. It goes on and on in my head like a warning of things to come. I hope you will recive this letter and come on home for I remane yor devoted sister,

Ivy Rowe.

My dear Daddy,

I think of you often, I miss you so. I am coming up ther to see you tomorry with Granny Rowe, she is coming after herbweeds, what all she needs. She says it will be pretty flowers and mountain grass now grown around yor gravehouse. I hope so. We have left yor pallet laying rigt up agin the fire, we culd not stand to move it, nor your shaving bag nether wich has hanged on the strop by the washbowl ever since you left us, now Babe has taken the razer I think. Oh Daddy, it is awful what all he does. And this is why I am writting to you, I do not know who to turn to, Momma has closed up her hart agin us all it seems. She dont care a thing for none of us and will not even kiss the littluns Johnny nor Danny whose so sweet nor even Beulahs baby John Arthur, named for you. And he is doing fine Im proud to say, he is a big large helthy baby whose the joy of Beulahs hart. Beulah is not as big as a minit now thogh, it is like that fat helthy baby is drawing the life rigt out of her. Beulah and Momma and me has liked to work ourselves to death, but ever day is as hot as the one that come before it, and this is not the worst by a long shot.

For Daddy, they is something terible going on here.

I do not know what it is nor how it comenced nor what to do about it nether, may be I am relly crazy myself like Tenessee or Mrs. Looneys daghter that stays in ther backyard all the time down in Majestic, you know we used to see her when we wuld go into town.

But Daddy, it is Silvaney.

She is hiding more now, she gets up of a morning and runs off in the woods and hides, I sware she is like a wild animal. She will grab up a bit of pone or a cold tater or something else crazy to eat and run off laghing, you can not ketch her nor slow her down, nor ax her a thing when she is like this. And talk! Lord she will talk to herself out loud, this is the scarriest part, and then she will cock her head just like she is listening to somebody, and then she will anser them back! Only aint nobody relly ther Daddy, and you cant understand a word she says. When I tell Momma this, she just says, Oh hush your mouth Ivy, you know how you embroider, honey, just hush.

And Silvaney has got a ligt in her eye now like a reglar fire, it is like her whole face is lit up from inside, like they is a fire in her head shining throgh, and its not long I think before this fire is going to burn her up.

Oh Silvaney Silvaney. She has that pale smooth skin you know and them big blue eyes like lakes, and it is like, rigt under ther is flames, flames. It is so scarry.

Momma says, Dont be so silly Ivy you are just full of notions, Silvaney is fine, fine, hush yor mouth, shut up shut up Ivy. Hush, just shut up for gods sake.

But Silvaney is not fine. And Daddy I see this, and I do not know who to turn to, nor what to say.

For it is all hooked up with Babe someway, I can not say. Silvaney has got worse since Babe come back. Somehow Babe is more than she can stand, you know Silvaney is dellicate. When did it all start I wonder, when Silvaney was little or when they was borned, them twins, Silvaney and Babe, do you reckon it culd of started that long ago? Granny Rowe allus said that Babe come out helthy with a big head of black hair but Silvaney was real tiny and come out blue and had to be shook upside down till she brethed good.

Do you reckon it started so far back? Or may be when they was five years old and Silvaney took the brane fever, Momma said she was out of her head for a week sollid and her head was as hot as a skillet on the stove and it burned out part of her brane. Oh Daddy were you ther when Silvaney took so sick, did you watch by her side? For I feel that I shuld watch ladies now, but I can not. I can not keep up with her now, sometimes I can not ketch her at all, I will heer her voice talking, talking in the woods, but when I come where she was, she is gone. Only a footprint or a broken leaf or her voice on the hot dry wind. Oh Daddy they is something terible hapening now, I can not say what it is. Were you ther when she walked in the fire? For Silvaney is doing these things agin now, I feel it, I can not keep up with her nor watch her ever minit wich I shuld.

Listen Daddy. The other nigt Babe come in drunk in the middle of the nigt. We had not seed him in days. He went out of the house to pee and fell offen the porch wich wuld of been funny if he hadnt of been so mad. So he just layed ther by the steps hollering and then he quit hollering and we knowed he had past out. But sometime later in the nigt, and I dont know what time it was but I know it was relly late, I woke up all of a sudden and sat up strate on the bed. I didnt know what had got into me. I was wide awake. So I got up out of the bed, I culd heer everbody brething around me, and gone over and pushed the door, and law you have never seed such a flood of moonligt in your life, all acrost the yard, it was nearabout ligt as day but a pale flat kind of ligt, the moon. And of coarse it was hot too, even up here, and not a breth of air stirring. I walked out on the porch.

And what did I see but Babe laying out ther drunk in the dirt, his head flung back and his mouth wide open. But the awful part of this is that Silvaney was out ther too, in her white shift with her hair hanging wild and ligt down around her sholders, bending over Babe, watching him sleep.

Silvaney honey, what are you doing out here? I asked her, and Silvaney said, Why hello Ivy, how are you?

I am doing fine, I said, now come on in. Finely she got up and come in the house and went to bed, but ther is something relly wrong Daddy, for it is like she does not need to sleep nor eat now, ether one. And ever after this nigt it has been in my mind, Silvaney sitting in the moonligt watching Babe, it was like she was part of him truely, like the other side of Babe who has so many plans and schemes, but she has none. Silvaney is so fair and he is dark. It scarred me to death and Ill sware it, I cant get it out of my mind how they looked in the moonligt like a statue in Mrs. Browns art book from France, how Silvaneys hair looked in all that ligt. Oh Daddy I miss you so much do not think I am crazy because I feel they is something terible starting to happen and you know it is dog days so whatever it is will go on happening, but I remane yo

My dear Molly,

Babe is dead.

He was shot in the back of the head by a man named Arlen Snipes, or so everbody says, we do not know it for sartin.

This is what all happend.

Babe had been gone from here upwards of a week, over to Kentucky trading or so he said, of coarse we never knowed where Babe went when he left nor what he was up to nether. I wuld like to know what he had to trade. He was up to no good, I reckon it is fair to say, and I dont care iffen I speak ill of the dead or not. Some men had been up here after him about some monney, while he was gone. But they say he had got in a whole nother ruckus over at Pineville about a mans wife that he had been messing around with for some time, and she run off from her husband after him, left two little old babys ther at the house, but when she got up with Babe he wuldnt have her, and sent her back to her old man, now this was Arlen Snipes. And so then Arlen Snipes come out after Babe, telling everbody in Pineville goodbye and that he wuldnt be back afore him or Clarence Wayne Rowe was dead, one. And his pretty blackhaired wife come out in the road crying and twisting her hands and begging him not to do it but he said, Gussie, get on back in the house now.

Who knowed what Gussie had in mind, or what she wanted to happen? Can you imagine this Molly I can not!

But the first thing anybody over here knowed about it was Tuesday after supper when it was just coming on for dark, and Granny Rowe was over here visiting, and we was all sitting out on the porch with the littluns, and all of a sudden we heerd a shot ring out in the nigt over the treefrogs and crickets, real close by. Then a horse started winnying.

Well did you heer that? Momma says, sitting strate up, and Granny Rowe says, It sounds like a shot to me, and not far off nether.

Oh no, Beulah says. Beulahs baby is sucking at her titty.

Sounds to me like it was rigt down the hill ther, says Granny Rowe. She is smoking her pipe on the porch, she has got smoke all around her head. The horse was down ther squeeling bloody murder at the creek.

Im going down ther, says Garnie who is morbid as you know, and he jumps off the porch and runs down the holler and Momma says, Ivy, go after him. He ougtnt to go alone. I have to say, I wanted to go down ther anyway, you know how I am so curios! So I took off running after Garnie, hollering Garnie honey, wait on me! But he wuld not wait for a thing. I ran along throgh a whole bunch of lightning bugs, it was like I was running throgh stars.

Then I heerd Garnie.

Ivy, Ivy, he hollered, Oh lord, Ivy come here, and I follered his voice across Sugar Fork to where he had come upon Babe laying on the creekbank down from the trail. This old horse he was riding had got itself all tangled up in a thornbush, it was raring and plunging and winnying, and culd not get away, wich was lucky for us as I will relate direckly.

Babe was laying half in and half out of the creek, it was so dark we culdnt hardly see him. The bullfrogs was making a racket all along the creek. Babe, Babe, I said and I pulled at his shirt and tryed to turn him over. When I got a good look at his face it was nearabout gone, nothing but blood, but when I layed my head on his back I thoght I culd heer his hart.

Garnie honey, I said to Garnie, you go on back to the house and get Granny Rowe and see can she do anything for Babe, and I am going to get on this horse and ride him down to Home Creek and get some of the neghbor people, it looks like a murder to me.

Ivy you cant ride that horse, Garnie said. Garnie was hunkered down looking at Babe, it was getting dark real fast.

Well I am going to, I said, and I said Whoa now to the horse in a big voice and reached in ther and got his bridle untangled and hopped alongside of him till I culd fling myself up on his back. He was not a real big horse or I wuldntve done it, also I used to ride a horse if ever they was a horse up here, or a mule ether one. So I got up on the horse and then he started bucking. I jerked him in evertime he jumped, and his shoes struck sparks from the rocks along ther by Sugar Creek. All rigt now boy, I said, lets go. He clumb back up the creekbank to the trail with me holding on for dear life. He stomped a little and looked around oncet he got up ther, and I got a holt of him good, and looked back down ther where Babe was laying in the dark with all them loud-loud frogs. Ill be back as soon as I'm able, I said not knowing iffen Babe culd hear me or not. Garnie had took off for home.

And do you know what I seed then, Molly, or thoght I seed?

I thoght I seed Silvaney slipping out from the pinetrees on the other side of the creek and coming acrost the creek so smooth on the steppystones like she was gliding, with her hair hanging down to her waist. Coming over ther to where Babe was laying. <u>No, Silvaney, go back!</u> I hollered. <u>Go back!</u> For I did not want her to see, but Babes horse rared up at that minit and I had to rassle his head down and when I looked back down ther I culdnt see her in the dark.

Git on then, I said to the horse. I gave him his head and let him pick his own way down Sugar Fork, and all that long way down to Home Creek too. My mind was going around and around. Now Babe is probly dead, I toled myself. It is what you have wanted all along, and because this was true I felt awful. I felt so bad. Oh Molly, dont never wish for nothing, for you are liable to get it. Granny Rowe says this and it is true.

So while I was riding down ther, the moon come up, the biggest prettest full moon come up just like it was any other nigt in the world, so ligt and lovely it like to took my breth. I knowed it wuld shine on no matter what, and this given me a turn. The moon dont give a damn, I said to myself, and it dont. The moonligt come down throgh the leaves as brigt as day, a cool white ligt, I culd see everthing just as clear when I come riding outen the woods and seen the neghbor peoples houses all in a nice little row. I felt like the highwayman come riding, riding, up to the old inn door. I have got terible news! I wanted to yell but I was too tired to yell. I turned in the saddle and looked back up on Blue Star Mountain wich looked huge and dark and full of mistery, even under that big full moon. You can not see our house from down ther on Home Creek, nor any sign of it. The moon had got up full by then. It hung real low and big in the sky over Pilgrim Knob, and it put me in mind of Silvaney, coming acrost the creek.

Babes horse was wellnigh foundered by then, twerent any problem to halt him at Delphi Rolettes, but when I got down offen him my legs buckled rigt out from under me and it was all I culd do to get acrost the yard and bang on the door.

Wake up wake up its me Ivy Rowe, I said, and my brother Babe has been murdered.

Well to make a long storey short, this was true, Babe having brethed his last about the time that I made it down to Home Creek I reckon, with Granny Rowe and Momma with him but it was too late, even Granny Rowe culdnt do nothing to stop him bleeding.

So it was early morning by the time that Mister Rolette and Mister Fox and the rest of them come back up ther bringing the law with them, this is Sargent Pope from Majestic, a little old fatbellied man that looks like a cookstove and didnt do nothing but write SHOT IN THE BACK OF THE HEAD on a piece of paper. I rember I went out on the porch in the early morning whilst Sargent Pope was examming Babe who was layed in the floor.

What will they do now? What will happen? This was Garnie out ther pestering all the men to death with questins.

Mister Delphi Rolette took a draw on his cigaret and said, Well Garnie its like as not that nothing will happen, may be they can not prove a thing.

Wich has turned out to be true! That Gussie has turned rigt around and swore it on a Bible that Arlen Snipes was laying with her all nigt long on the nigt in questin, and cant nobody disprove it. She knows wich side her bread is buttered on, Granny says.

But Momma cryed and said, Clarence has been looking for this bullet all his life, now it is finely his. When they layed his coffin in the ground she said, So holp me God I culdnt do a thing with this boy, and Early Cook said, Dont blame yorself now Maude, sometimes that is the way of it, you have had a hard row to hoe.

And I knowed he was thinking back to how Momma had run off from her home as a girl and how Daddy had layed in the bed for so long. Early Cook gave us Babes coffin for free, of coarse we culdnt of payed him a cent if we had to, and they berried Babe as quick as they was able, so quick it did not seem decent somehow. Nobody stood up by the coffin or toled any storeys. They berried Babe next to Daddy at sunset that same day but nobody built him a gravehouse nor mentioned it, it is awful I think to go throgh this world like Babe like a streak of lightning and nobody cares. Babe never had a thing to reccomend him but that grin I reckon, it is sad.

And the only one that loved him was Silvaney.

Now Molly, this part is awful. For Silvaney never showed up all that livelong day whilst they were signing the papers and berrying Babe, and nobody knowed where she was, you know she has took to wandering. And I culd not say for sartin wether I had seed her that nigt by the creek or not, things was confused in my mind. So I did not say a word about it. But I set out on the porch that nigt and wuld not sleep, looking for Silvaney, I wanted to be the one to tell her for I knowed it wuld upset her so. Finely thogh I just had to sleep, I was hurting all over from riding that horse, and so I went in and layed down on my pallet, and when I got up the next day it was plum noon and I was so sore I culdnt hardly move at first, but Momma was ther sitting in the chair next to me.

Mommas face looked all washed out and kind of purified and she said, Ivy I have got some more bad news to tell you, and I said, What, Momma? And Momma said, It is Silvaney, and my hart sank. For I had knowed it somehow I think, and I said, Oh Momma, what is it?

She said, Silvaney knows somehow, she has come back in here and cut at herself with the kitchen knife and run back out in the woods, so Granny says we must ketch her next time and try to holp her, and Granny is going to stay with us to holp out until we have done so.

Now this means that Tenessee is here too, wich is funny. For Tenessee has taken it in mind that Mister Early Cook who is a batchelder is sweet on her, and says that he is coming back up here for her direckly. So Molly, as I write this letter we are waiting. Granny Rowe and Momma and me are waiting for Silvaney, and Tenessee is waiting for Early Cook. She has got her little bead bag beside her chair. She says she is ready to go off to be maried. I will let you know what happens next for I remane yor devoted frend,

Ivy Rowe.

Dear Mrs. Brown,

I have thogt and thogt to myself, shuld I keep silent now or shuld I write and tell her my feelings about what she and Mister Brown have gone and done to Silvaney? And at first I thogt, I will not say a thing, for they have only done what they thogt was the best.

But then agin I thogt how Mister Brown used to push his eyeglasses back on his head and say, Girls, girls, search for the truth, for the truth is more presious than rubies, more dear than love. And Mister Brown read to us that death takes toll of beauty, courage, yuth, of all but truth.

So I will come rigt out and say what I think, it is as follers, I think you all have done a grave wrong to have brung old Doc Trout up here to sware out a warrant on Silvaney, and that little old stovebellied hateful Sargent Pope. If Daddy was still alive you wuld not have done so I will venture to say, nor Victor here nor Babe alive, ether one.

They did not <u>have</u> to tye her hands nether, to put her in the wagon, you know she walked down Sugar Fork so nicely, it was not nesessary to tye her hands. And she knowed what all was happening, she knowed it exactly Mrs. Brown, you yorself was not here to see her eyes when Doc Trout clicked to the mules and they started off, how she starred back at me and Momma and did not speak. I belive she knowed what was hapening, and gone of her own accord. She is no longer VILENT, yet this is what Doc Trout wrote on the warrant to send her away.

I was suprised that Momma let Silvaney go so easy, yet Momma is tired of figting, and all the fire has gone out of her since we berried Babe. <u>Momma, Momma, make them stop!</u> I said as old Doc he clicked up the mules, but Momma put her arms around me and said, Oh Ivy, perhaps it is for the best, Mister Brown thinks it is all for the best. Silvaney will get better bye and bye, and then she will come back to us.

But Mrs. Brown I will tell you the truth, I do not agree. Since Babe is dead, I feel that Silvaney wuld of quited down. In any case Silvaney is diffrent from all, she needs to wander the woods, and she needs some woods to wander. I cannot feature her in the Elizabeth Masters Home in Roanoke Va. it dont matter how nice it is, she will not learn a trade ther nether, as Mister Brown thinks. For I have tryed to teach Silvaney but she cant learn. She needs to be at home Mrs. Brown, up here on Sugar Fork where they is people to love her like she is, and where she can come and go as she will. She wuld of quited down before long, Mrs. Brown, but now that they have taken my Silvaney it is like they have taken a chunk of my hart.

So althogh you have done what you think is best, it is not best, it is wrong. And I remane yor truthful,

Ivy Rowe.

Dear Mrs. Brown,

To anser your questin, the man that brung that letter was my uncle, Revel Rowe.

Yrs.,
Ivy Rowe.

My dear Molly,

I have got some good news to tell you at last! For you will not belive what has happend.

First off I will start at the begining wich was last week when me and Beulah went to town for Court Day, I was thinking of you often on that day for I seed yor auntie who I have been mad at. Anyway me and Beulah set out walking in the morning afore full ligt, and it was a considerable chill in the air it being November, and when we got down to Home Creek Mister John Conaway spyed us walking and said, Girls, if you will wait for a minit, Ill hitch up the wagon and give you a ride to town, because I am going down ther for Court Day myself. Wich we did, and this is how we went in style and got ther early, we was bouncing up and down on the wagon seat and giggling. I have never seed such foolish girls, said Mister Conaway. I do not know what got into us Molly that we set to giggling so. Migt be that Beulah and me had not got off together away from them younguns afore. Migt be that Mister Conaway has a big goiter and a funny way of talking, he says girrels for an instance instead of girls. We got so tickled we like to have died! I rember I looked over at Beulah just as we was coming into Majestic and I thogt Law, she looks just like a girl, and then I thogt, Well I gess so, you crazy thing, she is a girl, but things has been so hard on her, I had like to have forgot it.

Then when we come by Mister and Mrs. Browns house I thogt of you Molly, and all the fun we had in the summer, I miss you so. Beulah and me rode in the wagon over Daves Creek where you and me used to look for gold. I hope the nuns will be nice to you, and yor momma will get well.

I have not said that Beulah and me was acting so silly because we was going to get storeboghten dresses wich we had not ether one had. Now this is because my uncle Revel has come back to town and is helping us, he come when he heerd the news about Babe, and he has stayed on in town where he has took a room over the drugstore. He had come up the holler one week prior, to bring Momma some things, and he toled us at that time to come into town on Court Day, that he wuld be trading mules and he wuld have some cash monney to buy us new dresses.

Now Revel, that is silly, Momma said. It will turn ther heads.

No Maude, I want to buy them dresses, Revel said, You see that they come into town on Court Day, and his horse rared up and he whistled to his dog Charly and took off down the holler leaving Momma on the porch with her mouth open.

So we had come. And since we was early we went by the Branhams house first to see Ethel, she was so suprised she like to have drapped ther baby. Lord lord, Ethel said. She bade us come on in the kitchen wher she was fixing to cook some breakfast for Mister and Mrs. Branham. We culdnt hardly get over all the dishes they had, and the silver. Ethel give us some coffee and sat down with the baby whilst Beulah made the biskit for her, Beulah makes the best biskit in the world, and we got in a good visit before Mister Branham come in to eat and Ethel took his wife her breakfast on a tray. She dosent hardly get up atall according to Ethel, she drinks her medisine out of a little bottle and seems real sad. I said, It looks pretty good to me getting to lay around like that. But Ethel says it is not. Ethel says Mrs. Branham is all the time crying.

Ethel has not changed a bit from living in town, she is still as funny and honnest as the day is long and the fancy life has not turned a hair on her head.

Mister Branham ate 7 biskits and allowed as how he wuld give us a ride to the courthouse, he said it was the leastest he culd do for such good biskits. So we hugged Ethel, and give her a kiss, and went on.

Now I had never been to Court Day, Mollie, and it is something belive you me! Folks milling all around everwhere, and horses and wagons, everbody selling everthing, you never have saw the like. And it is so cold that everbodys breths is making clouds in the chilly air. The lawyers is coming in by then, Mister Pobst and Mister Chilhowie that is famous in the courtroom for dressing fit to kill and making everbody cry, and the courthouse clock is chiming, and so I reckon they started. We went on around to the jockey lot in the courthouse yard, and sure enogh ther was our uncle Revel, trading to beat the band.

See, he had gone out to St. Louis and bought him some mules, and these mules had come in on the train last week wich had caused considerable intrest and consternation in town, and now he was fixing to sell them. Revel had him a red shirt and a black hat and a big cigar in his mouth. He grinned like he was tickled to death to see us.

You girls just sit down here a minit, he said, and he set us down on some old wood boxes he had ther. And hang on a minit he said, and you migt learn something. So we did.

That jockey lot was full of horses and mules winnying and hawing, and men looking at ther teeth. Ther breths was steaming in the frosty air. Me and Beulah sat on our hands to keep them warm. Revel sold two mules for cash monney and traded one for a horse he swore was a stumpsucker and not even worth a mule, he winked at us as he said it but the man didnt see him wink. A bigboned mule will more than apt to be lazy, Revel said to another man who said, These mules is too little, and A mule with hair sticking up on his head has not got any sense, he toled somebody else. You never heerd so much about a mule in all yor life! Me and Beulah was getting real tickled agin at how Revel was out-sharping everbody, when all of a sudden who come walking along, but yor auntie Mrs. Brown! All dressed up and walking along like she was at a fair insted of at the dirty jockey lot.

Why girls! she said, For heavens sake, what are you doing down here, it is so nice to see you, and Beulah how is that baby? Mrs. Browns cheeks was all red from the cold and she had on a little fur hat, she looked the prettest I ever saw her.

John Arthur is fine mam, thank you kindly, Beulah said, and I said, Revel is going to buy us some dresses.

Oh he is, is he, Mrs. Brown said real peart and Revel grinned at all of us.

Now this here is what I call a standard mule, Louisa, he said to Mrs. Brown. The best mules are out of Nebrasker where they breed the jacks to great big old Perchion horses, draft mules is what they call them, but our folks down here dont want any such of a large animal. They druther have a little easy mule like these which is cheaper and plenty of mule for the plow.

Do tell! Mrs. Brown said, and then we was all of us laghing, Revel too. I plum forgot I was mad at Mrs. Brown for sending Silvaney off, I gess I will always be mad about that but it is true I have missed Mrs. Brown, I had forgot how pretty she is also. Oh Molly, you are so lucky to have her for yor auntie, and to go to school! Then Mrs. Brown went on home and me and Beulah went to Sharps Mercantile with the monney that Revel gave us, and tryed on nearabout ever dress in the store until old man Sharp got real mean with us and finely we picked.

Oh Molly, I wish you culd see my dress it is so beutiful! It is green with puff sleeves and a round white coller, Beulahs dress is green too with buttons up the front and a kick pleat, Beulah says green will set off our red hair, she read this in a magazine.

Well well well looky here now! said old man Sharp, Lord have mercy, look out! he said when he seed us, and he got his old lady and her sister outen the back of the store to see how pretty we look. Beulah counted the monney. I was looking in the mirrer and trying to see, but it is dark in the back of that store and the mirrer is wavy. Old man Sharp put our old dresses in a poke for us to carry and Mrs. Sharp gave us a fried apple pie apiece and hugged us and cryed. I dont know why she was crying, she migt of been a little bit crazy it seems to me now.

Then we stepped back out the door. The town had got so full of people by then that you culdnt hardly walk. And the street just choked with wagons and cars, and people selling everthing outen the back of ther wagons. We boght a fascinator scarf for Momma from a blackheaded lady that looked like a gipsy, she was forren for sure. And when we was walking back around the square to the courthouse, everbody was smiling at us, all the men and the boys, and some several of them whistled. I felt crazy like I was drunk.

Now who is that? I thoght to myself as we turned the corner and waited in front of the pharmacy to cross the street. And Molly, it was us! Us in the winder looking like movie stars, me too. It was such a suprise I like to have got run over crossing the street.

But this is not all ether, and you will not belive what happend next.

We were going on back to the jockey lot to show Revel our dresses and see culd we find a ride home, when all of a sudden we hear a great shout, BEULAH! and it is Curtis Bostick, running after us hollering. Now Beulah has not set eyes on him for close on a year, since his momma had put her foot down.

BEULAH, BEULAH, Curtis Bostick hollered, pushing everbody out of his way. Beulah stopped and turned as white as a sheet. She held onto my arm till it hurt. Then Curtis Bostick had got up to us, and he grabbed Beulah around the waist and started kissing her rigt in the street!

Leave me alone now Curtis, said Beulah who was twisting her head all around, Let me go or Ill scream she said, but she was smiling.

Scream all you want honey, said Curtis Bostick, and then she stopped twisting and he kissed her on the mouth and everbody on the sidewalk set up a cheer. Molly, I thoght I wuld die, of coarse.

But then the crowd parted open like the Red Sea and here come Curtis Bosticks momma, mad as a wet hen. She is a spiteful little sharp-featured woman. Curtis! she said. You Curtis! You leave that hore alone! And she comenced to hitting both of them around the head with her pocketbook.

Well the day has past when Curtis wuld not speak up for himself, belive you me! He flung her pocketbook down in the mud and helt her back with one hand, and helt onto Beulah with the othern. Momma, he said, I aim to take Beulah and her sister on up to Sugar Fork now, and get my baby, and then we will be coming back home direckly.

You will not come to my house, his mother said. I forbid it, and Curtis said, All rigt then, and splunged off in the crowd pulling Beulah and me along with him and leaving his momma with her pocketbook down in the mud and her hat fallen off and her hair coming down from her hairpins. Curtis said he had been thinking and thinking about Beulah and the baby he knowed he had got, and the minute he saw her agin, it come to him plain as day what he had to do.

So Beulah is getting maried! Curtis has took her and baby John Arthur back down into town where he has rented that little house by the lumberyard wich is where he works, and he and his momma do not even speak. So Beulah is gone, and little John Arthur, and now it is only me and Momma and Garnie and the twins up here, and sometimes I get so lonesome, I feel like it is a million people gone. I keep thinking I see Silvaney but it is never her, it is only ligt in the trees, and so often I think I hear her talking but no one is ther, it is only the wind. It is getting cold here now and I am the one has to chop the wood, Garnie is no good for chopping wood or anything else except mealymouthing.

Momma and me can not keep up with nothing, we are living from hand to mouth on the kindness of Revel if the truth be known, and Victor has written to Momma and said he can not come home to help out as he has joined the Army, he said he did not know and he is sorry, and said to sell, wich she will not. It is John Arthurs land, she says, its all he ever had, and I will not even consider such a thing. Little John Arthur grows like a weed and Beulah is so happy, she has made some blue curtins and the Branhams that Ethel works for have given them a whole set of dishes, with roses on them, to start off with. It is a happy ending at last, like the Prince has come. And if you want to know where you put yor tonge Molly, I know this now, from looking at him and Beulah. It is, in each others mouths, if you can belive it.

And so I remane forever yor devoted,

Ivy Rowe.

Oh Molly, Molly,

I can not stand it. I can not belive the nuns will throw this letter away before you read it, I can not belive yor Father has said this, nor can I stand to think that any of you all blame us for what has happend. I do not know what to say. I think so much of Mister Brown and how he said <u>She was a Phantom of delight, when first she gleamed upon my sight,</u> and how he broght her those flowers up from the creek, I can see it so clear in my mind.

So I can not belive he tryed to hang himself on the willer tree by Daves Branch but evryone says it is so. And that Revel come along and cut him down and took him home and saved his life, so they say, Revel who was the cause of it all.

Oh now Mister Brown will surely have to kill Revel Rowe. They said it up and down the hollers, he aint got a choice in the world. But Mister Brown wuld not kill a flea, I said, and I was rigt. He wuld not touch a hair on Mrs. Browns head nether, no matter whose baby she is carrying.

They said Revel stood out in the snow for a day and a half after she toled him to go away, and hollered <u>Louisa, you know who you love,</u> but in the end of coarse he done what she said and went away after all but he hollered out that he wuld never love a nother and that he wuld do anything she said, anything in the world for her.

Then leave, Revel, just leave me now, she said from the door with her hair loose around her sholders and her face all wild.

Lord, they have talked it all over town, Ethel said. It was a reglar scandal. They said Mister Brown layed up in the bed and cryed, and wuld not eat a thing but boiled custard, and poor little Mrs. Brown had to do all the packing herself, and her pregnant. The Methodist preacher and his wife came out from town to help her pack.

When Revel left her finely he come up here to tell us goodbye, he said he wuld have to go away from this county now and try to find him a nother life, or else die, he wasnt sure wich. And him and Momma helt each other tigt and cryed and Revel said, <u>Ah Maude, if only.</u> Then Momma run out in the snow after his horse when he left but she did not ketch him. Do you know Molly, I halfway belive that Momma was a little bit sweet on Revel her self! And I belive I am too, and if you think that is awful, then you dont understand a thing. As Mister Brown him self has said, Love rules the court, the camp, the grove, and men below and saints above. He has said too, Tis better to have loved and lost then never to have loved atall but I do not belive this, do you?

Revel is a man born to love women, it is plain to see, and if I was Mister Brown I wuld not even feel bad that Mrs. Brown loved him. I wuld try not to take it too personal. And when I grow up and become a writter, I will write of such a love and I will write of a man like my uncle Revel who can come like a storm in the nigt and knock a born lady off her feet.

I am hoping to heer from you Molly I am hoping they will give you this letter and that you will sneak and write to me for I am so sad about all of this and in spite of all I will remane forever your devoted best frend,

Ivy Rowe.

My dear Daddy,

I reckon this to be the lastest letter I will ever write you in this world. And it migt be the last letter I will ever write ether. For I feel we have come to the end of all things. We are picking up and moving on, Momma says we have got to, I gess she is rigt but it pains me so, for all I have loved is here. Daddy Daddy I hate to leave you most of all. When I think of you laying up ther in yor little gravehouse it hurts me almost past baring it, laying ther by yorself all winter under the snow.

Now it is Febuary. It is the thaw. It has been a slow little gray rain for going on three days sollid. We are packing up all we own wich will not take long. Oh Daddy Daddy this letter is so sad it does not make sense I will bring it up and put it in yor gravehouse when we go to berry Danny, that will be this morning come full ligt. Oh Daddy this little gray rain blurs the edges of everthing, it is like all the world is nought but shadders and soft edges. I want to tell you what all has happend. Well you know that Babe got murdered and Silvaney got sent away, Victor is in the Army, Ethel is working in town where Beulah and Curtis Bostick is to be maried. See how many people this is, gone!

And I have lost my Molly, and Mister Brown and Mrs. Brown, as surely as if they was relly dead. They are dead to me now. Revel has gone away for ever too, it is the most unselfish of anything he has ever done he toled Momma. But Mrs. Brown toled him he wuld leave her if he loved her, so he done it. Revel says he will never love anybody else, nor settle down, nor be happy.

Granny Rowe is setting up by Danny now, she has set up all nigt by him, her and Tenessee. When Danny died, Garnie went out and rung the bell. Then he prayed and prayed over Danny but Momma said, Cut it out, Garnie Rowe! I dont know what Jesus ever had to do with usuns anyway. Then Garnie said he wuld pray for Momma too wich made her mad as fire. Garnie is a real case Daddy, and dont none of us know how he got this way.

But little Johnny is the one will miss Danny so much, it will be like me and Silvaney, when they took her away it was like they had took a chunk of my hart. I dont think Johnny understands yet what all has happend. Momma says that me and him and Garnie will go to school, the regular schoolhouse in Majestic not what used to be Mrs. Browns schoolhouse at Daves Branch, we will live in Majestic where Mommas frend Geneva Hunt has inherrited a big house, and Momma and Geneva will take in borders. Lots of folks have come in ther now with the lumber business, its a boom town Momma says. So we will go.

But Daddy I dont know as I will like it ther. May be I am like you, and need the pure high air, and a mountain to lay my eyes aginst. We will not sell this place, you can rest assured of that, Momma says she wuld die first. We will only leave it for a while. It is the chance of a lifetime, Momma says.

So I am writting you this letter Daddy, to say goodbye. We will be back before you know it! Oh Daddy Daddy when I think of all them that are dead and gone, and of all that has happend, I dont want nothing else to hapen to me, ever. I do not even want to be in love any more, nor write of love, as it is scarry. Too many things can happen in this world. It dont seem like no time since me and Victor and Silvaney and everbody was playing hide and go seek after supper, and putting lightning bugs in a mason jar, and playing Party, or since you was showing us how to make a froghouse in the yard. When I am quite it seems that I can still heer the notes of yor guitar on the air, and how you used to lagh and tell so many storeys before you got little and dreamy and took to laying up beside the fire. I think I can still see Whitebear Whittington laying under the tree. I can hear the awful sound of that ringing bell for sure. The neghbor people will be coming up the holler now, to berry yor boy Danny. It makes me so sad because Danny never was rigt he had no more chance in the world than a snowball in hell Granny said. He went throgh his life on a slant. I gess we will have to walk on up ther now in the rain, it is not a hard rain relly but more of a drizzle, it makes everthing look like its covered with dimonds. You ougt to see Tenessee she is wearing a great big hat, who knows where she got it ether.

It is time to go now. Oh Daddy dont you rember how you took us up the mountain ever year about this time to gather birch sap, it was so sweet and tart on yor tonge, and you said, <u>Slow down, slow down now, Ivy. This is the taste of Spring.</u>

I remane yor devoted daugter,

Ivy Rowe.

II

Letters

from

Majestic

To A Nurse.

Dear Madam,

Please read the enclosed letter aloud to my sister Silvaney Rowe,
she can not read unlessen you have taught her wich I never culd.
And I hope you are good to her too. I remane your grateful,

Ivy Rowe.

My dear Silvaney,

I think of you so much, and I wonder, now how is my Silvaney?
And how is she keeping today? I hope you are well, I have got
this adress from old Doc Trout, I went over ther and got it yesterdy
at closing time. His ofice is up a big long stairway over Sharps
Mercantile, they is nought but a door with a pane of frosted glass
up ther at the end of it. They was not a sole in the ofice, not even
a nurse, and dust everplace, you culd see the dust just whirling
around and around in these little bars of ligt that come down threw
his high funny winders. It is dirty to be a doctors ofice. He is not
much of a doctor if you ask me. Doc Trout, Doc Trout, I hollered
and I heerd a sound then but it was not exackly a anser nor yet
exackly a word, I culd not of said what it was. So I went on in
ther passed the chairs where you sit, now this was where <u>we</u> sat,
Silvaney, the day that we brung Danny to town and got his tonnick.
And then I dont know what got into me, I went passed those
chairs and strate on into Doc Trouts ofice where he sat with his
feet up on the desk drinking outen a fancy coffee cup, he was not
drinking coffee ether. Doc Trout looked at me real lazy. Well
Miss Rowe, is it not? he said, Is it not one of the Misses Rowe?
I can tell by that pretty red hair.

It is me Ivy Rowe, I said, and I have come to get the adress of
the Elizabeth Masters Home where you have sent my sister Silvaney wich I am still mad about. For I will take you out of ther
one day Silvaney and bring you back home to Sugar Fork. But
now we are living in town you know, and I will write you all about
it as soon as I finnish with old Doc Trout.

So he looked at me awhile and drunk outen his green china cup
and said, Well sartinly Ivy Rowe, you are braking my hart, and he

rumpled around in the drawer of his desk and come up with a envelop that had this adress in the corner and handed it over to me. Do you want it back I said, and he said, No, Lord no honey, you keep it and write to your sister Silvaney and tell her that old Doc Trout says hello ther why dont you, say hello from old Doc Trout. And then he comences to laghing a lagh wich you dont want to heer, it sounded just like a green persimmen tastes, a lagh like bitter gall. Go then Ivy Rowe, go on, he said, you had best make haste and get out of here, be on your way. Doc Trout was looking at me very hard, he is not so old ether. So I grabbed up the envelop and took off down his long dark stairway and run like hell all the way back threw the streets of town, feeling funny.

It is the same with the men at the bordinghouse Silvaney, I see them starring at me sometimes it makes me feel funny and bad. I know lots of girls my age is maried but I do not wish to be maried nor have them star untill it is like ther eyes are touching my boddy underneath my dress. I am reading a grate book Jane Eyre, about a orphan, wich I have borried from one of the lady teachers. Now Jane Eyre in the book is little and plane so far, she is like a elf or a fairy. I wish it was me, insted I am getting a bosom like Beulah, this is what they star at threw my dress.

Oh Silvaney, have you growed too? And wuld you know me? I know you can not write to me so I will dry my eyes up now and try to look on the brigt side as Geneva Hunt tells me to do. For I will come to get you bye and bye.

And in the meantime they is so much hapening, I will dwell on this, and tell you all, so you may feel that you are here in truth as well as spirrit. Well we come to town in a big March wind, Mister Delphi Rolette brung us down here with everthing we own piled up in his wagon, this is not much. This is me and Momma and Garnie and Johnny. It rained off and on that morning, I did not care if it rained or not, nor if I was wet nor dry, I was that sad to be leaving Sugar Fork. Momma sat on the seat by Delphi Rolette and starred strate ahead, I did not see her turn back oncet as we come down the holler. I rember I looked back when we crossed Sugar Fork for the lastest time and I seed that Blue Star Mountain was all covered in mist and low clabbered clouds, and then the wind blowed strong for a minute and I thoght I seed our house, then it was gone. I cryed all the way from Home Creek to Daves Branch, and Momma said nary a word. Finely Mister Rolette said Now Ivy, what ails you? Your mother will need you to be a big girl now, come on, you used to have so much spunk. And looking at Mommas face then I sat up and tryed to quit crying and tryed to say something back to Mister Rolette whose so nice, and something to Garnie and Johnny in the back of the wagon so good and quite. By the time we come into Majestic it had quit raining and the wind was whipping little stringy clouds around in the blue-blue sky and everbodys cloths was blowing on the line like people was in them dancing. The pale yaller sunligt shined offen tin roofs and mailboxes, and when we pulled up to Geneva Hunts bordinghouse, buttercups was blooming early by the gate. I had no sooner clumb down than here come Geneva Hunt herself tearing out of the house like she was blowed by the wind, I had never seed her in person afore this time.

Maude, Maude, she said pulling Momma up close for a hug— she is as big as two women, Geneva is, or as big as a big old man— Maude, Maude you look like the wrath of God, and you are so skinny, you look like something the cat drug in. We will soon fix that! Geneva cryed, for she is a famous cook. And look at these poor little old boys here, why this one is the spitting image of John Arthur she said, meaning Johnny for Garnie is not. Geneva says, I have got some speshal cookies back ther in the kitchen but I gess I will have to throw them out if I cant find no little boys to eat them. And Garnie says, where is the kitchen at? And then Geneva laghs a deep lagh, I think you wuld call it a chuckle. Ludie, take them on back ther, she says to a fat girl whose come out the door now, and Ludie does, and all of sudden the bordinghouse yard is plum full of people and it dont take a minute for so many hands to carry our things inside.

Oh Silvaney, I wish you culd see my room! For I have got a room of my own it is the firstest time ever as you know, nevermind it is not as big as a closet, Geneva says it is more like a closet relly. But Geneva says a girl needs a room of her own so I have got one! I love it so. It is at the back of the house on the third story, rigt under the roof. I can look out my winder over all the town. Here is a list of the things in my room. I wish you culd see them to.

   1 Bed, plane white iron with a fluffy blue counterpane too big, it comes down to the floor, it is like I sleep in the clouds!

1 little table, white wood panted, with a oil lamp on it of my own

1 chester drawers very beat up, and 3 hooks on the wall to hang your dresses

1 rag rug, old.

And Silvaney the bestest part is, they is <u>wallpaper,</u> for this was the house of Geneva Hunts uncle a very rich man who died. And I do not care iffen the wallpaper in my room is peeling off or not, nor if my cieling is very low and slants over my bed, I am rigt up under the roof as I said erlier. I love it when it rains, it is like a hundred million horses running on top of my head, it is like the Charge of the Ligt Brigade on this old tin roof. But I have not yet toled you of the wallpaper. It is the bestest part. The wallpaper is silver-gray squares with pink ribands running between, and in each square, they is a lady! These ladys are all alike very old fashened with high curly silver hair that migt be wigs, and the most beutiful big pink dresses with a skirt that resembles a bell. So I love them. I love my room. Geneva Hunt says it will get as cold up here as a witches tit come winter, but I dont care. I can go to the winder and push back my gauzy curtin and look out over all the town. <u>It is mine,</u> I say to myself then.

This town is mine, Majestic Virginia, U.S.A. The Presbyterian Church steeple is up on a level with me, and I can see the Methodist School down the way with hopscotch chalked out in the dirt. I watch them playing at recess time. I see rigt down on all the screen porches and backyards, the clotheslines and outhouses and sheds and gardens of Shady Lawn Street, and the livery stables way up at the end of it. If I lean way out and strane my neck I can see the roof of the Branhams house that is where Ethel lives. If I look strate down I see our own backyard with the storehouse and the old well and the clothesline and the fethery tree wich is called, Mimosa. It is very beutiful. If we still lived up on the mountain and played party this wuld be my name, Mimosa. But I will write no more of that as it makes me cry and ther is so much else to tell you, for an instance oncet I looked down and what did I see but that fat girl Ludie kissing a boy on the lips out behind the garage where Geneva keeps her automobile! Geneva has got a red touring car, they is not but about four other cars in town at this time. Ludie thinks noboddy can see her because of the forsithia bushes and the garage but this is not true, I can see her just fine! And I am watching now to see if she does it some more, I hope so.

Ludie comes from up in the mountains too near Smoky Gap, but she lives here now and cleans for Geneva. She is a fat girl with braids wound around and around on top of her head, whose looking hard for a husband. Also she is not very smart. Ludie cleans, and Geneva cooks her own self with two other women Mrs. Crouse and Mrs. Viers to clean up after her. Mrs. Viers has got big moles all over her face. Geneva makes the bestest chicken and dumpling in the world, and also pies. Her lemon merang pie is famous it is five inches high, she makes ten at a time in them big black cookstoves. People come to the back door from all over town and try to buy them a pie. Sometimes we will sell them, sometimes not. It depends on how many borders we have got, plus Judge Brack who takes his meals here and some others when Geneva will give them a place at her table. It seems like everbody wants a place at her table. So you wuld think that Momma wuld fatten up finely, but this is not the case. Momma is still as thin and as flat as a bord despite of Genevas cooking. Her black hair has got gray streaks in it now and she pulls it strate back in a bun on the back of her neck and it looks pretty good, I have to say, but her face is still halfway hanted. Momma is like she is scarred of fun. It is hard to see how her and Geneva got to be such good frends as they are so diffrent, but Geneva says when you grow up so close together like they done in Rich Valley, and are only children both of you, you are just naterally closer than kin. And I have read it in a book that oposites attrack, well Geneva is surely the oposite of our Momma! Geneva is so big and soft and easy-going with curly yaller gray hair and dimples and lots of chins, and she has spectacles on a gold chane around her neck, they rest on her bosom like it was a shelf. She claps her hands when she laghs and it seems to me that half the men at the bordinghouse wuld not mind to mary Geneva, that is the ones that are old enogh of coarse, but when I said as much she clapped her hands and laghed and said she wuld not have a one of them on a silver platter! Geneva has had three husbands, she says she is throgh with all of them and has washed her hands of men but I am not sure that this is true, I am watching to see what hapens.

I am watching everbody Silvaney, it is fun. We keep the teachers from the Methodist School, it is Mister Dudley Slade who is little and mean and we all hate, and Miss White who is old, and Miss Mabel Maynard who is rich I belive as she wears such lovely cloths. But Miss Maynard is moony and plane, and blushes at any attenshon. We have drummers that come to town to sell, such as rigt now some yung men Robert Street and Wayne Crabtree and a boy named Lonnie Rash who is with the lumber company. These are the ones that star at me as I serve, they look rigt throgh my cloths. Then we have lawyers that come to town on business and men from the mining companys and may be we will have a circuit rider, then you have to say grace at the table. One time we had the Methodist circuit rider and he said, Judge Brack, I have long been your admirer sir, I defer to you on this day of our Lord, and Judge Brack said, <u>Good food, good meat, prase God, lets eat,</u> and the circuit riders mouth dropped open. I got so tickled I like to of dropped the potatos.

Another time we had us a fancy preacher man here, Sam Russell Sage who is famous and holds camp meetings everplace and has a big head of curly black hair, he will be back for some more of Genevas vinegar pie for sure, he said. And yet another time when we firstest got here we had two big shots from Detroit who own one of the coal companys I forget wich, and come here to go up in the mountains hunting. Some company men had got the Green boys from Hell Mountain all lined up to take them, and the company men gone too, and they all come back after three days with a bunch of dead deer that Geneva says they will pack up and hall back on the train and stuff them and put them in ther liberries, have you ever heerd the beat of that? I belive it wuld look so ugly. And Geneva says it is a shame because a deer culd meat a mountain family for nearabout a year. But these Detroit men was full of the sites that they had seed and tales of a big bear up on Hell Mountain that had outsharped them, and said that they was coming back to get him another day, and I thoght to myself, it is Whitebear Whittington! but I never asked them if it was white. For I did not want to know, if it was NOT.

And soon they will build the railroad clear to Kentucky, and I reckon that more company men and more railroad men will stay here then, and so on. This bordinghouse is a busy place, belive you me! It is easy to see how Geneva relly needed Momma to look after the rooms and see that the washing and cleaning gets done, and even me thogh I only serve at table but sometimes on Sunday when Geneva has two sittings, this is hard. Sometimes my arms hurt awful. But then when it is done I can go in the kitchen and hang up my apron and come and go as I please for the rest of the day, for ther is so many people coming and going in a bordinghouse that a girl can slip away to come and go all over town, and see what ther is to see!

And this is a lot, belive me! For it is coming on to wartime and the econommy is booming, Judge Brack says. We have got the lumber business wich is booming, this is where Beulahs husband Curtis Bostick works, and the coal business wich is booming too. But Curtis Bostick toled Momma he will go into coal now he thinks as these mountains is dam near timbered out. The railroad takes out the coal, when you stand by the tracks the railroad men allways wave back if you wave.

But the logs go out on the river, and oh Silvaney, I wuld give a million dollars to go along. All winter they are halling in timber and cutting the logs and you can hear the high shrilly whine of the crosscut saw, from the lumberyard. This is where Curtis Bostick works in the ofice. They have to cut them up so they can tie them into rafts come spring. One time a man got his foot cut off and died and another time a man got his hand cut off but lived, Curtis Bostick showed me rigt where it happend, it was awful!

And they pile them up in log dumps all along the bluff above the river just past town, untill they is a reglar mountain of logs just waiting for the big spring tides that carrys them down to Kentucky. Ever day after breakfast is over and the dishes is done, I walk to the bluff and see. They is men ther watching the river, deciding when to go. The river is brown and swirly, it has waves and foams up the bank. When will you go? I ax them. The river is getting high. Not yet, they say. Not yet. And ther is a bunch of boys with ther sacks all ready to ligt out on the rafts when the river is risen enogh. They hunker on the bluff looking down at the foamy water, chewing tobaccy, waiting. They star at me. But oh Silvaney I wuld give anything to be one of them boys and ride the rafts down to Kentucky on the great spring tide! They pay you three dollars a day and you have to walk back wich takes four days, they pay you for walking back too. I will say I have even thoght of waring jeans and a boys shirt and shoes and trying to sneak along, but Momma and Geneva wuld have a fit.

Silvaney, they left today.

Something awoken me erly, I culd not say what it was. But I

waked up afore full ligt when all was pale and gray and I thoght to myself, It is today. Today is the day! Still I had half a mind to try and go as a boy and ride a raft myself but I said, Now Ivy you know you can not, you will never get away with it. So I jumped up and dressed and determined to run rigt out ther and see them off.

First I went down in the kitchen where Geneva was up all ready and boiling the coffee and said, Geneva I belive it is the day the rafts will leve. And she laghed her deep lagh and said Well go then Ivy, go on and watch it if you must, here take you a biskit to eat, and she given me a biskit that she had ther, and said I did not have to come back for breakfast atall! I will get Ludie to serve, she said, and I said, Thanks. Here now, she said and she given me one more biskit.

Ivy, you are a case, she said. And I taken the biskits and run out passed Mrs. Crouse just coming in, and I run out the front door and down the street and the sun was just peering out, and I run passed the iceman in his wagon and the milkman, and when I got close to the river I fell in with a whole bunch of peple going the same way because the news was all over town, It is today. When we got to the bluff I pushed threw and got up front where I culd see good. The river was wellnigh up to the bluff, brown and boiling it put me in mind of Genevas coffee. And it was covered bank to bank with patches of swirling mist. Get back! Get back! Everybody hollered. A whole bunch of men was on the bank pushing the logs down with canthooks and hollering Whoa now! and Watch out! when they hit the water. And men in the water is binding them into rafts with chains and tie-poles, then the boys wuld jump on hollering, two to a raft, and the river wuld seze them and spin them away, and off theyd go in the mist, bound for Kentucky, untill the whole river was full of rafts some from upriver too where they had took out the chaindogs and loosed the splash-dams. And off they went! It taken hours and hours.

I stayed and watched and thoght hard about going, and passing throgh mist, and diffrent towns, and not knowing what you migt find around any bend. By the time I left, it was wellnigh noon and I was plum wore out, I had thoght so hard it was like I had gone along. But when I got back to the bordinghouse they was a great group of folks on the porch around Bill Waldrop who had come in I gess with the mail, and Judge Brack who was reading a news-paper out to them all.

What is it? I said. What is it? and some several of them said, Hush Ivy, it is the news from France. It is the war news. It is very serious.

So Silvaney if it is war I hope I will still go to school for Momma has said may be come fall I can do so even if I am so very old all ready. At first Momma said No, ther is no sense in it, but Geneva taken her aside and then Miss Maynard, and now she says, May be. So I am fine Silvaney but I miss you so and I miss the house on Sugar Fork and the cloudy blue mornings up ther and the way things was. I think I will allways miss these things. But nevermind we are fine and all in all I gess its a pretty good thing that Geneva Hunt has taken us under her wing. I remane your loving sister,

Ivy Rowe.

Dear Molly,

Probly they will not give you this letter but I am writting it anyway to say, I am a town girl now, so do not pitty me if ever you are of a mind to do so. I will be in a fine school when fall term starts so I will know as much as you. And if ever you want to be my frend agin Molly I hope you will write to me at Geneva Hunts bordinghouse on Main Street, Majestic, Virginia. I will write back of coarse and tell you what all has happend, it is a lot! Sometime in this world I hope to see your face. And for now I remane your faithfull,

Ivy Rowe.

Dear Victor,

Doc Trout has said he will male this letter for me, he will contack the Army and make evry effort to see that it reaches you, I can only hope that this is so. I will write it short wich he said to, and on this thin paper wich he has given me free, Doc Trout is a nice man relly even iffen he is diffrent. But he taken this letter business to hart and said, You take your letters serios, dont you Ivy? I will not fale, he said.

So Victor we must get down to business, it is this. A fancy dressed man named John Reno has ben staying here at the bordinghouse off and on for a while. He is a agent for one of them big coal companys that is bying up land all around here. It seems crazy to me as they is not even a railroad yet anyplace near Hell Mountain nor Bethel Mountain nor Blue Star Mountain of coarse it is wild up ther, so how culd you mine the coal? But Mister Reno is bying up coal land rigt and left, and everbody is getting rich! For nothing it seems, as he is not going to do a thing with it nor bother them that lives ther in any way. So this is free monney, it is like picking monney offen a monney tree. Mister Reno comes and goes, he wears a blue-stripe suit and a good red tie and a hat, he has a gold watch on a chane. But he is nice, and talks to everbody on the nigts he is here, in the parlor or on the porch, and listens real careful, and sometimes he will write something down in his little book. John Reno smiles a lot, he has a nice smile but real bad teeth. So I think he is relly nice, but one time at Sunday dinner we were having pork roast and sweet tater pie, and Judge Brack stood rigt up from the table and said he wuld not eat with such a man as that and pointed his cane at John Reno and called him a son of a bitch! Then he up and left. John Reno smiled and went on eating, but ever since that day he has taken his meals down the street when he is bording, down at Miss Olivers who can not cook worth a damn, Geneva says, and him and Judge Brack do not even speak. But Geneva likes Mister Reno even iffen Judge Brack dont.

So one nigt about three weeks ago they was all out on the front porch rocking and she said, Say, John. I must be crazy as a coot, it has not ocurred to me to tell you that Maude here owns quite a property on the Sugar Fork of Blue Star Mountain. And John Reno turned and looked at Momma and said real easy, Is that a fact? Well may be if I am up that way in the near futcher I will look it over, now how much land is involved?

Momma said she culd not say, it migt be 100 or 200 acres, it is the watershed of Sugar Fork and up the ridge some, but she did not know. But it was John Arthurs land and I will not sell it, she said. It was all he had.

Why lord no Mrs. Rowe, I am not in the business of bying land, far from it, said Mister Reno. You wuld continue to own your own home and your land, why you wuld posess sole ownership of the surface now and forever into prosperity, said Mister Reno.

I am not interested, Momma said, and got up and went in to bed.

But about a month after that, it was in July I gess, Mister Reno come back and one night after dinner he spoke up and allowed as how he had ben up ther just by happenstance, that he had purchased the mineral rigts to a parcel of land owned by Delphi Rolette that he thoght we were aquainted with, and he had looked over our property as well since he was in the neghborhood so to speak, and since business was going good and Geneva Hunt was a partickler friend of his, he reckoned he migt do Momma a faver and pick up the mineral rigts to say, a hunderd acres as it wuld not put him out none. Four dollers a acre, Mister Reno said. Firm.

Momma and Geneva Hunt starred at each other acrost the table full of dirty dishes, Mommas eyes like dark burning holes in her face. No, she said.

Now Maude, you dont want to look a gift horse in the mouth, Geneva said, not sounding too serios, and I culd see Momma figuring out in her mind about all that monney. And I know she was thinking, then I culd pay Geneva back, and Stoney Branham at the store and old Doc Trout, and all I owe, for we owe monney all over this town.

Take it or leave it, its up to you, said Mister Reno like it was all the same to him. He drunk some more ice tea.

No, Momma said.

Now I have to say, Victor, I culd not keep my mouth shut no more by then, you know how I am! For I am sick and tired of being so poor, I wuld love so to have a nother storeboghten dress like the one Revel got me that is too short now, and a lether diary, and so many things. And I was clearing off the table as allways, and I heerd it all.

Momma, Momma, do it! I said. For Victor dont care, he is a man of the futcher, he said it himself, he has toled you this time after time. Victor wuld say, its the chance of a lifetime now you take it, I said, Momma you know this is true.

Mister Reno spred out his hands and smiled and said, I rest my case.

Just think it over Maude, said Geneva, and Momma looked down at the table and bit her lip.

We wuld keep the house? she said. And all the land?

We are not even talking about the house, said Mister Reno. Some of the holler going down into Home Creek is what I mean, but suit yorself, he said. I am not bying land at all but the mineral rigts and the likelyhood of exersising these rigts is sligt.

Momma started to cry. I dont know what to do, she said.

So Geneva jumped up and run around to Mommas chair and hugged her tigt. Do it! Do it Maude, she said. It will take a big load offen yor mind.

And so Momma said <u>I will then,</u> to Mister Reno, and he said, Thats the ticket, and it was done. He drawed up a deed and she sined it the follering day over at the courthouse and come back and layed down in the bed.

So Victor, as I write to you, it is done.

It is done and Mister Reno is gone, Geneva says he is a fast moving man who strikes wile the iron is hot. Geneva swares this is a smart move on Mommas part. Geneva was up to her elbows in flour yesterdy wile we were talking about it, she licked sweat off the top of her lip and smiled out the winder, talking about Mister Reno. And I smiled too for I knowed a secret, I had seed Mister Reno sneaking outen Genevas room, carrying his shoes! But I will not breth a word of it to Momma. And at any rate we have monney agin, I do not have to feel like Jane Eyre the orphan no more, even iffen Momma is so stingy wich she is. I will not have to be a shopgirl. I can go to school when the term starts back up. Ethel culd quit work and go to school too but she will not, she laghs when I beg her and says she is fine as she is and lerns more in a day than I can lern from a book. But still I am exited about school. And I thoght you wuld want to know that we have some monney now and what all has happend.

Victor I hope you are well and not shot, when the war comes you migt go to France Europe, this is what Doc Trout said. Oh Victor, I rember so well Mrs. Browns red book, I wuld give anything to go to France! But please be carefull and write to me soon for I remane your devoted sister,

Ivy Rowe.

Dear Beulah,

I will do the best I can to give you all the town news as you requested. You know you have got the right girl, for I love to write letters! I will try to make this one as happy and good as you, for I miss you so. It is hard for me to immagine you and Curtis over there on Diamond Fork, to immagine your blue curtins in the winders of a company house, or your rose dishes on your table in such a house. And I cannot immagine negros. But I know it is a good job for Curtis. May be you will like it better there as time goes by, I hope so. I do not know what to say about your new baby that is on the way, but I am glad if you are glad. I hate for you to get too wore out is all.

Here it is hustle and bustle. It is a boom town now, what with the price of coal and the war, this town is full of strangers. Business is booming at the bordinghouse, we are turning them away.

The big news is that Ludie just up and had a baby out of the blue and she is so fat we did not even know she was expecting untill this happened! She started hollering and bleeding in the night and Geneva sent me after old Doc Trout who come right away. It is a girl that Ludie is calling Little Geneva, and that everbody watches after. But if you ask Ludie who the daddy is, she bites her tonge and rolls her eyes and will not say. It may be she doesnt know, Geneva says. Geneva is fine, she is just the same, but Momma is just plain diffrent here. I guess you must of noticed before you left.

It is like all the fire and wildness went out of her when we come down off the mountain, I can not say. You know she was awful and scarry sometimes up there, but now she is very quite and dont say much atall. Instead of shooting sparks, her eyes are dull. Oh she talks to people at dinner, and on the porch, and sees to things for Geneva, but it is like she is not relly there, it is hard to describe. She has a pretty little white rocking chair in her bedroom you know, and when she is not busy she sits there and rocks, not doing a thing, looking out at the mountains across the river, with her hands folded up in her lap. Her hands are real thin. She has not ganed a pound since we have been here.

But Ethel is fine, as fiesty as ever, she is working some in Stoney

Branhams store now, too. He says he has never seed such a good hand at the cash register.

And little Johnny is fine, and Garnie is just a sight! Since he has been living in this bordinghouse, Garnie thinks he has died and gone to heaven! He loves to eat so much you know, and now he is getting real fat. He is the funniest fattest most serios little redheaded boy you ever saw. And now Sam Russell Sage has took up with him in a big way. Do you rember who he is? The famous preacher that comes to hold the big meetings, well he did this agian in August, and little Garnie went over there ever night and when the time come to go up and get saved, he went up ever time. He loves to go up and get saved.

So after a week of this, Sam Russell Sage taken Garnie aside, right out here on the porch, and said, Garnie, you can not do this no more. People are starting to talk and lagh, it is embarassing. Sam Russell Sage is a big huge man with curly black hair, Garnie is little and fat, it was some conversation! Then finely Geneva said, Why dont you give him a job then Sam, since he likes to pray so much, and so then Garnie got to pass the collection plate for the last part of the revival.

Momma would not go to see him, but I went over there with Miss Gertrude Torrington who had just arrived at the bordinghouse, I will write more of her later. She is very important.

But Beulah, it was scarry. Sam Russell Sage is not so bad at the bordinghouse but at the big meeting he is scarry. Did you and Curtis go to the one last year? If you did then you will know what I am talking about. For it is in a big tent acrost the river with folding benches that Sam Russell Sage carts around wherever he goes, and torches burning for light. You can see the flames in the water as you cross the bridge from town. The men sit on the right side, women on the left, I could see that this alone given Gertrude Torrington a turn as she had just arrived from Boston Masachusetts.

Sam Russell Sage walks back and forth, back and forth, preaching. As he goes he gets louder and louder and catches his breth with a ah! such as, You may think that death is far away, ah, but it is right here with us tonight, ah, death waits in the dark, ah, right outside the light of this tent, ah, oh he is so hungry, ah, he is hiding behind that big willer tree by the river, ah, he is licking his chops ah, oh he is hungry ah, he dont care if your old nor young nor saved nor dammed ah, he will take you when he wants to ah, he is out in the darkness right now ah, he is peeping in ah! It was something to hear. And folks on evry side of us started crying and then yelling out and I rembered something I heered way back, Whoso dies shouting happy will go to heaven.

You should have seen Mrs. Trenton Jones and Evangeline Matney and even old Wash Tuttle from the drugstore, acting crazy. And Mrs. Viers with all those moles on her face was ringing her hands and mumbling. And little old Garnie sitting up front on a chair with the Murphy family, this is the singers from Prestonsburg Kentucky, looking so serios. The Murphy family is two fat brothers and their gap tooth little sister. Garnie wore a suit that Sam Russell Sage had bought him at Sharps Mercantile. Then the Murphy family led us in singing That Beutiful Land with Sam Russell Sage himself lining out the words. In the beutiful land where the angels stand, we shall meet, we shall meet, we shall meet in that beutiful land. It is a real pretty song. Then I thoght about us berrying Babe, and how nobody sang. It made me so sad. Then Garnie got to pass the collection plate, he looked like a little old fat man. He would not look at me.

Then Sam Russell Sage was preaching agian and I have to admit, it started to get to me. I started thinking, now will I go to Heaven, or burn in the flames of Hell? I was getting so scarred I could not breth. Then the Murphys sung Ye young, ye gay, ye proud, you must die and wear the shroud. E-Ter-Ni-Ty! Eternity! Then youll cry, I want to be, happy in eternity. Time will rob you of your bloom, Death will drag you to your tomb, the Murphys sang.

Beulah, it was awful! For where will I go? I wondered. And, what will happen to me? I looked at Garnie and he was eating it up. But I was terified. Then Sam Russell Sage prayed agian and then he gave out the invitational while the Murphys sung real soft, Just as I am, without one plea, but that thy blood was shed for me. Come on, said Sam Russell Sage. Come right on up to Jesus. And people were screaming out and going up right and left, and he was hugging them. Oh lamb of God I come, I come, the Murphys sung. And I have to say, I almost done it too. For I could feel the firey hand of God clutching me in the stomach and I would of gone myself if it had not been for Miss Torrington who took a sick spell right then and there.

Ivy, she said, grabbing my arm, Ivy we must leave immediatly, and so we did, with Miss Torrington brething out of a little cut-glass bottle and holding tight to my arm. Once we were out of the tent and almost to the bridge we stopped for a minute and I looked back. The big-meeting tent glowed out smoky red in the night, on account of the pine knots. Miss Torrington swayed like she would fall, and bowed her head. I belive she was praying. And bye and bye as we walked over the bridge, the firey hand of God let go of my stomach, and it got to be plane old night agian, you could hear the bullfrogs in the river and then the piano from Hazels Entertainment.

So we got back home, but I have not been saved yet, so I hope I will not die anytime soon!

And now for Miss Gertrude Torrington. Beulah, do you rember the camio pin which Mrs. Brown used to wear all the time? Well, Miss Torrington favors the camio. She is so pale, with hair as light as Silvaneys and a long pale face with skin so fine and so thin you can see the blue vanes in it and almost the bones, and big deep eyes so dark blue they look purple. Her forehead is wide and white. She pulls her hair strate back in a bunch and wears no jewelry of any kind. Her voice is real high and grates on your nerves.

Miss Torrington is a misionary. This means that she has come from the Presbyterian Church in Boston to visit the school here, and describe the conditions. I cannot immagine what she will say. It seems to me that conditions are very good.

I am going to school now and I love it, I am the very first pupil Beulah, I hope you will be proud of this as Momma does not seem to care one way or the other. I am learning a lot. And Miss Torrington is taken a particular intrest in me! She is teaching me French which nobody knows but her, and plane geometry, and if I do real good she will teach me drawing. She asks me questin after questin, we talk evry day for hours and she is giving me many books to read such as Charles Dickens and Lord knows what all. Miss Torrington says that I am remarkable and wants me to go back to live with her in Boston and go to school there. So I may do this Beulah if Momma will let me go, its the chance of a lifetime I guess. I would dearly love to go to a school such as she describes, with a librery full of books. I would love to learn latin and become a teacher.

But something holds me back from saying YES I WILL GO, I am not sure what. I would like to be a teacher like Mrs. Brown but not like Miss Torrington. For she stands too stiff and pushes too close to you when she talks, it is hard to describe. She is not happy ether. She is strate as a poker and stars in your eyes too hard and she does not get along with Geneva. So I have not said Yes yet but how often I try to immagine the world beyond this town, I would love to go! Miss Torrington says that we could visit the Old North Church where Paul Revere started out in the poem I love, Listen my children and you will hear of the midnight ride of Paul Revere, and in the Boston Commons she says there is a lake with swan boats.

And now, a funny incidence about Geneva before I close. You know how Geneva has her red automobile which is the joy of her hart, and keeps it locked up in the garage? And sometimes she takes it out to go riding and sometimes she takes us too? Johnny just loves to go out riding. Well Saturday last she got it out and put on a fascinator and took Momma for a spin, out the old Poor-bottom Road towards Rich Valley, and had a head-on colision! There was not but one other car on the road and they run smack into each other, it was Marcus Rope who Curtis might know as he is a big company man. So Genevas fender is busted but her and Momma is fine and Geneva has made it a famous story now which brings a good lagh every time. And also Beulah, I belive that Sam Russell Sage has become her sweetie! But I will save this news for next time when I am sure.

And one other thing which will intrest Curtis I know, is what is going on right now, it has just started, in the bottom at the river bend. Do you rember Louis Judd? He is the son of Mrs. Rose Judd who lives in the yellow house but he has been gone for years, he is a mover and shaker as Geneva says, he will put you in mind of our uncle Revel. In fact he used to be a frend of Revels, it makes me very sad to write his name, REVEL. Anyway some say that Louis Judd has been to prison, some say not. In any case he has come back to town in a uniform, he is gathering up a regiment for the Army in the river bottom, this very minute! He has got him a whole Army camp over there with tents and guns and more men coming every day. To which Judge Brack says, Poppycock! But Louis Judd is doing it anyway. He is raising a company.

I wish I could join! For I think to myself, somebody has got to fight the Germans, they are cutting off babys hands. Well I hope you are happy about your new baby, Beulah. I relly do. I hope you and Curtis and little John Arthur take to it over there at

Diamond but for now I miss you and remane your loving sister in Majestic,

Ivy Rowe.

Oh Silvaney,

I feel I am bursting with news but I can not tell it to a sole, I have no one to talk to. It is so hard to say. But I feel that things are happening two times allways, there is the thing that is happening, which you can say, and see, and there is another thing happening too inside it, and this is the most important thing but its so hard to say. For an instance, I have just written a letter to Beulah, and every word I said was true, but there is so much I dare not say. Oh Silvaney my love and my hart, I can talk to you for you do not understand, I can write you this letter too and tell you all the deep things, the things in my hart. For sometimes, as Geneva says, a girl has just got to let down her hair! And it is like you are part of me Silvaney, in some way. So I can tell you things I would not tell another sole.

For I am bad, Silvaney. I am bad, bad, rotten clear throgh. I will tell you how bad I am. I have been knowing it ever since I went to the big meeting last August with Miss Torrington. A hand of fire clutched me in the stomach then Silvaney, it was the hand of God almighty, and it put me in mind at the time of something which has only now come clear to me.

It is, Mister Rochester in Jane Eyre.

When Mister Rochester kissed Jane Eyre she felt a firey hand in her vitals, this is her stomach I reckon. Well I know what she means. I think it is a warning that you are bad. For Jane would of given in and run away with Mister Rochester if it was not for God, but I have not been saved so I do not have him to turn to.

And I will tell you something else, if Sam Russell Sage is who God has sent, then I dont know if I even want to be saved ether, in spite of the firey hand! For I think Sam Russell Sage is awful. He is Genevas sweetie these days whenever he comes to town, and stays up in the room with her out of wedlock, and drinks whisky out of bottles which he brings, and cuts his mustache so messy that he leaves little black hairs all over the bathroom for me or Ludie to clean up. He does not even care what a mess he makes.

I have growed to hate the sight of those little black hairs all over the sink, and to hate the sight of Sam Russell Sage himself and that yellow touring car he comes in.

Judge Brack says he is a sharlatan and even Momma has said, Geneva, you ought to have better sense. To which Geneva just laghs and says, I would reccomend a dose of the same medicine for you, Maude.

And Garnie runs around after Sam Russell Sage like a little lap dog. He loves to polish his shoes. And I clean the room, and serve at table, and I see this. I see all of it. I see Ludie too who will go in the shed in the afternoons with any man at all when she thinks theres nobody watching. But I am watching. And from my bed-room window I can see fine. I can see the men come out zipping ther pants, looking to right and left.

This is not all ether. For there is a boy here named Lonnie Rash that I cannot stop starring at, nor him me. He is a young boy come to town to find work in the lumber business which he has done, but now he says he thinks he will go on over in the river bottom and join up with Louis Judds Army, but so far, he aint.

I know it is because of me. I know he has not gone yet because of me. I think he loves me. He stars at me all the time it is like he is touching me under my cloths, his eyes will follow me wher-ever I go. Whenever he is in the same room with me, I feel that firey hand again and cant hardly breth. I feel I have got to pee.

Lonnie Rash has got nice brown hair and kind of sand colored eyes with some green in them, and a broad strong face. Miss Torrington who hates him says he looks like a slavick boy. But I love Lonnies hands Silvaney, which are square and brown and strong, and the mussles in his arms are very hard. If you are curios how I know this, Silvaney, I have kissed him! I have run my hands down his back and his arms and let him put his tonge way down in my mouth and the firey hand grabbed me then for good. Me and Lonnie go walking out together after I am throgh with the supper dishes, and three times he has took me to the picture show to see western movies. This is the only kind of movie Lonnie likes. In the picture show he held my hand and rubbed it, I thoght I would up and die.

LONNIE RASH, LONNIE RASH, I write his name over and

over on everything. I draw flowers around the capitle letters and make a morning glory vine that climbs up the L and the R. He can make me laugh so hard. Everthing I say, he says, Yes? and Oh yes? and Is that so? untill he gets me laughing to hard to quit. So then he will tickle me some and then feel of my titty. I let him feel up under my skirt too and stick his finger in there, and two times he has took out his cock for me to see but so far we have not done anything else with it. Me and Lonnie do all this out in the shed back of the bordinghouse which is an idea I got from Ludie, I am scarred to death she will come in there with a man and catch us at it. Oh Silvaney, I know this is bad but it feels so good. We used to walk out in the woods by the river, but now it is too cold.

Lonnie wants me to sneak him up in my room but so far I have not, instead I have made some excuse. I dont know why but I dont want him up there, I dont want him to see in my room and see all my things or be there. LONNIE RASH LONNIE RASH I write it on everthing and I think of his strong brown hands and the way they feel. LONNIE RASH I write, but Lonnie Rash can not write, nor read ether one, nor will he learn. LONNIE RASH, I write in the ice on my window come morning, I think I am going crazy, now this is the truth! You know I am probly not too young to have a complete nervous breakdown like Jane Eyre when she got shut up in the Red Room.

A week ago Miss Torrington asked me to stay after school and I did, she was waiting for me in the big recitation hall with all the little panes of glass frosted over by the cold and the new steam radiators hissing. Oh Silvaney, I love this room! It is the room I love bestest in the whole world next to mine! The cielings are very high here, and the woodwork is old and curly around the big windows and the cieling and the door. I love the big slates on the wall and the way the eraser dust hangs in the air, and the oak table with the globe on it, and the pictures of Jesus Blessing the Little Children and Jesus Asending in Light. I love the way the schoolroom smells, the dusty somehow holy air. It seems as if the lessons quiver in the air, the sums and poems and conjugations we have learned by hart are all still there.

So I met Miss Torrington in the schoolroom Tuesday last, after school.

She was very stern. Her face seemed carved in pure white

marble, she wore a black dress. Now Ivy, she said. Christmastime approaches as you know.

Yessum, I said.

Say, Yes Miss Torrington, when will you learn to drop these backward customs? Miss Torrington said. For you are fast becoming a lady.

Yes Miss Torrington, I said.

She smiled. Her smile looked like a carved smile on a marble angel. And all of a sudden Silvaney I recalled the Christmas before Daddy died and how me and Ethel made angels in the snow. It seems so long ago! It seems almost like other people! For I am a town girl, a smart girl, and almost a lady.

Miss Torrington clasped her hands behind her back and walked across the schoolroom, her skirts went swish swish, swish swish, and the radiators went hiss, hiss.

Now Ivy, she said, I have some things to say to you and I want you to listen carefully and hear me out. In all my years of teaching in bording schools and colleges and churches, I confess that I have never come across a girl so remarkably tallented, so extrordinarily gifted in language. I feel it is a sin, Ivy, a great sin, if we do not use our tallents that God has given us, if we do not live up to our potenshal. In some ways it may be the greatest sin of all.

Miss Torrington quivered all over when she said, Sin.

Then she went on, And I confess to you I feel that God has sent me here to save you Ivy, to offer you a life which will enable you to use your gifts to his glory.

Amen, I said all of a sudden, without meaning to, it just came out, and Miss Torrington narrowed her eyes.

Laugh if you will then, she said, and I said, Oh no Miss Torrington, I was not making fun, I did not even mean to speak and please excuse me. I dont know what come over me, I said.

Miss Torrington stood up then very straight. This is precisely the point, Ivy Rowe! she said. Her voice was shaking. You need guidance, a firm hand. You do not know what comes over you, truer words were never spoken. You are buffeted about by evry wind that blows my dear, I can not stand by and see this happen.

See what happen? I asked then, for I did not understand what she meant.

Ah Ivy, Miss Torrington said. Do you think I am blind as well? I see you engaged in a flirtation which might very well end in disaster, for he is not suitable, your Lonnie Rash, nor is he your equal in any way. Deny this if you can.

And I had to hang my head and bite my lip then Silvaney, for what she said was so, and even Ethel has advised me aginst making eyes at Lonnie Rash. And yet the thought of his warm brown cheek came to me even then, even there in the schoolroom, I confess it. I walked to the window and stared at the snow. I could not look at Miss Torrington.

She said, Your mother has abdicated her duty it seems, and the less said about that paragon of virtue Miss Hunt, the better.

I opened my mouth and closed it agian. I could not say a thing. Snow blew into the windowpanes, no two flakes alike. But she went on.

I feel that you have been given to me by God as a sacred responsibillity, Miss Torrington said behind me. I am perhaps espeshally suited to help you fulfill your destiny, Ivy. I can educate you, I can dress you, I can take you to Europe. For there is everything, everything, to learn! I am a woman of some means, Ivy. I can give you the world.

A shock run all through me then Silvaney, at her words. It had grown nearly dark.

Miss Torrington continued, I could feel her breth soft as a whisper on my neck. And it would give me such enormous pleasure, she said. For it appears certain by now that I will never mary, nor bear a child, and yet I have so much to give a child, espeshally a young lady. Oh Ivy, do say yes!

I watched the snow.

When Miss Torrington spoke again, her voice was light. Just keep this in mind dear, she said. I depart for Boston in three days, my trunk has gone now, as you know. My report is finished.

I know, I said. I will think about it.

Together we went to the cloakroom and got our coats and our hats, and Miss Torrington got her lether gloves. I waited in the snow while she locked the door behind us. Now, she said and put the key in her purse and took my arm and we walked the short way back to the bordinghouse. My mind whirled around and around like the snowflakes around the gaslights. I thought of sliding on the frozen river in the snow, and of the lady sisters skimming home across the snow after they had told their stories, I thought of the story of Whitebear Whittington, and then I thought of all the stories I dont know yet, of books and books full of stories in Boston. I immagined their lether bindings and their deep rich covers and the pretty swirling paper inside the covers, like the snow. But to think of the lady sisters put me in mind of Granny Rowe and Tenessee, which made me feel bad.

For Granny Rowe came to town a day or so ago to sell sang which she does every winter, and Tenessee with her, and after they sold it to Mister Branham and said hello to Ethel, they came over to the school to see me. I was standing at the door, talking to Miss Maynard.

Lord God, how ye doing honey, Granny said, and I confess that for a minute I drew back, for here was Granny smoking her pipe and wearing her old mans hat, and Tenessee behind her giggling and clutching that filthy dirty crazy bead purse. I drew back. For all of a sudden they seemed to me strange people out of another time, I could not breth.

Excuse me, Miss Maynard said, and left.

And then I hugged them both and walked them back to the bordinghouse to see Momma and Geneva and have some coffee and vinegar pie, and did not think twice about it. But I was thinking now, walking with Miss Torrington. And I was ashamed of myself. And I thought, If I go to Boston, I will not see them, nor Beulahs new baby, nor Ethel grinning behind that big cash register in Stoney Branhams store, nor see my little momma any more, and I pictured her there in her rocking chair. Nor will I see Silvaney agian I thought, who is dearest to my hart, the one that I cannot picture at all having never been there to the Elizabeth Masters Home. Oh Silvaney! sometimes I think I made you up to suit me!

Me and Miss Torrington walked arm and arm through the snow, and then we were at the bordinghouse, where light spilled out the windows and shaddows moved behind the curtians in the sitting room. And one of the curtians moved and I thought it must be Lonnie Rash, looking for me. It was nearly suppertime.

The front door opened with a pop, and Geneva stuck her head out.

Ivy, is that you? she hollered.

Yessum, I said.

Well, where the hell have you been, get your ass right on in the kitchen this minute, we have got some extra company here that is stuck in the snow, Geneva yelled and slammed the door.

Miss Torrington and I paused by the foot of the stairs.

From someplace upstairs came a womans high pitched giggle and then a slamming door.

In her long dark coat, Miss Torrington looked very tall. Her thin pale face beneath the fur brim of her hat seemed pinched and white. Yet she was pretty. Oh yes, I thought then, oh yes the Ice Queen, and I remembered Mrs. Brown and all her books from long ago. Miss Torringtons hat was dusted with snow. She smiled.

I will come, I said all of sudden. My answer is YES, I said, and then we walked together up the stairs and crossed the porch and went inside.

I served dinner and dared not look at Lonnie Rash who starred at me. Tomorrow I will tell him, I said to myself. Tomorrow.

But oh Silvaney, I did not, for you will not belive what happened next!

We had extra places set at dinner for all the people who had got stranded in the snow, and it was a jolly table, everybody laughing. This was Miss Torrington, Miss Maynard, glummy little Mister Sledge, Geneva and Momma, Lonnie Rash and three other young men who are bording here now, Judge Brack, Miss Hazel Ridge who has come here from Roanoke to settle a estate, Mister Wiley a lawyer from out of town, and a man and a wife and his grown son from Lynchburg originally, who were motoring to Kentucky.

That is what the wife said when Judge Brack asked her where they were from, she said From Lynchburg originally. She was very fancy and I kept looking at her and thinking, Now is she a lady? And will I be like that? But finely Silvaney I decided she is not a lady, instead she is only rich. She ate in very little bites and acted too good for everybody else, but after while her husband and Judge Brack got to saying limmericks, and she had to laugh. For there is something about being inside around a table with good food on it and other people, while the wind is blowing outside and the snow is falling down, that will bring everbody together in spite of theirselves.

Only Miss Torrington did not relly join in, this is normal for her though, but even she looked happy with her white cheeks flushed pink from walking through the cold outside or else from Genevas hot potato soup. The pink spots on Miss Torringtons cheeks looked like they had been painted there. She said scarcely a word, but bunched up her lips from time to time as if to keep back a smile, and I could tell that she was pleased as punch that I had said yes and that I would be going back up to Boston with her.

I guess I will have to get used to the snow, I thought. They will be plenty of snow in Boston all right. I tried to immagine the State House or the Old North Church in snow, and to think that I would go there. Immagine, I thought, me Ivy Rowe in Boston!

Ivy are you feeling well? Geneva asked me and I said Yesm, just fine thanks, and she said Well then for gods sake pay a little more attention to what your doing, and I said Yesm. I could not immagine telling Momma or Geneva or Lonnie Rash.

Ivy, pay attention! Geneva said.

And then finely supper was over and Lonnie Rash follered me into the kitchen and said, Whats the matter Ivy? and I said, I will see you later. And Geneva and Judge Brack sang Alexanders Ragtime Band in the sitting room while little Johnny played the piano, he is getting to be a pretty good hand at this, he is learning it down at Hazels Entertainment from Blind Bill Smith, where Miss Torrington says he should not be allowed to go. Ludie and me and Mrs. Crouse did the dishes.

When we were finely done I walked back in the sitting room, thinking now I must speak to Momma and Geneva about all of this, but I did not because there was Miss Torrington waiting for me. Usually she leaves the group and retires to her room as she says right after dinner. But that night she stood with her back to the rest of them, watching it snow out Genevas front window, she turned when I came and said <u>Ivy,</u> only that, but the way she said it given me kind of a start. It was like she owned me.

But then she gave me a nice warm smile and said, while the rest of them were singing Shenandoah, that she was too wrought up to go right to sleep and consequently she thought it might be a good night for us to begin our drawing lesson.

And I said, <u>Oh yes</u> immediately, for this was something I had been hoping for. So we went up the stairs to her room while the rest of them were singing, I could feel Lonnie Rashes brown eyes burning holes in my back. I did not turn around ether.

I had never been in Miss Torringtons room, which is the large one in the front, right over the sitting room. It was neat as a pin. Miss Torrington was very businesslike. She moved her books and papers to clear a space at the writing table, and then from the wardrobe she took a lether box and opened it to reveal drawing pencils of every shade in the rainbow, it took my breth away! She layed the box open on the table, and come back with some thick white paper. Now then my dear, she said, and drew up the rooms two chairs to the table, and pulled the lamp over closer to us. She took a deep breth then picked up one of the pencils, charcole gray.

Now then Ivy, she said, and she began to draw, and in no time flat her page was filled. Roses in a bowl, a horse, a house, a mountain, a girl who looked like me. Her pencil moved so fast on the paper I could not see it move.

How do you do this? I said, How do you make the mountain seem so far away.

Ah, said Miss Torrington, That is perspective. You will need to learn perspective, Ivy Rowe.

Now, she said, and gave me a gray pencil like her own. Like this, she said, and we began. She drew, and I copied her lines, and the minutes flew past. We drew a house. Downstairs they were singing Alexanders Ragtime Band agian, I could hear Geneva belting it out and another high loud voice that I thought belonged to the woman who was from Lynchburg originally. We drew a tree. Yes, Miss Torrington murmured. Yes. I was very exited. Very good, Miss Torrington said. Now you just continue, and she stood behind me as I continued.

At first I was not even aware of her standing there, I was so wrapped up in what I was doing, putting more gray on one side of the tree to show that was the shade. Oh yes, she said, Exactly, and as she leaned over my sholder to look, I felt her breth on my neck. She rested her hand on my sholder. Like this, she said, and took my pencil for a minute and began to shade the tree, and then I saw how and she gave me back my pencil and I continued.

And then, Silvaney, Miss Torrington kissed my neck! I froze, Silvaney, right there with my pencil above the tree. I could not breth, I could not think what to do, but while I was still thinking it seemed, I found myself jumping up from there and in my haste I knocked over the chair and bumped the table so that all the drawing pencils went flying to the floor. And I flung the charcole drawing pencil across the room as hard as ever I could.

Miss Torrington sank down on her bed with her mouth in a wide round O. Oh what have I done? she said, and her hands flew up to her face and she started crying. I think she was just as surprised as me. Oh Ivy please forgive me, she said but I could not see her face.

Nor could I speak.

I lit out of that room as fast as I could go, and didn't even answer Geneva who had come to the foot of the stairs to say, Whats all the commotion?

I was just helping Miss Torrington pack, I finely said, and Geneva said Oh and went back in the sitting room where Johnny was playing piano. I knew I could not go down there. Instead I ran up one more flight of stairs to the third floor where you know my room is, and there was Lonnie Rash sitting at the top of the steps by himself.

Ivy girl, he said, Come here Ive been waiting on you for a hour it seems like. What is the matter with you, girl?

Why nothing at all Lonnie, I lied, because I knew I could not say, and oh Silvaney, I can never say! And then because I could not think what else to do next I let Lonnie kiss me standing there in the hall, and I liked it, and he put his hands on my titties like he was used to doing. Whats the matter Ivy? You are shaking, Lonnie said, and I said, I think I am getting a cold, but the fact is that I was real exited. I was real exited from the drawing lesson and from what Miss Torrington had done, which was awful. So then when Lonnie said Come on now Ivy, oh come on honey please, let me go in there tonight, which is what he always said, I said Yes.

And I took him in my room for the first time and closed the door behind us and took off all my clothes and layed down on the bed and let him do it to me. It hurt a lot more than I thought it would. I rember I layed there looking out across Lonnies hair and his white back in the light coming in the window, the light coming off the snow. It hurt a lot. But then Lonnie kissed me a lot and told me he loved me and said, We will get maried. Say you love me, Lonnie said, but I didnt say a thing, and then he tickled me and said Say it, say I love you Lonnie, and finely I gave in and said I love you Lonnie, but Silvaney I do not. Then Lonnie went to sleep but I could not sleep, I was as Miss Torrington said, too wrought up. I got up and washed between my legs with the water from the basin, in that light the blood looked black. But there did not seem to be too much of it.

Then I went over to the window and looked out at the town,

the way I always look out my window, at the Presbyterian Church steeple and the Methodist School where I go now and the backs of all the houses on Shady Lawn Street, and Genevas shed and our own backyard. Everything shone white in the snow, and the buildings looked all diffrent, and everything looked diffrent in the snow. The moon was about half full.

Lonnie layed in my bed taking up nearabout all of it. He brethed slow and deep and peaceful, like a little boy. I looked out the window at the moon and the mountains and the black slash of the river in the snow. Nothing moved. Lonnie was brething. All the streets and roads were covered by the snow. I looked out my window and felt so sad, and then all of a sudden I knew why, because I have lost it now, Majestic Virginia which used to be mine. And this room in Geneva Hunts bordinghouse is not my own ether, not any more, I have lost it too because of bringing Lonnie up here. I do not understand this Silvaney, but it is true. So I stayed awake awhile and looked out on the town but it aint mine any more Silvaney, it is not. I have lost it now. And my boyfriend Lonnie is very sweet. And even though so many things have happened I want you to know that I will always remain your loving and faithful sister just the same as I was up on the mountain,

Ivy Rowe.

Dear Miss Torrington,

I recieved the letter which you left for me, and the fountain pen which is beutiful. Thank you. I am writing with it now. I am glad I knew you. I hope you have a safe journey back to Boston and a good life in the future, for I will always remain your grateful student,

Ivy Rowe.

Dear Beulah,

No I am not going to be maried. I know what you have heard, and it is true I have a boyfriend Lonnie Rash, but I am not going to be maried anyway. And I am having a real bad time right now getting everbody to believe me, and stop bothering me about it. The hardest one is my boyfriend Lonnie himself who says, <u>Why not?</u> <u>Why not, Ivy?</u> If you love me then we should get maried before I join up with Louis Judds Army in the bottom, and go to War.

But Beulah, I do not love Lonnie, believe me. There is a strong feeling I get when I am with him, it is true, but when I am not with him I do not have this feeling, and if it was love, I would. Or I think I would, do you? For I used to marvel at how you kept on loving Curtis when he wasnt even there. Jane Eyre loved Mister Rochester so much that she could hear him cry out <u>Jane! Jane!</u> across the miles. It was like she was with him all the time. And I think of poor Momma who goes on and on after death loving Daddy so much it will finely kill her I think. Well Beulah, when I am with Lonnie he gets me tickled, and he is good looking, and sweet and nice. But sometimes right in the middle of when Lonnie is talking to me, my mind will wander off to think of other things, mostly of when we were all living up there on Sugar Fork, of Daddy and Danny and Silvaney, and of all the old stories. Sometimes I worry Beulah, that I can not just pick up and go on like you and Ethel do. Do you know what I mean? Or I will think of a song or a poem. And one time Beulah, I got to thinking about how to make a marble cake which Geneva is teaching me!

So I know I can not mary Lonnie Rash. But when he sits me down and looks me in the eye, I can not say why not. I can not say Lonnie, I do not love you, to his face. And it may be that I do love him in a way, sort of as much as I love, oh Garnie. I love him about that much. I know I am too honnest for my own good so you dont have to say it, Ethel has said it already! But I can not lie straight to his face, I love him too much for that. And yet I know it is not a love to die for, not like Revel and Mrs. Brown, it is not a love to stop the heart. So I have said, I have to stay with Momma now and help her out, we will get maried after the war.

I guess he will give up and join Louis Judds Army in the bottom before long, and I will be glad, believe you me! although I will miss him so. But right now I am living a lie which bothers me something awful. And this is not all. Lonnie Rash is not the only one bothering me about this. I am surprised to tell you that Geneva has told me I ought to go on and mary Lonnie while I have got the chance. I was surprised to death to hear her say it. You know she is one to talk! But Geneva says a husband is not a bad idea and may calm me down some and keep me from grabbing at straws, I am not sure what she means. She says Lonnie is as sweet as they come, and this is true I know, but Beulah I do not love him enough! Geneva says this will not signify, that love dont last long anyway, and I may as well get me a nice one while the getting is good.

And Miss Maynard has said I am ruint and can not come to help at the school any more, that I have learned all they have to teach me anyway, and I better look for another position. Miss Maynard is so mean to me now that I think she has hated me all along, and was jealous of how much Miss Torrington favored me. Miss Maynard said I am ruint one day after she saw Lonnie going down the steps from the third floor, she said it to Judge Brack before breakfast who laughed and said Oh I would not say ruint my dear but merely compromised. And little Momma says nothing Beulah, she looks out at the mountains and smiles a little and says Well Ivy, you certainly have got yourself in a stew now but I must say you have got a mind of your own, you take after old Granny Rowe who never did one thing she did not want to. But it is like Momma is talking to somebody else, not her own daughter, it is like she moves farther and farther beyond us in her mind.

So Beulah, what do you think? I am so curios to know. Do you think I am ruint or merely compromised? The only one on my side is Ethel who says I ought not mary Lonnie, he is too dumb! So I will stick to my guns agianst them all.

And speaking of guns, this will tickle Curtis, here is a funny story in the middle of all my trouble. It is what happened about Louis Judds Army lately and Judge Brack told it on himself. Geneva said, I dont know if I would tell that, Judge, if I was you! But it is so funny. This is what happened. Louis Judd has been coming over to town and comandeering his provisions, as he calls them, and charging them all to the U.S. Army. He writes U.S. Army on the charge slips, and takes what he wants, and that is all. Everybody is scarred to stop him, or say anything, because his men are armed to the teeth and he has got so many of them camping out there in the bottom. Plus Louis Judd keeps getting promoted or promoting himself, nobody knows which it is. But every now and then he makes a trip out of town and then comes back with a higher rank and a brand new uniform. Right now he is up to Captain. And he has charged up money all over town until all the merchants feel that they will lose their shirt. So a bunch of them, the ones that Louis Judd owes the most to, got together in a body and came to see Judge Brack and asked him to go over there please and try to find out what is the story, and when will they be paid.

So Judge Brack agreed to do it, and he went. He said that that camp is really something, very organized and military exactly like a real Army camp. He had to give his name twice to Judds men, once to cross the bridge and once to get to Judds tent where Judge Brack found to his great surprise, as he said it to us later, that Judd was inside seated on a folding chair and smoking a pipe while an orderly gave him a foot-bath.

Now listen here Louis, Judge Brack said he began without preamble for he had known Louis Judd and his family all his life. Stoney Branham and the others have sent me over here to ask you just exactly when and how you plan to honnor your debts.

It is good to see you Robert, said Louis Judd, We are honnored by your visit here today.

I have come to inquire about your debts outstanding Louis, Judge Brack said. Dont be so goddam friendly.

Now now Robert, said Louis Judd. I will respond to all your questions in due time. Right now I am having a foot-bath.

I can see that, Judge Brack said shortly.

Have you ever had a foot-bath, Robert? Louis Judd asked, and Judge Brack said that No, he had not.

This here is a outstanding foot-bath, Louis Judd went on to say. My boy puts something special in it. What is it that you put in here boy? he asked, and his orderly said, Epsom salts sir.

Epsom salts, Louis Judd said. I can highly reccomend the use of epsom salts in a foot-bath.

So this foot-bath goes on, according to Judge Brack, for a quarter of an hour, and the upshot of it all was that finely Judge Brack took off his own shoes and socks, and the orderly fetched him a fresh pan of epsom salts and hot water, and Judge Brack started having a foot-bath too. He said it felt so good he scarcely noticed when Louis Judd dried his feet and put his own shoes and socks back on, nor did he pay much mind when Louis Judd stood up and walked to the door of the tent and stood there looking out at his regiment. Judge Brack said he never thought a thing about it until the minute after that, when Louis Judd who was standing by that tent flap big as life, just up and <u>disappeared,</u> and his boy with him! Judge Brack said it was like that boy had vannished into thin air. Judge Brack got real mad as you might immagine, but it was too late by then because Judd and the boy were nowhere to be found and of course they had taken Judge Bracks shoes and socks with them. He had to walk back across the bridge barefoot and all through town, cussing every step of the way, and it just as cold as cold could be that day with a freezing rain falling. By the time he got back to Genevas his feet were bright red, I saw them myself. And now he has got a bad cold. But Judge Brack says to everybody at the end of this story which he has told and told, By god it was a hell of a foot-bath none the less!

And now the big news Beulah, which has just come while I was writing down the foot-bath part of this letter, the big news— Garnie came running in here first to tell it, and now it is all over town, so it must be true! is that Louis Judds Army is going to war, they are going for sure, they are packing up now and they will leave in three days, this is official. So Stoney Branham will be paid by the U.S. Army and Ethel will be so happy since she helps keep the books for him now, and everybody else will get paid too, and Lonnie will join them now I know, and leave here.

Lonnie has just been waiting to see if Louis Judds Army was on the up and up as he says. Beulah I confess it, I will miss him so much, and yet I am glad he is going. I feel both these ways at exactly the same time, I know it is awful! It is why I cannot mary him ether. I would end up acting like Emma Bovary which was awful, but I can see why she did it, I know I would do it too. I have said as much to Miss Maynard in fact who said Well Ivy you are an impossible girl, I guess this is true too.

However I do NOT believe that if you make your bed, you have to sleep in it for ever. Do you? Anyway they are leaving, Lonnie is leaving. This is the big news for now.

I remain your devoted but compromised sister,

Ivy Rowe.

Dear Silvaney,

Lonnie is gone.

He joined up with the Army just before they left. I walked with him all through town to the river, down to the bridge. Lonnie was walking very stiff-like with everything he owns in his old cloth bag that was his daddys, the one he came to the bordinghouse with. He does not own much, Lonnie, he is twenty years old today. He turned and grinned at me, You are so pretty Ivy, he said, and I smiled but inside I was screaming at him. Dont leave, dont leave, I dont even know you yet oh God I never took the time but what a nice looking stiff-legged boy you are, oh Lord I hate to see you go. I will miss your hands on my titties and how you can make me laugh. I will miss you, I will miss you I thought. It all came over me in a rush as we walked along, for I thought, May be this is the last time I will see you Lonnie Rash, this is it. When you come back from the war you will be all different, you will be a man. I just smiled at him.

The sun was real bright but skittish, sliding in and out of the fast-moving clouds. The sky was so blue. I thought, It was almost exactly a year ago, in March, that we came here. So many things have happened, it seems longer. It seems years. I have grown up I guess, although Miss Mabel Maynard would tell you I am no lady. Nevermind. In fact we passed Miss Maynard as we walked through town to the river, we passed right by the open door of the Methodist School just as Miss Maynard stepped outside to beat her erasers. She made an awful cloud of dust in the air and started coughing, then she turned and saw me and Lonnie Rash and stopped beating her erasers together and stood for a minute in the white cloud of dust with her hands raised up, not moving.

She looked at me and I looked at her.

Then I put my arm around Lonnie and we walked along like that together, out of sight.

You be good while Im gone now girl, Lonnie said. He squeezed me. We will get maried first thing when I get back. Oh Silvaney, I did not have the heart to tell him, I did not! For Lonnie is an orphan like Jane Eyre. Even though I remember so well what Mister Brown taught me and Molly so long ago, that truth is more precious than rubies, more dear than gold. But since that time I have learned a lot, believe you me, and now I wonder if Mrs. Brown had not been so honnest herself, if she had not told Mister Brown that she was pregnant with Revels baby, would he ever of found out that it wasnt his? For I can not see how. And I wonder, Must we always tell the truth, even if it hurts another very much? So I bit my tonge. For I thought, Lonnie is going to war, he does not need to feel bad. I can tell him when he gets back, that will be plenty of time. Silvaney, do you think this is awful? It is either awful or grown up, I am not sure which.

We walked through the town of Majestic which used to be mine, past stores and houses and the Methodist Church, gray stone, its steeple gray in the blue-blue sky. Everywhere, people were running in the street and yelling, and down by the lumberyard you could hear the whine of the circular saw. The new spring air was wet and clean. We got to the bridge. Lonnie set his cloth bag down. Then he put his arms around me, those arms which have been around me so much before. The river was up and the water went rushing past, it was hard to hear anything. Or see anything either—the sun came jumping out of a cloud right then and shone in my eyes, I couldnt see Lonnies face. I couldnt see his face, I dont know him, I never knew Lonnie really which seems so sad. He kissed me on the lips and I let him, I didnt care who happened by or what they thought. For I am compromised! I said to myself over the roar of the water, compromised! When he kissed me I felt that firey hand as always and kissed him back harder. I have always liked kissing Lonnie Rash.

Ivy, he said in my ear. I want you to have this. Ive got something I want you to have. And he reached in his breast-pocket and came up with a little box.

Oh no, I thought, I can not wear a ring. What is it? I said.

Open it and see, said Lonnie, I asked my sister Bonnie to send it and she did, it came in the mail yesterday, just in time.

In time for what, I said.

For you, Lonnie said. For me to give to you.

Lonnies sister Bonnie is a whole lot older than him. You will love Bonnie, he has told me many times, and I have not had the nerve to say, I will never know her.

Lonnie opened the little box and there was a round gold locket with flowers carved all over it. It is so pretty. Looky here, Lonnie said. He pressed a tiny spring and the locket popped open and there in one side was a picture of a kind of flat-faced woman with her hair piled on top of her head, and on the other side, a lock of the hair, brown, like Lonnies. This is my mothers hair, he said. This is my mothers locket. Then he closed it up and unclasped the chain and put it around my neck.

Thank you, I said.

I kissed him some more and then he left. I watched him walk across the bridge and check in with the soldier on the other side. He will look good in a uniform. He looked back once. I waved. He got smaller and smaller as he walked off into the bottom, into the bustling camp. Then he was gone.

The river roared and leaped, muddy brown but shining in the sun, about three yards below the bridge. Downstream, I knew, boys were waiting to ride the logs down to Kentucky, waiting for the great spring tide that would carry them clear to Catlettsburg, hunkered down on the riverbank watching the river and waiting to go. The water beneath the bridge spewed and whirled, it made me dizzy. Lonnie will cross the ocean and go to Europe. The water went around and around in little eddies, little whirlpools, and all of a sudden in my mind I saw Lonnie Rash walk away from me again and again and again, getting littler and littler as he went. Then he was gone. I blinked. Well, I thought, thats that, and with him gone it was like my whole self came rushing back to me again and I looked at the water and thought, Oh I <u>do</u> want to go to Boston, I do want to go after all!

And I recalled Miss Torringtons letter, how she said that there are kinds and kinds of love and that sometimes we confuse them being only mortal as we are, and how she said that she would never be other than my good true friend if I would reconsider coming.

<u>So I will go! I will!</u> I thought. My mind was as rambunctious and wild as the river. All the poems I ever knew came rushing and tumbling into my head, and the thought of losing Lonnie— for I have lost him, Silvaney, I know it—this thought put me in mind of the saddest lovelyest poem I ever knew which was Rose Aylmer <u>whom these wakeful eyes may weep, but never see, A night of memories and of sighs I consecrate to thee.</u> I thought <u>oh yes</u> for I have lost him now as surely as I have lost those others, Danny and Daddy and you, Silvaney, my lost one, my heart, and I thought

They are all gone into the world of light!
And I alone sit lingering here;
Their very memory is fair and bright,
And my sad thoughts doth clear.

Oh yes, I decided, watching the river, I will go, I will go, and if I do not like it there I can come back, I can always do that for I am grown up now even though I am compromised and no lady, nevermind I thought, I will go. And I felt then as if I had jumped the logs and ridden them clear to Kentucky! I am glad I am no lady now.

So picture me Silvaney, if you will. I want you to see me plain. It is spring and a skittery sunshiny day, I stand on the river bridge already missing my sweetie whose gone to the war, the river spews and boils like Genevas coffee, the wind blows hard and a bugle call comes across the river from the Army camp. I wear a dead womans pretty locket, I am free to come and go as I please. I will go to Boston and see what there is to see. Yet always I will be bound to you my love and my heart and I will come back for you one day soon and take you back to the mountain. I remain your loving sister,

Ivy Rowe.

Dear Miss Torrington,

I know you are surprised to hear from me but, I have changed my mind! I would like to come to Boston after all, if you will still have me. You know I do not have the fare, but I will repay you bye and bye when I am a teacher out in the world and earning my keep. So, do you still want me? And when should I come? I am too exited to write down here the steps which I have taken to arrive at this decision. Let us say instead, may be I have learned some perspective at last, and I rema

Oh Silvaney, Silvaney,

All is lost.

For I can not go to Boston, or have a new life, or do anything ever again.

This is what happened. I do not know if I said or not that I have been poorly lately from being upset I thought, what with everybody trying to mary me off, and from exitment and the war. Well right after Lonnie left, I was writing to Miss Torrington when I got to feeling sick at my stomach and when I came back from the bathroom, there was Geneva in her big blue satin robe looking serious.

Now Ivy, she said, we must have a talk. And she took my hand and led me back to the kitchen where she gave me a cup of coffee in one of my favorite cups, the white china one with the golden edges that we never use.

I sat at the table feeling puny while Geneva put sugar and cream in my coffee exactly the way I like it, looking at me. Then she got a cup of coffee for herself and made us some cinamon toast.

Thank you Geneva, I said, but then I had to get up and run out the back door and get sick again, this has been happening to me lately. When I came back in the door Geneva hugged me and sat me back down in the chair, and pulled her own chair up close so she could hold my hands.

Honey, how far along are you? she asked.

What do you mean, I said, for I did not know.

Oh merciful Jesus, Geneva said. She got up then and got herself another cup of coffee and got me another piece of cinamon toast.

I dont know if I can eat that or not, I said.

Eat it, said Geneva. You need to get your strength.

Why? I said, and Geneva said, Ivy honey, you are going to have a baby.

Her words exploded like a gunshot in my head, and then the whole kitchen whirled and then stood still. I can see it, smell it, feel it, yet—the kitchen so warm with the fires already going in the stoves, the coffee smell, the red and white checkered linolium cloth on the kitchen table, the salt and pepper shakers that look like little Dutch girls, the pale pearly light outside the kitchen window, Genevas fat kind wrinkled face above her satin gown. Oh yes, I thought, I have not bled for a long time, but I never did bleed too reglar anyway.

A baby, I said. Are you sure?

She hugged me then, I could smell her fancy perfume so strong I like to of got sick again.

Oh Ivy, Ivy, she said. I am pretty sure. You cant just rush into things the way you do honey, without them catching up with you sometimes. You have got to slow down, and not put yourself out so much, or you will frazzle your nerves before you are twenty.

I smelled Genevas strong perfume. Upstairs I heard people moving around, getting up. I heard Ludies baby going LA-LA-LA real loud. That was Little Geneva. Big Geneva drew back and smiled.

Well Ivy, she said, Let me think on this awhile. You go on now, and get cleaned up and dressed, and dont you tell a soul what we have said. You hear me? Not any one.

And I said, Yes.

I will talk to you after supper then, Geneva said. She kissed me on the hair and stood up and I stood up too and left. I went back up to my room and got dressed and went back down and served at breakfast and then slipped out. I walked by the river awhile, the bottom looked so funny all trampled down and muddy and trashy, and Louis Judds Army gone. It was funny how a place so bustling could be so empty now I thought, and I thought of the world of light. Then I went over to Stoney Branhams store to see Ethel who said I looked sick. I am, I said to Ethel. I am real sick. And then I went back to the boardinghouse and upstairs to my room and laid down in my bed and starred up at the ladies marching hand in hand along my walls, and kind of lost track of the time.

I felt of my stomach which still feels just as flat as ever beneath my skirt. At first I could not immagine the baby inside and then I could, you know I do have a good immagination. And I could see that baby as clear as day, tiny and pink and all curled up, and then it started beating with its little fists against my stomach, trying to escape. It hurt me. And then, I cannot explain it Silvaney, I was that little baby caught inside of my own self and dying to escape. But I could not. I could never ever get out, I was caught for ever and ever inside myself.

And then I felt I was all caught up in a cloud or a fog, like the fog that hangs on the top of Hell Mountain of a morning, you know we used to could see it from Sugar Fork. Then that changed and I felt I was riding a log raft down to Catlettsburg but the river got wilder, and Silvaney you were on the raft with me too in this dream but you fell off, and Granny Rowe was there holding out her hand but she was too far away and then she was gone too and I fell off, I went down and down in the muddy water and could not see. It was so dark. Then a beam of light came in the dark and crossed my bed and I sat up with my eyes itching. I guess I had been asleep. I guess I had slept all day long. I was real hungry. It was Geneva and old Doc Trout.

Geneva lit my lamp.

Ivy, she said, Doctor Trout is going to examine you now and then we will decide what to do.

I sat up. Is it night? I said, and Geneva said, Yes. Then Doc Trout came over and told me to lay out straight and put up my knees and hike up my skirt and I did so, but I could not stand to think of what he was doing so I looked at my ladies all in a row and thought about the play-parties we used to have and the flowers in our red hair. Beulah said we look good in green, with our red hair. Then he was done and I could put my knees down.

Well Geneva, Doc Trout said. You are right of course but she is not so far along that we cant take care of it.

Oh thank god, Geneva said.

Bring her over to the office tomorrow after supper, Doc Trout said. Then he leaned way down and pinched my cheek. Ivy honey, wheres your spunk? Where is that redheaded hellion I am so fond of?

I started crying. I dont know, I said.

Well you find her, he said. You get up with her and bring her on over to my office tomorrow night, you hear me? I will fix her up.

No you will not, another voice said from the door and we all looked up, and it was Momma. She stood there shaking all over like a leaf in the wind, in a long white gown with her long gray hair floating out around her.

For gods sake, said Doc Trout.

Now Maude, Geneva said.

Momma took one step closer. She looked real little. Ivy, you listen to me, she said. I am your mother.

But she looked more like the ghost of our mother. And the way she looked put me in mind of how she used to look up on Sugar Fork, how she went up on Pilgrim Knob and stood out in the snow and said, I am a fool for love.

She turned to Doc Trout. We will not be needing your services, she said. Thank you anyway. She said it real formal. Her face was pinched and white. She turned back to me.

Momma I am not going to get maried, I dont care what you say, I told her. I am not going to mary Lonnie Rash.

Well then we will raise this baby ourselves, Momma said. We will keep this child.

And though Geneva pitched a fit and Doc Trout talked till he was blue in the face, she would not change her mind and I could not go against her, Silvaney, Momma has been through so much.

You dont have to say for sure right now anyway, Doc Trout said. Theres plenty of time yet. But he is wrong. For I know already, the time is gone. Its gone. But Silvaney even though I am going to have a baby I will still remain your devoted sister,

Ivy Rowe.

Dear Beulah,

It is all I can do to write this sad letter.

Momma died in her sleep last Friday. When she did not come down for breakfast I started to go up there and get her but Geneva said No, wait a minute, Ivy, let me go. You stay here. And so I served at breakfast thinking no more of it until Geneva came back to the top of the stairs and called for Ludie and Mrs. Crouse. Then in a minute Ludie went running out the front door and everybody knew something was wrong. I believe I knew what it was right away. A great heavyness came over me, I had to sit down, I was so heavy that I couldnt even raise my head to nod to Doc Trout when he came back with Ludie. Johnny knew too. He came over to me and said, Is it Momma? and I said yes, and hugged him. It is a funny thing to me how you can know things without knowing them.

Beulah, I can not write too much of this. Momma looked so small in death, like a little child. All the lines in her face disappeared. Ethel and Geneva did her hair up so neat that she looked pretty too, and then you could see how she used to be a beutiful girl and how she had had such a big romance. Early Cook made her the prettiest white pine coffin, you know I think he was sweet on Momma always, and Geneva laid her out in the front parlor of the boardinghouse which upset Miss Maynard so much that she has had a sick headache for three days running. I dont care, as I hate her. But Beulah, people came from all over town even though we did not send for a one since you are so big now and it is so hard to get word to Tenessee and Granny. But the word got out someway to the folks from Home Creek and they all come, and men that Daddy used to know, and friends of Geneva who has so many friends. Sad as I am I was still glad to see Delphi Rolette and Mister and Mrs. Fox and all of them, and kissed them, I am not showing bad yet so they could not tell. Every one had something good to say about Momma the way you do when somebody dies but I wonder, Now how does anybody ever know relly what a person is like? Nobody ever did know Momma I think except Daddy, and that so many years ago before she was burdened by all her cares. You know I used to think all the time about love and it seems to me now that this was a great love Beulah, great and strange. I did not tell Ethel this as she would say, Poppycock. But there laid Momma with Daddy in death at last, surrounded by strangers. I think we were all of us strangers. I believe she went to join Daddy not God. She never cared for God. I said as much to Sam Russell Sage who came in trying to run things. <u>Dont preach,</u> I said, <u>and dont pray,</u> but then I got sick and I had to lay down and he did it anyway, I guess it does not matter much as she is gone.

I guess it does not matter how she looked, either. But Geneva and Ethel had dressed her up in a lacy blue dress that Ethel had bought at Sharps—Stoney Branham paid, and wasnt that nice?—and she looked real pretty, I have to say. But she would never of worn that dress in life. She did not look a thing like herself. She looked like a real lady, like somebody elses momma laying there. She did not look one bit desperate which she was dont you remember, all those years. But she looked like she died at peace. She died in her bed dreaming of Daddy and Sugar Fork, this is what I believe.

And we had all agreed that she would be berried on Blue Star Mountain with Daddy, and the men from Home Creek were going to carry her back up there directly but I was not to go Geneva said, it is true I cant hardly stand to ride anyplace it makes me so sick. Beulah, I do not see how you have stood it once already. I know I am not suppose to say this, but I do not.

Anyway there come a big rainstorm that next afternoon when they were fixing to leave, and so they all walked down the hill to Hazels Entertainment to wait for it to pass over, and I sat in the corner by myself, in the red wing chair by Mommas coffin, and thought about Lonnie Rash. Do you think this is awful Beulah? It is true. I could not get my mind off of him right then and I wondered, Where is he now? and, What is he up to? And I was thinking so hard that I failed to hear the knock at the door and I jumped when Ludie came running down the steps to let the old man in.

He stomped past Ludie real mean-acting and stomped across the parlor rug dripping water and mud everywhere and went straight to the coffin and raised up the lid which they had not nailed down yet. Oh my God, he said in a terrible voice. He wore a big black hat and his long white hair stood out in a wild way from underneath it. I stood up and tried to speak. He was dripping water on Mommas face. He looked at her for a minute and then let the top of the coffin drop and then he covered his face in his hands and made the awfullest sound I have ever heard. Lord Lord, Ludie was in the hall screaming. Garnie came running too but the rest of them had all gone down the hill to Hazels.

Who are you, I said finally, but then all of a sudden I knew.

It was our grandfather Mister Castle from Rich Valley that we have always heard tell of. His yellow face was old and mean and cut through by wrinkles as deep as the ruts in the road down Sugar Fork. His nose stuck out like Pilgrim Knob. One of his eyes was bleary and white, the other keen. He looked at me with that keen good eye.

She is mine now, he said. She will go with me.

He had three of his men along and one of them held me back while the other two carried her out to the truck in the rain. They carried her right past Ludie having a fit in the hall.

Beulah, I have been real sick with my baby as you know and I cant recall or tell the next part too good. It was thundering and lightning by then, this was the first big thunderstorm of the spring, and it thundered so loud right when they drove off that I couldnt hear the truck. It was raining cats and dogs too. I seem to forget what happened then for a while but soon they all came running back up the hill and milled around here hollering and deciding what to do next, and the upshot of this was that they got the sheriff and went over there to Rich Valley and got there just in time to find that he had berried her already in the family berrying ground over there with a wrought iron fence around it, right behind his big white house. Geneva said he stood out in the pouring rain with a gun and dared them to come any closer. But he was enjoined to put the gun down finally, by the law and common sense, and then he agreed to speak with Sam Russell Sage who went in the house and stayed for forty minutes while the rest of them stayed outside. And some several of Mister Castles men stayed out by the berrying ground in their truck which they had driven right across the yard. Geneva said Mister Castles house is beautiful but falling down.

Anyway Sam Russell Sage came out after while, by then it was getting dark and the rain had stopped, and addressed the crowd. He said that as Maude Castle Rowe was properly berried next to her own mother after all, he could find no fault with the arrangement although it had been wrongfully executed by the understandably distraught father. He said he thought it would cause more grief than good to dig her up again right then, especially in view of the circumstances, and said that everyone should get back in their vehicles and leave this sad spot immediately. He said that her soul was in Heaven anyway, and these earthly considerations meant nothing to God.

Beulah, you can immagine what I thought when I heard that! What about her berrying quilt? I asked, Laying in that chest up on Sugar Fork? But it is done. And now even Ethel has said, Oh Ivy, it is done.

But Judge Brack agrees with me, he says it is the worst thing he has ever heard of, and he said right to Genevas face, Your fancy man is nothing but a sharlatan my dear, and I will wager that a considerable amount of money changed hands that afternoon in the old mans house. Geneva has denied this of course, she was furious. But you know Geneva who has got so much good sense, does not have any sense at all when it comes to a man. She can run a boardinghouse like a genius but she cant see through Sam Russell Sage.

I will write more when I am feeling like it. I feel so bad now, like I too have been berried in a strange town among strangers, I can not say. I miss Momma. But I remain your devoted although ruint sister,

Ivy Rowe.

My dearest Silvaney,

I am writing to you in a hurry, in the middle of packing to leave. I want you to know always where I will be. Now it is with Beulah and Curtis, in the company town at the Diamond Mining Company on the back side of Diamond Mountain. Beulah wrote and asked me to come and now Curtis is here to fetch me. He is down below in the parlor right now with Geneva and all the rest of them, listening to Johnny play the piano, a new song he just picked up from a company man. The music comes up through the floor, it is like I can see the music waving in the air.

Out my window the mimosa tree is waving too, its branches like pink feathers waving in the air. It is so beautiful. The sun is going down now. I look out over this whole town which was mine, I check my room again and I check each drawer in my chester drawers but there is nothing left. Nothing. I have stripped my bed and folded my sheets and the blue counterpane at the foot of the bed so that Ludie can take them. Ludie had a baby. I will too. Curtis Bostick is waiting below. He has gotten real heavy and hooks his thumbs in his suspenders when he stands around, like he is a big shot, but he is not. I think he is practicing to be a big shot. Anyway you would never reconnize him as that skinny boy that used to come up the holler courting Beulah so long ago.

Down below they are singing <u>Oh how I hate to get up in the morning</u> which is about the war, it reminds me of Lonnie Rash. Johnny has got to where he plays the piano so good, I guess he got it from Daddy and uncle Revel who were so musicle. Johnny will stay here with Geneva and go to school, that is if she can get him to, he doesnt want to do a thing but play that piano. Johnny wears a mans hat. He picks up songs from the company men that come through, from people that come to stay in the boardinghouse, from the radio. Johnny is a town boy now, when I ask him things about Sugar Fork he cant hardly remember. Even the music he plays is different from the music we grew up on.

I will be glad to get back to the mountains myself even if it is not Sugar Fork. I have grown so sad here. But now, although I am glad to go, I am sad to leave. I am just a mess, I reckon.

Garnie will stay here too. He works for Sam Russell Sage and thinks he is really something, Sam Russell Sage has got him preaching now and calls him, The Boy Wonder.

So it is only me leaving.

Ethel will stay over at the Branhams. It is like they are her family now, and in fact we do not have a family any more Silvaney, we do not, they are all gone off into thin air or the world of light. The sun is going down now, I have to get a move on. Doc Trout came over this afternoon and stopped me on the porch and pressed my hands together and kissed them, I could not believe it! He said, Let me know if ever you want for a thing, you or that baby of yours, for you have made another conquest, Ivy Rowe. He is the strangest man Silvaney, I think he likes me better since I am ruint!

And so does Miss Mabel Maynard who came up to me today and said she wanted to wish me well, now that I am leaving, and apologize for her behavior, and then do you know what she did? She laid her hand on my stomach for a minute, and then bursted into tears, and ran away! Judge Brack is being real nice to me too, and Geneva. Everybody is very nice to me here but they think it is smart for me to leave since I am ruint. And there is another thing too, Geneva thinks I dont know it but I do. Ludie went in Mommas room today and put new linen and fixed the lamp, so I know Geneva has rented the room out to somebody else. I cant stand that. So I am glad to go. The ladies march in a line across these walls but I am no lady now. I can hear Genevas voice above the rest. Someday Im going to murder the bugler, someday theyre going to find him dead. It is a funny song. We are at war now. Our country is at war but I need a new start in life, so I am leaving. And I will tell you a funny thing Silvaney, this morning I got up real early and ran all over town like I used to do and spoke to everybody like I used to do, and then I came back here and took a sponge bath and stared at myself in the glass. My titties are big now and my stomach is getting big too, I can not wear most of my dresses already, it is like I am somebody else.

But I am not sick anymore. I feel strong. I feel real good, and I have to say I am excited to leave, for you know I have always wanted to travel. I am ready to get out of here! So I will close my trunk and pull my curtian and finish this letter, and go. Curtis said he wants to get on the road before dark. We will drive down the river towards Kentucky, and cross the new bridge. I think that travel by night is exciting. And I will tell you something else that may sound crazy Silvaney, I think my baby is excited too, I think I can feel her moving. And this is another thing. I know she is a little girl. I will raise her so good up on Diamond Mountain where no body will know her mother is your ruint sister,

Ivy Rowe.

III

Letters

from

Diamond

My dear Silvaney,

You will not believe it!

Here I am over on Diamond Fork with Beulah and Curtis having a new life, and guess what? The very day I got here Beulah had her baby, that was a week ago, it is another boy which they have named Curtis Bostick Junior. Big Curtis is tickled to death! He has been grinning up a storm and giving out cigars at the store. Curtis Junior is a long thin baby with a pointy head that I hope will smooth out in time. I hope my baby will not have a pointy head.

Beulah had him in a real medical way which was a good thing too as he come out a britches baby and Doctor Gray had to cut her and then stitch her up some. I hope my baby will not be a britches baby. Beulah is not feeling too good yet, either. The coal company doctor was the one that came down here, Doctor Gray who is a little old sad looking man with a very young wife that leads him a merry chase so everyone says. She gets herself up like a movie star. And this is how come Doctor Gray to live here, because of a scandal about his wife. Doctor Gray is from the North originally and talks like Miss Torrington.

And Beulah is acting real funny. Right when Doctor Gray was in the middle of stitching her up, she says, Ivy where's Curtis? and I said, He is out on the porch sitting with those men that have come over here, for I didn't know anybody's names yet. Are you sure? Beulah said, and I said, Yes. Then Beulah said, Doctor Gray, Doctor Gray! sounding very desperate. Her voice put me in mind, all of sudden, of Momma. Yes, Mrs. Bostick, said Doctor Gray. I want you to go ahead and fix me up so I can't have any more, Beulah said. Can you go on and do it right now? At these words Doctor Gray poked his head up from between her knees and looked over his spectacles at her and said, Now Mrs. Bostick, you know that is not possible.

I bet you could put something up in there while you are doing this, Beulah said, but he said No mam, I can not, in a definite Northern voice.

Oh merciful Jesus, oh god in heaven, Beulah started crying then—she was real brave up to that point—and she cried for the next three days, just crying and crying without let up or reason, and her milk did not come down. Finally then, on the fourth day, she quit and it did, and we did not have to have a wet nurse after all. I said I could nurse him, but they said, No you can't, it is bad luck before you have had your own baby, so I did not. But I have got milk in my titties Silvaney right now, I can feel it when Curtis Junior is sucking, they want to be sucked too.

And Beulah is <u>still</u> acting funny! When she was taking on so, I said to Curtis, lets get Granny Rowe to come around the mountain and give her something. For we are not too far from where Granny and Tenessee live.

No, I dont reckon that is a good idea, Big Curtis said real slow, but then he must of said something to Beulah about it because the next thing I knew, she was all upset and hollering at me.

Dont you <u>ever,</u> Beulah said, I mean <u>ever</u> Ivy Rowe, call old Granny over here with all her crazy old ideas. I wont have it. I will not. Beulah laid in the bed with her red hair splayed out on the pillow like a sunset. She is very beautiful. <u>I will not forget,</u> she said, <u>how we lived on Sugar Fork, how I bore that one</u>—she pointed at John Arthur, playing with a pan on the floor—<u>by myself on a cornhusk tick and cut the cord myself with the hatchet. I will never forget it,</u> she said. <u>And I will not have that for my boys,</u> she said, <u>or for me and Curtis, or for you Ivy, or for your baby. We will have more.</u> Beulah set her jaw when she said <u>more.</u> I looked at her good. She is serious, Silvaney. She <u>hates</u> Sugar Fork when she thinks of it, and yet I love it, now isnt this odd? us being from the same family and all. She hates Sugar Fork and all the old ways. She will not even talk about it. Still I do recall Beulah working her hands to the bone up there, and her with a baby to boot. She had a hard time. We all had a hard time, and that was all we knew. But I never thought about it—too busy thinking about myself all the time, I reckon! Poor Beulah.

With her jaw set like that, she put me in mind of somebody else, I could not think who at the time, and then that night when I couldnt sleep, I sat right up in bed all of a sudden and it came to me. It was Big Curtises mother! who used to be so bossy you will recall, until Curtis turned against her and married Beulah. To this day, they dont speak. And now Beulah is acting like Mrs. Bostick. And you would think that Curtis would mind this, but he doesnt. Despite of his size Silvaney, he is the kind of a man that <u>likes</u> to be pulled around by a ring in his nose. I guess some do. And Beulah has got big plans, you can see it in the set of her jaw and the steely shine in her gray-green eyes. I remember how much she loved to play Party. I remember way back when her and

Curtis first got married and she asked Ethel and me over there for supper in that little house by the lumberyard in Majestic, and everything on the table had a cream sauce, and Beulah had on black jet earrings, and after supper, on the way back, Ethel said, Beulah is putting on airs.

Well, now she is putting on more airs! She has got her hopes pinned on Curtis doing real good with the company and them moving him up to a better job someplace else. It is a good chance this will happen, as Curtis is a hard worker with a fine head for figures, and the kind of a man that other men like. Right now he works in the company store, which is why they have got a house up on the hill here.

You can tell how important somebody is by how far up on Company Hill they live. This whole town was built by the company, that is the Diamond Mining Company, they own everything here lock stock and barrel, and the name of the town is Diamond, Va. It takes up the whole holler. Down in the bottom by the creek is the company store where Curtis works. They say that he is standing in the store, which means that he is a clerk.

The company store is where you go to get your mail and groceries and clothes and damn near everything else, as Curtis says. It is a great big wooden building painted yellow like all the buildings here, now it is starting to turn gray from the coaldust. It has a wide front porch where everybody gathers to talk, the women of a day, the men of an evening, and to smoke cigarettes. The company store is the heart of this town, it is the heart of the world it seems, it is very important, and so is Big Curtis! This surprised me too.

The schoolhouse is down there in the bottom also—the company hires the teacher, and runs the school. The teacher is named Mr. Hyde, he loans me books. And now the company has even bought bats and gloves for baseball, and made a field. They say the superintendent is crazy about baseball. There is a company team, too. If a man can catch a ball then we will give him a good job in this mine, Big Curtis says with a wink. That is all it takes. And he wont have to mine too hard neither.

Then there is the company offices, and the community hall—this is for box suppers and meetings and cakewalks and such as that—and a barbershop, and a bunkhouse which is a long building like a giant chicken coop that the men sleep in who have come here to work but have not got their families, or may be they are single men, and then guess what! A <u>movie house,</u> where they run a new movie whenever they can get a hold of one. All these buildings look alike, yellow-painted wood, they are the last word in modern!

And then the houses start, they are all alike in long rows that fill up the whole south side of Company Hill, row upon row of little yellow frame houses with a porch in front built up on wood pilings so there is a space under the porch and most times dogs and kids up under there, and somebody will be sitting on the porch, a wife or her mother most likely, looking out upon the next row of houses, down the line of tin roofs shining in the sun. Oh there is a lot to see here, believe you me! In the lowest rows, the houses are so jam up on each other that you have not got hardly any breathing room, But no one cares of course for the money is so good. A man can make $7, $8, $10 a day in the mines if you can immagine this! And to think of how hard we used to live, just hand to mouth and never hardly laid eyes on cash money.

No wonder Beulah is getting so uppity. The houses start out being real little, two rooms I think, and then they get bigger halfway up. Beulah and Curtises house has got four rooms and a little dirt yard too. Beulah keeps everything pretty. We have got a pump out back that we share with three other houses and an outside toilet with a box to catch the shit in, that is between our house and the next one which is where some people named Gay-heart live. A colored man comes two times a week to haul the box away. I am not sure what the people down the mountain do for this, if they use in the woods or what. But we have got this colored man because Curtis is so important. The colored mans name is Earl Porter.

On up Company Hill above us, they have got some houses with five and six rooms and steam heat and I dont know what all, and above <u>them</u> is what you call Silk Stocking Row which is very grand. It is where the doctor and the engineers and the company men live, and their wives have got colored women to work for them so they dont have to lift a finger except to dress up and go to card parties, which they have a lot of. You can see the colored women climbing up there every morning with their heads wrapped up in rags. They live over in colored town, in another little holler, and sit by themselves in the movie house. You ought to see them, Silvaney! Some of them are black and some are brown, but they almost all have dark eyes. Their teeth and the whites of their eyes are <u>very</u> white and seem to shine out at you, and the inside of their hands is pink! They say their babies are born pink, and turn dark later. Sometimes at night you can hear the colored people singing, such songs as you have never heard. And also there is a bunch of other foreigners off to themselves in the other direction, down the Diamond Creek road, they have got crazy names and speak in another language. Curtis calls them hunks and wops. I have not seen any of these yet, or anyway not to know it.

But I have gotten off the track as usual, for right at the top of Company Hill is the superintendent's house, this is what I want to tell you about, it is really something! There is not a house in Majestic that can hold a candle to it, nor anywhere else even France, I immagine. For it was built by the owner—that is one of the richest men in the world, the company owner—for a summer place, and Beulah says it has a ballroom, and a conservatory full of flowers, and five bedrooms with mirror doors. How Beulah's eyes glitter when she describes it! The owner built it for his new wife as a surprise, and when she came here for the first time, they say she had 16 pieces of luggage which the colored men carried up the hill, and 14 hatboxes, and then two weeks later they carried everything back down because she hated it here, and said it is too depressing! So the owner never comes here any more, and Mr. Ransom the superintendent gets to live in the house with his wife who likes to put on the dog and does not find Diamond at all depressing. I would not either if I was that rich!

So this is it, Silvaney—Diamond, Va., picture it if you can. If you stand in the bottom by Diamond Creek looking up the mountain, as I did yesterday in the pale pearly early morning light when I had to run down to the company store for cornflakes, if you stand in the bottom and look up, you have to catch your breath, it is just fantastic! Row upon row of houses and people in every one like bees in a hive, you can not believe it is such a town! It seems to have sprung from the mountain already-made like mushrooms spring up on the mountain after rain. Or sometimes it seems to me like a toy town built by a big rich child. It is also like this for they have play-money here, or scrip which it is called. You can spend it in the company store just like money, it is good as cash. The company will buy you <u>everything</u> if you live here, and take it right out of your pay so you do not have to worry about a thing. It seems like a giant play town to me, or like paradise.

But I see I have forgotten the main thing probably, which is the railroad that cuts through this bottom like a knife following Diamond Creek and then the Big Sandy—next stop, Hazard, Kentucky. The train comes along every morning and every evening just about suppertime, and I reckon I will <u>never</u> get used to it! I still drop whatever I am doing and fly to the door to see it pass through town, the locomotive puffing out great clouds of white smoke and shooting up columns of red sparks. It gives you a real excited feeling to watch the train. And sometimes when I take little John Arthur downtown to get him out of Beulah's hair—for she has been short with him lately, ever since Curtis Junior has come—why then sometimes we will put our hands on the track and see can we feel it vibrate, or put our ears down there and see can we hear it hum. And little John Arthur gets so excited when he hears that whistle and then it really comes, he just has a fit. He puts his hands over his ears and holds his breath till his little face turns plum red—that funny face which looks so much like Daddy's—and jumps up and down all over the place. I have to hold onto the back of his belt whenever we are downtown and the train comes. And it only stops for a second.

The depot is right in the middle of town, next to the company store. The train stops with its brakes screeching and white steam hissing all around, and the bell ringing like crazy. The men sling the bags down onto the platform, mail and packages, and pick up whatever the station master has got for them, and sometimes a passenger will come down the steps brushing himself off and looking around, and sometimes a person will be waiting to get on. It is all very loud and exciting and fast. There is not but one passenger as a rule or two at most, company men on company business, for this is a coal train and make no mistake about it! It is the Norfolk and Western Railroad. Then they are off again with a whistle and a grinding roaring noise, and the white numbers flash by on the passing cars.

The caboose is full of boys that tip their hats and yell and wave to little John Arthur and me, but they do not look at me <u>like a girl</u> since I am so big now. I can not get use to it. You know I wrote to you how the boys would stare and stare at me in Majestic, those boardinghouse boys, but now if these boys look, they drop their eyes real quick or look away. I guess they think I am a married girl. My stomach is so big that my bellybutton pooches out, you cannot immagine it! The boys in the street look away, the boys in the caboose tip their hats like I am a hundred years old. I stand real straight and stick my belly out and dont care what they think! They dont know I am ruint, nobody knows, nobody knows me here. I look them all in the eye till they look away. Then the train is gone, around that bend yonder, to the mine.

You cant see it from here. And if you walk up there, past the company graveyard, you still cant see much—the tipple, loading coal into the railroad cars, the old tipple beside it falling down, a mess of cars and trucks and such as that, and jerrybuilt buildings and shacks scattered all around, and the old pony pen where they used to keep the mine ponies, and then the mine itself which is not a thing but a hole in the side of the mountain that looks like a big old cave. And that is it! It dont seem like much, not like anything to get all fired up about, or build a town for. But this is it, Big Blue Diamond No. 9. That's where the train is headed.

And then the train is gone and youre still standing there watching after it and the rails are still humming and youve got coaldust in your hair. It does get real dirty here in Diamond and thats a fact. Other than that, it seems like paradise to me!

Now it is summer of course and the mountains are pretty and green and you cant see the dirt anyhow. And it rains here most every afternoon, we have a thunderstorm, so all the houses and the fence rails and such as that gets washed off good. It would be a nice holler for a garden but you dont have to put in a garden, you can get what you want in a can from the store. Or those that did plant will bring you something, like that woman that brought Beulah some crookneck squash this morning. Oh, it is like paradise! So orderly and everything done for you, it is hard to beat. It is hard to believe the company will treat their own so good.

I said as much to Violet Gayheart, they live next door, yesterday when I was out stringing up our wash in the yard, and she was out there stringing theirs. Violet has got one baby and one big boy. Violet looked at me good. Huh! she snorted. Then she rolled her eyes up like a negro and busted flat out laughing. She has a high wheezing laugh like a horse.

What are you laughing at? I asked her. I didn't say nothing funny.

You, Violet Gayheart said. What is the matter with you? You are so ignorant. You act like you came from the moon.

What do you mean? I said. This here looks like a pretty good set up to me. It looks like the nicest place I have ever lived by a long shot, with a free doctor and all, and I think there is a good feeling of neighborness here too. Maybe you are just used to it, I said to Violet Gayheart. Didn't you say you all have been over here ever since this camp opened up?

Violet looked at me close and said, May be. Then she put her wash back down in her basket and took the clothespins out of her mouth and pushed back her curly black hair and said Listen here, honey. Violet Gayheart is tall and bony, with pale blue eyes and a wide full mouth. She wears red lipstick all the time. Violet is not too much older than me I would bet but she looks older, she seems older too. She is not from around here. She and her husband came up from someplace in East Tenessee I believe, and he has got a job about as good as Curtis I reckon, which is how come them to live as high up on Company Hill as Beulah. Violet's husband, Rush, sets timbers in the mine, he is in charge of that.

Close up, Violet's eyes look washed out and old. She licked her lipstick and put one hand on her hip and walked over towards me. I'll tell you the God's truth, Violet said, but I do not know what this is since just at that minute, Beulah came out on the porch and called me in because she was not feeling too good. Later she said she thinks Violet Gayheart is too rough. Rough! I was tempted to say. Rough! Well I don't care a fig for rough, since I am ruint anyway which is worse, but I held my tongue. For Beulah has got good intentions I know, and her and Curtis are so nice to take me in.

But it is a funny thing about being beholden, once you get beholden to somebody you are likely to hate them a little bit although this does not make a bit of sense as they are just being nice. I have been thinking about Daddy and the time he said to Mister Brown, We will not be beholden. Now I see why.

Anyway it is not long now, not long Silvaney, before my baby comes. I remember all the things we used to think about babies, do you? or that people used to tell us—like the hoot owl will bring you a baby, or a girl can find a baby underneath a cabbage leaf in the garden. I watched Momma get bigger and bigger with Garnie and didnt have no idea that's where he was, or that there was any baby in there atall! I remember how surprised I was to come in that afternoon and find Momma holding a baby, which was Garnie.

My baby kicks and kicks, she is full of life, sometimes she keeps me awake all night long but I will not take a sleepy dram from

Doctor Gray nor anything else that might slow her down. She is coming soon, I can tell it. She is riding low now and this makes me pee all the livelong day! I have already got a stack of little sacks for her to wear. And do you know what, Silvaney? I just cant wait to see her. And I know what I will name her too, but it is a secret so far. I have told no one. Her name is <u>Joli</u> which is French, it means Pretty and reminds me of Mrs. Brown. Because my baby will be pretty, and go to France. I will be so glad when she gets here! Because the truth is Silvaney, I am a little bit lonesome here in Diamond, Va. in spite of being stuffed in a four room house with Beulah and Curtis and little John Arthur and Curtis Junior, I know it sounds crazy to say so, what with so many people all around us living on this mountain like bees in a honey comb. So many many people, yet I am lonesome, and cant explain it. There is nobody for me to talk to here but when Joli comes, I will talk to her. And I cant wait!

Your loving sister,
Ivy Rowe.

Dear Miss Mabel Maynard,

I know you will be interested to hear from me because you acted so mean to me always and then you felt of my stomach the day I left, and ran off crying. You can not deny you did this, because you did. And since I got up here, I have had some time to think about it, and reflect. So I have something to say to you.

Miss Maynard, do not pity me.

Do not even bother to dislike me, nor pity me, nor anything else, because I do not need anything from you, nor want it either.

My little baby Joli Rowe was born September 10, 1918. She is all mine, I have never had a thing of my own before. She is the most beautiful baby in the world.

So, <u>I</u> pity <u>you</u>!

Your former aquaintance,
Ivy Rowe.

Dear Geneva,

It was sure good to get a letter from you in spite of all the bad news! For you know how much I love letters.

But I have to say, I can not stand to read the one you sent here from Lonnie, I sat and looked at it for three days solid and then I threw it in the fire. I have made my bed and I wish everybody would let me lie in it.

We were all surprised and sorry to hear about Lois Branham killing herself. I know it is awful for Stoney and the kids, but I hope in particular that Ethel is not too wrought up about it. I bet she is though. Their family must of become like her own family by now, I reckon. Stoney is lucky he has got her to run the store if you ask me. And as for Lois Branham herself, well I am real surprised! So is Beulah, we have been talking about it. It seemed to us both that Lois Branham was just one of those women without any get up and go, and a husband rich enough to where she could lay in the bed if she wanted. So I cant see it. She had everything a person could of wanted, it seems to me. I guess you never can tell. I will tell you one thing, though—if I was going to kill myself, I would never do it the way she did. You can just immagine the position you would be found in! And I can just immagine poor Ethel coming down the stairs to get breakfast started, and then smelling the gas. I can not believe it! It seems to me that it ought to take a really wild and dramatic person to do something like that, such as when Mister Brown tried it on the willow tree and Revel cut him down in the nick of time—but not a puny little lady like Lois Branham who was always getting Ethel to bring her some prunes for constipation.

I am also sorry to hear about Miss Maynard going all to pieces but to answer your question, I am sure it didnt have a thing to do with my letter. I think she has been spoiling for a nervous break-down all along. Dont you remember how she stayed in bed the whole time Momma was laid out in the sitting room?

Please tell Doc Trout and Judge Brack hello and give Garnie and Johnny a big kiss for me whether they want one or not! It is a funny thing to me how far away you all seem, for I am here in the house with my baby and that's about all. She is just beautiful,

Geneva, I cant wait for you to see her. I will bring her to Majestic bye and bye.

Did you know that old Granny Rowe and Tenessee came over here when she was born and stayed two days? Beulah was fit to be tied, but there is not a thing you can do with Granny once she settles her mind on a thing, and I was so glad to have her! I was so glad she was here. They just appeared, smack out of the blue, we were sitting on the front porch drinking ice tea, it was a hot night. What's that? asked Beulah real sharp, and it was Tenessee giggling. Big Curtis stood up. Why hello there, he said. Curtis is nicer in some ways than Beulah. You ladies have come from a long way off. Now come up here and sit for a spell. What are you all doing over here anyway?

Granny Rowe sat down and took off her hat, that man's hat she wears all the time, and lit up her pipe before she answered. I figured Ivy would be needing me, she said.

Then Beulah popped up and said, Why that is just ridiculous, Granny! You know nobody can tell exactly when a baby is coming, especially a first baby.

And I could almost <u>hear</u> Beulah thinking, Oh no, here they are and they will stay until this baby comes which might be weeks, for Curtis is too nice to run them off. <u>Oh no,</u> Beulah was thinking.

But Granny laughed, and in the dark you could see her pipe shine red when she pulled on it. <u>It's the full moon, honey,</u> she said. <u>Just look at it.</u>

And sure enough, right as she spoke, the moon came up over the top of the mountain as big as I have ever seen it in my life. It is funny how in a town like this, there is so much to see and talk about that you forget to notice things like the moon. I looked up at it that night and it was like I had never seen it before. It was huge.

Well, I wish you'd look at that! Curtis said. Now aint that pretty? And then Beulah gave up and went and got them some ice tea and some vanilla wafers which Tenessee just loves, and we all sat up late and talked, while Rush Gayheart fiddled right next door. And then after while I got up to pee and my water broke all over the porch.

So Granny was here and they never even went for Doctor Gray at all, which suited me fine, they got Violet from next door since Beulah turned too fainty to help much. And Joli is not a bit pointy-headed, she is beautiful, and she is all mine! So far I have not done a thing since she was born except look at her and count her fingers and toes—I even sit and watch her sleep. You know we were short on play-prettys, growing up—I do not recall but one doll-baby ever, and Silvaney used to grab her and run off. Well, now I have got a doll-baby all my own, and nobody can take her away. I sit out on the porch and nurse her and look down on the town which is very busy, what with the war and all.

Sometimes three or four trains will come through in one day, and they have put on a hoot owl shift at the mine now. The company has got too many people over here to put them all up so a bunch of men is living right out in the woods now, I dont know what will happen when it gets cold. It is getting rough around here, as Beulah says. It is a boom town. By the way, Oakley and Ray Fox are over here now, working, I saw Oakley down at the store and he looked just the same as he did when a boy, I would have known him anyplace. He said him and Ray have been over here for three months now but I didnt know it as I dont go out much, I stay home with Joli all the time. The only place I go is to the store for Beulah and down to the school, they will let you borry books every week now. You can get six, which I do. I read and read, you know how I love to read! I remember you and Momma saying it was foolishness. Well Beulah thinks so too, I can tell I am getting on her nerves. I know she thinks I ought to go out and get a job soon and so I will have to, but I can not bear to leave Joli just yet. You know I have lost so many that I love, I am determined to watch over this one good. And so I sit and rock her, and sit and read and watch her sleep. But I often think of you and thank you for your kindness, especially to Momma,

Ivy Rowe.

Dear Ethel,

Thanks for writing. Your letter was the first we had heard of it, as a matter of fact. You could knock me over with a feather! as Geneva used to say.

But I think it is fine, believe me. Anything that makes you

happy makes me happy too. I want what you want for yourself, Ethel, you ought to know that by now. And I still remember that you did not ever tell me to marry Lonnie Rash when everyone else did!

You never know what somebody else wants, that's all I have to say, and if you want Stoney Branham then I am glad you married him, even if he is 25 years older than you. I dont care. I dont care what you do as long as it makes you happy. Just hold up your head and dont listen to what all they say. Anyway it does not matter whether Stoney Branham was your sweetie or not before Lois killed herself, anybody honest would own he must of <u>needed</u> a woman for years, whether he had one or not, since his own wife was just laying up there in the bed crying and eating prunes. So my advice is, hold your head up high, Ethel, and shut your ears. For people will forget it soon enough. There is so much else to occupy their minds anyway, what with the war and the flu, by the way some several up here have got it, and two have died. I am not taking Joli out anywhere because of it. So, people will not be talking about you and Stoney Branham too long!

And as for Beulah, dont you worry about Beulah, because she will get over it.

I wish you all the happiness and love in the world, please tell Mister Branham—I mean Stoney. And I remain

Your loyal sister,
Ivy Rowe.

Mrs. Bonnie Rash Wilkes
15 John St.
Elizabethton, Tenessee

Dear Mrs. Wilkes,

I am sorry that it has taken me a long time to answer your letter, but as you see, I am living over here in Diamond, Va. now, and so I just got it a few days ago, and since then I have been broken-hearted.

To answer your question, yes I did love your brother very much, and so I am real sorry to hear of his death in France. I can not believe it. He was just a boy. And I am real sorry for you too. I know how much he loved you.

Yes it is true as he told you that we were to be married after the war. Everything he told you is true. I am sending your mother's necklace back to you. I know you will want to keep it. She was a pretty lady with such a sweet face. I am glad I got to wear it for a while. Do not worry about me sending the necklace back, as I still have something else to remember Lonnie by. And I will remember him always, as he was a nice boy so sweet and mild it seems impossible to immagine him dead in something like a war. I will remain yours in sorrow,

Ivy Rowe.

November 20, 1918

Oh Silvaney,

Lonnie is dead in the war, it has upset me so! For in my mind I keep seeing him in the countryside of France in Mrs. Brown's book, walking down a long straight road lined by trees that look like big fancy feathers, and fat round haystacks in the fields on either side, and a wide blue sky with puffy clouds, as in the book. There is not a road anyplace around here so straight, nor such a swatch of sky. And then in my mind the guns roar and the picture goes all bright with Lonnie's blood. I see it over and over again. I feel like this is my fault although Beulah says I am being ridiculous, that Lonnie would have gone to the war whether I married him or not. I guess this is true. But I do not feel ridiculous. I feel so sorry now. I feel like I <u>did</u> love him, though I did not. It is starting to get cold here now, I look out at the mountains from the window where I rock with Joli, and the leaves on the trees seem red with blood. May be I am crazy. But probably I am just contrary and spoilt, as Beulah says. She thinks it is high time for me to get out of here and find a job and earn my keep. She says that I have always been made too much of, may be this is true. Big Curtis thinks he can get me one down at the soda-fountain in the store, I guess it will be all right but I have gotten kindly shy from staying home so much with Joli. About the only outside people I see are Violet, next door, and Oakley Fox who is real sweet and comes by a lot. You remember Oakley.

You ought to see Joli, she is so beautiful! I hate to go off and leave her of a day. In fact I would not leave her if it was just Beulah here, because Beulah is too quick to get mad, and all these babies are a handful. I am the one that keeps them mostly, now. But Curtis has just gotten a raise and Beulah has hired a colored woman, Earl Porter's wife Tessie, to come in of a day and help out. So I will have to go out to work, and I am trying to switch Joli over to a little cup.

She does not look a thing like me or like Lonnie either one, she only looks like herself, although I guess you can tell she is a Rowe by the red hair. And hers is all curls, just like yours! She is smarter and bigger than Curtis Junior. When she sucks at my titty I know it is nearly the last time, nearly the end. Silvaney, there is something about nursing a baby that is like having a sweetie, you feel the same way I mean. And it feels so good and I hate to stop it, to stop nursing Joli or to leave her at home, I hate to leave her at all.

I want to tell you how it was when she was born. I will write it down plain for I want to remember it always, and I can tell I am forgetting it already, the way I am afraid I am forgetting some things about Sugar Fork and even Majestic. I think this is one reason I write so many letters to you, Silvaney, to hold onto what is passing. Because the days seem to go faster and faster, especially now that I have got Joli, the days whirl along like the leaves blowing down off the mountain right now. I remember Geneva saying that the older you get, the faster time goes by. Well, I want to stop it! I want to hold up its flight like you would hold up a train, and steal what I can from each day. But it is awfully hard to remember having a baby because your body wants to forget it right away, it hurts too bad, and if you remembered it all, you would never have another, Granny says. So you forget. You have to.

Here is what I do remember, though—first the water splashing on my feet and the great pushing opening tearing feeling, but it was like somebody pressing something heavy on my legs. My thighs hurt the worst, they hurt awful, and this went on for a long time and then right before she came out I could hear it, Silvaney, I swear I could hear my bones parting and hear myself opening up with a huge horrible screeching noise, and all the splashing down my legs felt cold, not hot. Beulah says I screamed so much I embarassed them all, but Granny says I did real good considering it was my first. So may be what I heard was me screaming, but I don't think so. I think it was my screeching bones.

And then Joli was out dripping blood and gore and making a funny little snuffly noise and Granny cut the cord with the kitchen knife and bound her with the strippy cloths and handed her over to me. She was big! And she grabbed onto my finger and held on for dear life, and squnched up her mouth and started crying. And all the poems I ever knew raced through my head, for she was the prettiest thing I have ever seen. Then Granny wrapped her up good and laid her in the dresser drawer propped up between two chairs, for we did not have another cradle yet, she was early.

Granny said, You will be fine, Ivy. For once you have had an easy time of something. She stroked my hair, pushing it back off my face. She smelled like tobacco, like woodsmoke, like snuff, like something old and tough I couldnt name you. The wrinkles in her face are so deep they are like cuts right down to the bone. In fact Granny looks like one of those dried-apple dolls now in the face—except for her eyes which are bright blue and twinkling and not filmed over in white like so many old peoples.

Granny poured me a drink of white liquor and then took some out on the porch for the rest of them. I heard Beulah say No thank you, and Curtis will have only one glass, Granny. But Granny said, Them that tries to rule the roost will find the cock has flown. And so Beulah said, Well pour me some then, and before long she was giggling as much as Tenessee. I think she will soften up on Ethel before long, too.

As for me I laid in the bed and watched the moonlight come across the quilt star by star—it was in the Heavenly Star pattern— coming toward me, and I could hear my baby snuffling in the dresser drawer, and then bye and bye Granny came and gave me some more liquor and took the rag packing out from between my legs and got some more. The blood smell was not so bad. It was sweet some way, it was not like anything else in the world, and now it will always be mixed up in my mind somehow with the moonlight and my baby, for then Granny handed her to me. I held her close by my side and looked at the moonlight on the closest star, red and blue and pink and purple, it seemed to glow out like the cathedral windows in Mrs. Brown's book.

After a while I could hear the rest of them coming in from the porch, and making up extra pallets and shifting people around, and then it got quiet, the quietest night in the world. Granny slept sitting bolt upright in a straight-back chair beside me. But I was all wrought up, I was far too excited to sleep, I would not have dozed off for the world. I kept thinking, <u>This is important, I want to remember this, it is all so important, this is happening to me.</u> And I am so glad to write it down lest I forget. I lay there real still while the moonlight slowly crossed my quilt, and listened to a hoot owl off in the woods, and little Joli breathing, and—come morning—the long sweet whistle of the train.

When we got up Granny fixed the baby a sweet tit, and by afternoon she was sucking on it, and then the next day she wanted some titty too, and Granny and Tenessee went on home and we began, Joli and me, and the rest of our days have been marked by when she eats and when she sleeps. She doesn't hardly cry at all. But now Silvaney, winter is coming on, and the war is over thank god, but these days are passing so fast. Big Curtis just came home and said I am to start at the soda-fountain on Monday, and so I will. But I remain your loving sister,

Ivy Rowe.

Dear Victor,

I am so happy to hear you are back from the war safe and sound and a hero, I am sorry about your leg though. Are you going to look for a place of your own now? Or stay on at Geneva's for a while? I know you are looking for work. It is a shame the Frank Ritter Lumber Company busted, they thought so highly of you I know.

Coal is the only thing over here, but the coal business is slacking off now and it looks like hard times on the way. Money has been so easy during the war that no body knows how to act without it. There is a big increase in drinking and fighting and spreeing around, since so many have been laid off. They dont know what to do with themselves. And Oakley says the company is shorting men on weight now up at the mine, but Big Curtis says it is not true. Curtis wont hear one bad word about the company! So I dont know for sure. But folks are mad about everything. My own job at the store gets me real tired but I am lucky to have it, I see that now. Everybody comes in spending that scrip, and then on payday there is no pay. Some of them owe so much to the store it looks like they will never pay it off. So this place is not paradise by a long shot. I used to think it was.

But the worst thing going on around here is the flu, and speaking of heros, you ought to see Oakley Fox and his little brother Ray! Dont you remember them, from down on Home Creek? Little Ray weighs about 300 pounds now. But he is just as nice as Oakley. And lately with so many folks dying right and left, Oakley and Ray and their daddy—who came over here a purpose to do it— has been working night and day laying folks out. Wont nobody else touch them, so the Foxes have got to wait on the whole town. Oakley says the company is paying them for their time. Everybody else is scared they'll catch the flu. Oakley says him and Ray wont catch it because they take a big bottle of horse temperature medicine and rub it across their lips. It is thick yellow-looking stuff which has made Oakley's whiskers yellow for good, I think. They are waiting on people day and night—they will wash them, dress them out, lay them out, put them in the casket and dig them a grave. Most families are making their own caskets since they cost $35 down at the store, where we have got a whole stack of them in the corner. They look awful, but you cant quit looking at them once you start.

Somebody will come in the store buying lipstick one day, then the next day they'll be dead. This is true. It happened last week to Trula Bond who bought Fire and Ice, I sold it to her. And the Fox boys laid her out, the way they are laying out everybody.

Only that time I happened to see it. They are burying them now in the company burying ground up on the mountain, not too far from the mine, and I walked up there yesterday evening with my neighbor Violet Gayheart and her two kids, to wait for her husband Rush to get off his shift. Violet goes up there every day and a lot of times I go too, I like to give Joli a breath of fresh air. Usually I look away from the burying ground because it looks so awful, with those new red mounds of dirt against the snow. So many have died.

But this time, it was right at sunset, there were the Foxes burying Trula Bond with that rickety wagon Mister Fox has had forever it seems, I believe it is the same one we used to ride in when we were kids. There was Oakley Fox and Ray Fox with yellow whiskers and yellow hands, and Trula Bond's family crying. Violet and me stood by the roadside and watched. Nobody sang or anything, they done it all real quick.

Then Oakley saw us and came over to me and I said, Oakley, how can you stand to do this? and he said, Ivy, somebody has got to, and then he walked me home. Oakley is real big and good to lean on. The sky was red and the mountains and the limbs of the trees were black against it. Sometimes I think a winter sunset is the prettiest kind.

Have you got any snow over there? We have got a lot here now, but it gets so dirty from the coaldust, you cant even make snowcream. Do you remember the snowcream Momma used to make up on Sugar Fork? I used to think it was so good. I want to make Joli some.

Victor, I know I go on and on sometimes in my letters, it is a great failing too. But I am trying to work around to what I want to say. Big Curtis has heard that you are drinking a lot these days, please stop, you know it runs in the family. Remember Babe and Revel. And I am sure you will find something real good to go into, bye and bye. Why dont you come over here and see us? Do not worry about us not having room, you can stay down at the bunkhouse with Oakley and Ray. It is not a palace, but I bet it beats the war. And I want you to see my baby.

Love from your little (Ha!) sister,
Ivy Rowe.

July 9, 1919

Dear Ethel,

I have had it with people trying to marry me off! Now it is Beulah and Curtis. This is what happened.

Every year on the Fourth of July, the company throws a big party, with a couple of bands, and dancing, and ice cream and fireworks. It is the only time all year, and the only place except the movie house, where the people from Silk Stocking Hill will mingle freely with them that goes down in the mines.

Now it soon became clear that this Fourth of July celebration was a big deal to Beulah, and you will see why in a minute!

But first—you should have heard her! She went on and on, she like to have dogged me to death. Now Ivy, what are you going to wear to the picnic? Now Ivy, you cant wear <u>that</u> for heaven's sake, here why dont you try on this old polka dot thing of mine! Oh of course you can, we'll take it up in the waist. No, dont go with Oakley, go with us. You can see Oakley when you get there. Now that is just silly Ivy, the fireworks wouldnt do a thing but scare those babies, and Tessie is perfectly willing to come. No, Tessie wouldnt be going to the fireworks anyway, none of the colored people go, dont be silly. Why, they dont even <u>want</u> to! Ivy, have you ever thought of bobbing your hair?—Which I would <u>not</u> let her do, Ethel, although she has bobbed her own hair and I guess it is right in style.

Anyway since it seemed to be such a big deal to Beulah, I left Joli at home with Tessie Porter and went to the Fourth of July picnic even though I had no real interest in it, I would of liked just one day to rest up and play with Joli. But I went, to please Curtis and Beulah.

I wore Beulah's white dress with cap sleeves and red polka dots and a red patent leather belt, and white high-heel sandals. <u>I thought we were supposed to look so good in green, with our red hair,</u> I said just to tease Beulah, but now Beulah says we look good in red! Beulah reads all the magazines, she keeps right up with fashion.

Joli waved her little hand bye-bye when we left. She is real smart I think she is smarter than Curtis Junior.

So Beulah and me and Curtis set off down the hill, all dressed up, and I must say the company had gone all out! The celebration took place in the bottom, on the baseball field, and they had stretched red, white, and blue bunting from here to yonder, and had two bands playing, and flags flying, and watermelon and ice cream and I dont know what all, and folks so dressed up you couldnt hardly tell who they were. The same folks I see every day in the store, I mean, now wearing their finest.

But you can tell the miners no matter what, from the black rings around their eyes like a possum. This is from coaldust. You cant wash it off. Oakley has got it too. It looks almost like makeup, as if he is a movie star, a shiek of Araby! And you notice it most particularly on Oakley who is so light complected otherwise, with those light brown eyes. I kept looking for him at the Fourth of July but I couldnt see him anyplace. A whole bunch of people were gathered around a truckbed, listening to a speech by a man in a blue-striped suit that Big Curtis said was famous. You could tell how proud Curtis was that the company men nodded to him, and spoke, and that he wore a tie, like they did. The miners wore open-neck shirts for the most part. It was hot, and getting hotter. Let us pledge anew in the words of Mister Wilson, the famous man said, to make the world safe for democracy! And everybody cheered. The famous man was sweating up a storm. But then when Mr. Ransom, the company superintendent, got up on the truckbed to make his speech, some men started whistling and he couldnt talk until some other men came and walked them into the woods. It was supposed to be no liquor there, but you could tell that a lot were drinking.

I was getting real hot and wishing I had put my hair up, and wishing I had brought Joli anyway, in spite of Beulah. I was too hot to eat a thing except one deviled egg. Finally I wandered off down the creek a ways while the rest of them were eating.

Nobody was around. I could hear bees buzzing, birds chirping, the faraway sound of the band. I was so hot I took off my shoes and went wading, even though the water in Diamond Creek is black as night because they wash the coal in it upstream. The water was shiny and cold and black. It felt so good, Ethel, and it struck me, this was the first time I had been by myself since Joli was born. So I sat down there on a big flat warm rock with my feet in the dark rushing water and kind of laid back and let the water run over my hands, too, and I might even of slept for a while when I heard somebody say, Hello there!

I looked up and saw a man in white pants and a striped shirt and a tie, the best looking man you can immagine! At first I thought I was dreaming. I couldnt see him too good for the sun in my eyes. So I sat up real fast but he said, Oh no, stay right there, you look so comfortable, and so I did. And he sat down on the rock beside me, real close.

You're Ivy Rowe, he said.

I felt a chill at that moment, in spite of the heat.

How do you know that? I said.

I came in the store Monday, he said, and saw you, and asked around and found out who you are. You had on a blue dress, he said, which was true. He leaned down real close over my face, grinning. He has very white teeth and dark eyes with the longest eyelashes ever, and perfect slicked-back black hair. He smells too good for a man.

Is that a fact, I said. I felt short of breath and couldnt think of much to say.

I've been looking for you, he said. I only came to this thing because they said you would be here. He took my wet hand in his hand and held it. His hand was the soft white hand of a man who has never worked in his life. He wears a gold wristwatch.

You seem mighty sure of yourself, I said, snatching my hand away. I dont even know who you are.

He laughed and leaned closer and brushed my cheek with his lips. You will, he said. I flicked some water in his face and laughed while he sat up and wiped it off with a clean handkerchief. I didn't care if I got him wet or not.

I like that, he said, grinning. I like my horses and my girls to have some spirit—which made me so mad that I leaned way over and splashed black water all over him and got his white pants dirty. Then I got up and ran off through the woods laughing, with him hollering curses after me. I didnt care either.

I ran home wet as could be but the breeze had nearabout dried me off by the time I made it back up the hill. My feet were killing me from running on the red-dog road, which is what you call a road made of the cinders left when a gob pile burns out. That's what the company makes roads out of. If Tessie Porter thought I looked funny when I got home, she never said a word about it, and Joli held out her little arms the minute she saw me.

So I watched the fireworks the way I wanted to in the first place, Ethel, sitting on the front porch holding Joli on my lap, and I bet it was the finest place in Diamond Va. to watch them from. They'd shoot up from the dark bottom, up and up and up the mountain side, and then burst open against the night sky so pretty you'd have to catch your breath. Little John Arthur came out and sat on his blanket—that blanket he carries everyplace—by my feet, and Joli never cried once. She laughed, though. She thought the fireworks were funny. I thought they were so beautiful. Pale green shining shooting sparks against the black, then red pinwheels, then pink, and then a shower of gold. I sat right there and watched them. I think the night air in summer smells so sweet, anyway. I like to sit out. Joli went to sleep in my arms and I carried her in the house and put her down. After the fireworks were over, a great cheer went up, and then you could hear car horns and glass breaking someplace, and somebody yelling. It was clear there'd be some fighting, that night. So I stood on the porch as bye and bye everybody came back up Company Hill, and lights went on, and you could hear kids crying and people arguing and carrying on, and music welling up all around so it seemed, from these dark close houses right up to the dark night sky.

Next door, Rush Gayheart started fiddling The Devil's Dream. He never says much, Rush, just fiddles and frowns a lot. Beulah and Curtis don't like him. They don't like Violet either. Curtis and Beulah think they are too good for the Gayhearts, but if they dont watch out, they will get too good for everybody if you ask me. That night, Curtis had stayed to play poker with some company men, so I reckon he was in hog heaven, but after while Beulah came marching up the hill by herself, fit to be tied.

Ivy! she hollered, and when I answered Yes real quiet from practically under her nose, she jumped a foot.

Hush or you will wake up John Arthur, I said, for I had made him up a pallet on the porch. Dont you remember how much we liked to sleep out on the porch of a summer evening? I asked Beulah, and she said Yes, and then burst into tears.

Well Beulah, whatever is the matter? I got up and hugged her and made her sit down on the step with me.

Oh everything! Her words came tumbling out like Diamond Creek running down the mountain over rocks. Everything. I try my best to get away from Sugar Fork and I never can it seems like, it's not fair, I've always got something like that right next door to remind me. I knew she meant Rush fiddling. I knew she was thinking of Revel and Daddy, like I was. Oh I want to leave here, she said. I want to go up in the world so bad, I want oh I want—but here, she broke down in crying. So I held her head and kind of rocked her, and then she said, Ivy, I am going to have another baby.

No! I said.

Yes! she said. And I have done everything I know to do, but nothing worked.

What do you mean, nothing worked? I asked.

I mean like a coca-cola douche or taking Milk of Magnesia, she said, and I said, Dont even tell me.

Dont tell Curtis, Beulah said. Then she flung something out in the yard—I couldn't see what, in the dark, and started crying again.

There's your shoes! she said.

Where? I was so surprised.

Out there, you dont care anyway, you left them at the creek, she said. You dont care about a thing but yourself. You are so selfish, she said. She cried awhile longer. Then she said, Ivy, dont you know who that was, down at the creek today? Dont you care? That was Franklin Ransom, that's who, the superintendent's son, he's just visiting here now. Curtis said he's been asking everybody who you are, and where you live, and finally somebody told him to ask Curtis, and Curtis told him. So see what a chance you had? and to throw it all away like that, like you always do—I cant stand it, Beulah said. It's like you get everything in the world on a silver platter, and then you throw it down in the mud.

How did you get those shoes? I asked her, and finally she said that she was in the store with Curtis, after the fireworks, when Franklin Ransom came in with them, and said to give them to me along with his kindest regards. You could tell he was mad, she said.

Then Beulah grabbed my arm so hard that her fingernails almost drew blood. Listen here, she said. This is one chance you will not throw away. Oh if I was you . . . if I was educated like you . . . if I'd had the chances you have—well, if he does come back, if he comes up here again, you be nice to him, you hear me?

So Ethel, that started it.

Of course he came back and took me riding in his car, and then riding again, and then out to the picture show. Big Curtis and Beulah are tickled to death.

And in the meantime, two funny things have happened. One is that Tessie, who never says one word, came up to me the other day and said Missy—this is what she calls me—Missy, I just want you to know, that boy is no good. What boy? I said, but Tessie was skittering off by then like a waterbug down the hill, scared to death. You knows which one, she hollered back over her shoulder.

And the other thing is that Oakley has pitched a fit. You know he is always so nice and so easy-going, Ethel—you know how

Oakley is. But he came over here Tuesday after he saw me out riding with Franklin Ransom, who has a blue Ford car, and busted right into the kitchen where I was washing my hair in the sink, wearing some old wrapper of Momma's.

Ivy! he yelled, and pulled me up by the hair so hard that it hurt, and I stood there dripping water on Beulah's floor. It's real bad to waste water because you have to haul it up from the pump yourself, so naturally I got mad at Oakley.

What's this about Franklin Ransom? he said. His whole face was black, he'd come straight from the mine.

None of your business, I said. I was about to cry because I had soap in my eyes, and Oakley was acting so high-handed.

You're my girl, Oakley said, and I said right back, I am not!

The hell you aint, he said, and pulled me over to him and kissed me. Now this was the first time he has kissed me since we were kids, Ethel. So you know I am not his girl. It made me so mad I pushed him, and he slipped down on the wet floor, and pulled me down with him. Right then Joli came toddling in and started laughing and I started laughing too. She thought we were all playing.

Oh come on, Oakley, I said, You are my best old friend, now dont be crazy. But he wouldn't laugh with me or even smile. He just stomped off, kicking the screen door on his way out, leaving me and Joli sliding around in the floor.

And Oakley has not been by here, or said one word to me since! He knows when I am working down at the store, and he walks by the soda-fountain sometimes but does not speak, he is so childish. How Oakley Fox thought for even one minute that I was his girl is beyond me! I am not anybody's girl, Ethel. And I know Oakley and me will be friends again one day.

But now Franklin has asked me to come up to his parents house for dinner, and Beulah is all excited. You would think it was her, not me. She says it is about time I made a good thing out of a man. She acts like I am an old maid not a girl of 19. But poor Beulah, she is pregnant again and not herself. I have not got the heart to tell her that Mr. and Mrs. Ransom are in New York City right now. So I know what will happen if I go up there. What would you do, if you was me? Well, on second thought, I know what you would do. You would do exactly what you wanted to! But I have Joli to take care of now, and I am beholden as well as ruint. I will let you know what happens.

And in the meantime, what about Victor?
Can you and Stoney do anything?
I remain your worried sister,

Ivy Rowe.

Dear Franklin,

To answer your question, Yes.

If you can keep a civil tongue in your head and your hands to
yourself for a change.

In haste,
Ivy.

Dear Geneva,

I have to say I am not sorry to hear about you losing Sam Russell
Sage, nor surprised either one. It is just what I would expect! A
man that taken with himself will try to get as many women as he
can, in my view, and that is a lot with the Lord on your side. I
still recall how awful he was, how he left those little black hairs
all over the sink and then acted like it was an honor for me and
Ludie to get to clean them up! I think Sam Russell Sage just uses
the Lord to get money and women. I think you are better off
without him but I am sorry you found out in such a way. What
was she like? What was her mother like? It takes a lot of nerve
to just come up and knock on your door like that. I would love
to have been a fly on the wall and heard you all talking and seen
you drinking a dope. I would love to have seen his face when he
walked in and found you all there! I am not surprised to hear
about Ludie or some of the others, not even the married ones
except for Mrs. Presley up the street, now that is a surprise to

me. I am also surprised that he pulled the wool over everybody's eyes for so long. I wish there was some way to get Garnie away from him, but Garnie is wellnigh grown now, as you say, and anyway I have come to think that anything is better than going down in the mine. Well, almost anything. Playing the piano in a roadhouse is certainly better, for who are we to say, maybe Johnny can go on from there. He may go back to school yet. I would rather have him playing in a horehouse than going in the mine, Geneva that's the truth!

When I first came here, I thought this was Paradise. Well, let me tell you, it is a far cry from Paradise. Now that the war is over they are laying men off left and right, and working part weeks, and taking off shifts, and people don't know what to do with themselves. They have given up their land, those hardscrabble places we all came from, and they have noplace to go back to. They have lived here so long they have forgot how to garden anyway, or put up food, or trade for goods, or anything about how they used to live. So they have got nothing now. They have got nothing but what they owe to the company which is so much they will never pay it off. The men lay around and drink in the daytime, and play cards and run cockfights up on the mountain, and get in fights themselves. They will bet on anything. If there's two birds on a washline, they will bet as to which one will fly off first. I heard a man say out loud in the store that he gets along so good with women because he makes it a practice to frail them with a stick. Nobody in there batted an eye when he said it, I believe this trashy behavior is common. There are outlaw people here now that care for nothing, and men that swap wives just like they are swapping horses. On payday, you have to stay in the house at night because everybody is milling around out there drunk, and most of them packing guns. I thought I was coming over here to raise my baby on this mountain like we were raised, but it is not so.

It is no good to raise kids here. The big ones run together like a pack of wild dogs, they get into everything. They climb all over the old tipple and slide down the chute, which is so dangerous, and yell at their elders, they don't know no better kind of life. The real bad boys get sent to the reform school over at Greendale where they whip them on a barrel I am told, until they come back and make good miners. You can go in the mine at 15. Go in the mine and never come out, is what I say! I am glad I have got a little girl. Now, that mine has come to look like a big old mouth, swallowing boys whole.

And I guess you can not expect too much from children that have been raised on this hill by their mamas who don't know any better themselves, who never see their men except to send them off in the pitch black morning to the mine, and try to get the coal-dust out of the house and keep up with the little kids all day long, this kind of a life will make you crazy. No wonder Myra Ramey down the road ties her baby to a chair leg so she can go to the store by herself. No wonder there's so many wives that drink, and marriages that break up here, it is not any kind of a life to have. Curtis and Beulah keep themselves above it all of course, they are looking to move on up in the company. But I work in the store all day, I see everybody, and know what's going on.

Violet Gayheart tried to tell me the truth when I first came over here and could have left I reckon, and she was right. Now I have seen Violet's husband come home from the mine when he has been working in water, with his clothes froze to where they will stand up by theirselves when he takes them off, like a headless man standing there in the kitchen floor. And now I have seen Oakley Fox's brother Ray, that is so sweet, get a facefull of little holes like the face of the moon, from shooting his coal too close. You carry a breast auger and drill a hole for every ton you want to shoot, and then you put four sticks of 40 percent dynamite in each hole, and shoot it. After you get your coal loose, you have got a fresh cut to mine, and a big man like Ray Fox can load 8 to 10 tons a day. But it is awful work. The safety rules have never been too grand, and now that times are so hard they are not paying much attention to them at all, and it is every man for himself and so much of the neighborness is gone. No wonder the wives get to drinking and crying, they are living in constant dread of that high-pitched whistle that means an accident, that a timber has give way or that the gas has caught on fire. If a man gets disabled, the company will move him out, just kick him right out of his house. But if a man gets killed, the company will let his wife live on in his house, and this hill is pocked with widows, Geneva. I know one that takes in washing and one that takes in men. Life is so hard here that it leads many right to church, Oakley and Ray Fox for an instance, and Beulah and Curtis too but they go down the river road to the Presbyterian Church because that is where the company folks go. But I am like Momma I reckon, and do not seem to have much use for church. What I like to do of a Sunday is stay home and play with Joli. Sometimes Violet and me will sit out in the yard on a quilt and play poker while Rush fiddles. I have gotten real close to Violet even though Beulah won't have a thing to do with her. So whenever Beulah and Curtis go someplace, I go next door.

For Violet is like you, Geneva, or like Ethel. She will call a spade a spade. I should have listened to Violet way back when. Instead I had my head all full of notions, it's the way I am, I reckon—full of notions. I wonder if I will ever get over it. One reason Violet is so bitter I think is that she had one baby that died before I moved over here, and now her little girl Martha has got something bad wrong with her. But the older boy R.T. is okay I reckon. Rush has lost his nerve though. This is how Violet describes it. She says Rush used to talk your ear off and cut up like crazy, that he was the biggest ladies man in East Tenessee when she met him, and famous for fiddling. Rush is right much older than Violet. But when his daddy died and left the farm to Rush's no-account brother, because of Rush carrying on so, then Rush decided to come over here and get in on the ground floor so to speak and make a quick buck to set him and Violet up in housekeeping. They did not figure on staying.

What happened, though, was that the very first month he was here, the methane gas—what they call the firedamp—built up in the shaft he was in and blew the man next to him all to hell and trapped Rush in there with that man's body on top of him for a day and a half. Can you immagine this? Can you think of what went on in his mind then, on that freezing cold wet mine floor with a dead man on top of him like a lover? I can not.

Rush came out of the mine a different man, and then right after that, their baby died. Now Rush is a shadow of himself, Violet says. He is still a big good-looking man but his coal-ringed eyes are so sad, they look dark and old. He is dreamy a lot. He owes too much to leave, even if he had the will to. They have still got a big doctor bill they are paying off, on the baby that died.

So Violet is real mad, she's been mad for years, but she can't get Rush to buck up and think of any way out of here. This seems to be the way of it. When you go down in the mine so long, something happens in your head so that you cannot immagine another life. It's the only thing you know to do, the only way you know to live. You get scared of the mine and scared of everything else.

Still and all, some times are real good. One day last week, Beulah and Curtis went off to town taking little Curtis Junior and the new baby Delores with them, and me and Violet spread a quilt in the yard between the houses like I was telling you, and laid out in the sun which felt so good after this long hard winter, and watched the kids playing in the yard. Joli is tough as nails I'm proud to say, and can hold her own with any boy. She is a sight, Geneva—may be she takes after you! She will go right up to John Arthur and grab whatever he's got that she wants. She is not scared of a thing. Anyway we were laying out there drowsing while Rush fiddled slow, and then he speeded up and we sat up, and Joli came over to play patacake. The sun laid over us like a blanket, although it was scarcely spring.

Listen here, Violet said all of sudden. I think it is Groundhog Day. She got up and ran in the house and looked in the almanac and sure enough, it was.

Well, what is it? she asked. I forget how it goes.

But I remembered of course, Lord knows I heard it from Granny a million times. If he can see his shadow, it's six more weeks of winter, I said. If he can't, it's an early spring. So I reckon that this here is just unseasonal, I said.

Hell fire, said Rush.

Play Ivy's song, Violet said, and then he fiddled and Violet sang

Just go and leave me if you want to
Never let it cross your mind
If in your heart you love another
Please, little darlin, I don't mind.

When Rush sings, you can see what a handsome man he used to be. Then he sang my verse.

When I see your babe a-laughing
It makes me think of your sweet face
But when I see your babe a-crying
It makes me think of my disgrace.

Then Violet took a dive and started tickling me, and we rolled over and over on the quilt laughing. I do not feel too ruint when

I am with Violet and Rush who have been through everything.

Then Oakley came by in a clean blue shirt, I bet he'd been doing something down at the church again. He never says much about going, but he's there every time they crack the door, he is faithful as the day is long. He is not a bit like Sam Russell Sage though, believe you me! And it don't seem to bother him that I won't go. Nothing I do seems to bother Oakley. In fact he is so nice that sometimes I want to hit him in the face, it's the same way I felt about him years ago.

Ever since I told Oakley I am not his girl, he has not said another word about it, or tried to kiss me again, or anything. But he does come by here right much even though Beulah is not always nice to him. Sometimes he brings things to Joli, a plastic brush or candy or a little book. She just loves Oakley. Sometimes he brings things to me, like Colliers Magazine. He still lives with his brother Ray in the bunkhouse and does not seem to want any more out of life than he has. He never asks me to go anyplace with him, and if he knows when I go with Franklin—he must know!—he never says a word.

Franklin does not come here ever, he sends me word where to meet him, or sometimes he will come by the store. Oakley never mentions Franklin, so I don't either. Why should I? But I am caught between a rock and a hard place, in all truth. Franklin is not any good and I know it. Oakley is real good but I dont love him. I don't. And anyway I can't quit on Franklin while Beulah and Curtis are still here, they still think Franklin is somebody for me to marry, and I am still beholden. Thank God they will be moving to Huntington soon.

Although, Geneva, just between you and me—I don't know how they will fare over there. Curtis is a good steady man, but Beulah wants so much that I don't know if there is enough in the world to satisfy her, I honestly don't. And also she is so scared, and ashamed of herself someway. Last week she got invited up to Mrs. Bolin's house to make an alter cloth for the church, this is the kind of thing that is so important to Beulah. But then she fretted and fretted so much that she would say the wrong thing, or do something wrong, that she ended up flat on her back with a sick headache, and missed it all. And yet to see her, you would think Beulah more of a lady than any of these. She reads all the magazines and gets herself up just so, you know how well she can sew and always could. But somehow it's like she is still playing party and doesn't believe it herself. So I don't know how she will do in Huntington, Geneva, I honestly don't.

I am glad I am ruint, and don't have to worry over such as that.

But I was telling you about Groundhog Day, when me and Violet were sitting out in the sun and Oakley dropped by. I said, I don't guess you want to gamble now do you? Oakley sat right down on the quilt and said Cut me in, honey, and Violet did while Rush fiddled Lonesome Valley. We played hand after hand and smoked cigarettes and had the best time, in spite of the gob pile that has caught on fire now and won't quit burning, sending the sulfur smell down here like boiling eggs. But I guess it is always something! And we had a fine time in spite of the sour yellow smoke and in spite of knowing that all this pretty sunshine means winter is coming back.

So I remain your faithful,
Ivy Rowe.

Oh Silvaney,

So much, so much has happened! and there is so much I can not tell to a living soul, I will write it to you instead. I hardly know where to start. I think I will do like Joli does with the crayons that Victor brought her from town—she takes the black crayon, and bites her lip, and outlines everything first. It takes forever, she presses down so hard. But then when she puts in the color, it's easy.

This is it. The mine fell in, and I got married.

I will fill it in later.

Because first I want to tell about Franklin Ransom, and I see that there is no place on the page here for me to put him, no black lines I can color him into. It was always like that. I never could see his outline clear. Franklin is the son of the richest man in Diamond, but yet he's needy. And he has been to more schools than anybody else around here except the doctor, but he hasn't got any sense. He likes to drink and laugh and play the fool, but he is sad inside. This is what he looks like, Silvaney—a long thin face with a large straight nose and a cleft chin and level eyebrows over dark eyes that look liquid. Franklin's eyes are very large and seem to be always moving on to the next thing, somehow. His skin is like a baby's, his hair is dark and fine, his fingers are long and thin. He doesn't have hardly any hair on his body to speak of, and wears the prettiest clothes. Shirts you want to rub between your fingers. His teeth are white and even—well, he looks like a movie star and I'll swear it. It's the truth. And he is a man that knows how to get around women, too. I guess if you are born looking like Franklin looks, and you are an only child since your brother died, well you would be just as spoiled as Franklin. I don't believe his mother ever told him No in all his life. But then of course he got so spoiled they didn't know what to do with him, so they sent him off to school at the age of ten and he has mostly stayed gone since then, off at one school or another or else with his grandmother in Kentucky, I believe this is the only person he really loves. It is his mother's mother, Nana he calls her, only Nana and his mother have not spoken for years since they had a big falling out.

Mostly, Franklin stays over there and fools with horses. But then he comes over here to see his parents, only they usually don't get on too good after a little while, and then he will leave again. He drinks a lot and has never had a paying job. One time his daddy decided that he would learn the mining business from the word go, so they set him to work running the mantrip, but he ran over his own foot on the track—you know you have to run a mantrip in the dark, mostly—and crushed two toes, and his mama got hysterical and said she could not permit him to go in the mine again, he is all she has. Doctor Gray had to go up there and give her a shot for her nerves. Her nerves is awful ever since Dennis—that was Franklin's brother—got killed when he was 14   [1] Franklin was 12.

Got killed or killed himself—there's those that will tell it both ways. In any case he fell off, or jumped off, the cliff on the other side of Diamond Mountain. Everybody says that Dennis was too adventuresome for his own good, and always had been. Too high strung.

So Dennis broke his neck and his mama's heart.

He also made it impossible someway for Franklin to grow up, and Franklin says that to this day he can still hear his brother screaming as he falls, or jumps, into Indian Creek. Franklin was right there when it happened. Franklin says he has to drink, to keep from hearing his brother scream. I guess if you come up in a big family like we done, you will lose one or two and take it as a matter of course. But I don't know. I don't know about that and I dont know about Franklin, either. I do know that he can tell you about his brother in such a way as to make you cry, and make you want to take your dress off.

For Franklin has that way about him which makes a woman want to make it better, all the time, and that way about him that makes you know you never can. And fun? Lord, Franklin is a lot of fun.

I remember one time I went up there. His parents were off someplace gallivanting, and we had the house to ourselves. He had asked me to dinner. Dinner? Shoot! All we had for dinner was corn beef out of the can and saltine crackers and bourbon whisky from Kentucky that went down smooth. Franklin wasn't studying dinner, nor was I. It was summer, hot as blazes. We turned on the overhead fans. Mrs. Ransom had covered all the furniture up with white sheets, which is what she did every time her and Mister Ransom went out of town, to try and keep off the coaldust. Her whole life is a battle with coaldust.

So I was up on top of the hill visiting Franklin Ransom in that fine house and eating saltine crackers and corn beef out of the can and drinking some, and when it started getting dark, all that white-sheeted furniture came looming up like ghosts, like islands, and Franklin went over to the phonograph and put on a record, Who's Sorry Now and said Ivy, come here.

What for? I said, and he said, I want you to dance with me.

Dance? I said. I can't dance like that.

Come on over here honey, he said, but I said no. I was sitting on the floor eating off the coffee table.

He came over and reached down for my hand. Ivy, he said, and I got up and danced and it was easy. I never have danced like that before, Silvaney, it was like movie dancing. And may be I will never do so again! But it was easy, easy.

The overhead fan blew down on us and Franklin swirled me around and around like the wind, in the dark, between all the looming rising mounds of white. I felt like I was dancing in the clouds, in the midst of a thunderstorm.

The music stopped but we went on dancing, and every time we would dance by the coffee table, Franklin would lean over and grab the bourbon and we'd take a drink straight out of the bottle. Later he took me in his parents bedroom and laid me down across the pale green satin bed. And later still, he turned on the bedside light and got me to look in the mirror door. I had never seen a mirror door before. I had never looked at my whole body all at one time.

And Silvaney, oh Silvaney, I am beautiful! Beulah said we look good in red but we look even better in nothing. I am beautiful!

Then there was a real storm, and then after that, Franklin and I sat out on the lawn chairs naked and smoked cigarettes, all I could see of him in the night was the glowing tip of his cigarette burning red, and then we made love again right there on the wet grass. It smelled so good. It brought me around, a little.

I have to go home, I said, getting up, but Franklin said, No Ivy, it's too late, they will be asleep and you'll wake them up. Just stay here.

I have to go, I said, but he wouldn't take me, and I was too crazy drunk to walk down the mountain myself and I knew it.

We slept in his parents bed, and in the morning, we did it again, and then he said Ivy, do you know what I like about you? This? I said. I got to giggling. No, he said, you are like me, Ivy. You will do anything. And I said, Franklin, that's just not true. But he said, Oh yes it is, honey. Yes it is. Franklin thinks he is quite a judge of women and horses. And he is fun!

I did not feel half bad walking the red-dog road down the mountain that next morning, in fact I felt like running and whooping it up, yelling and swinging on grapevines like we used to do up on Pilgrim Knob. Because it is a fact that if you are ruint, like I am, it frees you up somehow.

I walked in the house and Joli ran up and hugged me. Mama, Mama, where did you go? she said. Beulah was frying eggs with her baby propped on her hip. I have been visiting, I told Joli. Then I went over and took the egg-turner from Beulah and she sat down. Well, Beulah said. She looked at me and I could tell she wished it was her coming down the mountain ruint instead of me.

I certainly hope you will make sure to get what's coming to you, she said.

I immagine I will, I said.

Curtis came through then and said, Good morning Ivy, in a different way, a way I didn't like. But I didn't say a word. I decided that I had made my bed and I would lie in it, Silvaney, same as before.

I thought, I am getting to be a expert at making beds!

But even way back then, even that sunny morning that I felt so good, I knew Franklin had something wrong with him. He does not mind making a mess, but he won't clean it up. For instance I said, Now we have got to straighten up here, when I woke up and I wasn't drunk any more and I saw what we had done to the house. But he would not let me touch a thing. Stop it, Ivy! The colored women will do it, he said. But I never knew if they did or not. I believe he halfway wanted his folks to come back and find the mess. I never knew if they did or not.

Another time he tried his best to get me to wear one of his mama's dresses out to the Busy Bee roadhouse, where we used to go, but I would not. I think he wanted somebody that knew her to see me in her dress. She hated me, so they said. I don't know, myself. I never met her. I knew Franklin's daddy, Mister Ransom, who used to come in the store, and liked me fine. Anyway this was a rose-colored sheath dress that I would give my eye teeth for, but I wouldn't wear it, even when he tried to make me put it on.

Franklin is good-looking and fun, but he is so strange. He went to all those fancy schools and never read a book that he will own up to. He will be so sweet one minute, and then go funny the next.

I remember one time towards the end of summer when we were out riding in his daddy's car. We got to the new bridge, which is where we always turned back, and that day Franklin just kept on going. What are you doing? I asked. He said, Let's go on a little trip, honey.

I can't go on a trip, I said.

Why not? Franklin put his hand on my leg and turned in the seat to look at me. Silvaney, he is so good-looking!

When he drove across the bridge, I looked down and saw some little boys fishing and they waved.

I'm going to take you to Memphis Tenessee, Franklin said. He was drinking, had been drinking all that day. His daddy didn't even know he had the car—thought Franklin had driven it down to the machine shop to get Buddy Thigpen to change the oil.

I said, Franklin, I can't go to Memphis. You know I can't go to Memphis. That's crazy. He was driving fast and I was getting scared. He crossed the bridge, turned right, and headed south.

Franklin, I said. Turn around.

Instead he grinned at me. Honey, I am going to take you to Memphis, he said. I am going to buy you a new red dress and take you to the Peabody Hotel.

Turn around, I said.

They've got ducks in the lobby of the Peabody Hotel, he said. They swim in the fountain there. But I guess you wouldn't know about that. You haven't been there, of course. You haven't been anywhere.

Turn around, I said. Trees went flashing past us on both sides, now a house, now a glimpse of the river. The road stretched out straight in front of us like a ribbon in the sun with the end of it shining. It was August, and hot. Dust devils danced by the side of the road, and the end of it shimmered like fairyland. I think it was then that I started crying. Because I wanted to go, Silvaney, I really did! I wanted a new red dress. I wanted to see the ducks in the lobby of the Peabody Hotel, and see how funny they waddle, and find the end of that shiny road. Franklin finished off the bottle and threw it out the window and it sailed shining through the air into the woods at the side of the road. Hot air rushed past my face. I was having trouble breathing.

You've got to turn around, I finally said.

Stick with me and I'll take you places, Franklin said. You're my baby.

No! By then I was screaming. Joli is my baby. Because I knew that by then they'd be wondering where I was, what was taking me so long getting home from work, and Joli would be pulling on Beulah's skirt and asking where Mama was, and Beulah would be short with her, moren likely Beulah was still packing. Stop this car, stop it stop it. Turn around, I said.

Goddammit Ivy! Franklin skidded over to the side of the road and we screeched to a stop. Dust rose up all around us in great clouds and suddenly it was so quiet. The woods were thick and green around the car. Franklin jerked my skirt up higher on my legs and pulled my panties down.

I am not your baby, I said. I have got a baby of my own, I said. I could see her little face in my mind. I could hardly speak.

O.K., he said. O.K. He started the car again and pulled back out in the road with the tires squealing, and turned the car around. He never looked over at me once, driving back, and I didn't say a word. He drove too fast. Then when we got to the bridge, Franklin slowed down and started driving way over on the shoulder of the road.

I couldn't keep quiet then. Franklin, Franklin, what are you doing? I screamed. We'll go in the river, Franklin. We'll hit the bridge—and then, Silvaney, we did! Franklin ran his father's car into the bridge on purpose, and busted out the headlight on my side and tore up the fender. He meant to! And by the time we got to Diamond, that tire was flat too. We drove on the rim the whole way back. I don't know what all it did to the car. I don't know what Franklin's father said about any of it.

Poor Beulah. She always thought we were courting. I don't know what we were doing, Silvaney, but it wasn't courting! On August 16, Beulah and Curtis moved. Me and Joli rattled around that little house like peas in a pod, with all them gone.

Beulah left in a seersucker suit and a flat little hat, she believes in dressing up for a trip, in case you should die in a car wreck. Curtis looked at me hard, from the car, a look I couldn't read. John Arthur and Curtis Junior waved and waved. The company moved their stuff in a company truck. I reckoned they would move me out too, come fall. That's what they do. I knew I'd have to go in one of those little old houses down in the bottom, which is where the rough people live, and I was dreading it so. Still, I knew I had to hold onto my job, because jobs are so few and far between now.

Joli went over next door and got Violet's Martha, to spend the night with us. When Martha doesn't try to talk, she is just like anybody. I miss Beulah a whole lot even if we had our differences. Blood is thicker than water, as they say. And I don't know how she'll fare up there.

Anyway Beulah and Curtis moved out, and the next day Franklin showed up at the store grinning just like he hadn't done what I knew he had, like him and me was starting over from scratch, and he kept hanging around there giving me the eye, until after a while I found myself going along with him. He is the kind of a man you will go along with. And that night he showed up at the house late, drunk and crying, and told me all kind of sweet things. You see what I mean? I can tell you a lot about Franklin, I can put some of the colors in, but I can't get the outline right. He stayed the night of course and when Tessie came in the morning, she rolled her eyes and set her jaw to see him, and shook her head.

I was on my way down the mountain to work when all of a sudden I heard Violet calling Ivy! Ivy! after me, and I stopped.

Violet was out of breath. Her early morning hair was wilder and curlier than ever, that red lipstick gone. Her mouth looked pale and serious. It was still hot that morning but cloudy, looked like rain. Honey, she said, You need to think real serious about what all you are doing.

What do you mean? I said.

A man like that, he's not like usuns, Violet said. You haven't got any business fooling with him, honey. He is on the other side.

What side? I said. I don't know what you are talking about, Violet. I pulled away from her even though I knew she had good intentions, and ran off down the road just as the first drops started to fall, making big round splats in the dusty road like a silver dollar. For I am tired to death of people giving me good advice, even people with good intentions, it may be they are the worst of all.

I looked back up the mountain once and saw Franklin Ransom standing out on the porch with his shirt hanging open, watching me go, I reckon. I did not wave. Behind him on the mountain the dark clouds were piled up higher, and the thunder rolled, low and lazy. Lightning cut through the clouds. This is the next-to-last time I ever saw him.

I was in the store pricing baby clothes when it happened, three weeks after that. It was September 20, I will never forget that day. 1926. I had just drunk a cup of coffee and was talking to Mrs. Joines, who worked there too. She was complaining about her mother. Some of the people at the store had started treating me different ever since word had got out that I went some with Franklin, but not Mrs. Joines. She is common as the day is long. Of course she will talk your ear off, always has. She was telling how her mother won't eat any food except white food, like grits and potatos and light bread, when the whistle blew.

Mrs. Joines quit talking with her mouth wide open, and I laid the baby clothes back down on the counter. The whistle has never blown like that, between shifts, in all the years I have lived at Diamond. But it blew and kept right on blowing, and we all knew what it meant.

I walked out of the store and up the hill to Violet's. She stood at the door, as hard-faced as anybody I ever saw. The high shrieking sound of the whistle was all around us.

Go on up there, I said. I knew it was Rush's shift.

Violet took off running. She didn't wear a coat. She didn't take a thing.

The whistle kept blowing and blowing, like a nightmare. From houses all over Company Hill, people lit out running. Cars started up. Women and girls stood in the doorways holding little children's hands, like I held Martha's. The door was wide open behind us, letting cold air into the house. You couldn't even think with that whistle shrieking. Down in the bottom, folks milled around the store and the company offices. They looked like little dolls, like little toy folks from where I stood. They gathered on the porch of the company store. Cars came and went, toy cars. Horns blew. Then they let out school, and children came pouring out the schoolhouse door and started up the hill or joined those walking and running up to the mine, a line like a colorful snake going up the mine road behind the store and out of sight around the side of Diamond Mountain. I stood there and watched for Joli. She is real little for her age now. Not sickly, just little. When the whistle finally stopped, the silence was awful. Then Joli came running up the road, home from school, asking questions.

What is it, Mama, what is it? Joli said. Is it a fire? and I said Honey, don't you know? It is trouble at the mine. I believe it is big trouble. And Joli's pretty little face went sad. She has a pointy chin, and with all that red hair, sometimes she looks like a funny little fox. Is Martha's daddy down in there? she asked, and I said Yes honey, he is.

But Martha just swung on my hand and grinned. She didn't really understand it, she is older than Joli but simple.

We had no sooner gone back in the house than R.T. came busting in. This is Rush and Violet's big boy.

Where is Mama? he said, and I said, Up at the mine. Then he looked all over the house—he acted real scattered, I don't know what he was looking for—and then he bolted back out the door and said he was going up there too. Goddammit, goddammit, R.T. was saying. He was crying. He is a great big boy with light eyes and curly black hair like Violet.

I wanted to go up there myself.

I batted around Violet and Rush's house doing first one thing, then another. I made the girls some cinamon toast and washed Violet's kitchen floor but I couldn't bring myself to make the bed, it seemed too personal with Rush in the mine. Finally I couldn't stand it in their house any more so I took the girls over to my house, but that was even worse with Beulah and Curtis and everybody gone. I opened the cupboard and it was empty, all of Beulah's rosy dishes gone. Then I started crying for it seemed to me then that life is nothing but people leaving.

Mama, what is the matter? Joli said. Don't cry Mama.

And I said, Nothing honey, I miss Beulah and them, is all. Then I sat down and hemmed a skirt for Joli and darned some socks, then I got the little girls dressed up in sweaters and took them out in the yard and got them to scratching pretty pictures in the dirt with some sticks, and I swept off the yard real good.

Silvaney, you would not believe what a beautiful day it was! The prettiest day of September, the prettiest day of the fall! By then it had turned plum warm, with a light cool breeze, and the trees over on Diamond Mountain shone out like flaming jewels in the bright clear sunshine. Leaves were falling everywhere, but not in our yard where we have no trees. All we have is dirt, and I sweep it in pretty patterns. I took the girls out to the side of the road to look at our froghouses and they were still right there, standing fine.

Old Mr. Vance Looney came panting up the hill but when I asked him what the news was, he said, No word, no word. By noon you could see the smoke coming up over the top of Diamond Mountain. Mr. Looney said there had been a firedamp explosion, as near as they could tell, right after the seven o'clock shift started. They said it sounded like thunder rolling away off towards Kentucky, the way thunder sounds in the summer. But it was September of course. Mr. Looney said that some men came running out hollering that timbers were falling everyplace, and the mine-train rails had been blown all to hell and back, and the walls were caving in on the passage to the No. 8 face. Those who had been mining down the other two passages were walking out now one by one and two by two, straggling through the smoke, their faces black, coughing. But not a one of them came back up Company Hill. Somehow I knew they wouldn't. I knew they would stay there. They would all stay there until they got everybody out that was coming out. I stood on the porch—I just couldn't sit still anyplace—and the girls played paper dolls while I looked over at Diamond Mountain. Smoke drifted up lazy. It was such a pretty day. But I couldn't sit down. I couldn't keep my mind on a thing.

My mind went fluttering around and around like the yellow

butterflies in the Queen Anne's lace back up on Sugar Fork, not landing on something, not landing on something—what? Two neighbor women came by and asked me if I had heard any news and I said no, and then they left. I made some brownies for the girls and some soup beans for anybody that might want to eat them later. But I couldn't eat a thing.

When I went back out, the wind was coming up and the sun was lower. Now the toy cars were backed up all over the bottom and you could hear the steady low sound of so many voices, even up on the hill where we were. Relatives coming in, talking, waiting. People in trucks from god knows where. I saw a truck that looked like Oakley's daddy's, but from that distance it was hard to tell. My mind went fluttering, fluttering, it would not settle.

Then I couldn't stand it any more.

Come on, girls, I said. Martha, you run home and get your jacket. Joli, here's your coat. We're going up to the mine.

I don't want to, Mommy, Joli started whining. I'm too tired.

Oh sweetie, I said. I pulled her over and kissed her and pushed her hair back. Joli's hair is red as mine, curly as yours. I buttoned up her fuzzy pink coat which used to belong to one of Doctor Gray's girls. It has big square buttons.

I have got to go up there, I said.

Then I thought to pack some of the soup beans in a dinner pail. I took a sack of cornbread for Violet and R.T. who had not showed their faces since morning.

We walked down the hill at four o'clock, me and the girls, holding hands. It was getting colder. When we passed the store, some people were singing a church song on the steps. Rock of ages cleft for me, let me hide myself in thee. I could hear Bonita Munsey who has a real good voice. We got a cocacola from the store and went on, in a big crowd now. It was like they picked us up and carried us along, like we were riding a raft downriver. Past the baseball field, the pump, Mister Everett's house, the bunkhouse, the station, across the railroad tracks. Winding up the hill. I seen him coming from a long way off, somebody sang. I couldn't hardly breath which had nothing to do with walking. It was more like a nervous breakdown as in Jane Eyre. My butterfly mind went from Sugar Fork to Majestic to the black rushing water of Diamond Creek where I first met Franklin.

By the time we got up there, it was nearabout dark and they had dug through. They were bringing them out. The mine itself was a great charred gaping hole with smoke still coming from it, but they were pulling cars out hand by hand. There was an awful lot of smoke and yelling. At last, at last, the rope that pulled the cars would start to move, slow at first then a little faster. That meant a man was on the way out. The only way they could identify the bodies was by the check number on them. The men were black, smoking. But some of them came out alive. The groaning and suffering was terrible. And the rescue business is mighty slow. Doctors and nurses and men from all around were up there helping out. They had stretchers and tents and lanterns and carbide lamps. It was starting to get dark.

The rescue workers had roped the rest of the people off, up on the hillside right above the mine. You couldn't stand anyplace near the entrance, where they were bringing them out. Some of the women still had their cook aprons on from that morning. A line of men kept them back from the mine. Dragging Martha and Joli by the hand, I made it up there finally and found Violet, but she wouldn't eat anything.

Here, she said, Let this girl here have it, she needs it, Violet said and pointed to the woman beside her who had undid her blouse and was giving her baby some titty right there. I'd be obliged, the girl said when she got through feeding her baby, and then Joli held it for her while she ate. The girl's baby was just tiny. I couldn't believe Joli had ever been so little. I couldn't believe how long ago it was that she was born—eight years which had rushed pell mell, like high water under the bridge at Majestic.

It got dark. Below us, we could see the moving people black against the lights. Flares went up. And every now and then, they would come and call out the name of the man they were bringing out. Snead! Lowell Snead! Every woman there would strain forward and then fall back, and that man's family would let out a cry or a moan and a rush forward. Violet said that R.T. was down there working.

I always put plenty in his lunch bucket, Violet said almost to herself, just in case he got trapped again. And I always put some soda in there for his digestion, it cramps you to work bent over.

I hugged her.

You go on back, she said. Take the girls— who had fallen down in a pile like little animals, fast asleep. I looked down at them. Joli was sleeping with her mouth open, like always. I thought of that little poem she loves. What are little girls made of? What are little girls made of? Sugar and spice and everything nice, that's what little girls are made of.

I can't leave yet, I said, which was true. I said, Let the girls sleep. My mind was just fluttering as I stood there with Violet, waiting for Rush. Asa Horn! Raymond Childress! they yelled back the names. Some of them were walking out now, people said. There had been a whole roomful trapped that they'd just got to. Hope lifted, people stirred. But Violet said nothing. I think she knew even then that he was dead. The girl with the baby was praying out loud. Jeffrey Wayne Stacy! they called, and she said, Oh Jesus, oh please Jesus, and stumbled forward. I saw her clearly for a moment, all red in the light, then she was gone. Gayheart! Rush Gayheart! they yelled.

Go on back now, Violet said, and walked out slow.

But still I couldn't leave. My mind fluttered and fluttered and finally landed, and then I knew who I was waiting for—not Rush!— and why I couldn't leave.

It was close to dawn and not many were left on the hill when they called his name.

Oakley Fox!

I jerked the girls along crying down the hill, almost fell through the lanterns lined up like a ring of fire. The mine gaped. I didn't know if he'd come out dead or alive, covered up or walking. There was a row of bodies laid out to the right there, and women bent over them grieving. They were taking some of them away. The whole place was a mess of red light and darkness and movement and noise. Joli was crying hard. I half carried her along. And then I stopped. The huge black mouth of the mine yawned smoky and wide before me, and three men came walking out. One of them was Oakley. Limping and holding his arm funny, black-faced— still I could tell him, by the straight forward shock of his hair and his square shoulders, the way he held himself. It was like the mouth of the mine had opened up and let him go, like he had been spared, or like he had just been born.

Oakley! Oakley! I hollered. I could see him turn his head blindly toward my voice. But he couldn't see me. He couldn't see anything yet, you could tell. I think his mouth moved. Oakley! Oakley! I called, pulling Joli and Martha through the people, to Oakley at last who stretched out his arms as wide as the world when he finally saw it was me. The way he smelled made me choke when he hugged me, it was so bitter and strong, but then he held me back out and looked at my face and then hugged me again. His lip was bleeding and his whole collar was stiff with blood. Baby baby, it's you, Oakley said, and reached around Joli too. Then he leaned on me and we all walked out to the waiting cars together.

Just as we were getting into a car, I looked up—I will never know why, exactly—and there not three yards away, leaning against a truck, was Franklin Ransom. He was staring at me so hard I felt like his eyes burned holes in my body. Now, what in the world was he doing there? Helping out with the rescue? Just curious? I sank back into the car as they were getting ready to close the door after us, and looked down for a minute to make sure the girls fingers were not in the way, and when I looked back up, he was gone. The truck was still there but Franklin was gone, and I have never seen him again. I guess I never will. He is over in Kentucky with his precious Nana or so I hear, and his daddy is in big trouble over safety regulations, and his mother stays in bed all the time due to nerves.

Rush Gayheart was killed in the mine, along with Ray Fox Junior and 17 others.

Oakley and me got married.

And we will be leaving here.

We will go back to live in the house on Sugar Fork, and we will come and get you too Silvaney, and you and me will clean the house together and scrub the floors with creek gravel, and clear the dead leaves out of the spring. And we will get chickens and let them run up on Pilgrim Knob, and cut back the weeds, and plant the garden. I remember Daddy saying, Farming is pretty work. And when Oakley kisses me, it seems like I can hear Daddy saying, Slow down, slow down now, Ivy. This is the taste of spring.

Your happy sister,
Ivy R. Fox

P.S. It will not be long.

IV

Letters from Sugar Fork

Dear Victor,

I am so mad at you.

I have been fretting over my behavior for these last weeks and I declare, I am <u>still</u> mad at you. I have been studying on how to write you a letter. To tell you the truth, I don't know. Now I am writing you, but I still don't know! I am still mad. But Oakley says I owe you a apology. O.K., I am sorry. I am sorry I sulled up on everybody like that. I am going to write to Ethel and tell her too, and Stoney. For in all truth, it was real good of you all to come up here and help us. I don't know what Oakley and me would of done, either, if you had not helped us clear this land, and then Stoney bringing us the Gooch boys from the store too, and all those goods. So we are grateful to all of you, as well as Oakley's folks who have helped us out so much.

But to be perfectly honest Victor, I am sick to death of being grateful. I am tired of being beholden.

I want to be again like I was as a girl, you remember how I used to run these hills the livelong day and not say boo to a soul. But it may be that you do <u>not</u> remember, for you went away, you went off to work and then to the war in France.

So you and me, that used to be so close when I was little, have got disaquainted.

Well, let me tell you, I used to do just as I saw fit. And I went where I pleased and done what I felt like in Majestic too, even after I got ruint. So, although I am suppose to apologize, I will not act beholden. I don't feel like it. I have gotten too hateful and too sad. Mostly I am sad, over the way we have all got so split up by tragedy and the years.

But it <u>was</u> awful, how you told me about Silvaney.

I know I ought to thank you for going over there to find out about her after all this time, but it is terrible to me to learn the truth. I always thought she would get better, and would want to come home. Whatever I was doing, whatever befell, I always thought Silvaney was right there looking over my shoulder some way, I can't explain it, and that one day I would go get her and bring her home. I have felt like I was split off from a part of myself all these years, and now it is like that part of me has died, since I know she will never come. I feel like she has gone to a foreign land forever.

Victor, I guess I <u>am</u> sorry I got so mad! I know you are not suppose to get mad at the person that tells you the bad news, but I always do!

It seems like I wouldn't act this way. It seems like I would of growed up some, after all this time. I keep waiting for this to happen, but it has not. I remember as a child, I thought all the older people around us were <u>grown up.</u> Now I think they were just old. Because although I am a married woman now, I still feel like the girl that grew up here, the one I used to be. I still get too wrought up. But you do not need to worry about me, Victor, if you are, because I love Oakley, and him and me are doing real good, although I am working my fingers to the bone I am back where I have longed to be, where I belong. The garden is coming up now, so in spite of myself almost I am the happiest that I have ever been.

So I do apologize.

Your crazy sister,
Ivy R. Fox

June, 1927

Dear Violet,

Don't worry, we will be real happy to keep Martha over here for a while longer. Oakley says so too and means it. She is good company for my Joli. They are having the best time! You know I always thought I would have Silvaney with me, but now that she won't be coming, there is a place here tailormade for your Martha, believe me. So don't even feel bad. I don't know if I told you or not but this is a big house, bigger than the houses we had up on Company Hill—oh that seems like years and years ago to me, Violet, it seems like a dream—this here is a big double cabin with a loft on each side and a breezeway in between which had fell down but Oakley has shored it up now as good as ever. We set out there of an evening right where my daddy used to set to play a tune, and Oakley whittles which he is really good at, and I shell my beans which have come in good already, or I might sew some, or whatever. It is no end of work up here. But night comes in slow over Bethel Mountain and we watch it come, like it is sneaking in I reckon, stealing across the mountains ridge by ridge, they go blue and purple before your very eyes, and then the mist will rise. When it gets too dark to whittle, Oakley will quit doing it and come and sit on the floor by my chair and lay his head in my lap and we will stay there like that for a while. And then before long we will rise, and go to bed. The last thing Oakley does every night is stretch his arms, a big wide stretch that takes in everything before us, all these mountains ridge on ridge, and Home Creek down below in the noisy dark, and Sugar Fork, and all this little farm. Oakley says he has finally got him plenty of elbow room. Then he wraps me up in a hug as big as Bethel Mountain, and then we go to bed where we lay tangled in each other all night long. Sometimes we will wake to love then sleep to wake again.

All of this is a big surprise to me Violet. Having so many chores now gives me time to think, and I often think back on you and Rush, I believe you had such a deep love yourself, I did not understand it at the time. Sometimes I despair of ever understanding anything right when it happens to me, it seems like I have to tell it in a letter to see what it was, even though I was right there all along!

I have been thinking about Franklin too, and I know I was crazy to go with him so long. It seems to me now that Franklin was like a sickness that came over me and stayed. But I still can't feature what you told me about him getting caught in nigger holler with his pants down! Now I see what Tessie must of known, and why she never liked him. I didn't understand it at the time, like I was saying. But believe me, I am happy now. I am happy to have Martha here too.

So, you go ahead and do whatever you have to. But for God's sake be careful. You know that I will remain your good friend,

Ivy R. Fox

Dear Beulah,

I am writing again because you did not answer which makes me feel like we parted on a sour note, and I can't stand this since so many in our family are lost in light already, dead and gone. You know you have never wrote to me once not even after getting the letter where I told you that Oakley and me got married. Well, what do you think of that? You know we have ended up back here on Sugar Fork, and Oakley is farming which he has always wanted to do, so far it is hand to mouth but we are happy. I know how much you hate Sugar Fork, and I can see for why, but oh Beulah you would not if you could see it in the spring.

The apple trees behind the house were like a rolling sea of sweet pink clouds. The rosybush by the front porch steps is still in bloom, and the lilac by the back door never had so many flowers. It is beautiful up here. Try to think of me like this, in all these flowers, and don't be mad at me or disappointed because I failed to marry Franklin Ransom as you hoped, or make a schoolteacher either as Mrs. Brown and Miss Torrington wished. I guess I am too flighty to make a good schoolteacher anyhow—I still get all carried away! So I will just write my letters instead, for it means so much to me to keep in touch.

And as for Franklin Ransom, I am lucky I got out of that, believe you me! I am writing today to tell you what happened, in case you haven't heard. Well, it seems that Franklin Ransom had him a girlfriend in nigger holler all along, even when me and him were going out so much together, yes all that whole long time. Her name is Walterene Parrish. Franklin had daddied two little nigger babies on her, so they say. But after the mine disaster, when his parents left Diamond under a cloud, he went back over to Kentucky, and Walterene—now that's Tessie's sister's girl—took up with a big huge Northern nigger that had just come down here. But one day Franklin drove back over to Diamond and went knocking on Walterene's door again and she let him in same as always, and they were going at it for fair when this big new nigger got off of his shift and came home. And he up and pitched a fit! They say that Franklin said to him, You must not know who I am, you must not know your place either, and that nigger said, I don't give a damn who you are, you had better get your white ass out of my house right now, and then he shot Franklin in the rear end with grapeshot and made him run naked all the way down nigger holler to his car! I guess this Northern nigger had not yet learned how to act down here.

Anyway, folks did not take it laying down. You know how they are anyway, them that lives low down on Company Hill. They are so bad off theirselves that they have got to have somebody else to look down on, they have got to believe that there is somebody, someplace, lower than them. This is why they hate niggers so bad, in my opinion. This is why they done what they done, in my opinion, which was awful. Plus they are just naturally spoiling for a fight all the time. But what they done was awful.

A bunch of them got good and likkered up and went over there and lined both sides of that nigger holler just at dark, and let loose with a round of shooting you have never heard the likes of—and come morning, half of those niggers was gone. They had left out in the dead of night. They say that Walterene took off so fast, she left her beans in a pot on the cookstove, and her clothes flapping out on the line. Well, this is what folks say, anyway—so I am *glad* I failed to make a good thing out of Franklin, after all! I hope you will be glad too, and forgive me.

And times are still real bad over at Diamond, I reckon you have heard. I don't know what you have heard, though. The company side of it, I reckon. I swear, Beulah, I can't see it. I have to say I am all for the union myself, and Oakley says that not a day goes by but what he thinks of Ray, and blames the company for it. So I reckon you have heard what Violet is doing. We hear that the strike still goes on, and that the company has brought some thugs in there with Gatling guns to protect the scabs. So we don't know where it will all end, or when. But folks are leaving there in droves now, they can't hold out no longer. Violet is still right in the thick of things, her and her boy R.T. She is going to get run out on a rail soon, according to Oakley. She says that her and R.T. might go over to Harlan after this strike gets settled, and work for the union there. So Oakley and me are like to have her Martha for a good long time.

Speaking of children, how are John Arthur and Curtis Junior and Delores? Fine I hope. Give them all a big hug and a kiss for me, and do not let them forget me Beulah, especially John Arthur. Tell him how we used to go down the hill to see the train at Diamond. I think Oakley is real jealous of Curtis for having Curtis Junior. Oakley wants a boy the worst in the world, and says he needs one to farm with! Or may be two.

I was thinking the other day about you and about Curtis's awful mother Mrs. Bostick, and how mean she was to you. Have you all ever made up yet? My new in-laws are anything <u>but</u> mean. In fact they will kill you with kindness if you let them, Edith Fox will cook you to death and Ray Senior would give you the shirt off his back. You know we stayed with them down there on Home Creek until the thaw. Oakley couldn't stand to be at Diamond another minute after Ray Junior got killed. The Foxes are so nice they are almost <u>too</u> nice, if you know what I mean. At their table you have to hold hands and bow your head and say grace before each meal. And every night of the world, Ray Senior reads the Bible out loud. But since he can not read as good as me, he got me to read it while we were staying there. Oakley was real proud of me. He just looked at me when I read, and I could tell he wasn't listening to a word of it. I could tell.

We went to church with them too. Now this is the regular Primitive Baptist Church at Deskins Branch, you turn left there at the fork of Home Creek instead of going like you would go on to Majestic. My word, Beulah—they don't meet but twice a month, and so it goes on for ever. They start with singing, and Delphi Rolette lines out the words which he has been doing for twenty years, and then there is preaching and then more singing and then more preaching, it will wear you out. I kept thinking about Garnie through it all. I guess we have lost him too at least for now. We have given him up to God! After the service, the moderator will <u>open the doors</u> which means he will ask, <u>Are all in love and fellowship?</u> which they never are, and then anybody that has got a complaint, comes forward. If there is somebody that has not been coming to church regular, for an instance, they will notice him to come in and give an account of himself. Or they will church you for walking drunk. We went to church two times with Oakley's family and both times I was scared to death that somebody would say, <u>There is one here that don't believe!</u> meaning me. And I thought it might be Oakley's sister Dreama that would say it, she's real religious. I know it hurts Oakley a lot that I have not been saved, but when Mr. Rolette lines out the invitational and Oakley squeezes my hand, I do not feel a thing except Oakley squeezing my hand. But I have thought to myself, may be I <u>will</u> walk up there and get saved after all, and be baptized in the river, then if it is true I will go to Heaven and if it is not true, it won't matter anyway. And Oakley would be so happy. But finally, Beulah, I find that I can not—they could see it on my face in a minute if I was to lie and put on like that. For you know me, I can not lie—I could not fool a cat.

So the Foxes failed to save me but they fattened me up some which was a good thing too as it has been such hard work since we come up here.

I can't tell you how I felt, the day we came—it was early March, wet ground, cold wind, cloudy. When we came up along Home Creek I was sorry and surprised to see the trash that folks have throwed in the water alongside the road—for there is a road now, Beulah—and the lowdown kinds of people living any old way along there. The woods look ragged too, they have timbered out all the big trees, and it's not much along there now but scrub pines. The big tulip poplars are all gone. So I was glad when we left the bottom, and started up Sugar Fork. The trace had gotten so overgrown that we had to keep stopping to move logs and branches that had fallen across it, and Oakley's daddy said, Me and Delphi will have to come back up here and do some grading, and they have done it since. Now you can ride nearabout the whole way up here in your truck, if the water is not too high that is, you know you have to ford the creek twice on the way. But the water is still as cold and as pure as it ever was, the best water in the world, it tastes as good as it did to Momma when she and Daddy stopped to drink, riding Lightning. I was thinking about Momma and Daddy while I waited for the men to clear the brush, how brave Momma was, not knowing where she was going or what in the world she would find. Now I felt that way myself, but I did not feel brave. I felt cold and scared. And on the final turn, when we parked in the clearing beneath the he-balsam and I stood looking down the bank holding Joli's hand while they started unloading, then I thought of Babe laying dead right there in the creek, and of Silvaney stepping across the steppingstones to find him. Mama, Mama you are hurting me, Joli said for I was squeezing her little hand too hard. Come on honey, Oakley said then and we came, me wondering—I am wondering still—how I ever rode Babe's horse all the way down to Home Creek that night for help. Lord, it seems like a million years ago. It seems like another person, but it was me.

We had to walk through briars and branches to the house, our feet slipping on the wet stones. And then for a minute I got real scared—the way I used to feel when I looked at Momma's face in the wind up on Pilgrim Knob or heard Daddy breathing horrible by the fire—but then when I stopped to try to breathe, I looked down and seen something I had not seen since we left there, those little yellow beauties and blue-eyed grass that come first every year on the mountains, don't you remember too? And then I said to Oakley, Look here, spring is on the way for sure. Then we were home.

But everything is smaller than I thought, or remembered, or immagined. This may be because I was a child then, and now I am grown, but I find that all has shrunk some way, and I do not like it. The sycamore tree, for an instance, stands half its size! It does not take long for a house to fall in either, and Nature to take its course. The breezeway between the cabin halves was all to pieces, with ivy growing up the broken wood. Oakley has shored it up and added on, it is like a new breezeway now. Up in the loft, that first day back, I found a twist of tobacco that must of been Granny Rowe's, as dry as a piece of rope, and some several old gourds full of seed that was never planted, that seed rattles around in the gourds like little stones. Now I cannot bring myself to throw them out, I don't know why.

And I had clean forgot about the chest up in the loft, Momma's old chest, you will not believe what I found inside! The beautiful crazy quilt stitched together with golden thread, that Momma used to call her burying quilt. And I thought to myself, now Momma is dead and buried in Rich Valley these many years, so she will not need her burying quilt, and I am alive and making a house here with Oakley Fox, and we need a pretty quilt the worst in the world, and so I just snatched it up and aired it out and put it on our bed, now it is the prettiest thing in the whole house! And I will use the old chest for Joli's hope box. I thought I would not mention to Oakley about it being a burying quilt unlessen of course he was to ask me flat out, Ivy, is this a burying quilt? But he will not. It will not cross his nor anybody else's mind, and if you come up here, don't you tell it!

Oh Beulah, I hope you will visit us sometime. I hope you are not still mad at me, or at Ethel either one. I may have mentioned to you that her and Stoney Branham came up here to help us clear, plus Victor, and Oakley's folks and some other people— anyway, it was like a party. We cut the brush and pulled it up and piled it in big piles and burned it, and the pale blue smoke from the burning rose straight up to the blue-blue sky. The purple judas-trees were already blooming, and pink and white dogwood, and red and white sarvis even though all the trees were bare except for the greening elmtops. Cardinals were back already, calling Sugar sweet, sugar sweet. Lord, we got so dirty, got so tired. Victor is a big heavy man now, Beulah, and Stoney Branham is getting real old. Didn't either one of them work too hard, they mostly told these Gooch boys what to do. Stoney and Ethel acts so funny together, it would make you laugh to see them. They are a sketch. Mister Branham is what Ethel calls him still, and draws up her mouth so severe which will make him act evermore the fool. Now, now Mister Branham, Ethel says, real disapproving. He likes it, she likes it. I guess they cut up like that in the store.

Victor and them are partners now and he does not drink a thing except about two times a year, when he goes on a big spree and does all kind of crazy things according to Ethel and Stoney. Like he asked an old maid woman from Matewan to marry him, and so here she came with all her things in a car and her father to give her away, and Victor met them at the door and said, I am so sorry, miss, I cannot recall the incident in question. When he's sober, he's real serious. In fact sometimes he is too serious, he will go on and on when you wish he would just shut up. But I am not mad at him now.

Anyway they came, we cleared the field, we burned the brush, and then we plowed with the mule that Oakley's daddy gave us when we came up here, that's Sal, and the old bull-tongue plow that Oakley found out by the orchard, rusting in the weeds. I reckon Momma just left it laying there, halfway between the field and the house, when she didn't have the strength to carry it no further. Her and you and me was not enough to run this place, I don't know why she entertained the idea for even a minute. A farm is a lot of work, believe me. You need a man.

But you know Momma—bound and determined to have it her own way, and now that we are all getting older, I see how we take after her, Beulah, all of us. I know this is something that you don't want to hear.

Well, nevermind. Nevermind, it's all water under the bridge as Granny says. Anyway, when they were hitching up Sal to the plow, Victor stopped dead in his tracks and stared at the plow for a while, kind of puffing his breath in and out of his whiskers and mumbling something you couldn't hear. Victor is heavy now, he wears a straw hat and suspenders. He pushed that hat way back on his head. His face was all red from climbing up the hill.

I do believe that is Daddy's plow, he said finally, and Oakley said, Yes it is.

Well, humph humph, was what Victor said, or all you could understand. But Victor stood there looking at the plow for a while, all redfaced, until Oakley said, Well, let's get a move on, and we did. And now I wonder what all was going on in Victor's mind—if he had come back from the war sooner, we might of all stayed up here all along. Or if he never had gone to the war in the first place. Because it sure took the starch out of Victor in some way, I mean the war. He is not up for farming now, nor anything else much either. But I will tell you, he flung himself into the plowing, and Stoney did too, as much as they were able. Mostly they burned off brush and let the Gooch boys and Oakley hold the plow. After while Victor came up on the porch and visited me and Ethel, and we got to talking about the time we fooled Garnie with the chestnuts. I thought Victor would bust a gut laughing. Ethel was darning socks which I never get to, and making a lot over little Joli whose so pretty. But Ethel doesn't want no children of her own, not her! She says she has done took inventory, and they are already full up! Ethel is just as spunky as ever, she does not give a damn what folks think. And Ethel will make two of Stoney Branham, who has shriveled up while she has expanded. But Stoney is wirey, Stoney is game. He liked to work himself to death that day on the hillside, and said he will be looking for his share of the profits! He struts like a banty rooster, giving orders. Of course he is fooling, he doesn't mean it, but him saying it is good because it allows Oakley not to feel so beholden.

Oakley has got a little beat down, of late.

When the plowing was done, we drug the field with an evergreen bough.

By then it was sunset, and the field tilted dark and pretty against the wild red sky. We all walked down together, me and Oakley with our arms around each other's waists, the way we like to walk, and Ethel and Stoney, and Victor leading Sal, we walked down off the mountain, but I looked back once more to see that field, that sky. The field is so steep it looks like the side of the globe that Mrs. Brown used to keep on her desk, and it is curved like the curve of the earth. And all the sky beyond it is just huge. That night it was plum red, too. We walked through sarvis and dogwood and apple blossoms. Even the lilac bush by the back door had buds on it, you remember Revel brought it to Momma one time from far away.

Well, so much for the plowing.

We planted our potatos in the dark of the moon, later that spring, just Oakley and me. We planted when the signs were in the legs. Granny came by the house that afternoon to say, It is a fine night for planting potatos, so that is what we did. Only we got to giggling. Oakley says he doesn't believe a word of this plant in the dark of the moon stuff. But it is fun. First we got us a cup of blockade liquor that Oakley had put by someplace, and we drunk it down and checked on Joli and Martha. Sound asleep. Then we got the kerosene lantern and the seed corn, and set out for the field. It was so dark you couldn't see your hand in front of your face, and windy. Lord, was it windy! My hair was whipping around my face and my skirt blew up all around my legs, I felt like I was going to fly. It was the windiest, wildest night. Well, we got to cutting up, and Oakley grabbed me and gave me a big hard kiss, and one thing led to another. Before long we had fell right down there in that soft black field beneath the soft black sky. I know you don't want to hear this, so I won't tell it. But we did it, all the same.

Oh Beulah, Beulah, Beulah, write to me. I feel like I don't know you any more. But I am still

Your sister,
Ivy Fox

January 7, 1931

Dear Miss Torrington,

You can not immagine what a big surprise it was when the box arrived from Boston, nor how I felt to open it up and find the clothes, and the books for the children. My husband Oakley wants to join me in saying, Thank you. Please tell your nieces and nephews how much we appreciate the clothes. My daughter Joli reads the books aloud to Martha who can not read. But Joli is sharp as a tack! I know you would love to have her in your class. I try and fail to immagine your class, your school, or even you, Miss Torrington, after all these years.

To answer your question, I do not read much any more. I do not have the time. Sometimes Oakley gets me books from the Presbyterian School when he goes to town, or Ethel or Geneva will bring me a book when they come up here, but often I send them back unread, I confess it. Ever since my little twins were born, it is like I don't have near enough hands, or time either one. The time just slips away.

The twins are Bill and Danny Ray, born Christmas Eve 1929, now they are already one. They keep me hopping, believe me! They look just like my husband Oakley.

You are good to send these things, Miss Torrington. I hope from the bottom of my heart that you are well. I cannot immagine your life, no more than you can mine.

But I will always remain your thankful student,

Ivy Fox.

January 10, 1935

Dear Miss Torrington,

We thank you for the box from your school, it arrived just in time for

Dear Miss Torrington,

I am sorry I have not written to thank you for the boxes you sent us this Christmas and in the past. You are so kind.

I would like to announce to you the birth of my daughter LuIda, 1935, and of my baby Maudy, last summer. So you see how it is.

Happy New Year 1937, from

Ivy Fox.

June 10, 1937

My dear Silvaney,

It seems so natural to me now to write your name, yet it has been years since I have done so. Years. And in all truth I can not say why I have got my old yellow paper out tonight, nor my pen that Miss Torrington gave me so long ago. <u>Silvaney, Silvaney, Silvaney.</u> Lord it does feel good to write your name. Silvaney. Silvaney. I have missed you so. For years I could not get over the fact that you will never come to us here, I had sulled up about it, you know how mad I can get! My mind could not move around this fact, to write you a letter. You or anybody else. But now all of a sudden this time is past, I can not say how or why, and again I am dying to write.

It is the craziest thing.

Somehow, I have been dying to write to you ever since the lights came on last week, now this is the rural electrification project I am talking about. It is really something. They have put in poles and run electric lines all the way up Home Creek, it's the law! Some day they may come up this holler too.

Last Tuesday me and Oakley were sitting on the porch, just resting after dinner which I don't get a chance to do much of, and lo and behold, all up and down the bottom, lights came on! And you can see them shining on the lower slopes of Bethel Mountain too, they twinkle like stars. Oakley said Ho! and started praying.

But I said, Oakley, it is nothing to be scared of, or pray about. It is just the rural electrification which we have heard tell of. Praise be to God! said Oakley who has gotten real religious. I think you ought to say, praise be to the Appalachian Power Company, I said, and Oakley laughed. You are a sassy woman but you are mine, he said. We both got up and stood gripping the porch rail, looking out on this space that we have looked out on for so long, this side of Bethel Mountain that we feel like is ours for sure.

Who all do you reckon lives over there? Oakley asks real slow. I don't know, I told him.

But I know what he means. It is like we have owned that mountain, owned this view. It is like there has been nothing out there but what we have seen with our own eyes or heard in the night, nobody living there but what we made up in our heads. And now—lo and behold—there is lights all over the bottom of Bethel Mountain, there is somebody there clearly, people living in our view. I counted 14 houses, maybe more, it's hard to tell, the way the lights will cluster, the way they will twinkle through distance, in all that clear blue air between here and there. Who all do you reckon lives over there? I don't know. I can not immagine. But looking down the fork toward Home Creek, I can see the lights of the neighbor people's houses—the Rolettes, Oakley's folks, and the Breedings who live now where the Conaways used to live when we were growing up. Oakley went on to bed but I stood there, holding the rail real tight and staring. I stared down Home Creek and over on Bethel Mountain. I felt like I didn't know anybody. Who all lives there? It is a mystery. I heard Maudy start up fussing, start to cry, and I felt my breasts get tight the way they do, I unbuttoned my blouse to ease them and stood there in the breeze and looked out at the lights—it was just like Christmas across the bottom, like a lovely lady's necklace laid out on the side of Bethel Mountain. Oh, those lights! Maudy was crying hard. My milk started running down so I went inside and fed her, and then went to bed and laid there beside Oakley but I couldn't breathe right, couldn't think. In my mind I could still see the lights.

Then this morning I woke up early and started my letter to you. I will write more later.

Silvaney, I have been caught up for so long in a great soft darkness, a blackness so deep and so soft that you can fall in there and get comfortable and never know you are falling in at all, and never land, just keep on falling. I wonder now if this is what happened to Momma.

You know I used to have so much spunk. Well, I have lost my spunk some way. It is like I was a girl for such a long time, years and years, and then all of a sudden I have got to be an old woman, with no inbetween. Maybe that has always been the problem with me, a lack of inbetween.

For all of a sudden when I saw those lights, I said to myself, Ivy, this is your life, this is your real life, and you are living it. Your life is not going to start later. This is it, it is now. It's funny how a person can be so busy living that they forget this is it. This is my life.

But now I am so tired, Silvaney, just plain tired, tired unto death it seems. Maudy is the prettiest little baby I have ever had, but when she sucks it is like she is sucking my life right out of me. I am nothing but skin and bones now anyway, everybody says so. Oakley's mama Edith Fox keeps sending boiled custard up here for me and I eat and eat, but I can't gain. I can't seem to put on a pound. I am not old yet, Silvaney, 37—that don't sound so old! But I have fallen down and down and down into this darkness, I can see it all so clear now, and bits and pieces of me have rolled off and been lost along the way. They have rolled off down this mountain someplace until there is not much left but a dried-up husk, with me leeched out by hard work and babies. I feel like a locust—like a box turtle shell!

I hadn't ought to be so tired. I have worked all my life, you would think I'd be used to it by now. I was up cooking and washing dishes the third day after the twins were born. I milked the cow on the third day. I felt real fainty but there was not anybody else here to do it, I forget why. So you would think that with Maudy, I wouldn't of been so tired, but I was, even though Oakley's sister Dreama came up here and stayed a week to help me. After Maudy, I laid in the bed and slept like a rock, and did not dream. I never dream.

I never get out and go places any more, Silvaney. A woman just can't go off and leave so many children. So I don't hardly ever get out nor go anyplace. I dont go to church with Oakley except once in a blue moon—I've always got a baby to look after, anyway—and I don't get down to town but once every month or so. You know we have still got no near neighbors up here either, and

I dont give a fig to go off real far visiting. I keep up with Ethel and Geneva, and lord knows, the Foxes come up here moren I like anyway. I can't seem to take any interest in reading, which I used to, nor voting, which Oakley does. Oakley is all the time politicking around with somebody, he is a real good Democrat. One time he voted for a dead man because he was a Democrat.

But it seems like I don't want to do a thing when I'm not working, except rest. And when I rest, I lean back and shut my eyes and fall straight as a plum down into that darkness that I have been talking about.

I have been down in that darkness now for years.

Although in a way it seems short, like one long day that has lasted for years and years. I feel like I've been frozen, locked in time.

Oh Silvaney, all of a sudden I am thinking about that game Statues we used to play, and how you loved it. Don't you remember? Victor was the one that would fling us around, and however we landed, we'd have to stay. Beulah always used to try to land some fancy way. Beulah used to cheat on how she landed. Well, the twins play it now, right here in the dirt in front of the house, where you and me played.

Now I feel like I've been playing Statues and got flung down into darkness, frozen there. I see myself frozen this way, frozen that way.

I look down in my mind and see my statues.

The first one is me with Granny right before she died, only on the day in question I didn't know she was dying. This was early spring, I believe it was two years ago. You aint yourself, Granny had said to me, now hand that baby over to Dreama—this was LuIda, newborn,—and come along here with me. It was March again, and a cold wind blew in little fits and starts, it pulled Granny's long skirts up around her skinny ankles in the old men's shoes. She had tied a bonnet under her chin and it was hard to see her face, you had to look straight at her, head-on. She had her willow basket over her arm and her sharp little knife in her hand.

I am too tired, I think I said.

Hand that baby over and be quick about it, Granny said, and so I did. Tenessee went in the house and sat down in the floor and started making newspaper hats for the children. Get you a coat, Granny said, and so I did, and so we left. Little LuIda was crying when we left.

We went looking for sallet greens.

You have got to purify your blood, Granny said, and get your strength back. And she showed me how to find the little bunches of watercress growing in the rocky falls of Sugar Fork on up by Pilgrim Knob, and she showed me where to find the little green spears of poke, and how to cut them off right above the ground. They are real good if you cut them young, but if you let them get too big they are poison, and will kill you. We chopped dandelions no bigger than your little finger, and the fiddlehead ferns still curled up tight, and went along the sunny spots by the trace for lamb's quarter and dock. Before long Granny's basket was brimming plum over, and I had a stitch in my side from walking.

Lets us sit down a minute, I begged her. I am about to die.

So we sat in the sun above the creek and she told me what the greens are for, dock for the heart, dandelion greens for the liver. Granny says your blood gets dark and slow in the wintertime, and needs to be salivated. I got to looking around at the pretty day and thinking how we played party close to there, Beulah and you and me, with flowers in our hair.

Now Ivy, pay attention.

Granny's hand was like a claw on my arm. Look at me, Granny said. Here's how you boil your bitters, and I looked straight into her bonnet, at her apple-doll face. Remember, she said, and I have. I saw the clouds already forming in her sharp blue eyes, and I have always remembered, and now in the spring of the year I go out and gather the greens the way she told me, and boil them like she said, and give everybody a good dose of bitters whether they want it or not, to thin out their blood for the summer. And we never eat sallet greens, which I fix like she said with bacon fat and vinegar, sugar and salt, but what I think of her. The sharp bitey taste of the greens takes me straight back to that sunny blowing day by Sugar Fork when we sat on the rock ledge and Granny said, Ivy. Remember.

And I have remembered. I remember everything. But now that I am writing it all to you, Silvaney, it is coming over me real strong how bad I miss Granny since she died.

This happened the summer after that spring I was telling you about, nobody knows exactly how long she was dead up there in the cabin before Tenessee came down here to tell us, but it was some several days according to Oakley and his daddy who went up there later to do the necessary. I will never forget the night

Tenessee arrived, in a thunderstorm, it is no telling how she found her way to us in the night or why she chose not to wait until morning. But here comes a pounding on the door, and the dog barks and the baby cries, and Oakley says Hang on, Ivy, don't move and gets his gun, for we don't have too much company up here in the middle of the night as you can immagine.

And lord, it was Tenessee! all by herself, sopping wet with her hair straggling down in her eyes, clutching that little bead purse in both hands. As soon as Oakley opened the door, she rushed in and hugged me and set to crying. Behind her, lightning flashed and lit up the whole of Bethel Mountain, lightning branching out like a sycamore up in the sky.

It is Garnett, Tenessee finally said, and Oakley said What? Who? for I guess he had never heard Granny called by her given name in all these years.

Go get your daddy and go up there as soon as it gets light, I told him, and finally I got Tenessee to lay down although I couldn't get her to take off her clothes or give up that filthy purse. But I covered her up with a quilt and laid down beside her to warm her up, and I could hear her mumbling, mumbling as I fell back to sleep.

When I woke up again it was light, full light, and she was gone. Oakley was gone too, and so I thought Tenessee had gone back up there with him and his daddy of course. Immagine my surprise when Oakley came home that night and said, Why! Where is Tenessee?

I thought she was with you, I said.

She was here asleep when I left, said Oakley. That beats all.

It does, too.

For Tenessee got up in the early morning and snuck off from here, Lord knows where she went, either. She had no money that I know of, no food, and no clothes but the clothes on her back. Now do you think she went out looking for a man, after all these years? Maybe she finally found one. Tenessee is seventy if she's a day. And she is gone, gone for sure, as surely as uncle Revel is gone, him that suffered such a love as to spin him loose for ever in the world. I reckon Tenessee has suffered from the lack of such a love. Anyway, nobody in Majestic has seen hide nor hair of Tenessee since the day she left. We have not seen her either, nor has she been back up there to her cabin, there is a Mister Burley living there now, Oakley and his daddy have leased it.

So. Tenessee is gone, gone, and the statue I have of her when

I close my eyes is this—Tenessee standing still in the rainy door with the lightning branching out behind her head.

It's a funny thing, but I don't think she's dead. I think she's still wandering somewhere.

And Granny too, in a different way. For I did not go up to the burying ground with them when they buried Granny, so it don't seem to me that she has died really, but that she is off wandering too, with Tenessee. I have gone to Granny's grave since, on Decoration Day, and felt of the dirt with my hands, but it still don't seem to me that she is in there, it just dont.

Do you remember Decoration Day? It is the second Sunday in June, when you go and fix up the graves and put flowers in your mason jars and sink them down in the dirt to stay. The first time we went back up there, it was so much work to do. You have to tend a grave regular, Ray Fox Senior says. He knows all how to do it, too. Oakley's family is real good at keeping things up. Danny's grave is sunk in now and covered all over in violets, but won't nothing grow on Babe's, he was so mean. Babe's grave is hard red dirt. They laugh at me when I say this, but it is true.

Still, I can't get no feeling that Granny is dead, none atall, and sometimes when I am walking the trace, I think I will catch a glimpse of her long skirt swishing just around the bend ahead, or I think I smell her pipe-smoke in the air. And sometimes it is like I hear her talking in my ear. Just the other day for an instance, I heard her say to me just as plain, <u>A body can get used to anything except hanging.</u>

But I think this is wrong, Silvaney.

I think a body can get used to hanging too.

A body can get used to <u>anything.</u>

And even though she's gone, it's still like I can hear Granny talking in my ear. I can't get a feeling she is buried, nor the Cline sisters neither.

You remember them—the lady sisters, Virgie and Gaynelle Cline that used to come telling tales on Old Christmas Eve, and had told Daddy all the tales he ever knew, and he took us up there one time when they all lived on Hell Mountain and their house was so neat and they sat in those two little rush-bottom chairs on the porch. You wore a red skirt, Silvaney. I remember. It used to be Beulah's skirt. The sisters used to take turns talking.

Well, right before Joli went down to stay with Ethel, I got it in mind to go up there. I am not sure why either, except it had something to do with Joli leaving. I made her leave, I made her go on to school. But anyway, one pretty day last summer, Joli and me put some peaches in a poke and took off up Hell Mountain, leaving the younguns with Dreama and Martha. I was giggling like a schoolgirl that day. In my mind's eye I could see the lady sisters the night they left our cabin, flying over the snow. I told Joli about it, but she just laughed and said, Oh Mama. She didn't believe they flew. But that is Joli, she is more like Ethel some ways, and I am glad of it. I would not want her to be like me for anything.

So we climbed and climbed, and Joli kept saying Mama, you know they are not going to be up here. You know they'd be a hundred years old by now. This is crazy.

Oh just come on, I said. For I had got it in mind to go up there and take her. Before she left, before she went down off the mountain for good—for when Joli comes back she will be all different. I know. So I took her up on Hell Mountain while she was still mine.

But she was right.

I had a stitch in my side something awful by the time we got up there, and everything was gone. There was nothing left—nothing. And yet I was sure it was the right side of the mountain, the right cove. I remembered the chimney rocks on the way, and the two big pine trees behind the cabin. The pine trees were still there, blowing ever so gentle in the wind, with that sighing noise I remembered.

Oh Mama, Joli said.

Come here, I said. I dragged her over to where the cabin had stood and then we saw the heap of stones that was the chimney and the white roses running wild through the high green grass.

This here is it, I said. It is where they lived all right. They planted those roses, I said.

So Joli and me sat down and ate our peaches and they were so good, the best peaches ever, the juice ran all down my face and I didn't care. Bees buzzed everywhere among the roses and the long sweet grass. They say there is blue grass over in Kentucky but I have not seen it.

Joli laid back in the grass. She looks like a girl yet even though she is a full grown woman, almost nineteen. She has a sweet sharp pointy face and those big gray eyes. What all kind of stories did they used to tell? she asked me.

So this is a statue too, me in the grass at the old Cline place with Joli, roses blooming and bees buzzing all over. That day was like a day out of time, frozen fast. I was a girl again, that day. Joli and me were like girls together. I started telling her some of the old stories. It's funny how clear I can recall them. It is like they sit in a clear calm place in my head that I never even knew was in there. I told Mutsmag, Old Dry Fry, and how Jack fooled the smart red fox. Joli left a few days later, crying, mad at me for sending her away. Oakley drove her into town.

Then came fall, then winter, one of the hardest winters we have ever had, and I lost the baby I was carrying then, that day last summer when Joli and me went up Hell Mountain and sat in the grass. It was a boy, we buried him up on Pilgrim Knob.

And now for Oakley. The statue of Oakley is always working. Its back is always bent, its face is always turned away. For it aint no way to make a living from a farm. And you know, I must of <u>knowed</u> that somehow, it must of been down in my mind the same as those stories are, in the still place where you just know things. I must of knowed it from childhood, from watching it kill Daddy first, then Momma. But that is the thing about being young—you never think that what happened to anybody else might happen to you, too. Your life is your own life, that's how you think, and you are always so different. You never listen to anybody else, nor learn from what befalls them. And the years go so fast—oh lord, it seems like yesterday that we were plowing this field for the first time with Sal, who has been dead now seven years. It seems like yesterday that me and Oakley planted those taters in the dark of the moon. Well, we still plant them that time of the month. And Oakley still gets a deal of pleasure from this land, moreso than me, for when his work is done of an evening then it is <u>done</u>, for he don't have to mend the clothes or can the corn or feed the baby. I don't mean to sound like he lays around, neither—not like some. Oakley's statue is bent over like I said, working. But his face is turned away. So it would be hard at first to say what he might be doing, for he don't talk much and as times have got harder and harder, he has turned his hand to many a extry job. So he has lost the love of it that he used to have.

For instance, we don't grow cane now, as it was a pleasure crop. In the fall when it got ripe, Ray Fox Senior and Delphi Rolette would come up here and help Oakley cut it, and then cut the stalks out of the blades. You know it has the prettiest spike of red seeds that stand at the top of the stalk when the cane is ready— oh you remember, Silvaney, don't you? We used to grow cane up here in the old days too, before Daddy got sick, when we were little. And you and me and Beulah and Ethel would take those spikes and stick them in our hair for fancy hats. Well, Joli and Martha done the same, and Ethel got us to save her a pile of them to take down to sell in the store. She says that people in town will use them for decoration! I can't see that. But Ethel has got a good eye for what will sell. Ethel can sell anything, Stoney says. He says she could sell a bucket of mud if she took it in mind to, and I reckon she could! Anyway, we used to cut the stalks and save the spikes for Ethel, and borry the cane mill from Mister Gurney on Dogleg Branch, and then the men would dig the ditch and place rocks from the creek along the sides to hold it, and cut up wood to feed the fire, and then I'd scour the vat and we'd haul it in place, and word would go out everywhere—

A big stir-off!

Early that next day, Oakley would hitch up Sal and we'd all take turns walking her around and around while the mill crushed the cane and the green juice ran out in the trough. We carried it bucket by bucket to the vat, and Oakley started boiling it. It takes nearabout a day to boil it down. Meanwhile folks came from far and wide with their jars and bowls, to take some home. The children skittered like waterbugs all over the place, real excited, darting in to the fire to skim off the yellow foam with a spoon. They'd eat it till they got sick! We had fiddling too, and singing, and a lot of drinking, and dinner on the ground. We'd come out with about 8 gallons of molasseys, when all was said and done.

Not enough, Oakley says now, to warrant so much time and trouble, for then we would split those molasseys with the Rolettes and Oakley's daddy, of course. So after a while when times got hard, we stopped putting in the cane patch. But I miss it. I miss the stir-offs, and storebought molasseys is not the same. I loved the taste of that hot yellow foam and the ginger biskits that Edith Fox used to make with those molasseys, and I loved the notion of a day so different from all the rest.

You know what Granny used to call molasseys? the long sweetening.

Reach me some of that long sweetening, honey, she'd say at the breakfast table. I can just hear her now.

So we don't hold the stir-off any more. Too much trouble, Oakley says, turning his face away.

But I remember so well one night in October when we had

been back up here for about four years, we held it on the night of a big full moon—we had got going late because Sal had busted one of her sweeps—that is the long pole you hitch the mule up to—and so it was well into the night when the molasseys got boiled down good and thick. Oakley was there by the fire, stirring it with a long wood paddle and laughing at some men that had gathered around drinking. His face was red in the firelight, and the moon was red too when it come up at last over the top of Bethel Mountain. It was a windy, chilly night. I stood right outside the firelight, watching. Early Cook, who was a real old man by then and has passed on since, Early sat right up close to the fire in our daddy's ladderback chair and ate out of a vat with a tiny little spoon. He was so busy eating that he never once cracked a smile at the stories told. But Oakley! Oakley was laughing and laughing, stirring those molasseys. Then all of a sudden he looked around. His face got bright and full of yearning in the light.

Ivy, he called.

I hung back watching, I don't know why. Oakley looked from face to face around the stir vat.

Dreama, do you know where Ivy is? He asked his sister who has always been a little bit hateful to me purely out of spite, since she loves Oakley so.

No, Dreama said.

Ivy, Oakley hollered. Ivy! He hollered real loud and then I came running and Oakley caught me up and kissed me on the mouth right there in front of Dreama and his daddy. But I could feel him shaking under his old wool shirt.

Oakley, whatever's the matter? I said.

I lost you for a minute, Oakley said. He held me tight.

We made us a baby that night I believe, a baby which did not come to term and is buried now up on Pilgrim Knob, that was the first one we buried up there. Now I have got two little babies on Pilgrim Knob. I never gave them a name. But I remember losing them and getting them both, I remember everything. I remember the fire and the moon and Oakley's face, and exactly how we made that first little dead baby that very night, what I have come to call in my mind, the night of the long sweetening. It is like a curse, to remember as good as I do.

So you see why I am sad that we have stopped the stir-offs.

And you see that it was not always like this, with Oakley's face turned away.

But he has had a lot to contend with, it is true. For a man that likes farming as much as Oakley does, not to be able to do much good at it is awful. But it is not you, I keep trying to tell him. It is the times. It is the economy. We did good to get out of the mines when we did, that's a fact. It is worse over there. Why it used to be that a man couldn't make but a dollar a day in the mines, and the days they could work was precious few. It is a mighty big difference between the old days—those boom days— and these sorry times now. People from the coal camps are moving out in droves, going to Detroit, going back home to stay with their relatives and try to farm again. Like us. But they have mostly forgot how to do it, and so there's lots that are worse off than we are. At least we got out while the getting was good, which I keep telling Oakley and it is true.

Violet and R.T. are still up in West Virginia with the union, it is no telling when they will ever come back down here. So it looks like we have got Violet's Martha for good and I am so glad. Martha is simple but she's a fine hand to help out, I don't know what I would do without her. Martha runs and hides if a stranger comes up the holler, but she will come when you call her out. And loves a baby! She is so good to LuIda and little Maudy.

Oakley says, The depression dont make no difference up here. May be he is right too. But he and others have turned their hands to trapping and hunting sang these last years. Trapping pays pretty good, you would be surprised. A muskrat will bring a dollar, a mink up to 12 or 15. Gray foxes are easy to catch, but a red fox is hard to get and brings up to forty. A couple years back, Oakley got a red fox and didnt tell me, and came back from town with a new blue dress for me. He had picked it out himself at the Family Shop. It was blue velvet, too short and real impractical, but I never said a word, except Thank you. Oakley uses double spring traps because if you shoot, you mess up the hide. He is good at trapping. Most men around here, they wont do it despite of the money, they have not got the patience. They like to shoot too good. And you have to skin whatever you get, and case the hide. It takes time. It is the kind of work Oakley is good at, and likes. Oakley moves slow. He has got all the time in the world. The better you case the hide, the better grade you will get on it from the companies. Mostly Oakley takes his hides down to Ethel and Stoney's store and they pack them off to Sears Roebuck for him.

He goes after sang too, mostly in October when the leaves turn yellow so you can find it. Not that it is easy even then. There's some folks will follow others, to see where they get their sang. I have heard tell of one man leading another astray apurpose, so as not to let on where his secret place is. A man is mighty close-lipped on where he finds his sang. For a big bunch of it will bring a pickup load of meal and flour, bacon and salt and other goods. Just to look at it, you wouldn't think it would be worth a penny. It is a no-account plant with three large leaves and two littluns. But it is the root they use, and the root is shaped like a human body, like a little man. It gives me the creeps. It is the Chinese people that want it, lord knows what they do with it. Granny used to boil up sang to clear out your throat if you had a roomy cough as I recall, and also she said it would cheer the heart, comfort the bowels, and help the memory. Well, lord knows I don't need no help with the memory! My memory works overtime anyway. I just can't bring myself to boil up any sang, because I think about all those creepy little Chinese people liking it so, and somehow this puts me plum off of it. I feel like it is foreign stuff. So when Oakley has been out sanging, I tell him, Sell it all.

And you know, now as I am writing all this down, I wonder if this is what has made Oakley turn his face away, him going off by himself so much up in the mountains after hides and sang. For a man can lose the habit of talk and the habit of looking at you. Oakley looks down at his hands, whittling. A man can work so hard he gets caught way down inside of himself.

Another thing Oakley does is go around on carpenter work, particularly in the winter, building steps for some and sheds for others, and fences and gates, and what not. But you have got to watch him on this because he is like to do it for free, and will for sure if it is a widder woman or somebody bad off in any way, or somebody in his church. And while it is true that Oakley would give you the shirt off his back, it is also true that he would give the shirt off his back to anybody. This makes me feel bad. And I feel like Oakley works so hard, and stays so busy, that he has not got time for me! If he's not working, he's going to church. Ever time they crack the door now, there goes Oakley.

Come on and go with me Ivy, he says. Martha can keep the babies. You can't go if you are carrying a baby, of course. So I have got out of it a lot, that way! So sometimes now I go and sometimes I don't, but I'll tell you, I can't tell the difference. I swear I can't. I would not say this to another soul, Silvaney. It don't make me feel better nor worse, to go to church, except I get tickled sometimes at this Reverend Ancil Collins whose idea is that you have to get shut of your actual mind when you preach, just open your mouth and it will all come to you. He throws the Bible down on the floor and wherever it comes open, he takes his text. I was thinking the other day, I would love to know what Mister Brown would think of that! For he was a preacher too.

But I have not thought of Mister Brown in years and years, and thinking about him and her has made me weepy and given me the all-overs. For they were young when they lived here, and I remember I thought they were so old. Well, I am old now! I am older than they were then. It does not seem possible.

And sometimes I feel <u>so</u> old. I would a lots rather sit on the porch and think and look out at the world, than to go to church. I don't know why I have never got the hang of it. I guess the most religious thing about me is that I do say my prayers when I go to bed, you remember that little prayer our momma taught us which she learned in Rich Valley as a child. <u>Now I lay me down to sleep, I pray the lord my soul to keep, if I should die before I wake, I pray the lord my soul to take.</u> Do you still say this too? I think it is such a pretty prayer. But I would just as soon sit in the breezeway looking out at Bethel Mountain, as to go to church. I would just as soon sink into this soft warm darkness where I have been for years. I will rock my sweet Maudy and hum perhaps, and watch LuIda play with this babydoll that Miss Torrington sent, it has big blue glass eyes like marbles, and eyelids that open and close. LuIda is so cute with her babydoll. It is like, she's got her baby, and I've got mine. I don't know where Bill and Danny Ray are. Up to no good, I reckon, I can't keep up with those boys! In fact I can't keep up with a thing it seems like. Oakley ought to take more of a hand with the boys. I can hear Martha singing in the kitchen. But if I was to go in there, she'd shut up. She won't sing if you are in there with her. Martha loves the radio down at Ethel's and will sit by it for hours, and then can sing anything she hears on it, all the way through, and remember all the words. You can hear her singing all over the house. Yet if you ask Martha what month it is, she hangs her head and doesn't know. She sings so pretty now. My back hurts. It may be that I am going to start bleeding, whenever I bleed I get the blues.

Oh Silvaney. Silvaney. I recall one Sunday about a year ago when I was sitting here, Oakley was gone to church all day, to a baptizing I think, and when he came home he sat in that chair and we looked at Bethel Mountain together which we have done so many years and Oakley said, Ivy, you can look out on that Creation and know there is a God. I reached over and got his hand and held it. I couldn't see his face. And I couldn't see God's face neither.

But now, Silvaney, now we sit and watch the lights on Bethel Mountain twinkling like fairy lamps through this blue haze. I feel like there's a big change coming on somehow, when I look down this holler and see light. It makes me feel all electrified, myself! But it ain't got up here yet. So I remain

Your loving sister,
Ivy.

Dear Ethel,

Now that Joli has gone off to the Radford Normal Institute we want to tell you again, thanks for keeping her in town for high school, for I feel to the bottom of my soul that it is a good thing. I am not surprised that the state is sending her to college, neither. I have always said, Joli is real smart. And didn't she look pretty in her cap and gown? and just so solem, like a little owl. I thought my heart would bust. She was proud, too, you could tell. It will be such a good thing for her, in the long run. The hardest thing for her was leaving Martha. But Martha don't mind, as I have tried to tell Joli. Martha is real happy to be with you when you're here, but when you're not here, she don't notice. Martha has not got a sense of the passage of time, that's how she stays so happy. Five minutes or five years, it is all the same to her. Well, it is not the same to us. We still miss Joli real bad—especially Oakley who has a little game he always played with her when she was small. Every night he would say, Well, how is my little squirrel? and Joli would make a squirrel noise. Or, How is my old cow? and Joli would go, Moo. They have played this game for years and years. So at graduation, that is why I cried when Oakley went up and said, How is my little kitty cat? and Joli said Meow. And everybody else was laughing but I was in tears. Well, that is what was the matter with me!

Ethel, I guess you would think that when a woman has a lot of children, then each one means a little less. It is not so. Children will swell up your heart. I know you say you are glad that you and Stoney have not had none of your own, that hisn have been enough of a headache, but I would bet it is not true, Ethel. You just talk big, in my opinion. But you are as soft as a featherbed underneath.

Speaking of Joli's graduation, you know what I was thinking of? I would of given anything if Beulah could of been there. I think she would of been so proud too, it is the kind of thing that Beulah always wanted for us all. I know you say, Good riddance! but I can not. I wish so much that Beulah would send us a postcard at least and let us know where they have moved to.

Well, I am still right here! I reckon she knows it. She can get ahold of me anytime she wants, or you either one.

We are sorry to hear that Stoney is not feeling too good. I am not feeling too good myself. I don't know what gets into me sometimes. I am just wearing down, I reckon. Like yesterday, I was churning the milk which I always do, and all of a sudden I thought, Now I wonder how many times I have churned up butter in this churn? A thousand times? a million times? For it was Momma's churn before it was mine. I have done it so much that I don't even think about doing it any more. I don't even notice what I am doing. Nor making the butter into pats, nor stamping them down, nor cleaning the churn. And the minute I started noticing, and thinking about it, the paddle broke. I left it laying right there on the porch. I turned out the clabber into the hog pen, which I have never done before—I reckon the pigs were in hog heaven! Then I went in and laid down on the bed in the middle of the day! But I did not sleep. I laid there wide awake until the boys got home from school, then I got up and acted like nothing had happened. Well, nothing had! Or, nothing that you can put your finger on, nothing that you can name.

Then Oakley came in and cut me a new paddle and this morning I was churning again. I reckon that this new paddle will last me twenty years at least, I know the old one did. It seems like I can see the little pats of butter stretched out from here to yonder, a long yellow line. Don't you remember the story about little black Sambo, that ate up so much butter?

Lord, Ethel.

May be I am having the Change of Life early.

I will see you soon I reckon because Oakley says he is going to start him some hives, so we will be coming down to Home Creek to get up with that Breeding man that courses the bees, and then we will ride over and see you. I hope Stoney will be feeling better by then. Edith Fox always makes boiled custard for those that are weak in heart, you might give Stoney some. Thank you again for keeping Joli, I hope you have given her some good sense too! I remain

Your sister,
Ivy Fox.

July 6, 1940

Dear Silvaney,

You are the only one I can tell this to, for I know you will not tell a soul. You can <u>not.</u> But oh Silvaney, something awful is about to happen here.

And it looks like I can't do nothing about it.

It is a funny thing how much you have been in my mind, even before this started. I have been thinking about you lately. I don't even know if you recall how you used to not sleep good, nor eat, and run through the woods of a night with a light in your eye? And this used to scare me.

But now I must say, <u>I have these feelings.</u> And I too lie awake in the night with a strange pounding heart, I have to get up and walk a little. I don't know what has got into me, and I have been wondering—does this run in the family? For my boy Danny Ray is as wild as a buck and into everything, not like his brother Bill, nor like Oakley. For Oakley is a saint in this world, he has got no idea of what I am feeling. I won't tell him. I keep thinking, <u>This will pass. This too will pass.</u> And then I will be just plain Ivy again and not like I am now, somebody I don't know with my body took up by something wild I can not name.

Oh Silvaney. Those days when I sank into the easy darkness

took their toll. It is like I went so far I scared myself, and now I have to come back up. It is like I've had an electric shock. So now I am so much alive, I am tingling. I believe I know how you felt, Silvaney. For the first time, I know. I am on fire. I can feel it running through my veins and out my fingers. I feel if I touch kindling, it will light. I feel like fire itself. And I have felt this way now for several months, so I know it isn't Him. You see what I am saying? I felt this way before he ever came, before I ever saw Him. But in the long run Silvaney that may not matter, for he has been here two times now.

It is happening.

And yet you know that I love Oakley. He is my life. I love this farm, and these children, and Oakley, with all my heart. But there is something about a man that is <u>too good</u> which will drive you crazy, you can't hardly stand it. It makes you want to run or scream or roll down the hill in the leaves the way we used to do, never checking for rocks, nor thinking where we might land. It makes you want to dance in the thunderstorm like we danced up on Pilgrim Knob. For a long time I thought I was old, Silvaney. I sat in my chair in the breezeway like Momma sat in hers, feeling old.

But now I am on fire.

His name is Honey Breeding.

He got this name because he is a bee man. So I don't even know his given name. But he is a cousin to the Breedings that live now in the house on Home Creek where the Conaways used to live, next to Delphi and Reva.

Oakley—poor Oakley!—brought him up here. We had gone into town about a week before, and left word with Honey Breeding's people for him to come, and told him to get in touch. In the meantime Oakley made us some beegum hives which is just the kind of thing he likes to do. He went and looked at the Breedings hives to see how to do it. Then he told the kids he'd give a quarter to the one that could find a hollow beegum tree first, and they commenced to looking, and Bill found it and got the quarter. The beegum tree stood just above the treeline on Pilgrim Knob. Oakley took the boys up there when he cut it down. They used the old crosscut saw. It took a morning. I could hear them up there doing it while I stayed in the yard with LuIda and little Maudy. And sure enough about suppertime, they all came down dragging one of the beegums. This was a long section, hollow, right out of the tree. They were all tuckered out. The next day they cut it in two and made our beegums. Oakley bored four holes up close to the top of each one, and put two sticks in there to form a cross. The bees would make their brood comb on these sticks, Oakley said. I remember him telling me this.

Oakley seemed real sweet to me that afternoon, real young, drilling those holes. He was all excited about the bees. It is the kind of work he likes to do, close work in wood, where things can be made to fit exactly. It is more satisfying than farming I guess where you can't say if it will rain or not nor tell the price of tobacco.

Hand me that level, he'd say to the twins. Or, Sand this off. By the end of the day, we had the two prettiest beegum hives in Buchanan County. Oakley had put them up on a footing, to keep them dry, and built them both a heading, and a little slanted roof. He put them out back of the house in the orchard so the bees could get at the apple blossoms.

Along about dark, Oakley stood back and put his hands on his hips, which always means he is pleased with his work.

Now for the bees, he said.

At dinnertime, he explained to the kids what a bee man does. Now this here bee man, Oakley started, eating fried chicken. I remember it very well because me and Martha had killed a chicken that afternoon. She wrung the neck which I can't stand to do and she is good at. He don't live noplace. He don't have a home, said Oakley.

Aw Daddy, said Bill.

Nosir, that's a fact, said Oakley. Reach me another one of them wings. I love a wing. He winked at Martha and she passed him the whole platter. Oakley pinched me on the butt. Good chicken, he said. Oakley had not paid me so much mind in a while. He had got all worked up over his beegums, he had come outside of himself. And he is a fine man. It is just that you forget it sometimes, living with a man for years and years. It goes the other way too of course. A woman can get to be a habit as much as a man.

I slapped his hand away. Get on, I said, but I saw his eyes light up, I knew he would roll on me later and I was all on fire, eat up with fire as I mentioned, but not for that. Oakley has got to where he never talks nor pets me any, just does it and goes to sleep, while I lay there in the darkness immaginning god knows what, immaginning stars. I lay awake like that sometimes for hours.

Bill and Danny Ray were giggling.

What does the bee man do? Martha looked up from feeding sweet potatos to Maudy. Sometimes, Martha will surprise you.

He goes away back in the woods and finds a bee tree, Oakley said. Then he cuts it down and catches the swarm and brings it to your house and puts it in your hive.

Don't he get stung? Bill wanted to know.

Bees won't sting a bee man, Oakley said. He don't even wear a hat.

Dad-dy—Bill said. Bill is the smart one.

Oakley just grinned at him. It's a fact, he said. But if you was to try it, they'd liable to sting you to death. So you stay in the house now, you hear me, when he comes around.

Yessir, Danny Ray and Bill both said, but I will tell you right now that there is no way in hell to keep Danny Ray in or out of anyplace atall that he don't fancy. You can forget it.

Well, when is he coming? I asked. I put Maudy back down on the floor where she always goes straight for the dog, it is real sweet how he acts with her.

May be tomorry, Oakley said. Or it may be next week. He'll come up here whenever he catches us a hiveful of bees, he said.

Wait a minute, Bill said. Don't he do anything else? Don't he have to farm?

Nope, said Oakley. He goes around these mountains place to place, and don't stay nowhere long. There's always somebody needing bees, or needing to split a hive.

What's that? asked Bill.

You'll see soon enough, Oakley said. Have you all got any more of that chicken? he asked me, and I got him some. Oakley is sweet. What is going to happen is all my fault, but I can't help it. I can't be no better. I can't do no different, either, I swear it.

Is this bee man married? I asked all of a sudden to my surprise, and Oakley busts out laughing. Hell no he aint married, he says. He roams these hills like a coonhound, what I hear. I hear that he has daddied him some babies here and there though. Oakley winked at me. I could tell what he had on his mind, and we did it later of course, after Martha and me had done up all the dishes and bathed the babies and got the other kids to bed. Oakley sat on the breezeway smoking his pipe and staring out at the rural electrification, all this time. As soon as I sat down he reached for me but I jumped like a shot when he touched me. What ails you, Ivy? he says.

And I say, <u>Nothing.</u>

For it is not worth telling. It is not worth it to try to say how I want to scream all the time or when I look out at the mountains I want to reach out and rip them all away leaving only the flat hard sudden sky. That is crazy. So I didn't say any of this. We went to bed and did it, and the next day, Honey Breeding came.

I was down in the springhouse.

Now I have to explain this. When you're down in the springhouse, your eyes get set to the gloom. Oakley built this little house right down in the creek two years back and cut out the steps going down here where it's so steep.

And I love it here! Honeysuckle vines have grown up all over the bushes along the path, and wild white roses all down the steps. Sometimes I go down there just to catch my breath. It is like another world. Well, we had been looking for the bee man to come all day, but he had not, so we had gone on about our business and it had got to be nearabout evening again and Oakley had gone off to help his daddy with a load of bricks and I had gone down in the springhouse to take some butter. I had little LuIda with me, she loves the creek. She always paddles her hands in the water while I do whatever I need to. It's hard to get her to start back. So I had ahold of LuIda's hand and we were climbing the steep stone steps. The air down there is cool and green, it has to come down through so many leaves. The steps are cold, wet. I always go down them barefooted, it feels so good.

<u>Mam?</u>

He stood at the top of the steps, outlined against the sun.

<u>Mam?</u> he said it again. He has a soft low pretty voice that sounds like it's right in your ear even when it's not.

<u>What?</u> I said, putting my hand up to my eyes to try to see better. But the sun was a blaze behind his head, and I could not. The sun shot out in rays behind his head. LuIda started crying. She grabbed my knees and held on tight, and then I couldn't walk either.

<u>What is it?</u> I said.

<u>Where is your beegums, mam?</u> he said most polite. <u>I've got you a swarm up here in a sack.</u>

<u>Just a minute,</u> I said.

He stood right there while I made my way, pulling LuIda who cried and cried. He had somehow spooked her. I was out of breath when we got to the top.

You must be Honey Breeding, I said. My husband's been looking for you.

He might be sorry he found me. Honey Breeding was looking hard at me. Now I was right at the top of the steps, but he never moved. He stood in my way with his arms folded across his chest.

I came up on a level with him. He is not a big man, Silvaney, not near as big as Oakley. He is skinny, wiry, with pale thick curly gold hair on his head and thick gold eyebrows that nearabout grow together, and hair all over him like spun gold on his folded forearms. I thought about Rapunzel spinning gold. I thought about the Brownies in the McGuffey Reader. For Honey Breeding did not seem quite real. He seemed more like a woods creature fetched up somehow from the forest, created out of fancy, on a whim. Honey Breeding seemed like a man that I had made up in the cool dark springhouse, like a man I had immaginned until he came true. He rocked back and forth on the balls of his feet, grinning at me. His hair held all the sun. His teeth were real white. Animal teeth. I remembered Oakley saying, A bee man don't have no home. His eyes were pale blue. He was grinning at me. I could not breathe.

Let me pass, I said, but I couldn't help smiling.

Why yes mam, Honey Breeding said like a gentleman.

LuIda chose this very moment to cry even harder, clinging onto my legs. Children—sometimes it's hard to figure what gets into them. Mostly, LuIda is real even tempered.

Honey Breeding stood back a little, and bowed like a man in a play.

Now let me tell you what happened.

When I passed close by him, it was like a current jumped from him to me—or me to him and back, maybe. I don't know. Or it was like we both had it in us, and it just leaped out when we met, out of both of us—it arched between us through the leafy air. Oh lord, I think I thought. LuIda pulled on my legs then and I slipped on the rocks and nearly fell. Oakley and the boys carried all these rocks, for the steps and the springhouse.

Honey Breeding caught my elbow. Careful now, he said. His voice ran all through me like a song.

And then I was up on hard level ground again, and he stood staring. LuIda cried. I stared back, I lost myself down in his eyes, I don't believe I have ever seen eyes so light in a full grown man.

They are like cateyes. Granny used to have a cat with eyes like that.

The beegums are in the orchard back of the house, I said finally. But it didn't matter what I said.

All right, I think he said. He was looking at me. LuIda was crying. I picked her up all of a sudden and ran for the house, I could hear him laughing behind me, a nice laugh, a big laugh, like he had all the time in the world. I ran in the house and tore around doing first one thing and then another.

What has got into you? Martha asked me. Even Martha noticed. But I couldn't say.

Then directly he came by the house carrying his sack, and went up in the orchard among the blossoms. It is the best time in the world to start a beegum, Oakley had said. Early summer. The orchard was a sea of pale pink flowers, and Honey Breeding walked right through them like he owned it, swinging his sack. He was whistling. He could whistle like a bird!

That is the bee man, I told Martha. We watched him out the back door.

Honey Breeding laid down his sack in the high grass next to the beegums. Then he looked all around the orchard. He looked up at the house and nodded, as if he just knew we were watching him! This made me mad as fire. He took the head off one of the beegums and set it down on the ground. Then he untied the neck of his sack and reached down in there and came up with a big piece of dripping honeycomb and placed it down in the beegum, on those cross sticks. Then he put the head back on the beegum and licked his fingers. By then, some bees had got out of the sack. They were flying circles around and around his head. But Honey Breeding didn't wear a hat. He didn't have no gloves. He licked his hands again and looked back at the house, somehow he just knew we were watching. Then he grabbled around down in the bag for a little bit and came up with the Queen I reckon, or leastways with some bees he set right in the hole. He let the other ones go. They went buzzing around and around the beegum, around Honey Breeding. He grinned up the hill at us—at the house, at the window. He waved. He knew I was in there watching.

I'll be back, he called. You tell him. I'll be back.

By the next morning, those bees had all crawled in the beegum hive and settled. Oakley was tickled to death. But Danny Ray got stung real bad, three places, because he went down there when they were still swarming. We told him not to but he went anyway. I put soda on his bee stings, then tobacco, to take the fire out.

Did he say when he was coming back? Oakley asked, and I said, No. But he said he would. He just said he'd be here, I said.

And as for me, I was in a fever. First I'd have a cold sweat, and then I'd have a hot flash. I got to thinking, This must be the change of life. It must be. And I went about my days like I was walking through a dream, like the days were all happening under water, and I was swimming through them. It reminded me of when Daddy used to take us swimming down in the Levisa River, Silvaney, you remember. You could open your eyes under water and see the big fish. I thought about getting Oakley to take me and the kids down there like we used to, but it was too early in the year I decided, and besides—I was afraid I'd miss him.

I didn't even leave the house, for fear I'd miss him.

Which I did not.

It was the following Sunday that he came. Oakley had gone off to church taking Bill and Danny Ray with him. I myself had got out of going because I had to stay home and cook. All of Oakley's folks were coming up Sugar Fork for dinner after church, so I was cooking a ham and Martha was devilling eggs. By then it was flat out summer, getting hot. I was sitting out in the breezeway wearing nought but a shift, I had ironed my dress to put on when it got closer to the time for church to let out, and why not? Nobody up here but women and children. I sat in the breezeway rocking in my shift. I leaned back and closed my eyes. I was real tired. I'd been up since daylight, making potato salad.

Thinking about me? he said.

It was like he took shape in my mind. I sat bolt upright.

Lord, no, I said. What are you doing over here today? At first I was mad as could be, but then I found I was grinning at him. He stood there real easy, smiling, with one hand on the rail.

Come on and go with me this time, he said. It ain't far.

All right, I said. I stood up and hollered to Martha that I would be back directly, and left. Just like that. As easy as pie. I walked off down the path in my shift without thinking a thing about it, following Honey Breeding.

It was full June, the prettiest day.

How are you called? he said once, and I said, Ivy.

Well Ivy, he said, We are going right down here by the creek,

I seen some bees last time as I was leaving. You all are lucky, he said. This time it is going to be real easy.

We followed close by Sugar Fork, near where Granny and me had sat, and then when the path started down the holler and the creek went on, we went along by the creek. We went with it until it widened out into a little pool. Now I guess this pool has been here all along, but I can't swear it. It seems to me like I would know any pool along this creek, but I'll swear, I had never seen this one before.

Sit down, Honey said, pointing at a big flat rock in the sun by the pool, and I did.

Take your hair down, he said next, and I reached up and pulled out the pins. I have been wanting to cut my hair but Oakley won't have it, he says it's against his religion for a woman to cut her hair. Sometimes I sneak and trim it, but not so as he can tell. Anyway it is real long now and for the first time, that day on the rock, I was glad. I sat on the big warm rock with my hair falling all down around my shoulders. He had not looked at me yet. He had him a tub, a sack, some other things. The light came up from the creek and dazzled in my eyes, I could not see. It was dead on noon.

Bees love water, Honey said.

He took some corncobs soaked in honey out of the tub and put them on another rock, and then came and sat down next to me. We were waiting. While we waited, he fooled with my hair and my neck. I could not breathe. He never kissed me. But the funny thing is, it was like I had known him. For ever, for always, years and years and years.

We were old hat, him and me.

First one bee came to light on the corncob, then another, then another, more, until the corncobs were thick with bees, bees lighting, flying up, flying down, buzzing, buzzing. It made me dizzy.

Wait now, Honey said. He got up and they scattered, buzzing like crazy, and he followed them into the woods, not too far. I could hear him in the underbrush. Then I didn't hear him, and I figured he had found the bee tree. And sure enough, out he came after a while, with his swarming sack and the bees all around his head.

Stay back, he said. Let me go first.

I stood up like I was still in a dream. I had to shake my head to clear it. The sun off the water was blinding. I couldn't tell if I had been there for minutes or hours. I didn't care. I knew that

Oakley's whole family was coming for Sunday dinner but I didn't care, I couldn't think about it. I followed him back up the hill, not thinking about it, not caring, I followed him past the house where Martha stood in the breezeway holding Maudy, staring out at us. What was she thinking? What does she know? Martha's eyes are big and dark, like her mother's. Maudy waved to us, she loves to wave. I followed Honey Breeding around the side of the house and LuIda came down off the porch and followed us too, through the orchard, dragging her blanket that she carries everyplace. I believe it used to be Beulah's. The orchard smelled so sweet. You stay back, he said. We sat in the grass and I leaned back on my elbows and looked up. It was like a ceiling of swaying frothy pink blooms, like a moving ocean of foam. LuIda lay curled up on her blanket. She sang a little song. I watched while Honey settled the second swarm in the second hive. He worked fast, yet he never seemed to hurry. And he never wasted a move, that I could see. Above us was pink flowers, blue sky, sun. It was getting real hot, even there in the orchard. Maybe I slept for a minute. It was like I was in a dream.

Ivy, he said. Wake up. I'm going.

I looked up and he stood there right in front of me. He held out his hand and I took it. He pulled me up. We stood there real close to each other but not touching. We are exactly the same size. It's like he is me, some way, or I am him. All he did was look at me, nobody has ever looked at me like that before, or will again. I know this. Nobody.

I thought I would pass out, finally I had to look down. When I looked up, he was gone. Just like that, without a trace. I picked up LuIda and her blanket and walked back to the house thinking, I must make a picture. I must be a mess. With my hair straggling wild all down my back and grass stains on my shift.

Right before I got to the house, a bee stung me through my shift. It hurt like blazes.

I got in just before they all drove up. I could hear them down by the creek slamming the car doors, laughing and talking. Then I could hear them getting closer as they walked up the hill to the house. I was pinning up my hair when they got here.

Sweet heavy Edith Fox sat down in a chair and stretched out her legs, which are bad to swell. She started fanning herself. Hello there Ivy, she said. I have brung you some fried peach pies for dinner. Dreama, give her the pies. You look all thin and wore out, Edith told me.

Dreama handed me the paper sack and I took it on back to the kitchen and put the pies out on a plate. They looked real good. All of a sudden I was starving to death! I went ahead and took one and ate it in three bites with Dreama watching.

It ain't fair, Dreama said. You can eat all you want and you don't gain.

That is because I work all the time instead of living with Mama and Papa who do everything for me, I thought, but did not say it. For all of a sudden, I felt real sorry for Dreama, who is so pale and fat and hasn't got any eyebrows to speak of. Dreama will never feel as I felt this afternoon. Whether it is wrong or right she will never know it, never. She will be fat and bitter, and she will go to her grave this way. Dreama was married once, when she was real young, but he went off to the war and came back a different man. He shut her up in the wardrobe three or four times when he didn't like his dinner, and then he beat her with a mule harness and she ran home where she's been ever since. Oakley and Ray Junior went over there and liked to killed her husband. He left this county then and has been gone ever since. His name was Hubbard Looney. He has been a long time gone. Since then, Dreama has had some boyfriends, but she's too picky. This one's too lazy, that one's too fat, this one's got a gimpy leg. Now that she is well past 40, all the lines in Dreama's face go down. She gets harder and harder to please. The truth is, nobody can hold a candle up to Oakley or to Ray Senior, as far as Dreama is concerned. She doesn't really want a man. If you want a man, you can always get one, Geneva used to say. I believe this is true. They can tell when you want them, or when you don't. But Dreama still thinks she does. She was talking about a man from Saltville who is over here with the power company, that she had met at church.

Do you reckon I would run into him if I went into town myself to pay the light bill? Dreama asked, for they have got electricity now down on Home Creek, and I said, Well, I don't know. But then she said that his adam's apple sticks way out, which she hates in a man. She is so picky. I ate another peach pie. I put the ham and the potato salad and the devilled eggs out on the table. Every time I took a step, my bee sting hurt like crazy. But I didn't want to doctor it or tell anybody. I wanted to keep it a secret. Martha had already made the cornbread. I sent Billy down to the spring-house to get some more butter, and when he came back with it, I went out in the breezeway.

You all come on, I said.

Oakley always says the blessing at the table. But when his daddy is here, his daddy says the blessing and we all hold hands. That is how they do it down on Home Creek. So I held Oakley's hand on one side, his daddy's on the other. Oakley's daddy asked for rain, and peace in our time, and a good tobacco crop, and for Delphi Rolette, who has been real sick, to get better. Then he told God to say hey to Ray Junior in heaven, which he always says. Then he said, Make us ever mindful Lord of the needs and desires of others, in thy holy name we pray, amen, which is how he always ends a blessing. Ray Fox could have made a preacher. So could Oakley, of course. But I couldn't keep my eyes shut during the blessing. I couldn't stop thinking about Honey Breeding and how he had looked at me. As soon as Ray Senior was through, I raised up my head and helped everybody's plates and started eating like I was starved.

This is a mighty good ham, honey, Ray Fox Senior said, and I jumped a mile in my chair at the mention of his name.

Thank you sir, I said.

What all did you put on it? Edith asked, and I answered that I boiled it first, yesterday, then I put brown sugar and cider on it to bake it. I could hear my own voice talking but I didn't feel like it was me.

Well it sure is good, Edith said.

Thank you, Edith, I said. I kept thinking about Honey Breeding and how he stared. I could feel my bee sting swelling up beneath my skirt. It was starting to hurt real bad. The boys said they were through and could they go down the holler and play cowboys and Indians, and I said yes. I got up and got the jam cake from where I was keeping it down in the cold corner, away from the stove. Why, looky here! said Ray Senior. Those boys left too soon.

They can't sit still, I said. They'll get some when they come back. They will be back directly.

I don't like that Susie Ratliff, Dreama was saying about a woman at church. She is too stuck up.

I was rubbing my bee sting which was hurting. Then I looked up and found Oakley staring at me, with his calm brown eyes. You look kind of hot, Ivy, he said, or something.

I am okay, I said.

I was over at Maureen Gray's when she had a hot flash and shook like a leaf, Edith said. Can you pass me another peach pie? I ate another pie too. Oakley was watching me. I pulled up my dress and felt of the bee sting underneath the table, nobody could see me. Did I tell you what Bethy Rolette said to me when we were going in the door? Dreama asked her mother and her mother said, No. Well I can't believe I didn't tell you, Dreama said. Then she said, Bethy came right up behind me and said, Oh Dreama, you look so good from the back! Now, do you think I ought to be mad or not? Everybody was laughing, even Martha. Then Oakley was telling his daddy about the beehives. Maudy started crying in her bed. I stood up to go and get her. For a minute I just stood there though, and looked around the table. It was something like a hot flash, I think, though I did not shake like a leaf. Everything leaped up at me—Oakley's sweet face, his daddy's big wrinkled hands that never come clean, the shine off Edith's glasses, Dreama's wide white cheeks, Martha's dark pure eyes. Martha's black hair curls around her face, but Dreama and Edith both pull their hair straight back in tight little knots, it is their religion. I looked hard at everybody. Behind the table, out the open door, lay the orchard. I felt of my bee sting, secret under my skirt. I went to get Maudy. I just don't know what will happen.

Your sister,
Ivy.

July 21

Dear Oakley,

I am writing you this note to say that I have gone off on a little walk today. I will be back this evening. Do not worry about me as I remain your loving wife,

Ivy.

My dear Joli,

I do not know what you have heard about me by now, or what I can say

August 23, 1940

My dear Silvaney,

I was washing dishes when he came. I had the dishpan full of water, I was up to my elbows in soap. He came right in the front door without knocking and walked on through the house and came up behind me and poked me in the ribs. Gotcha, he said. I knew right away, without turning around, who it was. My heart has been beating too fast ever since I first saw him. When he came for me, it slowed down.

Hidy, I said, and he said, Hidy.

I turned around and looked at him good and he said, You are just as pretty as I remembered. But the cat had got my tongue, I couldn't say a thing. Martha was in there too, boiling water to scour the pans. She grinned at him. Hidy, he said to her, and she put her hand up to hide her mouth, she was giggling so. It was a bright hot day. Usually, Martha is scared of strangers.

I am going to borry the missus here for a hour or two, said Honey Breeding. I'll bring her back.

Martha giggled.

When is your old man coming home? he asked me. He never asked me whether I would go with him or not.

Before long, I said. Him and the boys have gone into town for some fence wire.

Well leave him a note, he said, and come on. We are going to take us a little walk.

I can't do that, I said.

Just take off that apron, he told me, and come on, and I did it.

I wrote Oakley a note and told Martha that I would be back after while. I could not afford to worry that she would tell Oakley who I had gone off with. I did it all like a dream. Here now, he said. He took my hand. He kept grinning at Martha who grinned back at him like she knew him some way, but she did not. They just hit it off, I reckon.

The paregoric is in the dresser drawer, I said to Martha, if you need to give Maudy some. It is in that little carved wooden box that Revel gave Momma. Maudy had a toothache.

Come on, Ivy, Honey said. I left the dishes in the sink and followed him out the back door past the lilac. Bye-bye, bye-bye, LuIda and Maudy called from the yard. They both love to say Bye-bye.

It was a bright hot afternoon.

Just where do you think we are going? I said, and Honey Breeding said, Up this hill.

So we set off on the path through the orchard, past the beegums, and then commenced to climbing Pilgrim Knob. Right here is where Momma used to keep her chickens, I said. I don't know how she did it. Ourn won't stay up here, they cluster around the house. But Momma's chickens were mountain chickens, you couldn't get them down to the house. If you carried them down, they'd run right back up here, I said. So we used to have to climb all the way up here to look for eggs, I said.

I reckon they were pretty hard to find, Honey said.

They were, I told him. Silvaney was the best one for finding eggs, that is my favorite sister Silvaney, she's gone from here now, I said. I have three sisters. Beulah lives up North now and Ethel lives down in Majestic with her husband, Stoney Branham. They run the store.

That's Branhams Merchandise? Honey asked me.

Yes it is, I said.

I've been in there, Honey said. There is a little old man that runs it, got kindly peppery hair and a moustache.

That is Stoney Branham, I said. He is a whole lot older than Ethel. My brother Victor works in there too. You might of seen him. He sits in the back a lot. He's real big and fat now, he lost his nerves in the war.

A lot of men done that, Honey Breeding said.

Did you go to the war? I asked.

I sure did, Honey said. His voice floated back to me over his shoulder. He pulled his shirttail up out of his pants.

Where did you go? I asked.

First I went to Germany, Honey said, and then I went to France.

We walked on. I had another older brother that died, I said, and then a little one that died young. And also I've got another one, Johnny, that I have not seen in a while that plays the piano, and yet one more that is making a preacher.

I couldn't believe I was talking so much, to a perfect stranger! My own voice sounded funny in my ears. It sounded rusty. I felt like I hadn't used it in such a long time except to say something like, The wooden paddle is broke, or Close the door.

See that rock? I said. My momma used to come up here and sit on it and cry.

What did she cry for? Honey asked.

Because my daddy was sick, I reckon, and things had not worked out like she thought.

They never do, Honey said. He walked on before me, up the path. His white shirt flapped in the wind, so white it was dazzling. I reckon it was new.

But she was a rich girl, I told him, who could of had a different life if she'd chose. Then I told him all about Momma and Daddy riding up Sugar Fork on Lightning, and about how Momma's daddy, my grandfather, came and took her back to him in death.

That's some story, Honey said, still walking. I was right behind him. And I wasn't one bit tired, or even out of breath. I told him all about Mrs. Brown and Revel too, while we walked up the mountain from Pilgrim Knob, and about my little dead babies buried over there. Right here is where you turn if you're going for chestnuts, I said. Victor, that's my brother I was telling you about that is in the store business now, he brung us all up here one time, and we fooled Garnie. That's the one that is preaching. I pointed to the path that forked off to the right, along the ridge. And there's a blackberry thicket over there. I came up here one time with Oakley when we were kids, I said. It was the first time he ever kissed me. I was talking about my own husband Oakley like he was somebody I scarcely knew! I couldn't believe it.

But we're going this way, Honey said, stepping off down the main trail.

Now I can't be gone too long, Honey, I told him. I felt giddy and crazy, climbing the mountain, I felt like a girl again. It seemed I was dropping years as I went, letting them fall there beside the trace, leaving them all behind me. I felt again like I had as a girl, light-headed, light-footed, running all over town. When I thought of my babies, I could see them real plain in my mind, their bright little faces like flowers, but it seemed to me that they were somebody else's babies, not mine. I was too young to have them. We walked on. Now we were not climbing so much, just walking the ridge. Honey went in front. A wind blew down from the mountain, in our faces, cooling us off. I was glad. This was the path that went to the burying ground. I hadn't been up here since Decoration Day. I said as much.

We came to the little bunch of scraggly pines where the trail forked again. That's the way to the burying ground, I told him.

Well, we ain't taking that path, he said. He went straight on, with me follering.

I reckon it was the wind picking up, but all of a sudden, I got a chill. I never have come up here, I said. I never have gone any further along this path. What's up here? I asked him. Where are we going, anyway?

Noplace in particular, Honey said. I just felt like walking.

I have never heard of such as that in all my life, I said. People around here walk to get someplace, and that is all.

Well, I am not from around here, Honey said.

Where are you from, then? I asked him.

Here and there, Honey said. Noplace particular.

You can't be from noplace, I said.

His laughter floated back on the wind. We were walking the top of the ridge now, above the treeline. The pines were all bent up, little and scrawny, and a low thick tangle of thorny bushes stretched away on both sides of the path. It was lots cooler. I knew I had never been up here before, yet suddenly it looked familiar. Maybe my Granny brought me up here looking for plants when I was little, I said.

There's not much in the way of plants to find, said Honey, once you get above the cliffs. I bet she never brung you this far.

We went on a ways, and I had to concede he was probably right. The ridge turned flat, almost like a meadow.

This here is what you call a bald, Honey said.

The bald was covered with little white flowers like stars, like a carpet of stars.

It sure is pretty, I said.

You sure are pretty, Honey said. But still, he had not turned to see me. Come on, he said. It's just a little ways.

What is? I asked.

Come on, he said.

He took my hand then and led me on through the flowers, over onto another path which stopped at the very edge of the mountain, on top of the highest cliff. From where we stood, we could see for miles. I thought I could see Sugar Fork but I couldn't be sure, there was lots and lots of hollers, and I saw them all, valley after valley, ridge on ridge, Bethel Mountain beyond—but now for the first time I could see over top of Bethel Mountain to another mountain, blue, purple, then mountain after mountain, rolling like the sea. It was so beautiful. A single twisted pine grew bravely up out of the rocks before us. Mile after mile of empty air stretched out behind it, the sky so blue, the sun so bright. And the wind, which kept on blowing all the time—now I recalled the famous endless wind on the top of Blue Star Mountain.

I know for sure I have never been up here, I said. I would remember it.

I bet you would, said Honey Breeding.

He dropped to the mossy ground and pulled me down beside him. See that hawk? He pointed to the right and I turned my head but when I did so, he kissed me. Mmmmmm, he said. What hawk? I said. Mmmmm, he said.

Oakley says you don't have a home, I told him.

I don't, said Honey.

But you keep your things down at the Breedings, I said.

Sometimes, he said. Some things. He was taking my hair down, unbuttoning my collar.

Tell me a story, I said.

What story? he asked me.

All about you, I said. Tell me all about you.

Nothing to tell, he said.

Tell me, I said. I am starved for stories.

Honey laughed real hard and sat up and looked out over the cliff. Well then Ivy, he said. Here is a story for you.

I laid back on the moss and closed my eyes.

Well I will tell you about my daddy and how he fell in love with a neighbor girl and came to a tragic end, Honey said. And this is how it happened. I was raised down in North Carolina, where all my father's people came from, in the shadow of the mountains. We had us a neighbor named Big Lute who had been to the far West of the state, and had spent a lot of time among the Cherokees. And then he came back home one day bringing a little baby girl, nobody knew where he got her, or who her mother was. And he brought in some Indian women to help him raise her. As she grew, she turned into the most beautiful girl in the county. Dark Catherine she was called. Well the story goes that my dad seen her only one time and fell in love so bad that he turned into a misery. She was just a girl, tended by Indians. And him a married man. He knew he couldn't have her, but he couldn't give her up. So he took to hunting a lot, going off to his camp in the woods, trying to forget her. Now I should say that he was a famous hunter, the most famous in that part of North Carolina. And he had two hound dogs that he was crazy about named Sally and Sam, that he always hunted with. Those were Plott hounds.

What's a Plott hound? I asked, for I had never heard of one.

It is a dog bred by old man Plott up on Grandfather Mountain, Honey said, and then I couldn't help laughing. I didn't care if he was lying or not. It seemed like years since I'd heard a story. I stretched out there on the moss, and the wind played over my face. It felt good.

Honey went on. Well, one night when he was out there at his cabin, a strange thing happened. A little old chicken came strutting in, and went right over by the fire, and ruffled up its feathers and started to dance, and bye and bye it swelled up to become an old woman. So these two Plott hounds, Sally and Sam, started barking like Kingdom come.

Tell your dogs to lie down, the old woman said to my father.

I can not make them mind, said he, for he was afraid of her.

Take this, she said, and she gave him a hair right out of her head. Tie them up with that, she said.

But he switched it and used a hair of his own instead, for he saw that the hair from her head moved in his hand. There, he said, lying.

Then as soon as she thought the dogs were tied up, she grabbed my daddy and started kissing him.

So Daddy commenced to holler and then the dogs jumped up and set upon her. These were two big severe bear dogs mind you, but she fought them tooth and nail. They fought in the cabin and out the door and down the side of the mountain, and finally the dogs ran her off. But she was a tough old lady, and it took considerable doing. It was bad luck, too—or so Daddy decided—because in the four days of hunting which him and the dogs done after that, they never saw a thing. No deer, no bear, no bird, nothing. It was unnatural. So after a bit, my daddy come on home all tuckered out.

But he walks in the house to find his old woman leaving, taking a chess pie, on her way out the door.

You are just in time, she said. Come on and go with me down to Big Lute's house, for his daughter Catherine is real sick and not expected to make it through the night. I'm taking this pie, she said.

Lord no! my daddy thought. So he got himself a snack and went along.

When Big Lute saw them coming, he came out and took the chess pie which he was fond of, and said he thanked them, but Catherine was so bad off that they couldn't see her. When Daddy carried on about this, Big Lute barred the door. But Daddy was crazy by then, and would not take NO for a answer. So he went out by the garden and pulled up a post and stove in the door with it.

And there she was—blackhaired and beautiful and raving mad. You could see that she was not long for this world. Daddy pulled the covers back and saw that her buttocks was plum tore off and her hips and legs were all tore up, and then he knew at once what had happened, that she had come to him in the shape of a hen and then in the shape of an old woman, and those Plott hounds had nearabout killed her. And he leaned over and whispered something in her ear.

Honey leaned over and kissed my ear and whispered something in it.

What? I said. I sat up.

We don't know, said Honey. She died that night. But he lived on and my mama bore him three sons and I am the third one. Everyone said that he was never the same after that. Then one night—after sitting at Dark Catherine's grave for hours—he walked up the hill behind our house and climbed the tallest oak tree there and crawled out on the stoutest branch, and hanged himself dead by the neck. That night there come an awful big storm, which is what always happens after a suicide. And after the storm passed and the morning light came, they found my daddy's body swinging with a smile on his face.

For in death he had joined her, I said. I felt like I was almost asleep.

Yes mam, said Honey Breeding.

And then what happened? I said.

Well then my mama, she died of the blues, and they farmed us boys out all over Kingdom come. The family I ended up living with, the old man tended bees, and he taught me the ways of them.

Is that the Breedings? I said.

That is some of them, Honey said.

And whatever happened to your brothers? I asked him.

My brother Bill is in the coal mines, Honey said, in Bluefield, West Virginia, but I have not heard a word about Roy in years and years.

That is like Beulah, I said.

And that aint all, Honey said, sounding very serious.

What? I asked him.

Ever time I see a sycamore tree, I have to run the other way as fast as my legs will go, Honey said.

Why? A thrill shot through me.

I get a big urge to hang, is why, he said. I reckon I take after Daddy.

Wait a minute! I sat up. You said it was a OAK tree, first! And now you are saying sycamore tree. I got to laughing. This is awful. I don't believe a word you are saying.

Well you said you wanted to hear a story. He was taking off my shirtwaist then and he got up and laid it real careful to the side.

Not that story, I said.

What story, then? He was playing with my titties.

The true story.

How are you going to know if it's the true story or not?

I knew he was teasing me. I will know, I said.

You will not, he said. And anyway, it don't matter. For you are a married woman, out here for the afternoon.

Married, I said after him.

Sugar Fork seemed far away, far off down the mountain. I leaned back and watched while he took off his pants. The sun was blinding me. I laid back while he did everything to me, everything. I watched the hawk gliding huge smooth circles out in the air. Now do this, he said, and I did. I had never even thought of doing such a thing before in all my life. I believe it's against the law. Then he stretched out on his back too, and closed his eyes and slept. I sat up on my elbow and watched him sleep. He had gold hair all over him.

I traced his thick blond eyebrows across his face. I loved him so much right then. I love you, I said.

He opened his bright pale eyes.

No you don't, he said. You just think you do. But this aint real, he said.

It is real, I said. I am here, aint I?

That's not what I mean, he said.

I love you, I told him again.

Don't love me, said Honey Breeding. Don't you dare.

I will if I want, I told him, which was true. So there! I got up and walked to the edge of the cliff and looked over. The wind lifted up my hair.

Honey sat up and shielded his eyes and looked at me. You are so beautiful, he said. You look like a Princess.

I'm too old to be a Princess, I said.

Then you look like a Queen. All of a sudden he got up and made a run at me. Gotcha, he called, and I leaped back at him. Gotcha back! I said. I believe it was the first time I had ever been naked in the sunshine in my life. I don't expect I will ever do it again, either. The sun seemed to burn into my whole body. But it felt wonderful. We played tag for a little while there on the bald on the top of Blue Star Mountain.

Fire on the mountain, fire in the sea—Honey ran back toward the bald—can't catch me!

But I am as big and as strong as he is, and I toppled him into the starry flowers where we laid face to face and leg to leg and toe to toe. He is just the same size as me. In fact I think he is me, and I am him, and it will be so forever and ever. What I did, I did it out of awful longing pure and simple. I did it out of love. Say what you will, and I don't care what anybody said then or might say now, it could not have happened otherwise. I had to do it, I had to have him. And even now I can close my eyes and see us laying naked in the flowers on the grassy bald, all tangled up together till you couldn't tell who was who. He reached down and grabbed my foot. Then he said, This little piggy went to market, this little piggy stayed home, this little piggy had root beer, this little piggy had none. This little piggy cried wee, wee, wee, all the way home. Then Honey rolled me over in the grass.

Speaking of home, he said, don't you forget about it.

Oh, I aint a-going home, I said. Then, that first time, he thought I was kidding.

He spread my hair out around me on the grass. You are the sweetest thing I ever saw, he said.

Sweeter than honey?

He was ticklish. Sweeter than honey, he said.

The sun had moved down lower in the sky over Bethel Mountain.

He was doing things to me with his tongue.

I said, I hear tell you're a ladies man.

What is that, a ladies man?

You know what a ladies man is.

Honey sat up then and I was sorry. I guess if the truth be told, I am more of a back door man, he said.

What do you mean, a back door man?

It is why you don't want to love me, Ivy, Honey said. A back door man is always going out the back door while the husband comes in the front.

What if she aint got no back door? I asked.

Ah, Honey said, grinning. Ah then, you are caught up Shit Creek! I'll tell you another story.

Is this story about you? I asked.

No honey, this story is not about me, Honey said. It is about a back door man, though. You will see what I mean. He got comfortable and started.

There was a man named Josh Raines that fell in with a married woman named Evangeline Matney, and he went home with her, and he was loving her up pretty good when they heard somebody pass the gate. Lord! this Josh Raines said, What'd I orter do? And she said, Hide in the scalding barrel. So he done it. Pretty soon in come the other feller, but it weren't her husband! It weren't no Mister Matney. It was a man named Long John Cates, is who it was, and he commenced to hugging and kissing and lollygagging all over Evangeline Matney. Then all of a sudden the gate slammed again, and this time it was her old man, Herman Matney. And so Long John Cates jumped back in his clothes real quick-like and did some fast thinking, and when Herman Matney walks in the door, he says, Well, hello there Mr. Matney! I just come over to borry your scalding barrel, we are aiming to butcher to-morry.

And Herman Matney didn't like the looks of things much, but he said, Well, there it is then, take it along.

When Long John picked it up, it was so dad blame heavy that

he liked to couldn't handle it, but he managed to roll it off down the road a ways, and then he stopped to rest.

He was congratulating himself some too, saying, Well, Long John, you sure did get out of that mess mighty slick, when all of a sudden Josh Raines pushed the top off the barrel and crope out! You sure did, Long John, he said, And I didn't do so terrible bad myself!

I got to laughing too hard to quit. It seemed like I had heard that story, or one like it, from Daddy—years and years ago. Honey Breeding was as good as Daddy or the lady sisters for telling tales. I rolled over laughing on the ground.

Then I thought of something and sat up. I just want you to tell me one thing, I said to Honey Breeding.

He said, What is that? His hair glowed gold in the sun.

Did you know me when first you saw me? I asked him. For I'll swear it on a Bible, I knew you.

What do you mean, he asked.

I don't know, I said.

He stared at me. Yes, he said. I watched him awhile longer. You put me in mind of something, I told him, for it was true.

What? He was picking the little starflowers and laying them out one by one in a row on the mossy ground.

I can't remember, I said. It is a poem.

A poem? He looked up. Sure enough?

I used to know a lot of poems, I said. I told you I took up with a schoolteacher that they had here one time, when I was young.

Shoot, Honey said. He was making a flower chain.

It was coming back to me then, or part of it. I said, Let us be—something—of soul, as earth lies bare to heaven above, how is it under our control, to love or not to love? I think that's it.

I said for you to quit that talking about love, Honey said. It aint nothing in it.

I won't quit, I said, and laid down in the grass while all the poems I ever knew came rushing back over my body like the wind. It was like they were all still there someplace, they had just been waiting. I felt I had got a part of myself back that I had lost without even knowing it was gone. Honey had given me back my very soul. But I knew better than to say it. I laid there with my eyes closed and acted like I was asleep. But I was not asleep. Sometimes I opened one eye a little, to see him. The way he was turned, I could see the line of his cheek and his jaw, how brown the skin on his arms was, his square strong back. He had golden elf-hair curling in his ears. His legs and his ass were real white, like I was real white all over. He set there whistling a tune through his teeth and fooling with the flowers he had gathered up. I couldn't believe it. I had never seen a grown man before that would fool around with little flowers. And here I was, on top of Blue Star Mountain, finally!

All of a sudden I thought, I could of climbed up here by myself, anytime! But I had not. I remembered as girls how you and me would beg to go hunting on the mountain, Silvaney, but they said, That is for boys. Or how we wanted to go up there after berries and they'd say, Wait till Victor can take you, or Wait till Daddy gets home. Well, I'll bet you made it up there yourself sometime or other, Silvaney, in all your wanderings, I feel sure you have been there too. And I had got up there myself at long last with a man it is true, but not a man like any I had ever seen before in all my life. Even his back was almost covered with little bitty golden hairs. He is like one of his own bees, I thought. I reckon he goes from woman to woman like a bee goes from flower to flower. I knew even then that I was only one of a lot of women that Honey Breeding had had or would have. But he was the last thing left to happen to me. So it didn't bother me a bit. I laid there and laughed to myself.

What's so funny? Honey said. I thought you was asleep.
I am sort of asleep, I said.
Well, wake up now. He leaned down and kissed me. It's time to go.
No, I said.
Get up now, I've got you a present, he said.
So I sat up. What is it?
He stood up and came over and put it on my head, a double starflower crown. You look real pretty, he said. Now stand up and walk, you will be a Queen. I stood up and did as he said, and the wind blew all over my body but my crown stayed put, caught up in my hair which is real heavy.

Here now, Honey said. He handed me my clothes. We've got to get a move on, if we want to get back before full dark. You can say you got lost, I reckon.
Why, what time is it? I asked.
For the sun still shone up there.
It is going on seven, he said, and it will take us two hours walking

back. The sun has set already down below. I looked out over the cliff. The hawk had disappeared. I felt the cold wind coming up my body to my face. I'm not going back yet, I said.

Now Ivy. Honey grabbed my elbows from behind, hard. Put on your clothes.

I will put on my clothes, I said, but I am not going to go back down there yet. I am not ready to go. I have not had my fill of you yet.

He laughed shortly. There is plenty that has had a bellyful of me already.

I expect so, I said.

Oh Ivy, Honey said. I am bad news. Anybody will tell you that. We can't stay up here.

We can stay awhile longer, I said, and I turned around and kissed him, and so we did. This is exactly how it happened that I ran off from home with a bee man and lived up on the mountain with him for a while, and would of stayed longer if I could have, if he hadn't gotten tired of me finally, and I hadn't of gotten sick. It was not his fault so much as mine. I was the strong one then. There is an old song Revel used to sing, He is just a heartbreak in pants. Well, this is true of Honey Breeding, and I reckon I knew it all along, but I didn't care. When I stood on the cliff with him that day in the last of the sunshine, I couldn't see nothing but him, nothing. I couldn't see the valley below, nor any part of the world. I was blinded and dazzled by his shape.

Come on then, he said, and we got dressed. We got dressed, but I knew we weren't going back. Something had passed between us. He walked me back across the grassy bald to the path which we followed still further then, along the ridge till we came to a cropping out place of big huge rocks, like a giant's toys. In here, Honey said, and I follered him in between two of the rocks to a cave that was big as a room. I couldn't see. Honey grabbled around in the dark and then I heard a flinty scratch and a match flared up red, and then he lit a candle. There was several candles laying on a rock ledge at the back of the cave, and an old blanket in the corner, and you could see where there had been some several cook fires in the floor.

You have come here before, I said.

Yesm. Honey's eyes were winking in the candle light.

Did you bring a woman here with you? I asked.

Nope, he said. And I am going to kick this one right out on

her hiney if she don't quit asking me questions and get to gathering wood.

I started laughing. We went out and got up all the wood we could find around there, and it was full dark when we got back with it. Honey had some dried apples and jerky and journey cakes that we ate for our dinner.

I remember looking across the fire at him that first night. I know what I'm doing, I said.

Naw you don't either, he said flatly, but he grinned at me, and he was right, but it did not signify. Nothing did. For I had to stay with him awhile. It could not be long, I knew that. We would have to go down off the mountain before long, I knew that too. But right then I didn't care. Can you understand this? I didn't care. We drank right out of a spring. We washed ourselves off in a little creek. We ate huckleberries and blue berries and nuts and greens and whatever Honey could catch—a squirrel, a rabbit. It was cold up there at night and a white mist covered the whole world in the morning. One time Honey was gone for a while and came back with some jimson weed and squeezed the juice right into his eyes—me screaming for him to stop, mind you, all the while—and died his eyes black for a couple of hours! I couldn't believe it. I had never seen anybody do that before, nor ever heard tell of it. But Honey Breeding was full of tricks, full of stories, full of songs. One that I remember was real funny. Here's your chitlins, fresh and sweet, who'll jine the union? Young hog chitlins hard to beat, who'll jine the union? Methodist chitlins, just been biled, who'll jine the union? and such as that, to make me laugh, and Poor Wayfaring Stranger to make me cry. I can't stand that one, it's so sad. I'm just a poor wayfaring stranger, travelling through this world of woe, but there's no sickness, toil nor danger in that bright world to which I go. I'm going there to see my mother, I'm going there no more to roam. I'm just going over Jordan, I'm just going over home.

Honey Breeding sang this song on the third day we were up there, late in the afternoon as we set by the mouth of the cave looking out on the rocky valley. It was misty, drizzling. It had been raining a little bit off and on all day. Don't sing that one, I begged him. It makes me cry.

Well then I won't, Honey said, and stroked my hair.

We set there together. He didn't sing. By then I knew all about him, he had told me the story of his whole life. How his parents had both died and he had lived for a while with a family where the old woman went sweet on him and he got run off, and then how he joined the Army and went to war and saw terrible things there, and came on home. And how he could not stand a city or a town, how he had to have mountains, and roam. If he got around too many people, he said, he heard them talking in his head. So he had give up one good job after another in order to roam, until he had hit on the bee business which suited him. He said he knew it was no kind of life for a grown man, but he couldn't help it. He said he had tried to live in a house with a woman twice, that is with two different women, and he said that they were real nice women and in fact he had married one of them, but in each case there come a morning when he woke up and looked around and knew it was time to leave there. That is just the way I am, said Honey Breeding.

I didn't even have to say, I know it.

I knew, he knew.

There would come that morning, and it came. It was hot and bright. We had got up early. I didn't have any idea how long we had been up there, I had kind of lost track of the time. The skirt of my dress was ripped and hanging by then, I remember that, and I was skinny as a rail. I could not keep a thing on my stomach. I could feel every one of my ribs and my hipbones were sticking out. I felt hot, dry, like I had a fever. Maybe I did. I kept drinking water but it didn't help.

We stood in the cave looking out at the day.

I reckon we will go on back now, Honey said. It is time.

No no, I said, or I think I said. Then I fainted or fell, down to the floor of the cave. Honey came over and pulled me up and kissed me and took me outside to sit on the rock that we always sat on, but when I felt well enough to look at him good, he was staring off down the rocky valley with his eyes set hard on distance. He had already left me, in his mind. The rest of it wouldn't be nothing but follow through.

And I'll tell you something else, Silvaney.

Something awful.

I would of stayed up there. I would of stayed with him until I starved to death and died, I reckon, living on love. I would have stayed right there with him if he hadn't of made me leave, and that's a fact. It doesn't even make me feel bad to say it. There has got to be one person who is the lover, and this time it was me, and one who is the beloved which was Honey. And I will tell you the truth—may be it's best to be the lover, some ways. Because even if it don't work out, you are glad. You are glad you done it. You are glad you got to be there, anyway, however long it lasted, whatever it cost you—which is always plenty, I reckon. We'll get to that. We'll get there. But right then me and Honey sat on a warm gray rock with little shiny pieces of mica in it, and I was glad I was me. I picked at the rock with my fingers.

Fools gold, I thought. Well all right. I remembered mining in the creek with Molly so long ago. And now it felt natural to me to be here, to have come up this mountain with this man. I guess that the seeds of what we will do are in us all along, only sometimes they don't get no water, they don't grow. Other times, well—you see what can happen. All of a sudden I felt my age. Forty. I thought about the old dry seeds that I found in the gourd up in the attic when me and Oakley moved back up on Sugar Fork, years ago. They were still there, still in the gourd, still in the attic. Who put them up there? Granny Rowe? Momma? It all went a long way back. Honey stood up. Come on Ivy, he said. And even though I cried and pitched a fit, I finally went.

I follered him down the mountain that morning, which was harder going than I expected. I was real weak. I was sick, as I said. I had to keep on stopping to get my breath, which caught in my side with each step. Honey walked ahead, light-hearted it looked like, sure-footed, whistling a little song. We went down a different path from the way we had come up there, it put us down off the mountain that afternoon by the hard road that goes from Majestic to Pound, where I didn't know anybody.

I stood by the road clutching at Honey's shirt. It was so hot— bees buzzed in the clover and the Queen Annes lace by the side of the road. A couple of cars went by, faces turned plum around, staring at us. I thought then about what we must look like, what they must think. I thought about Oakley, whose face came clear in my mind for the first time since I had been gone. Somebody blew their car horn at us. Dust hung golden in the air after each car passed. I would of given my life for a cocacola. A green truck passed us, then stopped and backed up. The man got out. Sir I am so glad you have had the kindness of heart to stop, for we have been in a big accident and—I heard Honey saying. Bees buzzed in the weeds. My ears were roaring. There was a taste in my mouth, sour and sweet. White honey comes from white clover,

Honey said in my mind, amber from tulip poplar. But the best of all is the sourwood honey, pale yellow and sweet and light. That is all I can really remember. I can't remember the truck ride back to Majestic at all, nor Honey leaving, nor Victor and Ethel driving me back up on Sugar Fork. I don't know if I spent the night with them or not, but it seems to me now that I must have.

Because it seems to me that it is morning again when I come back home. I am surprised at all the cars parked below—Oakley's family is up here, it looks like, and the Rolettes, and another car and a truck that I don't know. May be it is somebody from Oakley's church, I said right off the top of my head.

Ethel looked at me. She looked real tired. Why would you say that, she said.

I don't know, I told her. I reckon it just come to me. Oakley goes to church all the time now, I said. You just don't know the half of it.

Victor parked Stoney's car and we got out. Victor was huffing and puffing. He is a big man, and it was hot, and it seemed like he was building up to some kind of explosion. Sister! he said finally, pulling hairs out of his big thick beard which is what he does when he gets too wrought up. He always calls me sister. You hadn't ought to've done it! he said. You ought to've stayed at home!

Ethel turned on him in a fury. You crazy old man! she said. Don't you reckon she knows it? Ethel can be a spitfire sometimes. When Stoney Branham passes, which will not be long, Ethel and Victor will have themselves a time. You can see it coming.

I felt like I was with them but not with them, that morning. I felt like I had been gone for years, and then like I had never been gone at all. The air was clear and sweet up on Sugar Fork. Come on honey, Ethel said. She took my arm. I felt awful. I was wearing Ethel's clothes.

We crossed the creek on the steppingstones and started up to the yard. The rosybush was blooming by the steps. The yard had been swept clean. The breezeway and the porch were full of people, we could hear the low buzz of talking as we came. My sweet Bill was the first to see us, as him and Danny Ray came walking around the side of the house. Mama! he hollered. Looky here, it's Mama. And he came running, all skinny flying flailing arms and legs, a boy like a windmill, he nearabout knocked me down. Mama, Mama, he said, hugging me. His strawcolored hair smelled good.

Then Danny Ray was there, hugging me too. Where'd you go, Mama? they said. Where've you been? I hugged them and hugged them and then looked up at the house.

All the talk had quit. Those on the porch and the breezeway stood like statues, looking down. It was Oakley and his mother and daddy, and Dreama, and Martha holding Maudy, and some several people that I didn't know. Oakley looked at me with no expression atall on his face. Then he turned without a word and went back in the house.

Come on, Ethel said grimly, and we walked on up the hill.

Martha smiled at us shyly.

Hidy Ivy, she said. We killed a snake in the house while you were gone.

That's good, I said. I couldn't think what to say.

Maudy started struggling to get down. Mama, Mama, Maudy said.

Edith Fox has brought us a stack-cake, Martha said. It's real good too. She put Maudy down and we all watched as Maudy clambered down the steps and ran to me. She was bigger, fatter.

I got a new kitty, she said.

Martha was smiling, holding onto the rail, but nobody else was. Dreama was staring so hard that she liked to of bored holes in my face, I could feel her eyes.

The kitty's name is Susie. Maudy can talk so good for her age.

Dreama stood at the top of the steps like she was blocking them.

Wait a minute now! Just a minute now! Victor took off the straw hat he always wears and started fanning his face with it. Hold on! he hollered. Will somebody kindly tell me just what in the hell is going on here? Why are you all up here, anyway? I know damn well this is not a welcoming committee for Ivy.

Without moving her mouth, Dreama said, It is LuIda.

What about LuIda? Victor was huffing and puffing, short of breath.

LuIda is dead, said Dreama. We buried her this morning.

Just out in the orchard, Bill said. Me and Danny Ray helped to dig the grave.

Oh God oh God. I could hear, and yet not hear Ethel. I could not stand up.

What—I think I said. What—

Ray Fox Senior came down the porch steps then two at a time, and lifted me up. Oh Ivy honey, he said. I am glad to see you back.

LuIda was sick to her stomach, Bill said, but not real sick.

And she died? asked Ethel, old practical Ethel.

I reckon it was her appendix, Ray Senior told us. That's what they have all been saying. He led me up the steps and when we got to the top one, Dreama looked at me hard and started screaming and ran back in the house. Edith Fox went after her. Martha came over and hugged me, she had a big shy-looking boy follering at her heels that looked familiar. This here is Rufus Cook, Martha said, and then I knew who it was. It was Early Cook's son, who had come to make the coffin. I'm sorry mam, Rufus Cook said.

I pushed them all away and rushed through the breezeway to the back of the house but stopped dead when I saw the lilac. Granny's voice sounded strong in my ear. Never let a lilac bush grow tall enough to shade a grave, or death will come to fill it.

Up at the top of the orchard, right next to the treeline, I saw the pile of red dirt. I could not go up there. I sat down where I was on the back steps, and cried. I cried for a long time. I could hear people coming and going around me, car horns honking, somebody crying, somebody laughing down below, suddenly hushed. But they left me alone. They let me cry. Finally after a long time Oakley came up and stood behind me. I could feel him standing there. Then he said, Get up, Ivy, and take care of your children, and I did.

I am still doing so. I will continue. I will not be writing any more letters for a while though, as my heart is too heavy, too full. But somehow I had to write this letter to you Silvaney, to set it all down. I am still in pain and sorrow, but I remain,

Your sister,
Ivy Rowe.

V

Letters
from
Sugar Fork

August 2, 1942

My dear Silvaney,

It has been so long since last I wrote. Sometimes I think it is the longest time of my life and other times, it is the shortest, gone like the wink of an eye. Sometimes I think life is like that too, dreamed in a catnap. It don't make sense to me. It was summer when I left here with Honey Breeding, and summer still when LuIda died and I came back. A part of me died with her. This is true, Silvaney. I can't get it back. And now it is summer again and I can't get over it. It don't feel right to me for things to go on blooming like they always do, for the garden to come in, for me to make watermelon pickle and pickalily the same as always, or for the sun to rise or the rain to fall or the mist to hang over Bethel Mountain, or the days to go on like they do. It don't seem possible.

But Oakley is doing a lot of carpenter work now and Martha has got a boyfriend and we have got electricity and a radio. I can tick these things off on my hands. So time keeps on passing, all right. Ever since we got the radio, Oakley is crazy for baseball. You know he used to play some up at the mining camp where Franklin's daddy cared more about baseball than he did about mining, so they said. Oakley played shortstop. Now he is crazy about Joe DiMaggio who is hitting good this year. Oakley listens to the radio all the time, he has got it right out on the porch where he whittles. We had it inside when we first got it last winter and I will never forget Pearl Harbor, they talked about nothing else all that day on the radio while we gathered up around it like we used to gather around the woodstove. Wouldn't anybody leave the radio, that day. And now it is a war on, and the younger Rolette boy and one of Stoney Branham's boys—the one Ethel used to have so much trouble with—are gone into the Army, and folks are all riled up. It seems so far away to me, farther than France. I can not immagine Japan where they drink tea and eat rice and have such smooth closed faces. They look so calm and so mysterious to me. Closer to home, four people have been killed already in the Harlan strike, and we have had no word from Violet nor R.T. in over a year, or if we did I don't know it. I don't know if they are okay or not. I have missed a lot, I feel like I've been caught out in a catnap.

Silvaney, you will recall how smart I was when I was young. Well I am not that smart now! It has all got beyond me somehow. There is a war on and a big strike at Harlan right across the state line, but somehow I can not get past this little grave up here in the orchard on the hill. I can't get over it. For I know LuIda's dying is all my fault and if I had not run off with Honey Breeding it would not have happened, LuIda would be alive today, playing down at the creek with Maudy who I can see from here as I write. But little LuIda is pushing up grass, growing starflowers. I wish to God it was me instead.

I can not even die now.

Oakley said, Get up and take care of your children, and he is right. Today I am getting ready to can more shucky beans, we have put up a lot of beans already. But it is not right. I am canning beans but it is winter in my heart.

I know this is my lot. I deserve it all!

Geneva came over to visit right after I got back and said, Ivy, don't be ridiculous. You are not the first woman in the world to run off with a man nor will you be the last. Sit up girl, Geneva said. And take your medicine. My medicine is nought but bitter gall. I told her so. Oh hush! Geneva said. It takes time, you will come around. You'll see. But I will not.

I am a scandal, I told Geneva.

Ivy, just hush your mouth, Geneva said, fanning herself. This was right after I done it all. May be you are a scandal right now, she went on, but folks are all so wrapped up in themselves that they will forget before you know it. It won't be long. Nobody cares what you do. Not really. You'll see. Nobody in the world is near as important as they think they are, you included.

Then Geneva told me all about her new boyfriend, a man named Dr. Harvey T. Snow who had come to stay at the boardinghouse and never left. He won't either, Geneva said. He is just crazy about me. Geneva said that Mr. Snow is a retired superintendent of schools from Petersburg, Va. who came to town to visit his married daughter Mrs. Cindy Shreve who would not speak to Geneva right then because of this situation. She will, though, Geneva said. She'll come around. Geneva was rocking and fanning herself on the porch.

I used to be a scandal myself, Geneva said. Now I'm an institution. She winked at me.

Even sad as I was then, I had to laugh. Geneva is 70 if she's a day, and still up to no good. There is something in me which admires this, and wants to ride hell for leather down the high road of life like Geneva does. But I am somehow lacking in gumption and pluck, or else it is that I have got to think about things too much finally. I can't help it. You know I have always got to write my letters, and think about what's happened, and what I've done.

You worry too much, Ivy, Geneva said that day, rocking. Don't think, she said. She went on rocking in the heat and appeared to doze. Her glasses on their rhinestone chain fell down off her nose to the wide shelf of her bosom and she slept, Geneva, looking in sleep like any little old grandmotherly woman in the world, which she certainly is not. But I was wide awake. And I could not quit thinking. I can't help it—I guess I never could. I can't help what I do, either. It's like I'm pulled in two directions all the time.

All of a sudden I remembered one time way way back when Revel was taking us someplace in the wagon, now this was not too long after Daddy died and before Revel had to leave here. We were going to town in the wagon and a mad dog came up and started barking and the mules tried to run off in opposite directions. We had to hang on for dear life! I remember Beulah's screams, to this day. I remember how the mules' breath hung white in the frosty air. Then finally Revel shot the dog, and that was that.

But sometimes I feel I am caught in that wild bucking wagon yet, with no one here to shoot the dog.

Geneva mumbled as she dozed, that day in August, and a little smile crept around her lips. I reckon she was dreaming of Dr. Harvey T. Snow, and a good thing it was too, as he died not two months later. He had a heart attack in the Post Office. Geneva mourned like the devil for about six weeks, but now she is back to normal. Well I do have to cook for all these people, she says, after all.

And after all, Dr. Harvey T. Snow was not but a little dip, or a little hill, on the rolling field of Geneva's long life, and though she mourned hard and well, she has given it up now and moved on. I reckon this is my problem or one of them—I can't give up a thing! Nothing. I can't forget. I can't move on. I am having a heart attack all the time.

Now Geneva is up to her same old tricks, making her famous vinegar pies, considering her options. Judge Brack still takes his meals there though he, too, is retired, and Doc Trout is dead.

Mrs. Rose who came in to clean his office found him sitting straight up in his chair, dead as a post, last Febuary, with a coffee cup full of vodka still clutched in his hand. He was the only man around here that anybody ever heard of to drink vodka. Oakley says that is because you can't tell it on a person's breath, not like liquor. Well, he was sweet to me.

The Reverend Sam Russell Sage is dead too, died in a hotel fire in San Francisco, California, four years back. Geneva just found it out. And good riddance! is what she said. She has got so much gumption. And it's a funny thing how Little Geneva, Ludie's child, takes after Big Geneva even though they are not blood related—she is as sassy as can be, and paints her nails red, and talks back to everybody. She is a handful.

So is Danny Ray who can not sit still in a chair, he is restless like you and Babe were as kids. He is all the time in trouble, but smart. Miss McVey, the new teacher down at the school, says he is the brightest one she has ever seen but implores him to turn his talents to good not mischief. As it is, he spends a lot of time shining the windows with ammonia and newspapers, clipping the weeds, and doing whatever she can devise, for he finishes his lessons in no time flat. He is smarter than Joli they say, but Joli was so sweet and calm as a child, she is a different sort altogether. It always seemed like Joli had a soft warm glow around her.

Now Maudy is real silly and keeps us laughing even Bill who is serious like his daddy, he is not much good at school. Bill likes to whittle too, and do carpenter work, he is really his daddy's boy and takes after Oakley in every particular right down to the way he wears a hat.

And as for Oakley—Silvaney, what can I say.

You know that for a long time, Oakley's face was turned away.

Well, now he is paying attention.

He is looking at me dead-on.

I can't tell what he's thinking, though. I think he is waiting for something, but what it is, I couldn't say. May be he could not say either. In any case, one thing about Oakley which has always been true, is that he has got all the time in the world. This is why he was the best trapper around here. He can wait for ever. He is patient beyond belief. I have seen him move up on a frog for instance so slow that neither the frog nor I could tell he was moving. I have seen him sit on the porch and whittle for a whole long rainy afternoon without hardly moving, or saying a word, turning out one little animal after another, squirrels, turtles, bears.

In that way he is the flat out opposite of Honey Breeding who talked so much and acted so lively. Sometimes now when I think about Honey Breeding, it is almost like I made him up out of thin air because I needed him so bad. I can't think of him as real, somehow. I know he came, and I know I went off with him, and LuIda died because of it. I remember those moments with Honey as flashes of light.

And I am different now. I am changed in some way. It does not have a thing to do with Oakley either, and never did. I believe Oakley knows this. It has only to do with me.

So I am trying. I keep the house up good and try to help Bill with his schoolwork and try to keep up with Danny Ray. Maudy gives me a deal of pleasure. I do not go up on Pilgrim Knob, nor up in the orchard by LuIda's grave if I can help it. I can not look at the lilac. I keep busy. Martha and me are piecing a log cabin quilt and sometimes I help Ethel down in the store when Stoney feels too poorly to get out of bed. Victor has got a good job now at the Ration Board, so he is not at the store any more. On Saturdays and Sundays I go to church with Oakley sometimes, it is the only time I ever see a break in the lines of his face. For Oakley will get wrought up in church and holler out AMEN. Or he will close his eyes and bite his lips as if in prayer, swaying back and forth, it is clear then that he is carried away, and after church he is absent-minded in the truck going home, and seems thinner to me somehow, and purified. Sanctified, they say. Sometimes he goes up at the invitational, sometimes not. I have never gone yet, and now when they line it out loud, no one even looks my way. Either they all think I am saved already or else they have got used to me sitting there like a bump on a log, the same way we have all got used to old Mister Justice who sits in the back and talks to himself all the time, or Annie Woods who runs through town now asking for Mickey her son who died in a wreck two years ago come October, or old Paregoric Lou who goes along the sidewalks of Majestic looking for pocket change to buy her paregoric with.

Geneva was right. I am not a scandal now. The only one that still blames me is Dreama Fox.

Other folks are all took up with the war, and the war effort. They are busy knitting sweaters and vests for the soldiers, and raising a garden. Even folks that have never baked a cake in their lives are fighting over sugar coupons.

Life goes on, and I reckon now that I've got to live it.

But sometimes I think I am the only one that remembers from one day to the next what happens, may be because I am writing it all to you. It is true that time softens things. I feel now as I write that I am better than I was, even if Oakley will always be circling around me, and watching, and waiting. I don't know what he is waiting for. At least I am alive now, since I ran off with Honey, there is that, come what may. And I do have all these children to take care of.

Sunday.

This morning I got up early and set the coffee to boiling. I fried some sausage and made biskit, and cooked some hominy grits and eggs. Maudy sat in Martha's lap to eat, and Oakley got some church music on the radio. It was that old time gospel hour out of Bristol. And then, for a minute while everybody was eating, I felt like church. I mean I think I felt the way you are supposed to feel in church, which I never do. The back door to the orchard stood open and sunlight fell in a long solid block into the kitchen, touching Maudy's red curly hair. Little bits of dust went twirling in the sunlight which lay warm and restful on my new linoleum tablecloth which is all flowers, red and white roses entwined in circles that repeat and repeat and repeat. It is real pretty. Can I have some more eggs? Bill said. You can't fill him up! Danny Ray was reading a book which he does all the time and I said, Don't read at the table. He was reading, The Mayor of Casterbridge. Here's some more biskits I said and took them out of the oven and Oakley said, These are real good, Ivy. The Blue Sky Boys on the radio were singing Look on the Sunny Side of Life. I got us all some more coffee and sat back down and all of a sudden I thought how funny it was to have everybody there at the same time, usually they are off and running in a million different directions especially the boys. Where is the honey? Oakley said because it is new honey, he has just robbed the bees, and I got up and got a piece of it still in the comb and put it on a blue plate. It is pale, pale yellow honey, the lightest sweetest kind. Oh that is good, said Martha, and the children were chewing the comb, they act like it is candy. Don't reach, I said to Bill. Now you will just have to wash all over again, you are such a pig, Martha said to Maudy who had smeared it all over herself. Do piggy, Maudy said, and stretched out her fat little leg and wiggled her toes and Martha said This little pig went to market, this little pig stayed home, this little pig had roast beef, this little pig had none. Maudy was giggling, Oakley was staring out at the mountains the way he does, Danny Ray was reading The Mayor of Casterbridge. The gospel singers sang This little light of mine, I'm gonna let it shine on the radio. The sun felt warm on my forehead, like somebody's hand. Bill was eating up all the sausage. I put some of the new honey on a biskit and ate it myself. It was smooth and sweet. This is the best honey yet I said to Oakley who said it was because we'd had so much rain. This little pig cried wee wee wee all the way home, Martha said, pulling Maudy's least toe. Maudy started squealing and jumped out of Martha's arms and ran around and round the table. Gotcha. Oakley grabbed her. I ate another biskit, may be I will get old and fat like all the women in Oakley's family. Holding Maudy, Oakley was staring at me the way he does. It is clear to me now Silvaney that however much I may have wanted to die, I am stuck smack in the middle of this life.

I remain

Your loving sister,
Ivy.

October 12, 1942

Dear Garnie,

What a big surprise to hear from you after all these years! I have wondered so often where in the world you are, I have thought about you so much. Why did you never write before? You will have to do some fast talking to get out of that one! We have got so much to catch up on. For a start, I am not at Geneva's boardinghouse where you sent the letter, I am married to Oakley Fox who you will remember from childhood, and we live back up here on Sugar Fork where you were raised. Oh Garnie, I cannot wait to see you! For there is only some of us left now—Beulah is gone too, and Silvaney, and Johnny. We think that Johnny might be in New Orleans Louisiana because one of the Patterson boys claims to have seen him down there in a big hotel, playing the piano. But we don't know for sure. Anyway I am hoping he is alive and in New Orleans not dead in light as are so many.

Oh Garnie! It is only me and you and Ethel and Victor now, of all them that was here so long ago. This is why it means so much to me, for you to get in touch. We are the only ones that remember the same things like the day we went up the mountain after chestnuts, I bet you remember that as good as me! Those chestnut trees are all gone now. The blight got them. A lot has changed here. But you will see, you will see.

Don't you remember all those funerals we used to have, and how you preached, and how you made me sing? I am not surprised you have gone on to make such a fine preacher. An awful lot has happened here since you've been gone. I guess you will hear it all. But I will be so happy to see you and to meet your family.

Geneva says, Count on staying with her, and do not even <u>think</u> of payment.

They are putting up signs of your Crusade all over town.

I remain

Your Long Lost Sister,
Ivy Fox.

December 23, 1942.

My dear Joli,

It is two days before Christmas, and coming on to snow. The sky is low and gray with that special smell in the air that denotes S-N-O-W. After all these years, and old as I am, I still get excited! I feel like it <u>ought</u> to snow at Christmas. I sit down here to write letting all else go so that your daddy can take this letter to town as he goes, since it is clear that we will not get out of this holler later. He has got to go to town after Bill and Danny Ray's guns that are down at Ethel's store, and Maudy's doll which is put back over at Ernest Smith's Ben Franklin. It is the big one with the blue china eyes that she wanted so bad. The box from you is here already but we have not opened it yet, not even the outside wrappings. And another big box has come like clockwork from Miss Torrington bless her soul who must be as old as the hills by now. Yet I remember her stern face so plain, as if I saw her but yesterday. The radio plays A White Christmas, by Irving Berlin. I think he is real good. I will bet you have heard it too. The radio makes me feel closer to you, like we have got the whole world right up here with us. I am not sure what we did without it!

But I was just thinking about the way Christmas used to be and how it has changed now and is more storebought, that is progress! Still and all, I miss the Cline sisters, and all the storytelling on Old Christmas Eve. And I miss you. I understand that you can not leave there now what with the war and all, and I am so proud of you honey. Geneva says it does not snow by the ocean, is this right? You know the closest I have come to the ocean is to look out on these mountains from the porch. So I cannot immagine you there. Norfolk. It is clear across the state, it might be clear across the world as far as I can tell!

But it is about to start snowing, so I will get down to business.

I wanted to let you know that Stoney Branham died a week ago Tuesday, to no one's surprise as he has been sick a long time. The last couple of times I saw him, he reminded me of a locust shell, a little old dried-up husk of a man. When he died, Ethel went into a fury! She banged on his chest and got that new young doctor out in the middle of the night and kept rubbing Stoney's puny little body with Mentholatum long after it was clear that he was done for. Finally the young doctor had to give her a shot, so they could pull her away. For Ethel is a big strong woman. I never think of her that way, but I did then. She swatted them all away like they were flies.

Now come on, Ethel, Victor said.

You old fart! Ethel spit out at Victor, and some of them that were gathered around, hid a grin.

Ethel act your age, Victor said then which struck me as funny Joli, I confess it, even in that dire moment. So I laughed out, to the surprise of all, and Victor threw up his hands. There you go! he hollered. There you go! They will not act like they are supposed to, not a one of those girls, and never would. Victor said this to all assembled.

So after the young doctor gave Ethel a shot and they dragged her away from Stoney, Victor went down the street to Hazel's

Steaks and got drunk as a skunk. He was still drunk the next day at Stoney's funeral and the day after that when he done some terrible things which I won't go into, and now he is in the hospital. The word is out that Ethel went over there and slapped his face while he was laying in the bed hooked up to tubes, and said, Arent you ashamed Victor, to act like this? with Stoney not yet cold in his grave and all our boys dying in the war? And Victor set in crying which he does whenever somebody mentions the war. I am not sure sometimes if he knows which war it is, in spite of his job with the Ration Board that he has lost now because of what he went in there and said when he was drunk.

What will he do? I asked Ethel, meaning what will Victor do for a living now?

Do? Ethel said. Do? She was sitting at Stoney's desk in the back of the store, going through papers.

Then she said, I reckon he can start by sweeping up this floor when he gets back.

I looked at Ethel, who was smiling, and then I understood. It is like Ethel and Victor are all tied up in a knot which will hold no matter what. Ethel is as tied to Victor as she was to Stoney Branham, I see it now. Tough as she acts, Ethel is a puffweed underneath.

The old fool, Ethel said that day, going through the papers on her desk.

And sure enough, your daddy says that the last time he was in town, why there was Victor back in the store big as life and twice as ugly, wearing green suspenders and a red tie, giving out horehound candy free to children. The store was just packed with folks doing their Christmas shopping, your daddy said. And Ethel behind the cash register with her lips in a flat red line. Don't he look stupid? she said. But she kept on ringing things up.

Now here's what I think, Joli.

I think they have got it all worked out. Ethel and Victor will go on fighting all over town and grow famous for it. And it is a pretty good deal for all concerned.

You see, Joli, there are ties between a man and a woman that we have not got a name for, and plenty of them. I know something about that myself.

Which brings me to the other thing I want to say here.

You write that you are in love with your young man and that you may marry him before he leaves and I say, oh Joli, don't. You have to consider all your options in the words of Geneva Hunt. Don't marry him now, but wait, and see who he is when he comes back. See who <u>you</u> are! I have not asked a thing of you ever, but I am asking this. Love him all you want, honey, don't get me wrong. You can't help that anyway, if you are any kin to me! Just dont marry him too quick.

I am not going to mention this to your daddy, in hopes that you will keep your head. A uniform can turn it pretty easy, I know.

Your uncle Garnie Rowe is coming to town next week with his Gospel Crusade, I can't wait to see him after so long. He looks real fat in the newspapers. We all miss you honey. Take care of yourself.

I will stop here as it has started snowing. The first flakes that fall are always the biggest.

Merry Christmas from your loving,

Mama.

April 18, 1943.

Dear Silvaney,

I have to write to you, for I can tell no one. This is the story of how I was not saved.

Garnie has come back here now and he is awful he is no brother of mine as far as I am concerned, and if he is going to heaven then I will rot in hell and be happy about it. Back before I run off with Honey Breeding, I used to tease Oakley and sing that song that Revel taught us, <u>I know I've been a sinner and wicked all my days, but when I'm old and feeble, I'll think upon my ways.</u> But I will <u>not</u> think on my ways now, and I will not go to any Heaven that has got a place in it for Garnie Rowe. <u>Little Garnie,</u> as they call him. Ha! For he is not little at all, he is a pig, and looks like a pig, and does not take after any of the rest of us.

Let me get a deep breath and some more paper and a cocacola and start at the beginning.

The first time we laid eyes on Garnie and his family was down at the boardinghouse for Sunday dinner which was wonderful, ham and fried chicken and spoonbread and beans and pickled peaches. Geneva had outdone herself. At table we had Geneva, Judge Brack, me and Oakley and the kids, Little Geneva and Ludie, and Garnie and his whole family. The biggest surprise was Garnie's wife Ruthie, who looks like a movie star. Ruthie kept cutting her eyes around, and playing with her hair. All the kids looked down at their plates.

Geneva and her hired girl brought all the food in, and then Geneva sat down and settled herself. Will you say grace? she asked Garnie of course, and that was everybody's first mistake. For Garnie started praying and would not quit. He went on and on praying for all the sinners lost to God and all the orphan children of the world, and the end of the Yellow Peril. We know that you are a God of vengeance, Garnie prayed, and we beg you now to unleash your terrible swift sword upon the Yellow Peril. He went on and on real dramatic, like a man in a play.

Garnie seemed to be on great terms with God. I looked around the table without raising my eyes. Oakley was praying hard. I caught Judge Brack winking at Geneva, while Danny Ray snaked a thigh off the piled-up plate of fried chicken, and put it in his lap and fed it to himself in little bites. Garnie went on praying for the Allies and for each and every one of us. He has a real deep voice for such a small fat man. His pretty wife Ruthie kept her eyes squinched up tight like she was making a wish and so did his boys Corey and Michael and their little girl Mary Magdalene. They all sat as still as stones. Mary Magdalene looks like her mother with yellow corkscrew curls and skin so white you can see the blue veins through it. All of Garnie's family sat there just as quiet as church mice which they are. Judge Brack rolled his eyes. Bill yawned. Oakley never moved nor looked up, and Garnie went on, and finally when a skin was forming on the gravy, he was done.

I should of known then that something was wrong with him.

But the fact is that I set such store by family, and I was so happy to see him after this long a time, that I did not.

I couldn't tell it till he turned on me.

That first Sunday, Geneva piled up his plate and he started right in eating, which didn't slow his talking down a bit. Garnie told us all about how he had left here with Sam Russell Sage and gone West and stayed with him until Sam Russell Sage got jealous of his power—this is Garnie's power, mind you—which had occasioned a split between them in Kansas City after which I took the high road and he took the low, if you know what I mean, Garnie said, adding that the hand of God had come after that and set the hotel fire that burned Sam Russell Sage to a crisp along with his 18 year old consort who could only be identified later by her satin slippers and one gold tooth. She was a newspaper editor's daughter from Kansas City who had been missing for months, said Garnie. Garnie told us that as Sam Russell Sage grew older, he had succumbed more and more to the evils of the flesh and had become a devil. Garnie said he had witnessed it all. Then Garnie lowered his head and started in eating like crazy.

Geneva opened and shut her mouth a couple of times. Well that is mighty strong language, she said finally. You know those are very hard words, said Geneva who after all had shared her bed with this devil for years.

Yes mam, Garnie said looking right at Geneva, and my God is a hard God, and make no mistake about it.

Geneva's sweet sagging face turned pink.

I wouldn't mind some more ham, Garnie said, and some more of that red-eye gravy, and Oakley passed it along. Nobody said a word while Garnie ate. Ethel was off on a buying trip or she would have spoke right up and given him what for, the cat has never got Ethel's tongue yet.

Judge Brack stood up then and said he had to attend a meeting, and begged us to please excuse him, and as far as I know he never ate at that table again until after Garnie left. Judge Brack has gotten so thin now that his suits hang off of his shoulders like he is a suit rack, and flap around him when he walks. His hair is as white and fly-away as a dandelion fluff, and he always needs a haircut.

To break the silence I said, Well how did you all meet each other? meaning to get Ruthie to talk since she had not said word one, so far. She kept looking around and then when you'd catch her eye, she'd look down.

We had taken the message to Tullahoma, Tenessee, Garnie said, and Ruth here was among the saved.

I looked good at Ruthie who did not look very saved to me. Ruthie's skin was so fair it was kind of blue, but she had round patches of red rouge on each cheek. She had painted eyebrows on in thin half-circles above each eye which made her look real surprised, and her red lips were fixed in a perfect bow. In Oakley's church they don't hold with make-up at all, so I was surprised to see Garnie's wife done up like this. Her nails were long and pointed, red. Her hands did not look like she had ever washed a dish in her life and from what she told me later, this was wellnigh true. Garnie had always hired a girl to come in and do the housework, even when Ruthie was not much more than a girl herself. She is not so very old now either, which made me wonder about Garnie speaking out against Sam Russell Sage. If the shoe fits, wear it, Geneva always says. But Ruthie told me later that Garnie does not want any wife of his to lift a finger except to look good, and minister to his needs.

What do you mean, minister to his needs? I said. We were sitting out on the boardinghouse porch by then and I was getting a big kick out of the way folks looked when they came walking by and got a load of Mrs. Little Garnie Rowe.

Oh well, he, I mean, you know—Ruthie's answer trailed off in the breeze. Ruthie had a flat little Tenessee voice that came out of her nose but she could sing like an angel. That night at the First Crusade, she and Mary Magdalene were dressed just alike in pink ruffled dresses with pink bows in their hair and patent leather shoes. They sang Why Not Tonight together.

But that afternoon, I found out how she managed to get nylons in spite of the war. While Garnie was out seeing that every little thing about his Crusade was set up right, I walked by their open door with some towels and saw Ruthie in there with one foot up on a chair, drawing a line up the back of her leg with a grease pencil. She didn't have any nylons at all! Oh hi, she said real quick putting her foot back down, but not before I saw a flash of red silk underwear. She was wearing a fancy robe which Danny Ray told me later was Japanese, making Garnie at best a hypocrite and at worst a traitor. Danny Ray is too smart for his own good. Right then he was eyeballing Ruthie who paced back and forth in the hall wearing her robe and smoking Camels. I sent Danny Ray on down to the river with the rest of the boys.

I sure am glad to meet you, I said to Ruthie who jumped like a shot. She said, Likewise. She had long, long legs, real white. Don't you want to go back up on Sugar Fork with us after this Crusade, I asked her, and take the kids, and see where Garnie grew up?

If he wants to, Ruthie said in her high flat voice. If he wants to, I'd like it a lot, but he—he— She quit talking and started blowing smoke rings, something she did a lot.

When Garnie came back in from checking the set-up for his crusade I said as much to him. And furthermore, I added, Don't you want me to tell Ruthie all about Momma and show her where she died? It was right here, I said to Ruthie, in the corner room upstairs. In my mind I can see Momma so clear, sitting in her little chair.

Garnie shook his head back and forth like a dog coming up from under water. His jowls shook. Then he said, I am no child of hers.

I am a child of God, Garnie went on to say loudly, and I said Oh, and my heart sank for I knew then that the fat silly little Garnie I had loved was already dead and gone too.

Ruthie walked the hall smoking cigarettes, her long white legs flashing, and then it was time for the First Crusade, which Geneva did not attend.

But I went with Oakley to the First Crusade and it was neither better nor worse than I expected. I would rate Little Garnie Rowe about average as a preacher, and I'd bet furthermore that a lot of his fame has come from those that travel with him, such as Little Mary Magdalene in her pink dress, and this other young man that calls himself John Three Sixteen with a real deep singing voice, what Geneva calls a basement voice. But my own mind wandered the way it has done for years in church, and when it came time for the invitational, I enjoyed seeing everyone come forward and was not a bit surprised to see Dreama re-dedicating her life again. She cut her eyes at me but would not speak. She was wearing this hat, you should of seen her!

So Oakley and me drove home in the truck with the boys asleep in the back and Maudy asleep between us, her head laying in my lap.

Well, what did you think? I asked Oakley after a while, and when he didn't say a thing I leaned over in his face and asked him again.

Oakley sighed such a deep sigh that he seemed to draw it in from the night air all around us, from the very mountain. Ivy, I wish you believed, he said. We jolted on through the soft spring night with three of our children asleep in the truck and one dead, up under the apple trees.

I didn't say a word.

But when Garnie showed up on Sugar Fork the next Saturday, I was in a mood to listen even if he was a pig and a fool, and my own little brother to boot. First I heard a car door slam, down there by the creek, and bye and bye here came Garnie in a suit that made him look from a distance like a little black box, panting up the hill.

I was hanging out clothes, with the clothespins in my mouth. The boys had gone over on Deskins Fork with Oakley, where they were building Mrs. Clinton Jones a garage, and Maudy and Martha had gone off for a ride with Rufus Cook. So I was all alone there on the hillside, hanging out my clothes in the windy April day.

There was not a soul around to save me from being saved.

I remember I looked straight up at the patchy fast-moving blue spring sky with the clouds sailing past like kites, and I thought, May be. May be it is finally time. And I thought again of how it was that moment in the kitchen, when I felt like church, and how good that felt. Revel's crazy song came back to me too—

> I know I've been a sinner
> and wicked all my days
> But when I'm old and feeble,
> I'll think upon my ways.

I knew I had been a sinner all right, and although I have been a fool from time to time too, I am not a fool altogether, not so much of a fool that I expect a burning bush, I mean. I knew God could come in stealth and darkness and work in mysterious ways. So it hit me, there on the hillside, This could be it, after all these years. It could be God speaking out through your fat little brother Garnie, and why not? Stranger things have happened. But because I am so contrary, Silvaney, another part of me said, Well, if this is the vessel God has picked to carry his message, then it is a mighty damn poor one! Garnie stood on the big flat rock fanning himself with a funeral fan which I guess he'd brung up there from church, and sweating, all red in the face. Even his scalp was red, under the fuzz of his hair. I kept on hanging up clothes which was hard as the wind kept trying to jerk them away from me. I was not going to say a thing. I was going to make him work for it. Oh Silvaney, I am contrary!

But Garnie didn't say anything either, except Hidy sister, and I said, Hidy. Then he sat down on the rock and started flipping through this little white Bible that he carried in his breast pocket.

So finally I couldn't stand it and I said, How many have you saved this week, Garnie? for his Crusade had been going for a week. It had another week to go.

We have brought 19 souls to God, sister. Garnie said. Since Garnie got to be a preacher, he calls himself we.

I started adding up in my head. So that makes all together . . .

Seven hundred and forty-two, praise God! Garnie cried out in a loud voice. He keeps a running total. Then he took out a snow white handkerchief and mopped his face.

Which brings me to my message here today, he said in a quieter tone, but still sounding like a preacher.

Garnie, why can't you talk like yourself anymore? I said. For try as I might, it was only in little bits and pieces that I could see my brother in him at all.

Because I am not that Garnie any more, Garnie said, getting all worked up. I have been born again into the love of God and the bounty of his Kingdom. I have been washed in the blood of the Lamb, he hollered.

I was losing my will to be saved, and I knew it. I could tell I was closing my mind.

And that is why I have come up this holler today sister, Garnie said, for it has come to my ears that you have sinned and not repented, that my own sister is going to hell in a handbasket without remorse.

I didn't answer, still hanging up clothes.

Well! What have you got to say for yourself? Garnie said, almost hollered. He reminded me of that fat little feist-dog that Geneva used to save scraps for, down in Majestic. Ivy? What do you say? It was like he was jumping for scraps, and all red in the face.

Finally I took the clothespins out of my mouth and said, Well, I bet you've been talking to Dreama Fox.

It don't matter! Garnie yelled. It don't matter where the word comes from, as long as it comes!

But you, he said, hopping off the rock and coming closer, you are a whore and an abomination, and make no mistake about it! What you have done, oh what you have done . . . Garnie was getting so worked up now that spit made little bubbles at the corners of his mouth. I wished they would come back, Oakley and the boys or Maudy and Martha or anybody, I knew that moment I'd had when I might be saved had gone by as fast as one of those swift-moving clouds, and I dreaded what might come next. I wished somebody, anybody else would come to save me. For I was all alone on the hillside with Garnie, who stepped up closer.

I took a deep breath.

I'm glad to hear you saved so many souls, I said. And how much money did you take in?

Ivy you always were too smart which is the flaw in your tragic nature, Garnie sputtered.

I bent down to my basket to get some more shirts. I don't know what you are talking about, I said.

I will tell you Ivy right now, Garnie said. Of making many books there is no end, and much study is a weariness of the flesh. For God shall bring every work into judgement, with every secret thing, whether it be good or whether it be evil. That is the word of God in Ecclesiastes 12:14, Garnie said.

Amen. I was getting mad. I flapped out Oakley's jeans and hung them up.

Whoa now. Hold up honey! Garnie said. You had best not be so fast here. Well do I recall you as a girl and how you held yourself above your sisters and above us all, and see now where it has brought you, Ivy. It has brought you low, it has brought you down into the fiery pit of hell and into damnation, for as God has said in Proverbs 16:5, Every one that is proud in heart is an abomination to the Lord. Though hand join in hand, he shall not be unpunished.

I kept hanging up clothes, but I was getting scared. Garnie was nothing but a fat little feist-dog in a black wool suit and I knew it, yet what he said rung a bell in me someplace for I have been proud Silvaney, in my body and my mind, I am proud still, and if this is sin then I must claim it as my own. I thought of you Silvaney, and how you could not learn, and of Ethel who went without, and of Beulah that day at Diamond when she cried and told me I am the one that had everything, and then threw it all away. The wind picked up and the bed sheets flapped around my head.

Whoa! Garnie shrieked like the wind, it seemed that his voice was the voice of the wind. Listen here Ivy, now listen here! and I knew that he was going to read out of his little Bible although I could no longer see him, nor could I breathe, caught up in the flapping sheet. For a whore is a deep ditch, and a strange woman is a narrow pit, Garnie went on, These things doth the Lord hate, a proud look, a lying tongue, an heart that deviseth wicked imaginations, feet that be swift in running to mischief. And further,

Ivy, further—Proverbs 6:27, Can a man take fire in his bosom, and his clothes not be burned? Whoso commiteth adultery with a woman lacketh understanding. He that doeth it destroyeth his own soul.

What about the woman? I said through the blowing sheet. For that is all about a man.

In the mouth of the foolish is a rod of pride, Garnie said, you poor sinner woman you. Every wise woman buildeth her house, but the foolish plucketh it down with her own hands.

Listen then Ivy, said Garnie, for this is the story of a woman like you, a woman who thought she could take her fill of love until the morning, and our God has said of her in Proverbs 7:25, he has said it out loud and clear, Let not thine heart decline to her ways, go not astray in her paths. For she cast down many wounded, yea, many strong men have been slain by her. Her house is the way to hell, going down to the chamber of death. The chamber of death Ivy, where you dwell now and will dwell forever along with that sweet baby LuIda down in the cold damp earth with her flesh rotting off of her bones while you pull down your pants for any—

But right then, three things happened at the same time.

The first thing was that my heart gave the awfullest leap, jumping up in my throat and pitching me forward just as the sheet flapped up in the wind causing me to stumble and fall to the wet ground, and in that moment when I fell forward on my face in the dirt, in that very moment I had a full good look at Garnie who was unbuckling his belt with a furious face and drooling spit and panting out loud like a dog. I reckon he was fixing to whip me with his belt, but I don't know for sure because all of a sudden there in the middle of it all was Oakley who was the last thing I saw before I pitched forward.

Goddamn you! Oakley said, goddamn you, and Garnie grunted like a pig every time Oakley hit him. Then Oakley was helping me up and blood was running down my front from where I had bit my lip, but in spite of that I grinned to see Garnie stumble off down the hill like a fat little drunk, with mud on the back of his pants. He looked like a funny man in the movies. I was still holding Maudy's little yellow dress which I had been hanging up. It had got all muddy when I fell.

Well Ivy, Oakley said. Oakley had one arm around my waist

and held my elbow with the other one, very formal, as if we were going to promenade. This sure is some family I have married into, Oakley said.

We walked to the house like that, real slow and stately, and stopped at the back steps. My hair had tumbled down of course and kept blowing into my eyes. Oakley touched my hair, my bleeding lip. I looked back at the wash flapping on the line in the wind and it seemed to me like it was dancing, like all of my family and me was out there dancing to beat the band.

So I remain

Your loving, proud, and hellbent sister,
Ivy.

P.S. I have forgot to say that when Garnie left town with his Crusade, Ruthie stayed! For it turned out that Garnie beats her up, and makes her do bad things. She told Geneva all about it, and Geneva said Hellfire honey, it is no use putting up with that! Now she is making desserts for Geneva which she is real good at. One boy, Corey, stayed behind with his mother, but the other boy and Mary Magdalene went on with Garnie and John Three Sixteen and the rest of them. Garnie got ugly at the last, but Geneva stood up to him and threatened to call the sheriff who is one of her old sweeties. And Ruthie told Geneva that Garnie has not really done it for seven years! He <u>can't</u> do it, Ruthie says.

I found Garnie's little white Bible, that he lost in the fight, and I am studying it. It is pretty good. You know how I have always loved a story. I will write more later.

July 10, 1944.

Dear Joli,

I am writing to tell you about Martha's little wedding which we held here, at the house, a week ago. Of course this is not regular but since Oakley and his whole family just about keep the church in business, and since they have got a new preacher down there more broadminded than old Mr. Dent was, it could be done as Martha wished. You know Martha has never before expressed a preference for one thing over another in her whole life, so I said, Let her have her way for Gods sake! And we did. What Martha wanted was not surprising to me, as she has not been out of this house hardly ever in her whole life since we came back here, except lately when she has took to riding with Rufus in his truck. And Rufus is just crazy about her, Joli! It would make you cry to see it. For he dotes on Martha in every particular. He has built her a house down there on Home Creek which is exactly like this one right down to the blue rag rug, so she will feel at home there.

Martha smiles whenever Rufus comes in the room, and follows him everywhere with her eyes. As for Rufus, he grins like a fool. Rufus Cook is the homeliest boy that was ever to walk the face of the earth, I might of mentioned that. He has got a big hook nose like his daddy, and no chin to speak of, and the biggest adams apple you ever saw. It wobbles all the time, and gives him a real high voice. But Martha thinks he hung the moon.

It is a funny thing to me, Joli. For I have figured out that the change in Martha must of occurred when I went off, that time four years ago, me leaving meant that Martha had to jump right in with me gone, she had to do. And she has kept on doing ever since, much more than you would of thought! I do not mean that she can read a book of course nor anything like that, but she can come and go and drive a car and do a lot better than you would of dreamed, five years ago. It is like a miracle to me.

And also it makes me wonder—if you treat somebody as simple, does it make them simple? For that is how we treated Martha for so long.

And if you love somebody, as Rufus loves her, does that bring them out?

Anyway, Martha's little wedding was short and sweet and Rufus did not do a thing but wear a clean white shirt tucked in his jeans with his carpenters rule strung to his belt as always. Mister Blue, that is the new preacher, made it quick. Oakley's folks do not like Mister Blue because he said from the pulpit that he does not think that Catholics are going to hell for the worship of idols, not necessarily. Mister Blue is one of these new kind of preachers that has gone to school for it, not just got the call. Anyway, all he did was get Rufus and Martha to repeat the vows.

Maudy was so excited she liked to have died, you would of thought it was her getting married instead of Martha! Geneva had bought Maudy a sailor dress and we pulled her hair back with a big bow, she looked so cute, she looked like Shirley Temple in a movie, or somebody about to bust loose in a dance. You know she is 8 now, it don't seem possible. LuIda would of been 9.

And Martha is going to have a baby, so it all goes on, I reckon.

And speaking of young love, what are you going to do about yourn? Taylor Cunningham the Third I mean. He sounds like a King to me. Ha ha, just joking. I don't know what you mean, a good catch. I think you have been away from here too long, Joli. I think you ought to come back and let Geneva feed you some lemon chess pie and let me talk some sense into your pretty head. I guess I sound like old Granny Rowe, before long I will look like her too. Your daddy and me are getting old, Joli, it hit me yesterday as we were standing up there with Martha and Rufus and I thought how we stood up ourselves to marry, all those years ago. I looked over at him and I could tell he was thinking the same thing or damn near similar. He squeezed my hand. Your daddy breathes heavy now, you can hear him all over the house, I guess it is all those years in the mine. But he is such a good looking man, I think. He is better looking now than ever.

Anyway Joli, I hope you will think twice before you haul in this good catch of yourn. You better think if you could keep your job on the newspaper too, after the war I mean, or if you would have to just be Mrs. Taylor Cunningham the Third. It might be a full time job!

But here now.

I've saved the best for last.

Because Violet showed up, yes Violet Gayheart, Martha's mama, after all these years! I could not believe it and neither could anyone else. I would not of known her either. For Violet is all business and tough as nails, these days. You know she lost Rush in the mine. Now she has lost R.T. in the war, a year before it even started, on a Navy ship. But this has not slowed her down any, only made her more determined. For Violet Gayheart is a famous woman now, and looks it. She holds herself real tall and dresses up, nice seersucker suit, big black hat, and her face—which was always haunted, some way—has turned into a face you can not forget, for her eyes burn now with what she believes. It is like a part of who she was—the fun Violet I knew back in the Diamond days—has been burned clean out of her. She is a different woman now. I feel like she sees more than I do, and more than I want to see. This is true in fact as well, for she got into an argument right before she left with old Delphi Rolette and his boy Gus over the little truck mine that they are running now on some land they own down by the river. Of course they are not union! There is only five of them working it, and hauling it out in a truck. This is true all over the county which has never been big for the union as there is no real big mines here, not like over in Harlan for instance, or at Diamond. Not since Consolidated Coal pulled out. There is tipples falling down all over these hills.

Listen here, Violet said to Gus. You have got your rights too. You deserve better.

I deserve the right to make a living if I can do it, said Gus Rolette in no uncertain terms. Come on Daddy, and he pulled old Delphi away who did not understand what all the fuss was about or who this dressed up woman was that talked so fast and sounded so definite.

Nor did Martha! I introduced them on the porch before the service, and said real clear, Now Martha, this is your mother, who has come from a long way off.

I'm getting married, Martha said to Violet, who said, I know it, dear. That's why I came, and kissed her. Martha giggled, and seemed to know her then, and Violet helped me fix the flowers in her hair. Rufus sat out back on the steps smoking one Lucky Strike after another. We wouldn't let him come in until we were ready, then Maudy went out and got him.

To the surprise of all, the new preacher said right at the end like he was inspired, Let us not to the marriage of true minds admit impediment, and everybody stared at him. But I said without thinking, Shakespeare. It was like an old rusty door swung open in my mind. He—Mr. Blue—looked at me very careful and nodded. I felt a pain shoot through me, like an arrow in my heart. Oh Joli, you get so various as you get old! I have been so many people. And yet I think the most important thing is Don't forget. Don't ever forget. I tell you this now, in particular. A person can not afford to forget who they are or where they came from, or so I think, even when the remembering brings pain.

After the little service everybody gathered around for the Lady Baltimore cake that Ruthie had made, and ginger ale. We did not have any liquor out where you could see it because of Dreama

Fox and Edith Fox and Ray Senior, and of course the preacher—who might not of minded at all! I cut the cake and gave Martha a piece and she gobbled it right down without passing it around first, and everybody laughed.

That baby is going to be well nourished, the preachers wife said, laughing. She is a plain, cheery woman from the North.

Now pass it around, I said.

Would you like some of this cake mam, Martha said then, giving the next piece to Violet, you couldn't tell if she really knew who Violet was or not. And why would she? For Martha has lived with us all of her life while her mother acted on principle, which I have not.

Would you tell Ivy that I'd like another little piece of that cake? Dreama said to Oakley. She was wearing her awful hat.

I was right there, of course, not ten feet away from Dreama myself, serving the cake. But she will not speak to me.

Ivy, Oakley said, winking at me, Dreama says she wants another piece of cake.

Well she can damn well get it herself then! I flung down the knife and went off to hug Violet Gayheart who was leaving, even though she is not the kind of woman you hug. But Violet started crying and I did too, we go so far back together—to those crazy days at Diamond when I ran around like I was in a fever. I guess you call it youth. Violet smelled like cigarettes and good perfume. She lives in Pittsburgh Pennsylvania where I can not immagine her life. She strode off down the hill like a man going off to work, but stopped at the bottom and turned to blow me a kiss. Then she got in a black car that was waiting for her and they pulled off. I stood by the steps looking out at the misty June day and the blooming rosybush and the leaves of the trees like jewels. A little bit of rain makes all the colors deeper. Geneva ran down the hill arm in arm with Ruthie and they almost slipped, squealing like girls. Judge Brack was waiting for them in his Oldsmobile as he is too old to make the climb.

One by one, they all left including Mr. and Mrs. Rufus Cook in Rufus's new truck with the toolbox across the back and his two new hunting dogs in a cage in the back and Maudy sitting between them. She is going down there to keep Martha company for a while in her new house so she won't get lonely. Nobody seems to wonder if I might be lonely with them all gone, or may be they know I will not! With the new library down in town, I can get all the books I want. And I have got your daddy here to look after, and Bill who has quit school awhile back and works with your daddy now, and Danny Ray who is horsing to go in the Army. By the way there was a Patterson boy killed, I forget which one, at Saipan. Danny Ray says he wants to go in because he don't fit in here and there is nothing for him to do when he finishes high school, and I guess he is right. He has awful fights with his daddy who says he is wasting time reading, so I dont know.

After Martha's wedding, your daddy and me sat out on the porch taking a little drink until it got dark, which is not a bad way to pass the time. I was thinking about all of you. You know Joli, the older I get, the more it seems to me like you never can tell what will happen in this world. I bet you are like me and never thought—never thought for a minute!—that our Martha would up and get married. Now did you? But she has.

And so I remain up here on Sugar Fork

Your loving,
Mama.

June 26, 1945.

Dearest Joli,

You are sweet to want us to come to the wedding and please tell Taylor, he is real kind to offer to pay our way. Your daddy and I would give anything if we could come honey, but you know it is just too far. The fact is that your daddy has not been feeling good atall lately, he could not make the trip. So you will just have to get married without us present I reckon, if you can stand it! And we will be thinking about you all that day and wishing the best for you honey. I sure hope you know what you are doing! Lord knows you are <u>old</u> enough to know what you want by now, not like so many here who do it without a thought. I feel like they say, <u>Oh I might go to the store today, or I might get married</u>— and then they up and get married, with no more thought than that! Well, I was young myself once.

Ethel sends her love and so does Victor. And Geneva says to tell you some advice, it is, <u>Do not ever go to bed mad.</u> This is good advice and you ought to take it. Geneva may not be very good at marriage, but she is good at men.

So, have a fine wedding honey, and a real good honeymoon. I hope you can go before too long. I know you will love Paris France. Kiss the groom for me! And you all come home to visit when you can.

For I am thinking about you all the time.

And you can rest assured that there never was a daughter in this wide world that brought more joy to her mother's heart.

I remain your loving,

Mama.

Oh Silvaney,

I have just wrote Joli a letter declining to come to her wedding which has fair broke my heart. For I would love to go, and travel across Virginia on a train paid for by Taylor Cunningham the Third, and see what there is to see! But Oakley does not feel up to the trip, plain and simple. His breathing has not been good ever since we left Diamond, now it is worse. And it is more than that.

Oakley feels we <u>ought not</u> to go, and in my heart of hearts I know he is right.

Last night we went walking after dinner as we have taken to doing lately, down the holler to the road and down the road to where Bill has cleared the new field, and it was one of those summer nights when the mist rises up real thick and soft from the creek, and lots of lightning bugs were blinking. Maudy was back up at the house catching them, her and that little Rolette girl. They had took a mason jar and made a hole in the top and they were filling it up with lightning bugs for a lantern. Remember when me and you used to do the same? Bill is growing tobacco in the new field, it gives Oakley a deal of pleasure to see it grow. Him and Bill are building a little tobacco barn by that stand of pines, to cure it.

So Oakley and I were down there looking at the tobacco and watching the mist rise.

I was still thinking that we might make the trip. What do you reckon I ought to wear? I was saying. I bet I can borry something from Ruthie, for we are about the same size.

Now Ivy—Oakley took my hand.

What? I said, jerking my hand back, for I knew what.

I just don't believe we ought to go out there, Oakley said.

Why not? She wants us to come, she will send us the fare, she said so, I told Oakley. But I felt something settle in my chest.

Now Ivy, Oakley said again. She could of come here and got married if she had chose.

But she has got all her friends over there where she has been living for so long, I said.

Her whole family is here, Oakley said. I could not even see him by then through the mist, just hear his hateful voice, so calm and full of sense.

So you are saying that if she had wanted us at the wedding, she would of done it here, I said.

I am not saying a thing, honey, Oakley said. And it may be that Joli has not had too much to do with it anyway. I think you ought to let a sleeping dog lie. Anyway, didn't she bring him out here to meet us?

Yes, I had to say.

Well then, Oakley said. That is enough right now.

Then the hoot owls started up, there is a real old one that has been down there for years, someplace back in the woods close by the steppingstones.

Where are you? I said, and Oakley said, Right here, and we walked up to the house together. The hoot owls sounded like people calling back and forth through the trees. Other times they sound like cats, or like the inside of your head, screaming. That is what I used to think, the summer after LuIda died. Oh Oakley, I said, and he put his arm around me and we went on to bed early despite of Maudy and Ronda Rolette making fudge in the kitchen.

You know Silvaney, it is a funny thing, but that time I ran off with Honey Breeding helped not hurt, with me and Oakley. He has been new for me ever since, some way, and me for him, and even though I am way too old now to think on such things, I blush to say they come to mind often, they do! I am always ready for Oakley to lay me down. Back when I was lost in darkness, it was not so. For when you are caught so far down, you can not immagine the sun, or see a ray of sunshine any place. You can not get out of yourself enough to see even the outline of any one else. But now Oakley stands before me full in flesh, with those steady eyes and that one-sided grin and that same shock of hair that will not lay flat. He is the same old Oakley yet he is different, I can not explain it. I am yearning towards him always. Of course Oakley doesn't say much, he never did, but I have got used to it now.

I have just remembered something.

In my mind I go back to a time when I was a girl and Momma and Geneva and some other women, I forget who, were sitting out on the porch down at the boardinghouse talking about men. And one of these other women hove a big sigh and said, <u>Well, I will tell you girls, my marital duties have about wore me out.</u> She looked like they had too! And this other woman said <u>she</u> did not have to do it any more because of her spastic colitis. And I remember how Geneva winked at Momma, and even sad thin Momma could not stop a little smile from coming to her lips. Momma closed her eyes and leaned back in her rocker and rocked and smiled and rocked, while the other women talked on about men.

I was a little girl sitting on the porch steps, listening.

And now I am old. But Silvaney, it is still real good with me and Oakley, it is better than before, in spite of us being so old! I know you are not shocked by me saying this even though you are still a maiden lady, for you are my soul, and my soul is as wild as ever! I am glad of it too. Anyway Oakley went on to sleep right after we done it, and then the girls went to bed too. I could hear them talking for a while and then they went to sleep and it got real quiet. I could still hear the hoot owls down by the creek but soft now, like doves.

I got up and went out on the porch where I set for a while and smoked one of Oakley's cigarettes. It seemed like no time since that night that I come out here to find Babe passed out cold in the yard, and you sitting right there with him in the moonlight.

It seems like yesterday. I can still see the way your hair looked, rippling and long and light. Oh Silvaney, do you wrap it up around your head now, as I do? And is it not turning gray?

Maudy and the Rolette girl had left their lightning bug lantern out on the porch, so I picked it up and held it. It glowed and moved and changed, it was always glowing and always changing,

right there in my hands. I will tell you quite frankly, Silvaney—
Joli has broken my heart. For she is the child of my childhood,
and in losing her, I have lost my youth. I can not say it better than
that. I wanted her gone, I wished her godspeed, but now I am
about to die because she has took me up on it! Oh, I am contrary.
It is true! She has travelled far beyond me now. Martha is more
my girl, in all truth, and I do feel good when I think of her wedding.
I know she is in good hands with Rufus Cook.

I wish I could say the same for Joli.

But I was not impressed with Taylor Cunningham Three when
they came to visit. Joli was nervous, which put me off. You know
she has always been quick and changeable, this is her nature, and
the light comes and goes in her face like a lightning bug lamp.
But I had never seen her nervous. So what was she worrying about?
What was she afraid of? Did she care so much what Taylor Three
was going to think?

It would not have worried me none if I'd been here, for as far
as I could tell, he didn't think a thing! I mean nothing. Taylor
Three had one of those faces you have seen before on fine china
plates, white and exact, painted in tiny detail, too pretty. He has
a dimple in his chin, which I have always hated in a man. He has
a wide forehead and curly blond hair that is too brassy, fixed too
careful, and soft white hands that look like he has never worked
a day in his life. He is a lawyer. He grew up in Richmond and
went to the University. Joli says he is real smart, and this must
be so since he is marrying her! He must have something to
him. But I'll swear, I can't see it. All I know is that he has real
good manners and carries a leather cigarette case and makes her
nervous.

Bill liked him because Taylor Three asked him all about raising
tobacco, and listened hard to the answers. Then he asked Oakley
all about the mines and the union, and Oakley has never talked
so much nor so well, before or since. Joli looked from Taylor
Three to her daddy, back and forth, while all this was going on.
It made her so happy she was about to bust, you could tell. Don't
you think Daddy likes him? she asked me later, and I had to say
honestly, Yes.

But as for me, I am not so sure. I think Taylor Three is mighty
pretty, mighty cold. I think he might be the kind that will be real
interested in you for as long as you're offering what he needs, and

then drop you like a hot potato. I hope I'm wrong. But I can not bring myself to trust a man with soft hands and a dimple. Franklin Ransom had a dimple too.

That lightning bug lantern reminded me so much of Joli—not Maudy, never Maudy, who is a girl like a 100-watt bulb. I sat and held the lantern in my hands, listening to the owls, watching it glow, and change, and glow, and change. <u>Like all of us.</u> This thought came to me all of a sudden. For Danny Ray is back from Germany now and going to East Tenessee State, I don't know if I told you that or not, and our Bill has moved into a house down on Home Creek with a young widow woman named Marlene Blount whose husband did not come back from the war. She is ten years older than Bill if she's a day! And has two big old boys. Plus she is sort of fat. But she is real good-natured and keeps Bill grinning, I will say that. The other day when Oakley and me were driving to town, we went right by her house and there was Bill out in the yard throwing a baseball with her two boys, and she came outside and hollered them all in to supper! It beats all. It is like Marlene Blount has got one more kid. But Bill has always been real happy-go-lucky, just like a kid, and Marlene is a good mother. As for me, I'd never say a word against it anyway. I <u>couldn't.</u> Not after what I did.

So I sat out on the porch in the pulsing light of the lamp and after a while I started getting sleepy. But before I went back to bed, I unscrewed the lid of the jar and dumped the lightning bugs out on the porch. At first they kind of crawled around as if they did not want to go anyplace. But then they seemed to figure things out and they rose up together like a little blinking cloud—up, up, and out across the yard and up into the trees until they were out of sight.

And I remain your loving sister,

Ivy.

Dear Joli,

I know Ethel has called you up on the long distance telephone which I could not bear to do.

So I know that you know about your daddy.

We buried him yesterday. But somehow it did not seem real to me, not even then. It does now, for I am writing you this letter.

I will try not to go on and on as is my want.

The funeral was preached by Rev. Ancil Collins, the old preacher they used to have who came back here special to do it, as he said he has never known a better man than Oakley Fox in all his life. Rev. Collins uses a cane now and can't hardly see. He was assisted by Mr. Blue and by Delphi's boy Cord who has got the call. Cord told about how he knew your daddy from a child and how your daddy carved him a little horse when his pony died. I had never heard this story before. It was real sad. Everyone was crying and fanning themselves. The little Ramey's Chapel Church was full to overflowing, with folks sitting out in the grass and standing back in the shade of the trees. Somebody had dug up ferns from along the creek and filled the whole front of the church plum up with them. It looked so pretty and was fitting for your daddy too, who loved these mountains so. Dreama cried and fainted dead away when they carried him out. She has always got to be the center of attention. Your grandmama Fox could not come as she is in the hospital down at Majestic. Your grandpa came to the church but could not make the climb to the house nor to the burying ground.

All I will say about the burying is, there has never been so many people up this holler before, not ever. And it so hot, with a thunderstorm coming up! But yet they came, all the folks from church and town and Home Creek, more besides. You would not think a quiet man would know so many, nor be so loved. For a man who did not say much, he got around a good bit! All kinds of people come up to speak to me and Ethel and Bill and Danny Ray and Victor, telling stories of how your daddy fixed their bridge after it got washed out, or how he gave them some money when their old man died, or he gave them one of those little carved bears to give to their boy for Christmas, or he drove them into town to see the doctor or catch the train and I don't know what all.

You can rest assured of one thing.

I believe your daddy was the best man in the county, bar none. If there is a heaven, your daddy is right there.

His grave is up high next to my own father's, facing East so he will see the sun rise and can look upon Bethel Mountain as always. I have to stop now. Because I have written this letter to you, it is real now.

In grief I remain your loving,

Mama.

Oh Silvaney,

It has been over a month now, it is September and the leaves start to fall, a big yellow sycamore leaf landed all of a sudden on the porch yesterday. It was like a blow to my heart. And when I went walking, I saw where the horsechestnut has changed to red, a red fan of spiky leaves just blazing amongst the green.

Oakley was too young to die.

And I am too young to be a widow woman even though some days I feel old as the hills themselves which I walk among now almost without ceasing, I know they are saying it up and down the holler that I am crazy, crazy like Tenessee, may be that is right. For my grief is so long and so cold, as cold as Oakley's cheek when they put him in the grave oh he had the prettiest coffin Rufus stayed up two nights running to make it, Martha says he couldn't hardly see to hit a nail, for crying. You have got to cut this out Ivy. You can't go on like this, Geneva came up here to say and took Maudy down there with her for a visit. You have got to get a hold on yourself, Geneva said. But I wake in the early light and walk, I can't help it, I go again and again to the ridge where we picked the berries and the berries is up there still, now spoiling on the bushes for folks has no longer got time to climb up there and pick them and cook. Folks can just buy what they want at the store, and do so. But I go and stand in the little cave nearby, where he first kissed me, and whenever I close my eyes I can see him coming out of the mine at Diamond, and feel my heart leap up to see his face. Oh Silvaney, I never knowed how much I loved him until I left him, and that's a fact. And now I have lost him again and this time it is for good. No it is not for good. It is for ever. Life seems contrary to me, as contrary as I am. I feel like you never say what you ought to, nor do as you should, and then it is too late. It is all over. I have spent half of my life wanting and the other half grieving, and most often I have been wanting and grieving the same thing. There has been precious little inbetween.

Oakley's preacher Mr. Blue came up here but nothing he said made me feel any better, and when he said, Now let us bow our heads in prayer, Mrs. Fox, before he left, I just looked down and noted the dust devils everyplace in this house which I have not touched for a month nor will I let Martha nor Marlene Blount come up here to clean it for me. Oakley's absence is filling it up, this is why I have to leave and go walking. And I know he loved the mountains where I walk.

Oh lord Silvaney, over and over I see in my mind the night he died, he woke up with a pain in his chest, he knew he was dying.

Ivy, he said, turn on the light, and I did, and his face was as gray as his hair. Ivy, my Ivy, he said. I had to bend down to his mouth to hear the words. Ivy I love you, he said, and then, My God.

So then he died, and God has got him now not me.

It was so hot walking up that hill. I kept thinking I saw Granny Rowe around the bend ahead. I thought I saw her long black skirt go swishing, and smelled her pipe smoke in the air. Two others besides Dreama passed out that day from the heat and we left them and gone on up there and got him in the ground as the black clouds were piling up in the sky and the air grew green and still.

Amen, I remember Mr. Blue said Amen just before the thunder cracked and everybody started back down. By the time we hit Pilgrim Knob, the rain was falling hard and big drops were splatting like silver dollars in the dusty yard. They left then, everybody except Ethel. I made them go. Ethel laid down on the bed to rest when the last one left, Mrs. Johnnie Sue Rasnick who is always the first to come and the last to go. She loves a funeral.

It started raining nice and steady, and I went out on the porch. I had sat there so long, over so many years and years, with Oakley, I didn't hardly see how I could sit there by myself. I looked at Oakley's rocker which Rufuses daddy had made and gave to Momma years ago, that old rushbottom rocker with the seat now curved to Oakley's shape. One of his knives was laying right there, and some little pieces of wood, and shavings all around his chair from where he whittled. You know he was always whittling, mostly those little bears. He made them doing everything! Running, sleeping, sitting up, playing. I can't tell you how many people have asked for a little bear to remember him by, but when I went out to the old tobacco barn to find some more, I couldn't find a one. He had given them all away. They are all over this county now. But that is how Oakley was. And then I felt so <u>mean</u> because I used to bitch at him for helping folks for free, or for getting shavings all over the porch! I looked over at Oakley's chair for a while as the rain started pouring harder, and then finally I sat down in my own chair.

It got almost dark—dark green air, and the heavy rain smell came up from all around me. It was like the earth was steaming. Then I cried. I cried a long time. I cried until finally Ethel came to the door and said, <u>Come here Ivy, I want to show you something,</u> and then she took my hand and led me in the kitchen and showed me what all was still there, even after so many folks had come and gone. Meat loaf, a carrot cake from Ruthie, Geneva's fried chicken of course, and Marlene Blount's potato salad. Ethel got her a plate of that and me a plate, and sat down.

<u>Sit down,</u> she said to me, and I did, and she took a bite and I did too. <u>What do you think?</u> she said, and I said, <u>Too much onion.</u>

<u>I don't guess he is marrying her for her potato salad,</u> Ethel said, and I said, <u>What do you mean, marrying her?</u> for that was the first I had heard of it.

<u>Well I don't know that for sure,</u> Ethel said. <u>But I betcha.</u>

So we ate the potato salad and then some boiled custard and carrot cake.

Then Ethel turned on the radio which still makes me cry as it reminds me of Oakley so much. He was just crazy to hear all about Jackie Robinson.

Well, Ethel stayed up here with me for a while and then she left and I took up walking as I said, and now I am about walked out. I am ready to go down and get Maudy back from Geneva's and may be sell off another little piece of this land if I can do so. Corey is offering to come up here and stay for a while, and Martha says she will loan me that little boy of hers and Rufuses who is cute as can be. But I have said no to all that. I will not be lonely. Even if it is just me sitting on this porch, I will not be lonely.

Although I know that not one hour for the rest of my life will go by without me missing Oakley and that's a fact. But I will tell you another fact which is just as true, it hit me yesterday.

I can read every book that John O'Hara ever wrote.

I can make up my own life now whichever way I want to, it is like I am a girl again, for I am not beholden to a soul.

I can act like a crazy old woman if I want to which I do.

I can get up in the morning and eat a hot dog, which I did yesterday. I don't know what I might do tomorrow!

But for sure I will remain your loving sister,

Ivy.

July 11, 1952.

Dear Joli,

Sure.

Send him on.

You know I will be happy to have a boy around here again as I have lost too many, I can use one. It will keep me young. The road is real good now from here to town and Maudy can drive him to school when it starts. Ethel and Victor got her a car for her 16th birthday it is a powderblue Sprint convertible. Maudy makes you say powderblue instead of just blue. She is a majorette. Maudy is a sight in this world and she has got a job in the dime store selling make-up and records. So, David can walk over to Geneva and Ruthie's after school and then Maudy will pick him up when she gets off work, and bring him up here. We have got it all figured out. Ethel has already got him a slinky to play with. So you just send him on, and we will be tickled to death.

Now then. There is not a reason in the world for you to feel bad about getting a divorce, Joli. The divorce like the T.V. is the wave of the future it seems to me! And if people could of done it way back when—if they had of known they could do it, I mean—why there would be a lot of them divorced today instead of just crazy. This is a fact. Instead what happened is they just stayed together for life until one of them got sick and died, that's what, like Stoney Branham and his first wife. Or like Delphi Rolette who would of left that crazy Reva in a minute if he'd thought he could. And him such a handsome man. But he was stuck, as so many are stuck.

You know I would be the last one in the world to get on to you for something like this. I am glad you are going back to school too. And if you want to be a writer, I am glad. I know where you get that from, Ha!

I only have one thing to say to you Joli, about all of this. It is, do not feel bad about Taylor Three, and do not think that it is your fault or any fault with you. It is not your fault. Do not listen to that mother of his either. Forget it. Forget her. It was in his nature, and that is that.

I was thinking today about something your daddy said one time. I think you will like to hear this. We had been out walking in the woods down by the creek and he saw this old stump and drug it home. Then he just set it in the middle of the yard and walked around and around it, whistling. It was an ugly thing, with roots poking up ever which way, all gnarly and old.

What are you aiming to do with that, Daddy? Are we going to chop it up? asked Bill and Danny Ray. They loved to chop things up.

No siree, your daddy said. He kept circling the stump and whistling.

I went in the house and got some beans and some newspaper to string them on, and came back out there and sat down and started stringing them and watching him. Finally I couldn't stand it any more and I said, Oakley honey, what are you doing?

And your daddy said, I am studying the nature of this stump.

This was the first animal he ever made, Joli. This was that floppy eared dog that he gave to that kindercare center that Ludie runs. But later, a lot later it must of been several years, he said almost the same thing to the newspaper lady that came up here taking pictures of his animals.

She said, Mister Fox, where do you get your ideas from? I can see her yet in my mind's eye, licking her lips, with her pencil ready to write.

Oakley took his time answering her. He looked over at Bethel Mountain for a while, and then he looked at his animals, and then he looked at her. Finally he said, I am bad to find the nature of a stump. I will never forget it. <u>Bad to find the nature of a stump,</u> he said.

For it is so, Joli.

The true nature will come out whether or no, we have all got a true nature and we cant hide it, it will pop out when you least expect it. I never thought I would walk up the mountain my dear with Honey Breeding, and once I got up there, I never thought I would come back down. Nor that I would turn into an old mountain woman like I have, and proud to be so.

Honey, honey. Now I mean <u>you,</u> Joli. This is Taylor's nature that is all, may be it is not even so unnatural as we all think! The older I get, the more different things seem natural enough to me. I take a real big view! Just remember that it is no reflection on <u>you,</u> and then forget it. Put him behind you and go on. I did not think he was your kind anyway, Joli. I thought he made you nervous. So keep that in mind for next time. If a man makes you nervous at all, if a man makes you feel uncomfortable even for a reason you can't name, then that is not the one.

Do not worry about sending money as I have sold off a little more land, we will get by fine.

I am fixing up the boys old room for David. I am painting it aqua blue! Rufus is bringing him a new little desk over here tomorrow. He made it.

Take it easy.

I remain your loving,

Mama.

March 21, 1954.

Dear Joli,

Put down everything you are doing right now and listen to me. I mean it. Make yourself a cup of coffee and sit down and put your feet up.

The first thing is, I did not raise you, nor any one of you, to be a quitter. For you take after me and Ethel and Beulah, who are spitfires as you know. Your hair is as red as ours was! Remember this, Joli—if you act like a rug, everybody is going to walk on you. You are not the first one to get a divorce nor will you be the last, a woman does not need to have a man around all the time anyway!

So, buck up. Here is some money from me and a check signed by Victor which is really from Ethel, now do not be stupid. Go on and cash it. Get yourself a new pair of shoes. Geneva always said, A new pair of shoes will make anybody feel better! But do not take any money from Taylor Three's mother at all, we will not be beholden to her in any way. I can see her feeling guilty since he has run off to California with that person. I guess she is embarassed too, I would be! But I would just steer clear of them all if it was me honey, I think she sounds crazy. She can start David a trust fund if she has got a mind to do something, this is what Danny Ray is suggesting. You know the government is paying for him to go to law school now, so we might as well take his advice on the legal. He is going to call you up on the long distance telephone and talk to you about it. So you listen to him good, and cash this check, and do not be so stubborn trying to make ends meet. If you work all the time, you won't be able to study, nor to write anything at all.

And I am counting on you now to be a writer which I never was. I read the best book the other day that Marlene brought me up from the drugstore, it was Gone With the Wind, I guess you have all ready read it. I stayed up all night long for two nights, reading that. It seemed so real, it seemed like it was happening right down there on Home Creek. Oh Joli! It is no time atall that you and me were sitting out together in the sweet long grass and I knew what all you had read and what you'd not. And now you have gone on past me down the road. It is too late for you to turn back, honey. You have got past the point where you can do that, past the point where you could ever come back here and live. I know it and you know it. So you have got to keep on keeping on. I know it is hard sometimes.

But your David is fine, we get the biggest kick out of him! The fact is, Ethel and Victor and me are all fighting over him, he is so sweet. He is real good company. He likes to play with Marlene Blount's boys, Ernest and John and Bobby, they would tumble around out there like monkeys all day long if we would let them. By the way, Marlene is going to have another baby now which is

Bills of course, he is tickled pink! It is time he made an honest woman of her, too. Bill and Marlene put all of them boys in the back of his truck and took them clear to Richlands to see a movie in 3-D. David has talked and talked about it. He wears those crazy 3-D glasses all the time. And Maudy has taught him how to dance the jitterbug. I think it is fair to say, he is having a real good time here. He does so good in school, too. His teacher is Mrs. Price Johnson who was Betty Duveen that is one of the Duveens from up on Six and Twenty Mile Branch. Anyway his teacher thinks he is so sweet. The thing about a grandchild is, you do not feel like you have got to raise them up so careful for you know it will not do that much good anyway (Ha). So you get a real bang out of them instead, or I do mine.

I don't know if I wrote you or not, but all the school kids have to take a little towel and lay down on it for an hour at lunchtime, so they will not get polio. David likes to take a red towel with flowers. I guess it is a good idea for them to lay down at lunch.

Now I will tell you the funniest thing David did down at Geneva's the other day at Sunday lunch. We had corn on the cob and David just loved it. He ate about three ears. Then after lunch when he was helping them to clear the table, he said to me, Mamaw, Mamaw, where do I put the bones?

Why, what bones, honey? I said, for we had had chicken pie.

These corn bones! David said, and all present just about died laughing. He is so cute. He has not growed a bit since he has been here but he eats like a horse, I reckon he will start to shoot up before long.

Here is some real news. Since Victor has more and more trouble getting around, Ethel says she is going to sell the store and move him down to Florida where he has always wanted to go, he says. I think Victor just thought this up lately, so he would have something to talk about all the time and devil everybody with. You know how he is. I bet he is surprised that Ethel has took him up on it. But you know Ethel! She will do anything. Plus she has been saying that the Magic Mart is putting a big dent in her business and she wants to get out while the getting is good. Anyway, she has sold the store to Hawk Matney for a good sum, and they are going. I cannot picture them in Florida at all. There is one of Stoney Branham's boys down there that has found them a little house, dirt cheap. That's what Ethel says. She says it is pink and has a lime tree in the yard. Ethel says she wants to fish off a dock, and sit out under a palm tree, and watch the world go by. She says she wants to paint her fingernails and eat key lime pie. I don't know what in the world Victor thinks he will do down there. I bet they will be back up here in no time flat. Ethel says to me, Ivy, you ought to come too, and I did think about it some, but I said No. I cannot feature me being there, and said so.

I belong right here, I told Ethel. I've got things to do!

And that is all the news for now except that Judge Brack just lays in the downstairs bedroom at Geneva's without even moving a muscle. He will not eat a thing either but mashed-up bananas and oatmeal which I guess a person could live on if they had to. Geneva has hired a girl to sit right by him when she can't be there, but mostly she is.

Anyway, you study hard and don't worry about David, I am not going to go to Florida anytime soon. David is no drain on me honey, but the perfect joy of my heart. When the time comes, I will hate to send him back.

I remain your loving,

Mama.

Sept. 7, 1956.

Dear Ethel,

I am sorry to hear that Victor is not doing too good, but as long as he stays off the bottle I guess that is all we can hope for. May be he was just too old to move, and too set in his ways. Or may be you all just want something big to fight over! I did not think he would like it down there. I am surprised to hear that you like it as good as you do. I guess it helps to have the job, you always were a good hand to sell things, it ought to keep you and Victor out of each other's hair some. It is just like you Ethel, to retire down to Florida and start working all over again! You are as bad as me.

But I am writing today because I have got some sad news to tell you. Beulah is dead. She has been dead for a year now. Of course she has been dead to us for years anyway. However it is tragic, to learn that this is real. The way I know this is Curtis Bostick, who came up here to visit in a big gray car that had fishtail fins on it.

Here is how it all happened.

Maudy was up here Saturday playing her record player, Heart-break Hotel by Elvis Presley who I like almost as much as she does. I think he is so good to his mother. Anyway, Maudy was playing Heartbreak Hotel over and over and kind of dancing around the house like she does, she is the flittingest girl! And bye and bye she stops dancing and stands looking out the open door and says, Mama, they is a strange man coming up here. He has parked his car down the holler.

What kind of man? I said, and Maudy starts giggling. A big old fat one, she says.

What kind of a car? I says, trying to figure it out.

The biggest Buick you ever saw, Maudy says. Gray.

So I go over there and stand looking down the holler. It is a cloudy, edgy day.

Who is it? Maudy asks me.

I said, for I knew him right off the bat, I swan. It couldn't be.

Couldn't be who? Maudy says, who is dancing.

Curtis Bostick, I said, but she could not hear me over Elvis who was singing, I'm so lonely, I'm just so lonely I could die. Curtis climbed the hill real slow and dignified. If he looks like anybody it is Herbert Hoover. So you can immagine, Ethel! But it is a funny thing, I would of knowed him anyplace. Lord he has gotten fancy however. I guess he has come up in the world. He has finally gotten as important as he thought he was! He wore a striped suit with a gold watch chain hanging out of his pocket, a black hat, a red silk tie, soft black leather shoes that were getting muddy. Curtis Bostick ought to of known better than to wear such shoes up here!

That is your uncle, I said to Maudy. The husband of your Aunt Beulah that we have not set eyes on for years and years.

Since the dinosaur days, Maudy said. She did not seem one bit interested which made me recall what she told Mr. Jennings, her ninth grade history teacher, that she did not want to learn about anything that happened before she was born. Well Maudy, that cuts out a lot! Danny Ray said then.

I did not have time to get fixed up.

I stepped out on the porch just as Curtis Bostick reached the steps.

Ivy! he said. He just stood there staring. He liked to of stared a hole through me. Then he held out his hands and I went over there and took them. Curtis Bostick's hands were as soft as a pretty woman's.

I've thought—he started to say. Lord I have immagined—he said.

Then to my complete surprise he started crying, sobbing just like a little boy. This even got Maudy's attention. She came and stood out on the porch to see him cry. It's down at the end of Lonely Street, it's Heartbreak Hotel, Elvis sang.

Honey go turn that down I told Maudy, who did.

I took him by the hands and led him to the steps and sat him down. Curtis, it is so good to see you after all these years, I said even though that remained to be seen at the time. Now where is Beulah? I asked him for I could not wait to know.

But I read the answer in his face before he spoke.

Beulah is dead, he said. She died a year ago next month. He wiped his face with a fine handkerchief that had his initials on it, C.N.B. Try as I might, I couldn't remember what the N. was for. I bet he made it up so he would have three initials.

Maudy, go get us some ice tea, I said.

Then I asked him, Dead of what?

Curtis took a deep breath. Well, it is hard to say, Sirrosis of the liver primarily, but it is more than that.

You know how bad she wanted to leave Diamond, he said.

I remember, I said.

Well it may be that we should not have done it, Curtis said slowly. Because in some way she was never again the same woman that she was here. Charleston was too much for her, he said. The rest of her life was too much for her.

What do you mean? I asked.

Her nerves went bad, Curtis said. I blame myself for it. I was so busy at the time, working day and night, but I thought Beulah was happy. Hell, she should have been happy! She wanted so many things, and I gave them all to her. I gave her everything. She had everything she ever wanted, Ivy, believe me. Everything! A big house on the hill, a cook, a hired girl, the best of everything for those kids. Summer camps, private schools—

Curtis fumbled around in his pocket and got a cigarette out of a silver case, and lit it, and went on. But I don't know, Ivy—it was like, the more she had, the more she wanted. Not things—I see that now—I just thought it was things. I was killing myself, buying them so many things.

What did she want then? I asked. Thank you honey, I said to Maudy who had finally brung the ice tea.

I don't think she knew, Curtis said. But I think she was desperately lonely.

She never wrote me back, I said. We never heard word one.

I think she was scared to. Beulah wanted to get away from her past, from where she'd come from, what she'd been. From you. From all of you. She felt like the past was holding her back, Curtis said. She wouldn't let my mother visit either, or my brother Ricky, and she wouldn't let me talk about any of you-unses or find out what you were up to.

Curtis had got so worked up that he said <u>you-unses</u> like he had never left this county. But I don't think he even noticed it. It was like she couldn't find enough things to fill up her day, he said. Why, she was the head of every club in Charleston, there for a while. She was real important.

<u>But,</u> I said.

<u>But she was drinking,</u> Curtis said. Drinking sherry all day long. For years I didn't know it. Nobody knew it except the cook. But then there came the years when she was sick so much, when finally I did know, and everybody else knew too.

What did you do then? I asked.

Well, there wasn't much I could do for a long time, Curtis said. Beulah denied that there was any problem at all, and the kids were growing up fine on their own, we had sent them away to school because of the situation, and of course I did not want to embarass Beulah. You know how much she hated to be embarassed, Curtis said, and I nodded. Well I remembered that! <u>And I was working double time, what with the war and all</u>—Curtis took the last drag of his cigarette and threw it out in the yard—<u>Anyway, finally, her liver went. Just like that.</u> Curtis snapped his fingers and looked around. Then he seemed to remember something. He reached in his breast pocket and pulled out a little parcel wrapped in tissue. I looked at him. <u>It is for you, Ivy,</u> Curtis said.

I took it and unwrapped it carefully.

It was Momma's brooch, that little spray of violets with tiny purple stones, held together by the pretty golden bow.

Did Beulah say for you to give this to me? I asked Curtis, for you know that Beulah and I had not parted on the best of terms.

I am giving it to you, Curtis said. It belonged to your mother.

I know, I said. I pinned it to my dress. Curtis watched me.

Did she say anything? I asked.

When?

When she died.

Curtis lit another cigarette and thought for a while.

Not right then, he said. But about three days prior, she sat straight up in the bed and said, A true lady will not let a silence fall.

Beulah said that?

Curtis nodded. I think it was from a book she had.

I could see that book in my mind's eye still—red, worn, with illustrations. The ladies in the illustrations were very thin.

That sounds like Beulah! I had to smile.

Curtis had been staring at my yard. Now he stared at me.

What are you doing with all these crazy animals up here, Ivy? he asked.

Those animals were made by my late husband, I said.

Your late husband, Curtis repeated.

Yes, I said.

Well, he said after a while. I'm so sorry.

But I didn't think he was. Don't you remember Oakley Fox? I said. From down on Home Creek? That was my husband, I said.

I never had the pleasure, Curtis said.

He was looking at me again, the way he had stared when he first came up here. It made me feel so funny. I wished Maudy would come out on the porch but I could hear her back in the kitchen, banging things around. This is how Maudy cooks, she will mess up every pot and pan in there to make one thing.

I was getting nervous. Tell me about your children, then, I said real cheerful. I wanted to know in particular about John Arthur since I used to take him downtown at Diamond, to see the train.

John Arthur is a banker now in Pittsburgh, Curtis said. He is much like me, God help him, Curtis said.

I let that go. And the others? I asked.

Curtis Junior died in the Korean War, Curtis said. He had turned wild and had gotten into a lot of trouble, so I paid him out of it and forced him to enlist. I forced him. Sometimes even now at night before I sleep, I hear that conversation over and over in my head. I made him go. I killed him, Curtis said.

Oh Curtis, I said. Then I asked, Delores?

Delores is a housewife in Cincinnati, Curtis said. She married a doctor.

Well that sounds good, I said. I reckon.

Then he fell silent. But I had run out of things to say too, and I hated that awful staring.

What about Franklin Ransom? I asked finally, surprising myself.

He's dead too, Curtis said, he has been dead for six or seven years now. You remember how wild he was.

I nodded. I had to smile.

Well, he got himself a private plane and took up barnstorming, Curtis said. Lord, he flew everyplace! And there was no trick he couldn't do. In fact he was in a fair way to get famous right before the war, but then he enlisted of course, and came home a hero with one foot gone. He had been shot down over Italy. He was a genuine war hero.

Then what happened?

Hell, Ivy, I don't know. He has been quoted as saying that it was all nothing after the war.

What was all nothing? What did he mean?

Life, I reckon, Curtis said. He was the kind of a man that needed a war to fight in, and once the war was over, he couldn't stand it. The lack of a war was what killed him, in my opinion.

How did he die? I asked.

Curtis took a deep breath. He flew that pretty little red plane into the face of the cliff at Stone Mountain, Georgia, in the middle of an air show. A thousand people watching. I'm surprised you didn't see it in the paper, Curtis said. It was in all the papers.

I don't read too many papers, I said.

You used to read a lot, Curtis said.

Yes, I answered.

There was a lot of talk about it at the time. They are sure it was suicide, Curtis said.

I just sat there. I could see it all in my mind real clear—I could imagine Franklin flying, flying, doing tricks—turning over and over in the clear blue Georgia air and then all of a sudden pointing his plane at the gray cliff face and crashing, burning. I could see it all. I could see how he did it and why he wanted to. And I could immagine Beulah drinking herself to death out of little bitty crystal glasses and never once allowing, to herself or anybody else, that it was happening. I remembered, as if it was yesterday, how Beulah stuck her little finger out when she held a glass, how she had done it that way her whole life long, even way back when we used to play Party.

It runs in the family I reckon, I said, and when Curtis looked at me hard, I said, Drinking.

Curtis stood up very formal and pulled me up too, beside him. He cleared his throat.

Oh no! I thought, for in that moment I knew—though I could not have said how I knew it—what was coming next.

Ivy, my life is empty, Curtis said.

One thing about Curtis is, and you will remember this, Ethel, I know—whatever he says, he sounds like he is making a speech.

Back when you were living with us up on Diamond, he went on, I wanted you. I wanted you so much. Don't you remember? And you were going with that sorry Franklin Ransom?

Oh yes, I said. I remember. And I did too. I remembered the way Curtis looked at me that morning I came in after I'd stayed up at the Ransoms all night, and the way he looked at me the day they drove away.

Well, Curtis was saying now. All of a sudden his whole face seemed to break up into a million pieces, so all I could see there was need.

Nobody ever gets really old, do they, Ethel? I guess we are alive until we die.

Well, what about it, Ivy? What do you say? Will you give me a chance? Curtis Bostick's face was the funniest mix-up of young and old.

And as for me, I felt a stirring that I had not felt since Oakley's death. Yes! For that old, fat man. I turned away.

I remember one time when I came back from work early and you were in the house alone washing yourself, Curtis said. You had your blouse pulled down to your waist. I stood in the door, he said. You never saw me.

I stood looking out in the yard, at Oakley's stump-creatures.

Curtis, Curtis, we are too old, I said. The time is gone. It is too late now, I told him.

Ivy, please. Curtis had begun to cry. It looked so funny to see such an important gentleman crying. You could tell he wasn't used to it, either. It was like it hurt him. I went over to him and held him for a long time, and after a while he quit.

Ethel, Curtis begged me to go back up to West Virginia with him, but of course I would not go. So that possibility is done with.

Oh I will admit I was tempted. But only for a minute, because Curtis Bostick and me are as different as day and night, and both of us know it. If Beulah was too high-falutin for him, I am not high-falutin enough. He is going to have to find himself a woman in between. But you know he won't, because he doesn't really want one. If he really wanted one, he would not have come searching me. He would have come after somebody suitable. What Curtis held about me—what brung him all the way up here—was a notion he had. Men are like that. They will do anything on the basis of a notion, even old men. May be they are the worst! For poor old Curtis Bostick would not want me at all if he knowed me, which he does not. All he has got is an idea, which is more important to him than I could ever be. Naturally I did not explain this to him, nor even try.

But Curtis stayed on for an hour or more, catching up on all that had happened, and Maudy came out with some pizza pie which she learned to make on the M.Y.F. trip to Myrtle Beach. I never heard of it before she started making it, now I think it is real good. Curtis left at 4 p.m. He is a serious man, I think he is a good man. It grieves me to know, as I do, that I will never see him again.

And so, Ethel, I remain,

Still Single!
Ivy.

May 18, 1961

Dear Joli,

I don't reckon David has got himself in any trouble that we can't fix. Send him on, honey. I am liable to slap his face first then give him a big kiss and set him to working with Rufus. It is good for a boy like that to work with wood. Don't worry. We will get him straightened out bye and bye.

And thank you for sending your book which I sat down and read in one sitting, it was pretty good although I think you could of used more of a love interest. Or may be that is just me! Anyway it was real good even if they do just think an awful lot. You might put some more plot in it next time, for an awful lot does happen in this world, it seems to me. Oh honey, I am real proud of you! But I wonder, why don't you write about New York City, since you have been up there for so long? Or about Norfolk and the newspaper life? It seems like that would be more exciting than these mountains which nobody wants to read about, honey. By the way I read a good book the other day, The View from Pompey's Head by Hamilton Basso, there is also A Tree Grows in Brooklyn by Betty Smith, both have plenty of plot and kissing. Raintree County is another one, it's a real humdinger. But this is all just a thought. You know I am behind you one hundred per cent.

And now for some news. I have got some good news and some bad news, as the man said.

Ethel finally had to put Victor in the V.A. Hospital down there in Florida.

But, he likes it fine! Ever since the war, Victor has been lazy without much aim in life. He likes to be waited on hand and foot, and since Ethel hates to wait on anybody, this has kept them busy fighting for twenty years. But now in the V.A. Hospital, he is waited on plenty and Ethel does not have to do it. Plus he has got a whole bunch of old men to talk to, which is what he loves. Ethel says when she goes over there to see him, he is just about too busy to see her. He's out back in the sandy lot under the scrub pines at this table they've got set up out there, dealing five card stud, wearing a baseball cap. Orioles. Somebody gave it to him. She says he looks up and grins and says Hey there Ethel! real jaunty, like he used to do. Ethel says that the way they sit around that table reminds her of how the old men used to sit around the stove in Stoney's store, Victor right in amongst them of course. He never got over those days, and now he has got them back.

Ethel herself has been up here with her new husband Pete Francisco, lord you ought to get a load of him as Maudy says. He is real fat and about a foot shorter than Ethel, with long white hair that looks like a wig or like a star's hair. In fact Pete Francisco looks like a star. He looks like somebody on the Opry. He was wearing a big-weave white suit with a white tie and a dark shirt, I think it was black, kind of shiny. He smiles all the time, but I think it is a real smile, nonetheless. He seems to be so pleased with Ethel, who dresses just as plain as she ever did, and seems as sour and practical as ever.

Ah Ethel! Pete Francisco says, shaking his head and making a tch-tch noise with his teeth. What can you do with such a woman? he asks, spreading his hands wide, after he tells a tale about how he bought Ethel a fur coat and she took it straight back to the store. Fur in Florida? Ethel snorts. She thinks it is crazy. Pete Francisco grins and shrugs. All the movements he makes are big movements, like he is in a movie. That's because he is Italian, Ethel says. Bill and Marlene think he is Jewish. He is something foreign, in any case. And Ethel is pleased as punch with him, you can tell. When he went out of the room for a minute, she said Ivy, isn't he a sight in the world? and I had to agree, he is!

Pete Francisco used to run a trucking business out of Memphis Tenessee. Now he has retired to Florida where he runs this Quik-Pic that Ethel got a job in, which is how they met. I guess it is a case of opposites attract. For although they are so opposite, I can not now immagine one without the othern. Ethel and him stayed down at Ruthie's hotel. I can't get over Geneva dying, even now. It does not seem right to say, Ruthie's hotel. But anyway. Ethel and Pete Francisco did not even have a reason for the trip! I think Ethel just wanted to show him off, what I think. She knows everybody in town, from standing in the store so long. So she got Pete Francisco all dressed up and set him out on the porch Sunday afternoon, so folks could see him. She was like a big child at Christmas, with a new little toy.

Ethel was also pleased to see she sold the store in the nick of time, for Hawk is about to go broke with it. The Magic Mart is taking all of his business. And with the road finished finally, folks can just drive over to Richlands and go to the shopping center if they've got a mind to, which they do. Ethel got out while the getting was good.

But it is getting real built up around here, Joli, and real tacky. People are throwing these jerrybuilt buildings up anyplace, even out into the river which is not a good idea as they say that's what caused the flood—that and all the strip mining. But Bill says you can't stand in the way of progress. This makes me sad to hear. I wish he hadn't of quit farming, and let that tobacco field fall to weeds. I keep thinking about this land and how Daddy said, Farming is pretty work. It hurts me to see the scrub pines taking over what used to be the garden. Do you remember how steep it was? I have got me another little garden up close to the house now, but it's not the same.

Bill and Marlene are doing real good in the real estate business though, Marlene turns out to be one sharp cookie. She works even harder than Bill if you ask me. I keep their little Ellis a lot, he is a precious angel in the world. Marlene's two oldest boys are going off to college on football scholarships, both of them. Ernest is going to Kentucky and John to East Tenessee State. Bobby has got one more year to go in high school, like David.

Honey, just send him on, and do not worry about him too much. It is a boy's nature to get into things, and one of those things is trouble. A boy will get into trouble if he can. I never will forget the time I had with Danny Ray, and look at him now! A lawyer! It beats all. Of course I know from T.V. that there is a lot worse stuff for them to get into now than there used to be. One thing to remember about a teenager is this—they will not believe a thing you tell them, not one word of it. A teenager has got to do it all himself, or herself, as the case may be. Maudy was a case too. But they all grow up, believe me. They all grow up. So, send him back over here. I will do my best to straighten him out. I will put Bill and Rufus on it too.

That is all the news for now except I guess you read in the papers about Francis Gary Powers and the U-2 plane, well he is from right around here. He is one of those Powers from over at Hurley. He used to play football for Hurley. And speaking of news, what do you think of Jackie Kennedy, I think she is too thin, and bowlegged. But Maudy thinks she is just perfect, in fact Maudy has bought a little round hat like Jackie wears. Maudy reminds me of Beulah, the way she likes to dress up. Dress up and then drive around in the car, that's all she does. Mark won't let her work. I don't think she is all that happy with him either, if you want to know. He is gone so much. But now she says she is going to teach twirling at the Charm School in Richlands, and how to walk. Part time. One thing you can say for Maudy is, she walks great! Mark wants to have a baby but Maudy does not yet, she is on birth control pills.

I said to Maudy, Those birth control pills are great. They are the greatest thing since drip dry. You ought to get yourself some,

Joli, just in case. You can't ever tell when a love interest might come along. I would, if I was still young.

Send David.

And speaking of love interests, don't forget to put a bigger one in your next book. People don't like to have too much thinking in a book. Mister Rochester in Jane Eyre is my idea of a good love interest, Joli. Or Heathcliff. I would have him be smoldering.

And I remain your loving,

Mama.

Dear Molly,

I could not believe it, to hear from you of all people, and after so many years! In a way it seems like no time atall since we jumped rope together and mined for gold. In another way it seems like more than years. It seems like lifetimes and lifetimes ago. For we are old now Molly, old—leastways, I am! My face has got lines all over it especially the eyes, and it is hard to tell my hair was ever red. Yet sometimes I feel just like that girl again, and even more so. I still get all wrought up about writing my letters, as you see. When I can get the time! I have got so many grandchildren around here now, they are like to drive me crazy. They want to stay up here with me all the time, they like it up here since I do not <u>bug</u> them as they say. Ha! So I do not have much time to sit and enjoy my old age, to read and think of things, as I would like to do. I have got plenty of thinking saved up to do when I get the time, believe you me.

But if you really want me to, I can help you some with the settlement school. I can tell you who to hire around here and who not to, for sure. Lord knows it is a good high school, you know my Joli graduated from there, the one that is a famous writer, and Danny Ray that is a lawyer, and Maudy my least girl. So I think that putting in a college down there is a fine idea and needed. I am so glad to hear that you are the one coming back here to do it, for you know us, and our ways. You will have to go slow, you know. You remember how we are so proud here, and what Granny

Rowe used to call <u>techious</u>. But we need an education, these children around here needs the light.

Ruthie will send me word when you get here. I will try and help you all I can Molly, if an old mountain woman's help is what you want.

In spite of the years I remain your long lost friend,

Ivy Rowe.

Dear Danny Ray,

I am writing to give you a piece of my mind. For I think it is high time I did so. You have got a nerve, going into politics <u>over there.</u> What is the matter with this county, I would like to know? I guess that wife of yours is too good for the likes of us. Just don't forget your raising, Danny Ray. I did not raise you to be a fat cat, or a Republican. Stick with the Democrats.

Oh honey, I do not blame you, and I am proud of you too. When I look at those pictures I am proud as punch. I like the one of you all in front of the fireplace with the twins in the armchair. Little Elizabeth favors Maudy, don't you think? I don't know as I like Louise's hair so short, but she is <u>your</u> wife after all, so what? She is such a pretty little thing, to be so smart. You better watch out, or she will make more money than you do! Head doctors are <u>in,</u> what they tell me. But I like Louise. Don't you remember how her and me sat up all night talking, that last time I came to visit and could not sleep and got up in the middle of the night and cleaned the bathroom? <u>A fine new bathroom like that, it ought to stay clean,</u> I remember saying. <u>Besides, I wasn't doing anything else.</u> Louise said, <u>Except sleeping!</u> Lord how we laughed.

The truth is, Danny Ray, I don't sleep good anywhere but right here in my own bed on Sugar Fork where I have spent my life. And I don't sleep <u>much,</u> either. It seems like I have got too many things to think about, to sleep good. I have got a lot on my mind!

When you get old, the time draws shorter and shorter for you to figure it all out.

And I'm an old woman now. I can say what I want to, and this is what I want to say. Now that you are a big politician, I want you to know what is going on over here. For sometimes it seems to me that we might as well not be in Virginia atall, or any other state. We are like a kingdom unto our own selves. Everybody has took everything out of here now—first the trees, then the coal, then the children. We have been robbed and left for dead. I mean it—I can name you who all is on this mountain now. All the young ones have up and gone, including you, Danny Ray.

Or take Home Creek, for an instance. You can walk up and down Home Creek now and not find hardly a man that works. You will recall how it used to be when you were coming along and we would go down there to see your daddy's folks, and how Edith Fox used to make a pie and send a piece to each and every, up and down the creek, and everybody had a garden with a hollyhock or a sunflower in the yard, and there was such a feeling of neighborness. Don't you remember those big sunflowers that the Rolettes grew? It is all gone now.

Let's start at the head of the creek. Charlie Rue died young of his lungs and so his wife Rowena lives in the house now, on his social security and his union check, and she has raised up a passel of younguns one after the other, mostly her grandchildren. Every one that turns sixteen, before you know it, is out and gone. They have lit out for Detroit or someplace else, you can't blame them, they is just not a thing for them to do here.

It is crazy to me that Joli's boy David wants to come back so bad. He says he is coming here after college, to live. In a pig's eye! I said. You will be back just like your mama and Danny Ray, I said. No, I mean it, Mamaw, he said, grinning real big. I aim to farm. He sounded just like his grandaddy, years ago. Don't you know that nobody does that any more? I said. I am not nobody, David said, and I reckon he is right in that. He is just David, and not nobody else, that's for sure. Calls his mama Doctor Mom now. I've got this pain in my left side, Doctor Mom, he says. Oh go on, David! says Joli. Of course she is a Doctor of English not the medical. But you can't get too put out with David, which is why he used to get away with as much as he did. He could get away with murder, just like you.

Anyway you can walk the streets of Majestic now on a Saturday and not find hardly a one between high school age and old, unless they are out of work. It's true, yet you recall how Majestic used to be come payday, or Court Day—all the hustle and bustle, so much happening. There was so much _life_ here then. Well it is gone now. Like chimney smoke into thin air.

Now we have come to the Rolette house which has been took over by Musicks since Reva and Delphi passed and Gus went to jail. This is Clell Musick that got his arm cut off at Blue Star Number Six a while back and has got so many children. I imagine he gets a check from the state but he would not get one from the union, he was never a union man. So many in this county are not, you know.

There is nobody in the Foxes house at all but Dreama who is still mean as a snake, and just as stuck up as ever. As for the Copes and the Charleses, there is two men both too old to get a job yet too young to retire. So they are stuck in the middle. Stuck and out of work! They got laid off when Panther Coal put the new machine in over on Hell Mountain, and they have been laid off ever since. Folks do say that Luther Charles is real bad to drink. And I say, Who is to blame him? So you see how it is here.

Bert Cope is the one that Molly sent up before Judge Grant for not sending his children to school. I said, Molly, don't do this, he can't help it or they would be here, but she done it anyway. There is something about a maiden lady that makes them head-strong as a girl. So the Judge sends out a warrant, and then it is Bert Cope's day to come to court.

Let's just go over there, I said to Molly, and see what he says. For I wanted her to hear it.

Nothing he says can justify keeping those children out of school. So says Molly, who has gotten right set in her ways with old age. I think a person will go one way or the other, don't you? Either they will get more set in their ways, or they will get all shook up. I am shook up, myself.

Anyway, the upshot of it was, we went, me more or less dragging Molly. First the county attorney appears, to prosecute for the state, which is Molly. The county attorney is a young whippersnapper from someplace over in Kentucky, who has not been living here long. Then the truant officer, Bob Wright, says that Bert Cope is the father of six children that ought to go to school, and hardly do. They have not been to school for a month. The county attorney asks the court to impose a fine or a jail sentence, whereupon Bert Cope just starts laughing. He is about fifty years old and you can tell from the tilt of his back that he has spent his years in the mine. His hands are big, fingernails black with coal dirt.

He spreads his hands and says, I agree with everything that has been said. Hell it's true, it's all true, and everybody knows it. Nobody wants my kids to go to school any more than I do, they are driving me crazy. And my old woman, she is crazy, I reckon. I punched Molly, for I had heard this too. I've been out of work for nigh on to four years now. I've been all over this coalfield and over into West Virginia looking for work. Well there aint none to be had. I drawed out my unemployment over three years ago and all what I've had since is just day work here and there, when I can get it. But I am old for day work, and it's hard to get. I sold my car, my shotgun, my radio and even my pocketwatch that my daddy left me, to get money to feed those kids. And now I don't have a thing in the world that anybody would want. I'm dead broke and wore out. We are over a mile from the schoolhouse and I have not got the money to buy my kids the shoes and clothes they need to go to school. Me and my oldest boy has got this one pair of shoes between us and that's all. Bert Cope holds up his foot, wearing shoes that look sorry to me. When my boy wears em I don't have any, and when I wear em, he don't have any. If it was not for these rations the government given us, I guess our whole family would of starved to death long afore now. So if you want to fine me sir, why go ahead! Bert Cope grins a big grin that shows some missing teeth. I aint got a penny to pay it with, so I reckon I'll have to lay it out in jail. This is fine with me. So if you think that putting me in jail will help my younguns any, why you go right ahead and do it, and I'll be glad of it. I need me a good long rest. And if any of your fine gentlemen will find me a job where I can work out something for my kids to wear, then I'll be much obliged to you for all the days of my life.

By the time Bert Cope had finished saying his piece Molly was crying, not making a sound, into her lace handkerchief. Judge Grant cleared his throat and asked Bert Cope some more questions. Bert said he had a fourth grade education. He worked in the mines for twenty years and spent three years as an infantry soldier in the war against Japan. He had not gotten wounded, though. If he had gotten wounded, then he would be getting a check from the V.A. But he did not. Then Judge Grant asked him whether he had any skill but mining coal, and Bert Cope said, No. Then Bert went on to say,

Judge I'm not the only man on the creek that is in this fix. You know it is true. Miss Molly here will back me up in saying it. There's other children along the creek don't go to school, for the same reason mine don't. Now you all aim to make an example of me. You all think if I go to jail for a week that they will get the money to get their kids to the schoolhouse, but it aint so. It aint so atall. Aint that true? Bert Cope asked Bob Wright, who nodded.

Judge Grant is not a fool.

He looked all around the courtroom. He looked for a long time at Bert Cope and then at Miss Molly Bainbridge. Well you do your best, he said at length to Bert. If they don't go to school, they will be in as bad a fix as you are in now. Case dismissed.

Bert Cope smiled a long smile which did not reach his eyes, and put on his hat, and left. He has a long stride, I thought as I watched him cross that courtroom, a stride like a mountain man. And I felt then as I have often felt since, that I do not belong down there in Majestic myself, but up here on Sugar Fork where I am from. Molly thinks she needs me at the school, but she don't. About all I do down there is tell her who is who and where they live, and she is getting to know it all now anyway. So I might retire! My car, this old Chevy that Bill give me, is about give out anyhow. But that's another story. We'll see.

The upshot of it all was, now all those little Copes are coming to school of course, for Molly has bought them shoes. And now she is going to start a foundation, and maybe an orphanage. I want you to tell people about it, Danny Ray. You might as well be good for something!

As for the rest of Home Creek, it is more of the same. Except for Rufus and Martha who have got another problem as they live too close to the mouth of the creek, and it nearabout flooded them out last month. It did flood, over on Jump Creek. I went over there with Molly to look. It was the awfullest sight in the world. The thing about a flood is, it don't destroy. It is not like a fire. It just ruins everything, and then you are left with what all is ruint. We went in one house and there wasn't hardly a thing left except this little old T.V. going and these children huddled up all around it. They were just as dirty as could be, and scrawny. Big eyes like holes in their heads. Molly gave them some apples. On the T.V., there was a butler. A butler! How do you reckon it makes them feel, watching that? For there are no shows about such as us. Molly says it is awful, the way folks that have not got even a toilet will beg, borrow or steal to get a T.V. I do not think it is awful though. I can see why.

Anyway, the water in Home Creek did not get that high last time, but it bears watching. The T.V.A. says it is just a matter of time before the Levisa River has a flat out flood. Down in Majestic, it covers the back road with every big rain. Myself I recall the days when the river ran clear and deep with great fish in it, and folks rode the log rafts clear to Kentucky. When I was a girl, oh how I longed to go! But now the river is hardly there, a dirty little trickle, or else it is like a flood. I am lucky to live up high in the holler, I say!

Well Danny Ray, this is what is going on where you are from, I guess you have got an earful! I hope so. I hope you will think on these things, and tell people. For I remain your loving and feisty old,

Mama.

October 9, 1965

Dear Maudy,

Well congratulations. I guess. Of course I am real proud of your Maureen for being Little Miss Tri-City, thanks for sending the picture of her in the newspaper. She looks so delicate. She takes after her aunt Silvaney the most, I believe. All that fine pale hair. Did you make her dress, or buy it? Remember how you used to sew in high school. I don't know if I would go on to put her in the Little Miss East Tenessee Pageant or not, if I was you. I would think twice. Because she does look so delicate, and it might be too much of a strain. How is she doing in that little school, anyway? And speaking of that, Maudy, why don't you go back to school yourself? Did you ever think about it? Joli did, you know. I was always sorry you married so young and never went, you are a smart girl, even if you did not sound so smart in your last letter.

Honey, hold on to your hat.

I would think twice before I left a perfectly nice husband and a redwood ranch house just because my husband looked funny to me all of a sudden. What do you mean anyway, <u>looked funny</u>? All you wrote is that you were laying out in the sun in the backyard and Mark came home from work and walked across the patio and you took off your little cotton eye patches and watched him come closer, and he <u>looked funny</u> to you. Honey, that is not enough! It might of been the sun. Of course it is true that Joli got a divorce but it is also true that she had a good reason, it was more than just having Taylor Three look funny to her. I mean, Taylor Three <u>was</u> funny. Ask Joli. And just think about it.

Besides, who would drive Maureen over to Knoxville for the Little Miss East Tenessee Pageant? Who would teach those girls how to walk? Settle down. Oh Maudy, a person can not just go through the world doing whatever the hell they want to, whenever they want to do it. I know this better than anybody.

Take a course down at the new college, why don't you? Go out and get yourself a pantsuit. Paint the bedroom. Or, why don't you start a store, and sell clothes? You would be good at that. And I have always thought you took after Ethel in knowing exactly what folks would want next. Plus you and Mark could take out a loan real easy, I'm sure of it.

And speaking of Ethel, let me just tell you what Pete Francisco has gone and done now. He has bought Ethel a motorboat and named it <u>The Ethel!</u> Can you stand it? She says it is stencilled in gold on the side. For the life of me I cannot picture Ethel sitting up in a boat, riding through the blue waters of Florida with Pete Francisco in The Ethel.

But Maudy. Think it over. You have always had a flair, honey. In any case I will remain your loving,

Mama.

Dear Joli,

It was <u>chicken gizzards,</u> but why you need to know is beyond me. Are you going to put it in a book? Or have you got one?

Anyway, what you do is peel the outside off of the chicken gizzard and rub it on the wart. Then you bury the gizzard and forget all about it. When you forget, the wart will be gone.

If you <u>don't</u> forget, I won't promise a thing!

And don't forget the love interest.

I remain your fond old,

Mama.

Dear Silvaney,

I have quit the settlement school now in spite of the pleas of all, it is hard to say why. For I liked it down there, and the people, and they do a lot of good especially at the new orphanage. But I am old and crazy, I have a need to be up here on this mountain again and sit looking out as I look out now at the mountains so heavy with August heat in this last long hot spell before the fall. I can feel the season changing, in my heart. I have been reading the Bible, Silvaney, that fancy white Bible that Garnie left up here so long ago. I have been sitting out in the heat with three of Oakley's animals placed just so around my chair for company, and reading this white Bible, and watching dust devils rise up in the yard.

I do not like Proverbs which is what Garnie quoted to me, all those years ago. The proverbs are mean-spirited which is probably why Garnie liked them! And the Song of Solomon is dirty. It reminds me of Honey Breeding who I have not thought about in years, and how it was with him. I don't know where he is, or if he's still alive now. But I have not forgot him either. It's a funny thing to me how some folks can pure tee vanish off the face of the earth, Revel is another who has done so. And Johnny—although they say he is a jazz man now and goes by the name of J.Q. Rivers, I don't know. This is what Joli thinks.

But Ecclesiastes is good and makes sense. I like to read Ecclesiastes 3 and run my hand along the fine-grained wood of this deer that Oakley cut out of a poplar stump, it makes me think I am close to him. To every thing there is a season, and a time to every purpose under heaven. A time to be born, and a time to die, a time to plant, and a time to pluck up that which is planted. A time to kill, and a time to heal, a time to break down, and a time to build up, a time to weep and a time to laugh, a time to mourn, and a time to dance, a time to cast away stones, and a time to gather stones together. A time to embrace, and a time to refrain from embracing, a time to get, and a time to lose, a time to keep, and a time to cast away, a time to rend, and a time to sew, a time to keep silence and a time to speak, a time to love and a time to hate, a time for war, and a time for peace. I have copied it down out of the Bible. It makes sense to me, Silvaney. Lord knows I have had my time to dance and my time to mourn. Now I think it is the time for me to cast away, and get about my business, if only I could tell you what it is (Ha).

I have been having a lot of stomach trouble lately, I think my age and these hard years are catching up with me. It will leave for a while but then it comes back. I won't go into the particulars! But it makes me want to keep silence and think hard, it is time for that. So far I have not been to the doctor but brewed up plenty of bitters which has helped me a lot. I have fallen off some in the course of it however. The other day I put on some old pants I had not had on in a while, and they just hung on me. I had to gather the waist up with a belt. My breasts look like those bean bags that I used to make for the kids.

Molly cried when I told her I was quitting down there, but she took both of my hands in hers and said Ivy, Ivy, you have been such a help to me! You will always be my friend, and this is true. But she is a grand lady now, with a bosom like a dove and a big desk full of important papers. Congressmen come to see her.

And I am a mountain woman whose time has come to cast away stones which I told her, and she hugged me tight. Why Ivy, you are just skin and bones! she said then. You have been working too hard. Go then, back up on Sugar Fork, and rest some. You have certainly earned it. For we are well begun here—and Molly gestured with her hand, a square hand like a man's, at the old school building and the new school building and the brick dormitories they are putting up down by the creek. In shop class, the boys are making a big wooden sign that says <u>Majestic Mission School.</u> They are carving out the letters one by one. They are real proud of it. A man from a New York newspaper is coming next week to do a piece on Molly and the school.

Just think, Silvaney—this is my little friend Molly, from childhood! And Violet Gayheart has gotten famous too, she is a union organizer, and Joli is the writer which I always wanted to be. I am so proud of them all that I am like to bust over it. But this is not for me. I have got things to think on, and letters to write. Such as to the Peabody Coal Company that is augering up there on the mountain behind me, and making my creek flood. Marlene and Bill just called to say that they are going to bring a new color T.V. up here for me to watch in my retirement and I said <u>No thanks</u> but they are likely to bring it anyhow. Marlene will not take No for an answer. She reminds me of me! Then Rufus and Martha called up and said why didn't their middle girl, this is Johnny Sue, come up here and keep me company? And I said, <u>Thanks but no thanks. I am going to live up here alone and get used to it,</u> I said. <u>Them that wants to see me, can come up here.</u>

I remain your (thin) and loving sister,

Ivy.

Sept. 5, 1974

Dear Danny Ray,

Martha says you called up long distance while I was laying down. I have not been feeling too good, I guess she told you. Well, there is not too much to say about me and the Peabody Coal Company! I am surprised you saw it in the paper. Although Joli did too, she called me up crying and wanting to come down, but they told her I am not feeling good, and not to come right now.

I did it for David, of course.

You know he lived with me two times, once when he was little and once when he got into trouble in his teens, and he loved it over here, and said he was coming back after college. Then—I don't know if you know this or not—he got into all that trouble in college, it was something about drugs I believe although Joli never would say, and then he got kicked out and drafted, and sent to Viet Nam. I cannot even immagine it over there, nor my little David carrying a gun. They used to make fun of him up here, Martha and Marlene's kids, because he couldn't stand to hurt a thing not even a butterfly, and refused to go hunting.

I remember he hurt Bill's feelings when he was 16 and Bill came up here to give him a brand new shotgun for his birthday and expected him to go over to Matewan with him and some other men, hunting bear on Hell Mountain. I still recall David's answer, and how his face looked, to this day. He was standing out in the yard and it was starting to rain, a cold rain, November the first it was, that was his birthday. And Bill right there, a heavy man, a man that still wears a crewcut. And you know how good-hearted he is!

David grinned as big as life. He ran his fingers down the slick stock of the gun. This is a beautiful gun, he said. But I don't believe I'd use it enough to take it.

You mean you don't want it? You could tell that Bill had never heard of such a thing. When you all turned 16, he wanted his own gun worsen anything.

You would be wasting your money, Uncle Bill, David said. Go on and give it to Ernest or one of the others. I wouldn't use it enough, he said. I am going back up to Doctor Mom's before long anyway.

You are? I said. For this was the first I had heard of it. Joli had a boyfriend youngern her, and David didn't like it.

I reckon so, David said to me. I guess I ought to finish high school up there, so I can take some more French.

French! Bill said it like a cuss word.

Your mama went to France on her honeymoon. All of a sudden I remembered that.

Didn't do her much good either, David said. He handed the gun back to Bill. Let me just go over there on Hell Mountain with you all, he said, and NOT hunt. I'd like to go over there, David said.

You could see Bill thinking it over, figuring what he would say to the other men to explain a boy that would not hunt.

Do you reckon you will get up close to any real bears? David asked. Or is that all talk? I guess you will drink some whisky, he said.

Bill laughed. Now we might see a bear or we might not, he said. Depending.

Depending on what? David asked. On how much whisky you drink?

On that and other things, Bill said. There's bears still up there, though. Nobody has mined that mountain because old man Hide Johnson owns it all, he still owns it, Bill said, spitting. But he lets us go up there because this one old boy that goes with us, that is his son-in-law. And there's bears still up there, believe you me. They're cornered up there now.

Well, I would be proud to go along then, David said, grinning. That's what I want for my birthday.

Then you got it, Bill said. Of course he did! You couldn't refuse David a thing. Nobody could, he had this way about him. Bill left and David came over and hugged me. Mamaw! he said. I reckon you knew I would have to leave here sometime.

I reckon, I said, but in all truth I had got so used to his presence that I had kind of forgot. When I hugged him, he was all bones. Bones and freckles, that was David. Red Rowe hair. Why do you want to go up there anyway? I asked him, meaning up on Hell Mountain after bear with a bunch of men as rough as a cob.

I just want it, David said. I want to go everyplace I get a chance to. But I'll be back here before long. David said this to me the day he was 16. Okay, Mamaw?

And I, hugging all those bones and angles, I said, Okay. Honey. Okay.

So you see, Danny Ray, I did not have a choice. You know how Momma had sold some of the mineral rights to this land years and years ago, to John Reno when we were living at the boardinghouse with Geneva bless her soul, and so hard up for cash. I don't blame Momma for it. Everyone else done the same then. Nobody knew any better. And it has looked for all these years like the Peabody Coal Company was not going to exercise those rights anyhow, so I had kind of forgot about it. Then they done the augering up by the blackberry clifts, and messed up the creek, and then they up and brung a bulldozer in here to strip the outcrop. There is not enough coal in there to warrant it either. So this was where I had to do something, and fast! For if they had done what they were intending, they would of mined out that whole clift right up beyond Pilgrim Knob, and left us just sitting in a watershed. Come the first spring rain, this whole place would of washed right down the mountain! Now Danny Ray, I know this! I am not guessing. I have been out and about enough with Molly, I have been all over this county, I know what I am talking about. I have seen it happen again and again, to others bettern me.

The first thing I did, when I heard of it, was put a No Trespassing sign on the road down there by the creek so they could not come up here, but they come up with the first dozer anyway, up as far as the steppingstones. So then I went out there and said, You had better not come any further. I had Oakley's old thirty-ought-six with me and it was not loaded, but this bulldozer man, he didn't know that. He was a Northern negro. His eyes got as big as silver dollars.

Lady, please put that gun down, he said. He spread his hands, the insides of which were pink. I had not seen a negro since Tessie.

You can't come up here any further, I said. I mean business.

I reckon you do, he said. He grinned a big white grin and climbed down off the dozer, leaving it right there shaking like it had the palsy even after he turned it off. I am not about to mess with you, this negro said.

So the upshot of it was, he told it down in town, and they was a big whoop-de-do over it and Molly hired me some fancy lawyers and we were going to court, but then we could not get to court in time. The company planned to strip it before we could get the restraining order. This is what Bill came up to tell me.

But I wish to God that you would lay off of this, Mama, he said, instead of raising such a ruckus. I don't see why you want to carry on so. This farm is not worth saving, he said. Bill is into real estate now, him and Marlene, they know all about land values. Let it go, he said. Come on into town now and live with us. We'll take good care of you, Bill said. He was wearing a khaki suit, twisting his hat in his hands. He did not say, Since you are sick.

What I did not say was, I wouldn't live with you and Marlene Blount if you were the last people in the world despite your good intentions. For I don't believe in real estate, or in good intentions, and I won't live in town. I will never again be beholden. It is a time to keep. So I did not say.

Please Mama. This is embarassing for me.

I did not say, I know I am sick. I have nothing to lose.

I did not say, My grandson is fighting in Viet Nam while you are running the Kiwanis Club.

I said, I will think about it.

But when they brought that second dozer up here, I was ready for them. I knew they were coming, Corey had heard it in town and called me. I went out before daybreak, all dressed up. I knew they'd be taking pictures. So I put on some lipstick that Maudy had left over here, and a pantsuit Joli sent me which I had not worn yet, it was way too big. I took a book to read, Exodus by Leon Uris which I had bought at the Rexall, and a whole bunch of nabs to eat, and went out there in the pitch black dark. If I'd had some whisky, I'd of took that too!

I climbed up on the seat of the dozer and sat there. I was not going to move. After a while I could hear the other dozer coming up the trace. I could hear the engine rumbling, and the crack it made every now and then breaking a branch. I wondered if it would be that same negro, or another one. I ate a nab. My back was hurting real bad. Then I separated out another sound, another engine, and here came Martha and Rufus in their old car, ahead of the dozer. They parked and came over to me. It was still real dark, I could hardly see them.

I am not getting down, I said.

Rufus started laughing. Who says you have to? We just came along to keep you company, Rufus said. He lit a cigarette, and the match flared up in the dark.

You better watch out you don't blow us all up, I said.

That is the spirit, Rufus said.

Then Corey showed up with a chainsaw and cut down a pine tree so it fell right across the trace. That will give them some pause, he said.

And then the sun rose, and then that second dozer got up to the pine tree, down there by the steppingstones, and it stopped, still going chug-a-chug-a-chug, and the bulldozer operator—who was a big white man this time—put his hands on his hips and looked up at us, across the pine tree, and scratched himself. He shook his head. Then he turned his back on us and folded his arms and waited for the rest, who were not long in coming. It was a pickup and a car full of company men in navy blue suits, all of them fat. Then there was another car right behind them with three reporters in it and one of them taking pictures. All the reporters were thin. I was just glad I had on that lipstick. <u>Hot Pink,</u> this is the lipstick Maudy wears.

Well, you know the rest. They backed off at the sight of those reporters. They backed off for good. This land will be here waiting for David when he gets back.

You know the rest. You saw the story in the newspaper. You saw the pictures.

But it's a fact that there was not enough coal in that outcrop to justify them going up there after it, anyway. They were just going to mine it because they <u>could,</u> pure and simple.

What did you think of my lipstick?

Love,
Mama.

Dear Maureen,

Thanks for your letter. I am sure you will get the letter-writing badge if you keep it up so good. You can write to me anytime honey and I will write back, I am a fool for letters. Your mama will tell you that! And speaking of your mama, tell her that you can stay over here with me anytime too, whether she is going to the Darlington 500 again or someplace else. I will be <u>glad</u> to keep you. I will tell you all the stories that you ever want to hear. I am glad you like the family ones. I do, too. They are the best! But I have to say, I was surprised to learn that you have never heard tell of your great-great-uncle Revel. Then I thought, well why <u>would</u> she? And did I tell you he had a dog? The name of his dog was Charly.

Now here is a story that Revel used to tell when we were girls, it never failed to scare the pee right out of us.

There was a poor little girl—and he would name the little girl <u>Ivy,</u> say, if he was telling it to me—there was a poor, poor little girl that went out walking in the woods one day looking for something to eat, and she found a chunk of meat right there on a big flat rock. And so she snatched it up, and ran right home with it, and put it in the beans, for they had not had meat in that house for days and days. And it got to cooking, and the whole house smelled good, and all the children were happy.

But then all of a sudden came a big awful growling outside and a terrible voice said, WHERE IS MY CHUNK OF MEAT?

So the little old woman gets under the featherbed. And the little old man gets under the featherbed. And all the little brothers and sisters gets under the featherbed. And then the girl hears the gate-chain rattle, and then she hears something climbing up on the porch roof clawing on the house-roof.

WHERE'S MY CHUNK OF MEAT? The terrible voice says again. And soot commences to fall down the chimbley. So the girl goes over and looks up the chimbley and sees a BIG OLD HAIRY BOOGER sitting up there on the smoke-shelf.

And the little girl asks, What you got such big eyes for?

The hairy booger says, Stare you through.

And the little girl asks, What you got such a bushy tail for?

The hairy booger says, Sweep your grave.

But when the little girl says, What you got such long sharp snaggly teeth for?

The hairy booger says, EAT YOU UP!

And he does so in a flash.

This is where Revel used to yell and grab me. Lord I was scared! I used to love stories such as that, when I was your age. I liked to get real scared. And I loved hairy boogers.

Now I remain your loving old,

Mamaw.

Dear Joli,

I will make it short since I am feeling real bad today.

The quilt you are talking about was Momma's burying quilt which she did not get to use since she died down in Majestic at the boardinghouse, and she was robbed in death and carried over to Rich Valley by her mean old daddy Mister Castle and lies there yet beside her daddy's body, the way he planned it all along, in a little cemetery with a wrought-iron fence around it. I hear they are putting in a mall right up the hill. I have always meant to get somebody to go over there and dig her up and bring her back to the mountain, but somehow the years have slipped by and I have not done so, till now it seems worse to move her than to let her lay. Anyway, it was Momma's burying quilt, first.

And then when your daddy and I moved back up on Sugar Fork, I found it in an old cedar chest that was made by—I believe—Early Cook, Rufuses daddy. Anyway there was the quilt, folded just so. Never used.

And because I love a crazy-quilt and hate a waste, I took it out and put it on our bed. We used it for years and years. I know you remember seeing it on the bed when you were little. It held up real good. I used it until the Christmas that Ethel gave us those new drapes and the comforter she had ordered off for, in the Early American style. That old quilt was getting pretty worn out, anyway! Then when Martha and Rufus got married, I gave it to them along with everything else I could find around here that we weren't using, so Martha could set up housekeeping. And you know Martha—she likes the old ways, and for everything to stay the same as it always was, so I bet she is using it still, on her and Rufuses bed. I would not be atall surprised by that.

All this is by way of saying <u>NO</u>, honey, I can't send you the quilt for your exhibit, I am sorry. Now I am going to quit writing this letter and lay down. More and more lately, your face has come into my mind, the sweet way you looked as a girl. You looked like a little fox! I hope you will be able to come and see me soon.

For I remain your loving, loving,

Mama.

Dear Maudy,

I don't know what you mean, a bad influence. You will kindly remember who you are talking to, Miss Priss! That is what your daddy used to call you. He loved you so much honey. And I do too.

But it will do her more harm to be in the Little Miss Gatlinburg Christmas Contest than it will to hear a good story. Mark my words.

I would write more, and give you a real piece of my mind, but I am not feeling too good today. It must be something I ate. I hope you will send Maureen over here again soon. We had a real good time.

Even though I am a Bad Influence, I remain your loving,

Mama.

Dear Ethel,

I will make this short.

I am still over at Bristol in the hospital but going home soon. About the only thing that gives me any pleasure here is the roses from you and Pete, thank you so much, they are beautiful. I am so happy that you all are coming for a visit. You will find me at home! I do not intend to stay over here despite what the doctors are saying, it is no use in it, they know it as well as me. I do not plan to spend my last days laying up in a strange bed and not knowing a soul, like Victor. So I have said, Forget it! And they are all giving me a fit, especially Joli and Danny Ray who think they know everything. I hope you will be on my side. I have lived like I wanted by God, I will die that way too. Plus, doctors don't know everything. I might just up and get well and do something crazy! Anyway I am going home as quick as they will let me leave here, although I don't know as I will recognize the place since Marlene Blount and Maudy have gone up there and cleaned the house from top to bottom, so I hear. I reckon it needed it, but I do not appreciate anybody going through my things like that, would you? Lord it is hard to be old. It is hard to <u>act nice,</u> the way folks expect you to.

Anyway Ethel, thanks again, you know how I love white roses and have since a child.

You will find me back up on Sugar Fork where I belong.

Love,
Ivy.

My dear Joli,

I <u>know</u> I am worrying you by staying up here by myself. I am sorry for it honey, but I can't do nothing else. It will not do you any good to try and hire anybody either, I will just run them off the way I run off Martha, and I <u>love</u> Martha. But there does come a time when a person has got to be by theirselves. May be you will understand this, and may be you will not, when you get to my time of life. I know it is hard for you now, caught up as you are in the great roiling churn of things, to consider any other way to be. But it comes to us all, honey. It comes to us all.

Joli, you ask about the letters.

I don't know if I can explain this to you or not. I will try, though. Because you are a writer, I will try. I <u>know</u> that your aunt Silvaney died in the Elizabeth Masters Home in the great flu epidemic that took so many lives. Of course I know it! I am not a fool. I have been knowing it ever since Victor came home from the war and went over there and found out about her death. I got so mad at him I liked to have died, for telling me! I did not want to know it then. For it didn't <u>matter.</u> Silvaney, you see, was a part of me, my other side, my other half, my heart.

So I went on and wrote her letters, all the years. I put them in the cedar chest which is where Marlene and Maudy found them.

And you know what I have done with those letters now?

I gathered them up and took them out back to the firepit, where we used to lay the kettle to boil our clothes when I was a girl, it taken me several trips as I move so slow now. I cleared out the snow in the firepit and took my big old kitchen matches out there and burned the letters every one. Now and then I would stop and look all around, but you know how quiet the land lies in the snow. And it all looks different. The shape of Pilgrim Knob looked different, and Bethel Mountain down below hung in wreathy mist, and even the slope of the orchard looked different, strange and new. I don't know—it was kindly exciting! It was a new world, with even the shape of it changed. The clouds hung low and dark and puffy. My breath hung in the air. The smoke from the burning letters rose and was lost in the clouds. It took me upwards of an hour to burn them all. With every one I burned, my soul grew lighter, lighter, as if it rose too with the smoke. And I was not even cold, long as I'd been out there. For I came to understand something in that moment, Joli, which I had never understood in all these years.

The letters didn't mean anything.

Not to the dead girl Silvaney, of course—nor to me.

Nor had they ever.

It was the writing of them, that signified.

So now I have sent them up in smoke and given the cedar chest to Maureen for a hope chest (I hope she will not grow up to be Miss America!) and I remain forevermore your loving,

Mama.

My dear Silvaney,

I know you have not heard from me in a long time, I am so sorry for it. I have been sick. Today I am better thogh. All throgh my sickness I have been thinking, thinking, and now I am dying to write I am dying to   oh Silvaney, today is the lastest snow! You know a March snow brings good luck, and a pretty spring. It will be gone by noon. Right now I am looking out the window at it. It is real pretty, laying like lace all over the yard, down by the steps I see my crocuses poking through gold and purple, purple and gold the colors of royalty and church. The whole round world is so bright with the sun, and the snow melts before my eyes, a hundred little rivers running down the yard and all of them shining. I hear Dreama back there in the kitchen banging things around. She is all the time trying to cook up something I will eat. She is a real good cook like her mama was but I don't have a taste for much these days except Orange Julius which people bring me from the mall. I guess it has gotten all around how much I like Orange Julius. Just about everybody that comes up here now, brings me one. Dreama is cooking bacon, I can smell it. I wont eat a bite. What Dreama will do, is fix me up a breakfast plate, and then she will eat it all up her ownself! We are like Jack Sprat and his old woman, I get thinner and Dreama gets fatter, I bet she is pushing 200 now. Silvaney admit it, aint you suprised to hear that Dreama Fox is up here now taking care of me? She has rented out her house to a third grade schoolteacher with real short hair. This is what happend. I had not been home from the hospital but about one week when there came this knock on the door and Bill goes to open it and there stands Dreama big as life and twice as ugly, wearing that hat, carrying a matched set of Samsonite luggage. It suprised Bill so bad he just stepped back without a word and she came right on in not saying hidy nor bye-your-leave nor nothing, and marched straight on back to the back room, where she has been ever since. She calls up Bill or Corey to bring us food from the store. Or she will just call the Piggly Wiggly if she cant get any of them on the phone, and say who she is and what she wants, and sure enogh they will send it up here directly. They dont deliver to anybody else. But you know there is not a soul in this county that will tell Dreama no. She tickles me. Even as sick as I have been, she tickles me. Of course we do not speak. Lord no. Not one word. Dreama Fox still thinks I am a fallen woman, I reckon. She has not spoke to me for years and years, and she is not about to start now. And its a funny thing—I would of run anybody else off that any of my younguns tried to put up here to take care of me, just like I told them I would, but I can put up with Dreama. Dreama is okay, I couldn't say for why. And it is okay with me that she still won't speak, because I have got so much on my mind these days, and no time to waste on talking. Right now I can see the forsythia blooming under the snow. Don't you remember how we used to make angels Silvaney, until we were wet clear throgh? A heavenly host of angels all across the yard. The ice is melting. The Ice Queen walks in beauty like the

night of shooting stars and cloudless skies. There's a big hawk
circling in this blue, blue sky. Lord it is a pretty day, it reminds
me of my daddy and how he gave us that birch bark to lick and
said <u>Slow down now, slow down now Ivy. This is the taste of</u>
<u>spring.</u> I never have slowed down. But oh how Oakley loved the
spring   when I close my eyes I see him always Oakley always
coming out of the black and smoking mine, bearing his own sweet
face like a present, I seen him coming from a long way off, and I
see Lonnie Rash the day he left for war, and all the high muddy
water rushed under the bridge   <u>there is a time for war</u>   I
see Franklin the night we danced and danced in his fathers house
while the fans whirled overhead and the furniture covered in sheets
loomed up from the darkness like so many ghosts   <u>there is a</u>
<u>time to dance</u>   and I see you and me Silvaney on Old Christmas
Eve when the lady sisters came and flew away across the snow and
we stood in the door to watch them go while the moonlight turned
the snow to diamonds all around   <u>and there is a time to be</u>
<u>born</u>   when Joli came it was moonlight too, moonlight ad-
vancing slow across the quilt   square by square   she was
little and perfect, sugar and spice and everything nice in the moonlight her new skin as pale and perfect as Mrs. Browns camio   Mrs.
Brown my first love which passeth understanding oh who ever
loved, that loved not at first sight? I used to think I would be a
writer. I thought then I would write of love (Ha!) but how little
we know, we spend our years as a tale that is told I have spent
my years so. I never became a writer atall. Instead I have loved,
and loved, and loved. I am fair wore out with it. I see Miss Torrington so severe her kiss like fire on the back of my neck yet
first born of all my kisses all my life, I thought once I would go
to Boston and see the sights, instead I have lived here on this
mountain   I climbed it once, I went as high as you can go
following Honey's white shirt up and up and up past the treeline,
Honey's hair shone golden in the morning light. It is all so long
ago. We ate rabbits, squirrel   my David will not hunt   Whitebear Whittington lives yet up on Hell Mountain   He lives there
even now I tell you and he is wild, wild. He runs throgh the night
with his eyes on fire and no one can take him, yet he will sleep
of a day as peaceful as a lullaby   Wyncken Blynken and Nod
one night sailed off in a wooden shoe, sailed on a river of crys-
tallight and into a sea of dew   I do not want any bacon. I do
not, I am too busy   <u>there is a time for every purpose under</u>

heaven   The hawk flys round and round, the sky is so blue. I think I can hear the old bell ringing like I rang it to call them home   oh I was young then, and I walked in my body like a Queen

With very special thanks to Kathryn Stripling Byer, whose fine poems inspired this novel and sustained me while I wrote it; to Dan Patterson, for his help in finding old-time gospel music; to my cousins Randy Venable Sinisi and Melissa Venable Poynter; to Anna Jardine, for her heroic copyediting of the manuscript; to Clyde Edgerton and Wilton Mason; and to Hal, for everything.

I have gathered Appalachian legends, history, songs, and tales from people I know and also from the following sources:

More Than Moonshine, by Sidney Saylor Farr, University of Pittsburgh Press, Pittsburgh, Pennsylvania. Reminiscences and recipes: a wonderful book.

Our Southern Highlanders, by Horace Kephart, University of Tennessee Press, Knoxville, 1976. Original copyrights 1913, 1922, The Macmillan Co., New York.

Grandfather Tales, edited by Richard Chase, The Riverside Press, Cambridge, Massachusetts, 1948. It was in this volume that I came across the stories of Whitebear Whittington, Mutsmag, Old Dry Frye, and Chunk O Meat.

The Southern Highlander and His Homeland, by John C. Campbell, reprinted by The Reprint Company, Spartanburg, South Carolina, 1973, from a 1921 edition in the North Carolina Collection at the University of North Carolina at Chapel Hill. With permission of the Russell Sage Foundation.

Growing Up Southern: Southern Exposure *Looks at Childhood, Then and Now,* edited by Chris Mayfield, Pantheon Books, New York, 1980.

Such as Us: Southern Voices of the Thirties, edited by Tom E. Terrill and Jerrold Hirsch, University of North Carolina Press, Chapel Hill, 1978.

My Appalachia, by Rebecca Caudill, Holt, Rinehart & Winston, New York, 1966.

Voices from the Mountains, collected and recorded by Guy and Candie Carawan, Alfred A. Knopf, New York, 1975.

Where Time Stood Still, by Bruce and Nancy Roberts, Collier Macmillan, New York, 1970.

Our Appalachia: An Oral History, edited by Laurel Shackelford and Bill Weinberg, Hill & Wang, New York, 1977.

About the Author

Lee Smith has written eight novels, including *Oral History*, *Family Linen*, and the recent *The Devil's Dream*, and two collections of short stories. A recipient of the 1991 Robert Penn Warren Prize for Fiction and the John Dos Passos Award, among other honors, she lives in Chapel Hill, North Carolina.